# A Visit to the Holy Land Egypt and Italy

## IDA LAURA PFEIFFER

Published in 1852

# TABLE OF CONTENTS

# PREFACE BY THE VIENNA PUBLISHER

For two centuries the princes and nations of the West were accustomed to wander towards the land of the morning. In vain was the noblest blood poured forth in streams in the effort to wrest the country of our heavenly Teacher from the grasp of the infidel; and though the Christian Europe of the present day forbears to renew a struggle which, considering the strength that has been gradually increasing for the last six hundred years, might prove an easy one, we cannot wonder that millions of the votaries of Christianity should cherish an earnest longing to wander in the paths the Redeemer has trod, and to view with their own eyes the traces of the Saviour's progress from the cradle to the grave.

In the generality of cases, however, the hardships, dangers, and difficulties of such a journey were sufficient to overthrow the bravest resolution; and thus the wishes of the majority remained unfulfilled.

Few men were found to possess the degree of strength and endurance requisite for the carrying out of such an undertaking; but that a delicate lady of the higher classes, a native of Vienna, should have the heroism to do what thousands of men failed to achieve, seemed almost incredible.

In her earliest youth she earnestly desired to perform this journey; descriptions of the Holy Land were perused by her with peculiar interest, and a book of Eastern travel had more charms for her than the most glowing accounts of Paris or London.

It was not, however, until our Authoress had reached a riper age, and had finished the education of her sons, that she succeeded in carrying into effect the ardent aspiration of her youth.

On the 2d of March, 1842, she commenced her journey alone, without companions, but fully prepared to bear every ill, to bid defiance to every danger, and to combat every difficulty. That this undertaking should have succeeded may almost be looked upon as a wonder.

Far from desiring publicity, she merely kept a diary, in order to retain the recollections of her tour during her later life, and to impart to her nearest relatives the story of her fortunes. Every evening, though often greatly exhausted with heat, thirst, and the hardships of travel, she never failed to make notes in pencil of the occurrences of the day, frequently using a sand-mound or the back of a camel as a table, while the other members of the caravan lay stretched around her, completely tired out.

It was in the house of my friend Halm that I first heard of this remarkable woman, at a time when she had not yet completed her journey; and every subsequent account of Madame Pfeiffer increased my desire to make her acquaintance.

In manners and appearance I found her to resemble many other women who have distinguished themselves by fortitude, firmness of soul, and magnanimity; and who are in private life the most simple and unaffected, the most modest, and consequently also the most agreeable of beings.

My request to read our Authoress's journal was granted with some timidity; and I am ready to assert that seldom has a book so irresistibly attracted me, or so completely fixed my attention from beginning to end, as this.

The simple and unadorned relation of facts, the candour, combined with strong sound sense, which appear throughout, might put to shame the bombastic striving after originality of many a modern author. The scheme and execution of the work are complete and agreeable; strict truth shines forth from every page, and no one can doubt but that so pure and noble a mind must see things in a right point of view. This circumstance is sufficient in itself to raise the book above many descriptions of travel to the Holy Land, whose authors, trusting to the fact that their assertions could not easily be disproved, have indulged their fancy, seeking to impart interest to their works by the relation of imaginary dangers, and by exaggeration of every kind, for the sake of gaining praise and admiration. Many such men might blush with shame on reading this journal of a simple, truth-loving woman.

After much trouble I succeeded in persuading the Authoress to allow her journal to appear in print.

My efforts were called forth by the desire to furnish the reading public, and particularly the female portion, with a very interesting and attractive, and at the same time a strictly authentic picture of the Holy Land, and of Madame Pfeiffer's entire journey.

# A VISIT TO THE HOLY LAND EGYPT AND ITALY

## CHAPTER I.

I had for years cherished the wish to undertake a journey to the Holy Land; years are, indeed, required to familiarise one with the idea of so hazardous an enterprise. When, therefore, my domestic arrangements at length admitted of my absence for at least a year, my chief employment was to prepare myself for this journey. I read many works bearing on the subject, and was moreover fortunate enough to make the acquaintance of a gentleman who had travelled in the Holy Land some years before. I was thus enabled to gain much oral information and advice respecting the means of prosecuting my dangerous pilgrimage.

My friends and relations attempted in vain to turn me from my purpose by painting, in the most glowing colours, all the dangers and difficulties which await the traveller in those regions. "Men," they said, "were obliged gravely to consider if they had physical strength to endure the fatigues of such a journey, and strength of mind bravely to face the dangers of the plague, the climate, the attacks of insects, bad diet, etc. And to think of a woman's venturing alone, without protection of any kind, into the wide world, across sea and mountain and plain,—it was quite preposterous." This was the opinion of my friends.

I had nothing to advance in opposition to all this but my firm unchanging determination. My trust in Providence gave me calmness and strength to set my house in every respect in order. I made my will, and arranged all my worldly affairs in such a manner that, in the case of my death (an event which I considered more probable than my safe return), my family should find every thing perfectly arranged.

And thus, on the 22d of March 1842, I commenced my journey from Vienna.

At one o'clock in the afternoon I drove to the Kaisermühlen (Emperor's Mills), from which place the steamboats start for Pesth. I was joyfully surprised by the presence of several of my relations and friends, who wished to say farewell once more. The parting was certainly most bitter, for the thought involuntarily obtruded itself, "Should we ever meet again in this world?"

Our mournful meditations were in some degree disturbed by a loud dispute on board the vessel. At the request of a gentleman present, one of the passengers was compelled, instead of flying, as he had intended, with bag and baggage to Hungary, to return to Vienna in company of the police. It appeared he owed the gentleman 1300 florins, and had wished to abscond, but was luckily overtaken before the departure of the boat. This affair was hardly concluded when the bell rang, the wheels began to revolve, and too soon, alas, my dear ones were out of sight!

I had but few fellow-passengers. The weather was indeed fine and mild; but the season was not far enough advanced to lure travellers into the wide world, excepting men of business, and those who had cosmopolitan ideas, like myself. Most of those on board were going only to Presburg, or at farthest to Pesth. The captain having mentioned that a woman was on board who intended travelling to Constantinople, I was immediately surrounded by curious gazers. A gentleman who was bound to the same port stepped forward, and offered his services in case I should ever stand in need of them; he afterwards frequently took me under his protection.

The fine mild weather changed to cold and wind as we got fairly out into the great Danube. I wrapped myself in my cloak, and remained on deck, in order to see the scenery between Vienna and Presburg, which, no doubt, appears lovely enough when nature is clad in the garment of spring; but now I only saw leafless trees and fallow ground—a dreary picture of winter. Hainburg with its old castle on a rock, Theben with its remarkable fortress, and farther on the large free city of Presburg, have all a striking appearance. In three hours' time we reached Presburg, and landed in the neighbourhood of the Coronation-hill, an artificial mound, on which the king must stand in his royal robes, and brandish his sword towards the four quarters of the heavens, as a token that he is ready to defend his kingdom against all enemies, from whatever direction they may approach. Not far from this hill is situate the handsome inn called the "Two Green Trees," where the charges are as high, if not higher, than in Vienna. Until we have passed Pesth, passengers going down the river are not allowed to remain on board through the night.

March 23d.

This morning we continued our journey at six o'clock. Immediately below Presburg the Danube divides into two arms, forming the fertile island of Schütt, which is about forty-six miles long and twenty-eight in breadth. Till we reach Gran the scenery is monotonous enough, but here it improves. Beautiful hills and several mountains surround the place, imparting a charm of variety to the landscape.

In the evening, at about seven o'clock, we arrived at Pesth. Unfortunately it was already quite dark. The magnificent houses, or rather palaces, skirting the left bank of the Danube, and the celebrated ancient fortress and town of Ofen on the right, form a splendid spectacle, and invite the traveller to a longer sojourn. As I had passed some days at Pesth several years before, I now only stayed there for one night.

As the traveller must change steamers here, it behoves him to keep a careful eye upon the luggage he has not delivered up at the office in Vienna.

I put up at the "Hunting-horn," a fine hotel, but ridiculously expensive. A little back room cost me 45 kreutzers (about one shilling and eightpence) for one night.

The whole day I had felt exceedingly unwell. A violent headache, accompanied by nausea and fever, made me fear the approach of a fit of illness which would interrupt my journey. These symptoms were probably a consequence of the painful excitement of parting with my friends, added to the change of air. With some difficulty I gained my modest chamber, and immediately went to bed. My good constitution was luckily proof against the attacks of all enemies, and waking the next morning, on

March 24th,

in tolerable health, I betook myself on board our new steamboat the Galata, of sixty-horse power: this boat did not, however, appear to me so tidy and neat as the Marianna, in which we had proceeded from Vienna to Pesth. Our journey was a rapid one; at ten o'clock in the morning we were already at Feldvär, a place which seems at a distance to be of some magnitude, but which melts away like a soap-bubble on a nearer approach. By two o'clock we had reached Paks; here, as at all other places of note, we stopped for a quarter of an hour. A boat rows off from the shore, bringing and fetching back passengers with such marvellous speed, that you have scarcely finished the sentence you are saying to your neighbour before he has vanished. There is no time even to say farewell.

At about eight o'clock in the evening we reached the market-town of Mohäcs, celebrated as the scene of two battles. The fortress here is used as a prison for criminals. We could distinguish nothing either of the fortress or the town. It was already night when we arrived, and at two o'clock in the morning of

March 25th

we weighed anchor. I was assured, however, that I had lost nothing by this haste.

Some hours afterwards, our ship suddenly struck with so severe a shock, that all hastened on deck to see what was the matter. Our steersman, who had most probably been more asleep than awake, had given the ship an unskilful turn, in consequence of which, one of the paddles was entangled with some trunks of trees projecting above the surface of the water. The sailors hurried into the boats, the engine was backed, and after much difficulty we were once more afloat.

Stopping for a few moments at Dalina and Berkara, we passed the beautiful ruin of Count Palffy's castle at about two o'clock. The castle of Illok, situate on a hill, and belonging to Prince Odescalchi, presents a still more picturesque appearance.

At about four o'clock we landed near the little free town of Neusatz, opposite the celebrated fortress of Peterwardein, the outworks of which extend over a tongue of land stretching far out into the Danube. Of the little free town of Neusatz we could not see much, hidden as it is by hills which at this point confine the bed of the river. The Danube is here crossed by a bridge of boats, and this place also forms the military boundary of Austria. The surrounding landscape appeared sufficiently picturesque; the little town of Karlowitz, lying at a short distance from the shore, among hills covered with vineyards, has a peculiarly good effect. Farther on, however, as far as Semlin, the scenery is rather monotonous. Here the Danube already spreads itself out to a vast breadth, resembling rather a lake than a river.

At nine o'clock at night we reached the city of Semlin, in the vicinity of which we halted. Semlin is a fortified place, situated at the junction of the Save with the Danube; it contains 13,000 inhabitants, and is the last Austrian town on the right bank of the Danube.

On approaching Semlin, a few small cannons were fired off on board our boat. Unfortunately the steward did not receive notice of this event early enough to allow of his opening the windows, consequently one was shattered: this was a serious misfortune for us, as the temperature had sunk to zero, and all the landscape around was covered with snow. Before leaving Vienna, the cabin stove had been banished from its place, as the sun had sent forth its mild beams for a few days, and a continuance of the warm weather was rashly relied on. On the whole, I would not advise any traveller to take a second-class berth on board a steamer belonging to the Viennese company. A greater want of order than we find in these vessels could scarcely be met with. The traveller whose funds will not permit of his paying first-class fare will do better to content himself with a third-class, i.e. a deck-passage, particularly if he purposes journeying no farther than Mohács. If the weather is fine, it is more agreeable to remain on deck, watching the panorama of the Danube as it glides past. Should the day be unfavourable, the traveller can go, without ceremony, into the second-class cabin, for no one makes a distinction between the second and third-class places. During the daytime, at any rate, it is quite as agreeable to remain on deck as to venture below. Travelling down the river from Pesth, the women are compelled to pass the night in the same cabin with the men; an arrangement as uncomfortable as it is indecorous. I afterwards had some experience of steamers belonging to the Austrian Lloyds, on whose vessels I always found a proper separation of the two sexes, and a due regard for the comfort of second-class passengers.

The cold was so severe, that we would gladly have closed every window, but for the close atmosphere engendered by the number of poor people, mostly Jews, who form the larger portion of passengers on board a Hungarian steamer. When the weather is unfavourable, these men are accustomed to hasten from their third-class places to those of the second class, where their presence renders it immediately desirable to open every outlet for purposes of ventilation. What the traveller has to endure on board these vessels would scarcely be believed. Uncushioned benches serve for seats by day and for beds by night. A separation of the two sexes is nowhere attempted, not even on board the Ferdinand, in which you enter the Black Sea, and are exposed to the merciless attacks of sea-sickness.

Considering the high rate of passage-money demanded on this journey, I really think the traveller might expect better accommodation. The first-class to Constantinople costs 120 florins, {23} the second 85 florins, exclusive of provisions, and without reckoning the hotel expenses at Presburg.

March 26th.

Last night was not a period of rest, but of noise for us travellers. Not one of us could close his eyes.

Semlin is a place of considerable importance as a commercial town: above 180 cwt. of goods were unloaded here from our vessel; and in exchange we took on board coals, wood, and wares of various descriptions. The damaged wheel, too, had to be repaired; and every thing was done with so much crashing and noise, that we almost imagined the whole steamer was coming to pieces. Added to this, the cold wind drove in continually through the broken pane, and made the place a real purgatory to us. At length, at six o'clock in the morning, we got afloat once more. One advantage, however, resulted from this fortuitous stoppage: we had a very good view of Belgrade, a town of 20,000 inhabitants, situate opposite to Semlin. It is the first Turkish fortified city in Servia.

The aspect of Belgrade is exceedingly beautiful. The fortifications extend upwards on a rock from the Danube in the form of steps. The city itself, with its graceful minarets, lies half a mile farther inland. Here I saw the first mosques and minarets. The mosques, as far as I could observe from the steamer, are built in a circular form, not very high, and surmounted by a cupola flanked by one or two minarets, a kind of high round pillar. The loftiest among these buildings is the palace of Prince Milosch. From this point our voyage becomes very interesting, presenting a rich and varied succession of delightful landscape-views. The river is hemmed in on either side by mountains, until it spreads itself forth free and unrestrained, in the neighbourhood of Pancsova, to a breadth of 800 fathoms.

Pancsova, on the left bank of the Danube, in the territory of Banata, is a military station.

As the stoppages are only for a few moments, little opportunity is afforded of seeing the interior of the towns, or of visiting most of the places at which we touch. At such times all is hurry and confusion; suddenly the bell rings, the planks are withdrawn, and the unlucky stranger who has loitered on board for a few moments is obliged to proceed with us to the next station.

At Neusatz this happened to a servant, in consequence of his carrying his master's luggage into the cabin instead of merely throwing it down on the deck. The poor man was conveyed on to Semlin, and had to travel on foot for a day and a half to regain his home. A very pleasant journey of two hours from Pancsova brought us to the Turkish fortress Semendria, the situation of which is truly beautiful. The numerous angles of its walls and towers, built in the Moorish style, impart to this place a peculiar charm. As a rule, the Turkish fortresses are remarkable for picturesque effect.

But the villages, particularly those on the Servian shore, had the same poverty-stricken look I had frequently noticed in Galicia. Wretched clay huts, thatched with straw, lay scattered around; and far and wide not a tree or a shrub appeared to rejoice the eye of the traveller or of the sojourner in these parts, under the shade of which the poor peasant might recruit his weary frame, while it would conceal from the eye of the traveller, in some degree, the poverty and nakedness of habitations on which no feeling mind can gaze without emotions of pity.

The left bank of the river belongs to Hungary, and is called the "Banat;" it presents an appearance somewhat less desolate. Much, however, remains to be desired; and the poverty that reigns around is here more to be wondered at, from the fact that this strip of land is so rich in the productions of nature as to have obtained the name of the "Garner of Hungary."

On the Austrian side of the Danube sentries are posted at every two or three hundred paces—an arrangement which has been imitated by the governments on the left bank, and is carried out to the point where the river empties itself into the Black Sea.

It would, however, be erroneous to suppose that these soldiers mount guard in their uniforms. They take up their positions, for a week at a time, in their wretched tattered garments; frequently they are barefoot, and their huts look like stables. I entered some of these huts to view the internal arrangements. They could scarcely have been more simple. In one corner I found a hearth; in another, an apology for a stove, clumsily fashioned out of clay. An unsightly hole in the wall, stopped with paper instead of glass, forms the window; the furniture is comprised in a single wooden bench. Whatever the inhabitant requires in the way of provisions he must bring with him; for this he is allowed by the government to cultivate the land. Throughout the Russian territory the soldiers at least wear uniform.

Our journey becomes more and more charming. Frequently the mighty river rushes foaming and roaring past the rocks, which seem scarcely to allow it a passage; at other times it glides serenely onwards. At every turn we behold new beauties, and scarcely know on which side to turn our eager eyes. Meanwhile the ship sails swiftly on, gliding majestically through wildly romantic scenery.

At one o'clock in the afternoon we reached Pasiest, where there is nothing to be seen but a large store of coals for the steamers and a few huts. Of the town itself nothing can be distinguished.

A couple of miles below Pasiest we enjoy an imposing spectacle. It is the solitary rock Babakay, rising from the midst of the waters. Together with the beautiful ruin Golumbacz, on the Servian shore, it forms a magnificent view.

March 27th.

How unfortunate it is that all advantages are so seldom found combined! We are now travelling amid glorious scenery, which we hoped should recompense us for the manifold discomforts we have hitherto endured; but the weather is unpropitious. The driving snow sends us all into the cabin. The Danube is so fiercely agitated by the stormy wind, that it rises into waves like a sea. We are suffering lamentably from cold; unable to warm ourselves, we stand gazing ruefully at the place where the stove stood— once upon a time.

At four o'clock we reached Drenkova without accident, but completely benumbed: we hurried into the inn built by the steamboat company, where we found capital fare, a warm room, and tolerably comfortable beds. This was the first place we had reached since leaving Pesth at which we could thoroughly warm and refresh ourselves.

At Drenkova itself there is nothing to be seen but the inn just mentioned and a barrack for soldiers. We were here shewn the vessel which was wrecked, with passengers on board, in 1839, in a journey up the Danube. Eight persons who happened to be in the cabin lost their lives, and those only who were on deck were saved.

March 28th.

Early in the morning we embarked on board the Tünte, a vessel furnished with a cabin. The bed of the Danube is here more and more hemmed in by mountains and rocks, so that in some places it is not above eighty fathoms broad, and glides with redoubled swiftness towards its goal, the Pontus

Euxinus or Black Sea.

On account of the falls which it is necessary to pass, between Drenkova and Fetislav, the steamer must be changed for a small sailing vessel. The voyage down the stream could indeed be accomplished without danger, but the return would be attended with many difficulties. The steamers, therefore, remain behind at Drenkova, and passengers are conveyed down the river in barks, and upwards (since the accident of 1839) in good commodious carriages.

To-day the cold was quite as severe as it had been yesterday so that but for the politeness of a fellow-passenger, who lent me his bunda (great Hungarian fur), I should have been compelled to remain in the little cabin, and should thus have missed the most interesting points of the Danube. As it was, however, I wrapped myself from head to foot in the fur cloak, took my seat on a bench outside the cabin, and had full leisure to store my memory with a succession of lovely scenery, presenting almost the appearance of a series of lake views, which continued equally picturesque until we had almost reached Alt-Orsova.

A couple of miles below Drenkova, near Islas, the sailors suddenly cried, "The first fall!" I looked up in a fever of expectation. The water was rising in small waves, the stream ran somewhat faster, and a slight rushing sound was to be heard. If I had not been told that the Danube forms a waterfall here, I should certainly never have suspected it to be the case. Between Lenz and Krems I did not find either the rocks or the power of the stream much more formidable. We had, however, a high tide, a circumstance which diminishes both the danger of the journey and the sublimity of the view. The numerous rocky points, peering threateningly forth at low tide, among which the steersman must pick his way with great care, were all hidden from our sight. We glided safely over them, and in about twenty minutes had left the first fall behind us. The two succeeding falls are less considerable.

On the Austro-Wallachian side a road extends over a distance of fourteen to sixteen miles, frequently strengthened with masonry, and at some points hewn out of the solid rock. In the midst of this road, on a high wall of rock, we see the celebrated "Veteran Cave," one of the most impregnable points on the banks of the Danube. It is surrounded by redoubts, and is admirably calculated to command the passage of the river. This cave is said to be sufficiently spacious to contain 500 men. So far back as the time of the Romans it was already used as a point of defence for the Danube. Some five miles below it we notice the "Trajan's Tablet," hewn out of a protruding rock.

On the Turco-Servian side the masses of rock jut out so far into the stream, that no room is left for a footway. Here the famous Trajan's Road once existed. No traces of this work remain, save that the traveller notices, for fifteen or twenty miles, holes cut here and there in the rock. In these holes strong trunks of trees were fastened; these supported the planks of which the road is said to have been formed.

At eleven in the forenoon we reached Alt-Orsova, the last Austrian town on the military frontier of Banata or Wallachia. We were obliged to remain here for half a day.

The town has rather a pretty effect, being composed mostly of new houses. The house belonging to the steamboat company is particularly remarkable. It is not, however, devoted to the accommodation of travellers, as at Drenkova. Here, as at Presburg and Pesth, each passenger is required to pay for his night's expenses,—an arrangement which I could not help finding somewhat strange, inasmuch as every passenger is made to pay twice; namely, for his place on the steamer and for his room in the inn.

It was Sunday when we arrived, and I saw many people proceeding to church. The peasants are dressed tolerably neatly and well. Both men and women wear long garments of blue cloth. The women have on their heads large handkerchiefs of white linen, which hang down their backs, and on their feet stout boots; the men wear round felt hats, and sandals made of the bark of trees.

March 29th.

After having completely refreshed ourselves at the good inn called the "Golden Stag," we this morning embarked on a new craft, the Saturnus, which is only covered in overhead, and is open on all sides.

So soon as a traveller has stepped upon this vessel he is looked upon as unclean, and may not go on shore without keeping quarantine: an officer accompanied us as far as Galatz.

Immediately below Alt-Orsova we entirely quit the Austrian territory.

We are now brought nearer every moment to the most dangerous part of the river, the "Iron Gate," called by the Turks Demir kaju. Half an hour before we reached the spot, the rushing sound of the water announced the perilous proximity. Numerous reefs of rocks here traverse the stream, and the current runs eddying among them.

We passed this dangerous place in about fifteen minutes. Here, at the Iron Gate, the high tide befriended us, as it did at the former falls.

I found these falls, and indeed almost every thing we passed, far below the anticipations I had formed from reading descriptions, frequently of great poetic beauty. I wish to represent every thing as I found it, as it appeared before my eyes; without adornment indeed, but truly.

After passing the Iron Gate we come to a village, in the neighbourhood of which some fragments of the Trajan's Bridge can be discerned at low water. The country now becomes flatter, particularly on the left bank, where extend the immense plains of Wallachia, and the eye finds no object on which it can rest. On the right hand rise terrace-like rows of hills and mountains, and the background is bounded by the sharply-defined lines of the Balkan range, rendered celebrated by the passage of the Russians in 1829. The villages, scattered thinly along the banks, become more and more miserable; they rather resemble stables for cattle than human dwellings. The beasts remain in the open fields, though the climate does not appear to be much milder than with us in Austria; for to-day, nearly at the beginning of April, the thermometer stood one degree below zero, and yesterday we had only five degrees of warmth (reckoning by Reaumur).

{30}

The expeditious and easy manner in which cattle are here declared to be free from the plague also struck me as remarkable. When the creatures are brought from an infected place to one pronounced healthy, the ship is brought to some forty or fifty paces from the shore, and each animal is thrown into the water and driven towards the bank, where people are waiting to receive it. After this simple operation the beasts are considered free from infectious matter.

Cattle-rearing seems to be here carried on to a considerable extent. Everywhere I noticed large herds of horned beasts and many buffaloes. Numerous flocks of goats and sheep also appear.

On the Saturnus we travelled at the most for two hours, after which we embarked, opposite the fortress of Fetislav, on board the steamer Zriny.

At five o'clock in the evening we passed the fortress of Widdin, opposite which we stopped, in the neighbourhood of the town of Callafat. It was intended merely to land goods here, and then to proceed immediately on our voyage; but the agent was nowhere to be found, and so we poor travellers were made the victims of this carelessness, and compelled to remain here at anchor all night.

March 30th.

As the agent had not yet made his appearance, the captain had no choice but to leave the steward behind to watch over the goods. At half-past six in the morning the engines were at length set in motion, and after a very agreeable passage of six hours we reached Nicopolis.

All the Turkish fortresses on the Danube are situated on the right bank, mostly amid beautiful scenery. The larger towns and villages are surrounded by gardens and trees, which give them a very pleasant appearance. The interior of these towns, however, is said not to be quite so inviting as one would suppose from a distant view, for it is asserted that dirty narrow streets, dilapidated houses, etc., offend the stranger's sight at every step. We did not land at any of these fortresses or towns; for us the right bank of the river was a forbidden paradise; so we only saw what was beautiful, and escaped being disenchanted.

Rather late in the evening we cast anchor opposite a village of no note.

## CHAPTER II.

March 31st.

We started early this morning, and at eight o'clock had already reached Giurgewo. This town is situate on the left bank of the Danube, opposite the fortress of Rustschuk. It contains 16,000 inhabitants, and is one of the chief trading towns of Wallachia. We were detained here until four o'clock in the afternoon; for we had to unload above 600 cwt. of goods and eight carriages, and to take coals on board in exchange. Thus we had time to view the interior of this Wallachian city.

With what disappointed surprise did my fellow-passengers view the ugliness of this town, which from a distance promises so much! On me it made but little impression, for I had seen towns precisely similar in Galicia. The streets and squares are full of pits and holes; the houses are built without the slightest regard to taste or symmetry, one perhaps projecting halfway across the street, while its neighbour falls quite into the background. In some places wooden booths were erected along each side of the street for the sale of the commonest necessaries of life and articles of food, and these places were dignified by the name of "bazaars." Curiosity led us into a wine-shop and into a coffee-house. In both of these we found only wooden tables and benches; there were hardly any guests; and the few persons present belonged to the humblest classes. Glasses and cups are handed to the company without undergoing the ceremony of rinsing.

We purchased some eggs and butter, and went into the house of one of the townspeople to prepare ourselves a dish after the German fashion. I had thus an opportunity of noticing the internal arrangements of a house of this description. The floor of the room was not boarded, and the window was only half glazed, the remaining portion being filled up with paper or thin bladder. For the rest, every thing was neat and simple enough. Even a good comfortable divan was not wanting. At four o'clock we quitted the town.

The Danube is now only broad for short distances at a time. It is, as it were, sown with islands, and its waters are therefore more frequently parted into several streams than united into one.

In the villages we already notice Greek and Turkish costumes, but the women and girls do not yet wear veils.

Unfortunately it was so late when we reached the fortress of Silistria that I could see nothing of it. A little lower down we cast anchor for the night. At an early hour on

April 1st

we sailed past Hirsova, and at two o'clock stopped at Braila, a fortress occupied by the Russians since the year 1828. Here passengers were not allowed to land, as they were considered infected with the plague; but our officer stepped forward, and vouched for the fact that we had neither landed nor taken up any one on the right bank of the river; thereupon the strangers were allowed to set foot on terra firma.

By four o'clock we were opposite Galatz, one of the most considerable commercial towns, with 8000 inhabitants,—the only harbour the Russians possess on the Danube. Here we saw the first merchant-ships and barques of all kinds coming from the Black Sea. Some sea-gulls also, heralds of the neighbouring ocean, soared above our heads.

The scene here is one of traffic and bustle; Galatz being the place of rendezvous for merchants and travellers from two quarters of the globe, Europe and Asia. It is the point of junction of three great empires— Austria, Russia, and Turkey.

After the officer had repeated his assurances as at Braila, we were permitted to leave the ship. I had a letter of recommendation to the Austrian consul, who accidentally came on board; after reading my letter he received me very kindly, and most obligingly procured quarters for me.

The town promises much, but proves to be just such a miserable dirty place as Giurgewo. The houses are generally built of wood or clay, thatched with straw; those alone belonging to the consul and the rich merchants are of stone. The finest buildings are the Christian church and the Moldavian hotel.

Though Galatz lies on the Danube, water for drinking is a dear article among the inhabitants. Wells are to be found neither in the houses nor in the squares. The townspeople are compelled to bring all the water they require from the Danube, which is a great hardship for the poor people, and a considerable expense for the rich; in winter a small tub of water costs from 10 to 12 kreutzers (about 4d. or 5d.) in the more distant quarters of the town. At every corner you meet water-carriers, and little wagons loaded with tubs of water. Attempts have frequently been made to procure this indispensable element by digging; water has, indeed, in some instances gushed forth, but it always had a brackish taste.

In Galatz we made a halt of twenty-four hours: the delay was not of the most agreeable kind, as neither the town itself nor its environs offer any thing worthy of remark. Still I always think of these days with pleasure. Herr Consul Huber is a polite and obliging man; himself a traveller, he gave me many a hint and many a piece of advice for my journey. The air of quiet comfort which reigned throughout his house was also not to be despised by one who had just endured many days of privation; at Herr Huber's I found relief both for body and mind.

April 2d.

The scenery round the town is so far from being inviting, that I did not feel the least inclination to explore it. I therefore remained in the town, and went up hill and down dale through the ill-paved streets. Coffee-houses appear in great abundance; but if it were not for the people sitting in front of them drinking coffee and smoking tobacco, no one would do these dirty rooms the honour of taking them for places of entertainment.

In the market and the squares we notice a great preponderance of the male sex over the female. The former are seen bustling about every where, and, like the Italians, perform some duties which usually fall to the lot of the softer sex. We notice a mixture of the most different nations, and among them a particularly large number of Jews.

The bazaar is overloaded with southern fruits of all kinds. Oranges and lemons are seen here in great numbers, like the commonest of our fruits. The prices are of course very trifling. The cauliflowers brought from Asia Minor are particularly fine. I noticed many as large as a man's head.

In the evening I was required to repair to the harbour and re-embark.

It is almost impossible to form an idea of the confusion which reigns here. A wooden railing forms the barrier between the healthy people and those who come from or intend travelling to a country infected with the plague. Whoever passes this line of demarcation is not allowed to return. Soldiers, officers, government officials, and superintendents, the latter of whom are armed with sticks and pairs of tongs, stand at the entrance to drive those forcibly back who will not be content with fair words. Provisions and other articles are either thrown over the barrier or left in front of it. In the latter case, however, they may not be touched until the bearers have departed. A gentleman on the "plague" side wished to give a letter to one on the other; it was immediately snatched from his hand and handed across by means of a pair of tongs. And all this time such a noise and hubbub is going on, that you can scarcely hear the sound of your own voice.

"Pray hand me over my luggage!" cries one. "Keep farther away! don't come near me, and mind you don't touch me!" anxiously exclaims another. And then the superintendents keep shouting—"Stand back, stand back!" etc.

I was highly entertained by this spectacle; the scene was entirely new to me. But on my return, when I shall be one of the prisoners, I fear I may find it rather tedious. For this time I was not at all hindered in the prosecution of my journey.

On the whole, these timid precautions seemed to me exceedingly uncalled for, particularly at a time when neither the plague nor any kind of contagious disease prevailed in Turkey. One of my fellow-passengers had been banished to our ship on the previous day because he had had the misfortune to brush against an official on going to see after his luggage.

At seven o'clock the tattoo is beaten, the grating is shut, and the farce ends. We now repaired to the fourth and last steamer, the Ferdinand. From first to last we changed vessels six times during a journey from Vienna to Constantinople; we travelled by four steamers and twice in boats; a circumstance which cannot be reckoned among the pleasures of a trip down the Danube.

Though not a large boat, the Ferdinand is comfortable and well built. Even the second-class cabin is neatly arranged, and a pretty stove diffused a warmth which was peculiarly grateful to us all, as the thermometer showed only six to eight degrees above zero. Unfortunately even here the men and women are not separated in the second-class cabin; but care is at least taken that third-class passengers do not intrude. Twelve berths are arranged round the walls, and in front of these are placed broad benches well cushioned.

April 3d.

At five o'clock in the morning we steamed out of the harbour of Galatz. Shortly afterwards basins and towels were handed to us; a custom totally unknown upon former vessels. For provisions, which are tolerably good, we are charged 1 fl. 40 kr. per diem.

Towards ten o'clock we reached Tehussa, a Bessarabian village of most miserable appearance, where we stopped for a quarter of an hour; after which we proceeded without further delay towards the Black Sea.

I had long rejoiced in the expectation of reaching the Black Sea, and imagined that near its mouth the Danube itself would appear like a sea. But as it generally happens in life, "great expectations, small realisations," so it was the case here also. At Galatz the Danube is very broad; but some distance from its mouth it divides itself into so many branches that not one of them can be termed majestic.

Towards three o'clock in the afternoon we at length entered the Black Sea. Here the arms of the Danube rush forward from every quarter, driving the sea tumultuously back, so that we can only distinguish in the far distance a stripe of green. For above an hour we glide on over the yellow, clayey, strongly agitated fresh water, until at length the boundary is passed, and we are careering over the salt waves of the sea. Unfortunately for us, equinoctial gales and heavy weather still so powerfully maintained their sway, that the deck was completely flooded with the salt brine. We could hardly stand upon our feet, and could not manage to reach the cabin-door, where the bell was ringing for dinner, without the assistance of some sailors.

Several of the passengers, myself among the number, did little honour to the cook's skill. We had scarcely begun to eat our soup, before we were so powerfully attacked by sea-sickness, that we were obliged to quit the table precipitately. I laid myself down at once, feeling unable to move about, or even to drag myself on deck to admire the magnificent spectacle of nature. The waves frequently ran so high as to overtop the flue of our stove, and from time to time whole streams of water poured into the cabin.

April 4th.

Since yesterday the storm has increased considerably, so that we are obliged to hold fast by our cribs to avoid being thrown out. This misfortune really happened to one of the passengers, who was too ill to hold sufficiently tight.

As I already felt somewhat better, I attempted to rise, but was thrown in the same instant with such force against a table which stood opposite, that for a long time I felt no inclination to try again. There was not the slightest chance of obtaining any sleep all night. The dreadful howling of the wind among the masts and cordage, the fearful straining of the ship, which seemed as though its timbers were starting, the continual pitching and rolling, the rattling of the heavy cables above us, the cries, orders, and shouting of the captain and his sailors, all combined to form a din which did not allow us to enjoy a moment's rest. In the morning, ill as I felt myself, I managed to gain the deck with the help of the steward, and sat down near the steersman to enjoy the aspect of that grandest of nature's phenomena—a storm at sea.

Holding tightly on, I bade defiance to the waves, which broke over the ship and wetted me all over, as though to cool my feverish heat. I could now form a clear and vivid conception of a storm at sea. I saw the waves rush foaming on, and the ship now diving into an abyss, and anon rising with the speed of lightning to the peak of the highest wave. It was a thrilling, fearful sight;—absorbed in its contemplation, I soon ceased to think of my sickness.

Late at night the violence of the storm abated in some degree; we could now run in and cast anchor in the harbour of Varna, which under ordinary circumstances we should have reached twelve hours sooner.

April 5th.

This morning I had leisure to admire this fine fortress-town, which was besieged and taken by the Russians in 1828. We remained here several hours. The upper portion of the ship was here loaded with fowl of all descriptions, to such a degree that the space left for us travellers was exceedingly circumscribed. This article of consumption seems to be in great demand in Constantinople both among Turks and Franks; for our captain assured me that his vessel was laden with this kind of ware every time he quitted Varna, and that he carried it to Stamboul.

April 6th.

The shades of night prevented my seeing one of the finest sights in the world, in anticipation of which I had rejoiced ever since my departure from Vienna—the passage through the Bosphorus. A few days afterwards, however, I made the excursion in a kaik (a very small and light boat), and enjoyed to my heart's content views and scenes which it is totally beyond my descriptive power to portray.

At three o'clock in the morning, when we entered the harbour of

Constantinople, every one, with the exception of the sailors, lay wrapped in sleep. I stood watching on deck, and saw the sun rise in its full glory over the imperial city, so justly and universally admired.

We had cast anchor in the neighbourhood of Topona; the city of cities lay spread out before my eyes, built on several hills, each bearing a separate town, and all blending into a grand and harmonious whole.

The town of Constantinople, properly speaking, is separated from Galata and Pera by the so-called "Golden Horn;" the means of communication is by a long and broad wooden bridge. Scutari and Bulgurlu rise in the form of terraces on the Asiatic shore. Scutari is surrounded, within and without, by a splendid wood of magnificent cypresses. In the foreground, on the top of the mountain, lie the spacious and handsome barracks, which can contain 10,000 men.

The beautiful mosques, with their graceful minarets—the palaces and harems, kiosks and great barracks—the gardens, shrubberies, and cypress-woods—the gaily painted houses, among which single cypresses often rear their slender heads,—these, together with the immense forest of masts, combine to form an indescribably striking spectacle.

When the bustle of life began, on the shore and on the sea, my eyes scarcely sufficed to take in all I saw. The "Golden Horn" became gradually covered as far as the eye could reach with a countless multitude of kaiks. The restless turmoil of life on shore, the passing to and fro of men of all nations and colours, from the pale inhabitant of Europe to the blackest Ethiopian, the combination of varied and characteristic costumes, this, and much more which I cannot describe, held me spell-bound to the deck. The hours flew past like minutes, and even the time of debarcation came much too early for me, though I had stood on deck and gazed from three o'clock until eight.

I found myself richly repaid for all the toils of my journey, and rejoiced in the sight of these wonderful Eastern pictures; I could only wish I were a poet, that I might fitly portray the magnificent gorgeousness of the sight.

To land at Topona, and to be immediately surrounded by hired servants and hamaks (porters), is the fate of every traveller. The stranger is no longer master either of his will or his luggage. One man praises this inn, the other that. {40} The porters hustle and beat each other for your effects, so that the custom-house officers frequently come forward with their sticks to restore order. The boxes are then searched,—a ceremony which can, however, be considerably accelerated by a fee of from ten to twenty kreutzers.

It is very advisable to fix on an hotel before leaving the boat. There are always passengers on board who are resident at Constantinople, or at least know the town well, and who are polite enough to give advice on the subject to strangers. By this means you rid yourself at once of the greedy servants, and need only tell a porter the name of your inn.

The inns for the Franks (a term used in the East to designate all Europeans) are in Pera. I stayed at the hotel of Madame Balbiani, a widow lady, in whose house the guests are made comfortable in every respect. Clean rooms, with a beautiful view towards the sea, healthy, well-selected, and palatable fare, and good prompt attendance, are advantages which every one values; and all these are found at Madame Balbiani's, besides constant readiness to oblige on the part of the hostess and her family. The good lady took quite a warm interest in me; and I can say, without hesitation, that had not my good fortune led me under her roof, I should have been badly off. I had several letters of introduction; but not being fortunate enough to travel in great pomp or with a great name, my countrymen did not consider it worth while to trouble themselves about me.

I am ashamed, for their sakes, to be obliged to make this confession; but as I have resolved to narrate circumstantially not only all I saw, but all that happened to me on this journey, I must note down this circumstance with the rest. I felt the more deeply the kindness of these strangers, who, without recommendation or the tie of country, took so hearty an interest in the well-being of a lonely woman. I am truly rejoiced when an opportunity occurs of expressing my sincere gratitude for the agreeable hours I spent among them.

The distance from Vienna to Constantinople is about 1000 sea miles.

RESIDENCE AT CONSTANTINOPLE.—THE DANCING DERVISHES.

I arrived at Constantinople on a Tuesday, and immediately inquired what was worth seeing. I was advised to go and see the dancing dervishes, as this was the day on which they held their religious exercises in Pera.

As I reached the mosque an hour too soon, I betook myself in the meantime to the adjoining garden, which is set apart as the place of meeting of the Turkish women. Here several hundred ladies reclined on the grass in varied groups, surrounded by their children and their nurses, the latter of whom are all negresses. Many of these Turkish women were smoking pipes of tobacco with an appearance of extreme enjoyment, and drinking small cups of coffee without milk. Two or three friends often made use of the same pipe, which was passed round from mouth to mouth. These ladies seemed also to be partial to dainties: most of them were well provided with raisins, figs, sugared nuts, cakes, etc., and ate as much as the little ones. They seemed to treat their slaves very kindly; the black servants sat among their mistresses, and munched away bravely: the slaves are well dressed, and could scarcely be distinguished from their owners, were it not for their sable hue.

During my whole journey I remarked with pleasure that the lot of a slave in the house of a Mussulman is not nearly so hard as we believe. The Turkish women are no great admirers of animated conversations; still there was more talking in their societies than in the assemblies of the men, who sit silent and half asleep in the coffee-houses, languidly listening to the narrations of a story-teller.

The ladies' garden resembles a churchyard. Funeral monuments peer forth at intervals between the cypresses, beneath which the visitors sit talking and joking cheerfully. Every now and then one would suddenly start up, spread a carpet beside her companions, and kneel down to perform her devotions. As no one of the male sex was allowed to be present, all were unveiled. I noticed many pretty faces among them, but not a single instance of rare or striking beauty. Fancy large brilliant eyes, pale cheeks, broad faces, and an occasional tendency to corpulence, and you have the ladies' portrait. Small-pox must still be rather prevalent in these parts, for I saw marks of it on many faces.

The Turkish ladies' costume is not very tasteful. When they go abroad, they are completely swathed in an upper garment, generally made of dark merino. In the harem, or in any place where men are not admitted, they doff this garment, and also the white cloth in which they wrap their heads and faces. Their costume consists, properly speaking, of very wide trousers drawn together below the ancle, a petticoat with large wide sleeves, and a broad sash round the waist. Over this sash some wear a caftan, others only a spencer, generally of silk. On their feet they wear delicate boots, and over these slippers of yellow morocco; on their heads a small fez-cap, from beneath which their hair falls on their shoulders in a number of thin plaits. Those Turks, male and female, who are descended from Mahomet, have either a green caftan or a green turban. This colour is here held so sacred, that scarcely any one may wear it. I would even advise the Franks to avoid green in their dresses, as they may expose themselves to annoyance by using it.

After I had had more than an hour's leisure to notice all these circumstances, a noise suddenly arose in the courtyard, which produced a stir among the women. I considered from these appearances that it was time to go to the temple, and hastened to join my party. A great crowd was waiting in the courtyard, for the Sultan was expected. I was glad to have the good fortune to behold him on the very day of my arrival. As a stranger, I was allowed, without opposition, a place in the front ranks,—a trait of good breeding on the part of the Turks which many a Frank would do well to imitate. In a Turk, moreover, this politeness is doubly praiseworthy, from the fact that he looks upon my poor sex with great disrespect; indeed, according to his creed, we have not even a soul.

I had only stood a few moments, when the Sultan appeared on horseback, surrounded by his train. He alone rode into the courtyard; the others all dismounted at the gate, and entered on foot. The horse on which the Sultan rode was of rare beauty, and, as they told me, of the true Arabian breed; the saddle-cloth was richly embroidered with gold, and the stirrups, of the same precious metal, were in the form of shoes, covered with the finest chased work.

The Sultan is a slender slim-looking youth of nineteen years of age, and looks pale, languid, and blasé. His features are agreeable, and his eyes fine. If he had not abandoned himself at so early an age to all the pleasures of the senses, he would, no doubt, have grown up a stalwart man. He wore a long cape of dark-blue cloth; and a high fez-cap, with a heron's plume and a diamond clasp, decked his head. The greeting of the people, and the Sultan's mode of acknowledging it, is exactly as at Vienna, except that here the people at intervals raise a low cry of welcome.

As soon as the Sultan had entered the temple, all flocked in. The men and the Franks (the latter without distinction of sex) sit or stand in the body of the temple. The Turkish women sit in galleries, behind such close wire gratings that they are completely hidden. The temple, or more properly the hall, is of inconsiderable size, and the spectators are only separated from the priests by a low railing.

At two o'clock the dervishes appeared, clad in long petticoats with innumerable folds, which reached to their heels. Their heads were covered with high pointed hats of white felt. They spread out carpets and skins of beasts, and began their ceremonies with a great bowing and kissing of the ground. At length the music struck up; but I do not remember ever to have heard a performance so utterly horrible. The instruments were a child's drum, a shepherd's pipe, and a miserable fiddle. Several voices set up a squeaking and whining accompaniment, with an utter disregard of time and tune.

Twelve dervishes now began their dance,—if indeed a turning round in a circle, while their full dresses spread round them like a large wheel, can be called by such a name. They display much address in avoiding each other, and never come in contact, though their stage is very small. I did not notice any "convulsions," of which I had read in many descriptions.

The ceremony ended at three o'clock. The Sultan once more mounted his horse, and departed with his train and the eunuchs. In the course of the day I saw him again, as he was returning from visiting the medical faculty. It is not difficult to get a sight of the Sultan; he generally appears in public on Tuesdays, and always on Fridays, the holiday of the Turks.

The train of the young autocrat presents a more imposing appearance when he goes by water to visit a mosque, which he generally does on every Friday. Only two hours before he starts it is announced in which mosque he intends to appear. At twelve, at noon, the procession moves forward. For this purpose two beautiful barges are in readiness, painted white, and covered with gilded carvings. Each barge is surmounted by a splendid canopy of dark-red velvet, richly bordered with gold fringe and tassels. The floor is spread with beautiful carpets. The rowers are strong handsome youths, clad in short trousers and jacket of white silk, with fez-caps on their heads. On each side of the ship there are fourteen of these rowers, under whose vigorous exertions the barge flies forward over wave and billow like a dolphin. The beautifully regular movements of the sailors have a fine effect. The oars all dip into the water with one stroke, the rowers rise as one man, and fall back into their places in the same perfect time.

A number of elegant barges and kaiks follow the procession. The flags of the Turkish fleet and merchant-ships are hoisted, and twenty-one cannons thunder forth a salutation to the Sultan. He does not stay long in the mosque, and usually proceeds to visit a barrack or some other public building. When the monarch goes by water to the mosque, he generally returns also in his barge; if he goes by land, he returns in the same manner.

The most popular walks in Pera are "the great and little Campo," which may be termed "burying-places in cypress-groves." It is a peculiar custom of the Turks, which we hardly find among any other nation, that all their feasts, walks, business-transactions, and even their dwellings, are in the midst of graves. Every where, in Constantinople, Pera, Galata, etc., one can scarcely walk a few paces without passing several graves surrounded by cypresses. We wander continually between the living and the dead; but within four and twenty hours I was quite reconciled to the circumstance. During the night-time I could pass the graves with as little dread as if I were walking among the houses of the living. Seen from a distance, these numerous cypress-woods give to the town a peculiar fairy-like appearance; I can think of nothing with which I could compare it. Every where the tall trees appear, but the tombs are mostly hidden from view.

It took a longer time before I could accustom myself to the multitude of ownerless dogs, which the stranger encounters at all corners, in every square and every street. They are of a peculiarly hideous breed, closely resembling the jackal. During the daytime they are not obnoxious, being generally contented enough if they are allowed to sleep undisturbed in the sun, and to devour their prey in peace. But at night they are not so quiet. They bark and howl incessantly at each other, as well as at the passers-by, but do not venture an attack, particularly if you are accompanied by a servant carrying a lantern and a stick. Among themselves they frequently have quarrels and fights, in which they sometimes lose their lives. They are extremely jealous if a strange dog approaches their territory, namely the street or square of which they have possession. On such an intruder they all fall tooth and nail, and worry him until he either seeks safety in flight or remains dead on the spot. It is therefore a rare circumstance for any person to have a house-dog with him in the streets. It would be necessary to carry the creature continually, and even then a number of these unbidden guests would follow, barking and howling incessantly. Neither distemper nor madness is to be feared from these dogs, though no one cares for their wants. They live on carrion and offal, which is to be found in abundance in every street, as every description of filth is thrown out of the houses into the road. A few years ago it was considered expedient to banish these dogs from Constantinople. They were transported to two uninhabited islands in the Sea of Marmora, the males to one and the females to another. But dirt and filth increased in the city to such a degree, that people were glad to have them back again.

The town is not lighted. Every person who goes abroad at night must take a lantern with him. If he is caught wandering without a lantern by the guard, he is taken off without mercy to the nearest watch-house, where he must pass the night. The gates of the city are shut after sunset.

In proportion as I was charmed with the beautiful situation of Constantinople, so I was disgusted with the dirt and the offensive atmosphere which prevail every where; the ugly narrow streets, the continual necessity to climb up and down steep places in the badly-paved roads, soon render the stranger weary of a residence in this city.

Worse than all is the continual dread of conflagration in which we live. Large chests and baskets are kept in readiness in every house; if a fire breaks out in the neighbourhood, all valuable articles are rapidly thrown into these and conveyed away. It is customary to make a kind of contract with two or three Turks, who are pledged, in consideration of a trifling monthly stipend, to appear in the hour of danger, for the purpose of carrying the boxes and lending a helping hand wherever they can. It is safer by far to reckon on the honesty of the Turks than on that of the Christians and Greeks. Instances in which a Turk has appropriated any portion of the goods entrusted to his care are said to be of very rare occurrence. During the first nights of my stay I was alarmed at every noise, particularly when the watchman, who paraded the streets, happened to strike with his stick upon the stones. In the event of a conflagration, he must knock at every house-door and cry, "Fire, fire!" Heaven be praised, my fears were never realised.

CHAPTER III.

I chose a Friday for an excursion to Scutari, the celebrated burying-place of the Turks, in order that I might have an opportunity of seeing the "howling dervishes."

In company with a French physician, I traversed the Bosphorus in a kaik. {48} We passed by the "Leander's Tower," which stands in the sea, a few hundred paces from the Asiatic coast, and has been so frequently celebrated in song by the poets. We soon arrived at our destination.

It was with a peculiar feeling of emotion that for the first time in my life I set foot on a new quarter of the globe. Now, and not till now, I seemed separated by an immeasurable distance from my home. Afterwards, when I landed on the coast of Africa, the circumstance did not produce the same impression on my mind.

Now at length I was standing in the quarter of the earth which had been the cradle of the human race; where man had risen high, and had again sunk so low that the Almighty had almost annihilated him in his righteous anger. And here in Asia it was that the Son of God came on earth to bring the boon of redemption to fallen man. My long and warmly-cherished wish to tread this most wonderful of the four quarters of the earth was at length fulfilled, and with God's help I might confidently hope to reach the sacred region whence the true light of the world had shone forth.

Scutari is the place towards which the Mussulman looks with the hope of one day reposing beneath its shade. No disciple of any other creed is allowed to be buried here; and here, therefore, the Mahometan feels himself at home, and worthy of his Prophet. The cemetery is the grandest in the world. One may wander for hours through this grove of cypresses, without reaching the end. On the gravestones of the men turbans are sculptured; on those of the women fruits and flowers: the execution is in most cases very indifferent.

Though neither the chief nor the tributary streets in Scutari are even, they are neither so badly paved nor quite so narrow as those at Pera. The great barracks, on a height in the foreground, present a splendid appearance, and also afford a delicious view towards the Sea of Marmora and the inimitably beautiful Bosphorus. The barracks are said to contain accommodation for 10,000 men.

THE HOWLING DERVISHES.

At two o'clock we entered the temple, a miserable wooden building. Every Mussulman may take part in this religious ceremony; it is not requisite that he should have attained to the rank and dignity of a dervish. Even children of eight or nine stand up in a row outside the circle of men, to gain an early proficiency in these holy exercises.

The commencement of the ceremony is the same as with the dancing dervishes; they have spread out carpets and skins of beasts, and are bowing and kissing the ground. Now they stand up and form a circle together with the laymen, when the chief begins in a yelling voice to recite prayers from the Koran; by degrees those forming the circle join in, and scream in concert. For the first hour some degree of order is still preserved; the performers rest frequently to husband their strength, which will be exerted to the utmost at the close of the ceremony. But then the sight becomes as horrible as one can well imagine any thing. They vie with one another in yelling and howling, and torture their faces, heads, and bodies into an infinite variety of fantastic attitudes. The roaring, which resembles that of wild beasts, and the dreadful spasmodic contortions of the actors' countenances, render this religious ceremony a horrible and revolting spectacle.

The men stamp with their feet on the ground, jerk their heads backwards and forwards, and certainly throw themselves into worse contortions than those who are described as having been in old times "vexed with a devil." During the exercise they snatch the covering from their heads, and gradually take off all their clothes, with the exception of shirt and trousers. The two high priests who stand within the circle receive the garments one after another, kiss them, and lay them on a heap together. The priests beat time with their hands, and after the garments have been laid aside the dance becomes faster and faster. Heavy drops of perspiration stand on every brow; some are even foaming at the mouth. The howling and roaring at length reach such a dreadful pitch, that the spectator feels stunned and bewildered.

Suddenly one of these maniacs fell lifeless to the ground. The priests and a few from the circle hurried towards him, stretched him out flat, crossed his hands and feet, and covered him with a cloth.

The doctor and I were both considerably alarmed, for we thought the poor man had been seized with apoplexy. To our surprise and joy, however, we saw him about six or eight minutes afterwards suddenly throw off the cloth, jump up, and once more take his place in the circle to howl like a maniac.

At three o'clock the ceremony concluded. I would not advise any person afflicted with weak nerves to witness it, for he certainly could not endure the sight. I could have fancied myself among raving lunatics and men possessed, rather than amidst reasonable beings. It was long before I could recover my composure, and realise the idea that the infatuation of man could attain such a pitch. I was informed that before the ceremony they swallow opium, to increase the wildness of their excitement!

The Achmaidon (place of arrows) deserves a visit, on account of the beautiful view obtained thence; the traveller should see it, if he be not too much pressed for time. This is the place which the Sultan sometimes honours by his presence when he wishes to practise archery.

On an open space stands a kind of pulpit of masonry, from which the Sultan shoots arrows into the air without mark or aim. Where the arrow falls, a pillar or pyramid is erected to commemorate the remarkable event. The whole space is thus covered with a number of these monuments, most of them broken and weather-stained, and all scattered in the greatest confusion. Not far from this place is an imperial kiosk, with a garden. Both promise much when viewed from a distance, but realise nothing when seen from within.

THE TOWER IN GALATA.

Whoever wishes to appreciate in its fullest extent the charm of the views round Constantinople should ascend the tower in Galata near Pera, or the Serasker in Constantinople. According to my notion, the former course is preferable. In this tower there is a room with twelve windows placed in a circle, from which we see pictures such as the most vivid imagination could hardly create.

Two quarters of the globe, on the shores of two seas united by the Bosphorus, lie spread before us. The glorious hills with their towns and villages, the number of palaces, gardens, kiosks, and mosques, Chalcedon, the Prince's Islands, the Golden Horn, the continual bustle on the sea, the immense fleet, besides the numerous ships of other nations, the crowds of people in Pera, Galata, and Topana—all unite to form a panorama of singular beauty. The richest fancy would fail in the attempt to portray such a scene; the most practised pen would be unequal to the task of adequately describing it. But the gorgeous picture will be ever present to my memory, though I lack the power of presenting it to the minds of others.

Frequently, and each time with renewed pleasure, I ascended this tower, and would sit there for hours, in admiration of the works of the created and of the Creator. Exhausted and weary with gazing was I each time I returned to my home. I think I may affirm that no spot in the world can present such a view, or any thing that can be compared with it. I found how right I had been in undertaking this journey in preference to any other. Here another world lies unfolded before my view. Every thing here is new—nature, art, men, manners, customs, and mode of life. He who would see something totally different from the every-day routine of European life in European towns should come here.

THE BAZAAR.

In the town of Constantinople we come upon a wooden bridge, large, long, and broad, stretching across the Golden Horn. The streets of the town are rather better paved than those of Pera. In the bazaars and on the sea-coast alone do we find an appearance of bustle; the remaining streets are quiet enough.

The Bazaar is of vast extent, comprehending many covered streets, which cross each other in every direction and receive light from above. Every article of merchandise has its peculiar alley. In one all the goldsmiths have their shops, in another the shoemakers; in this street you see nothing but silks, in another real Cashmere shawls, etc.

Every dealer has a little open shop, before which he sits, and unceasingly invites the passers-by to purchase. Whoever wishes to buy or to look at any thing sits down also in front of the booth. The merchants are very good-natured and obliging; they always willingly unfold and display their treasures, even when they notice that the person to whom they are shewing them does not intend to become a purchaser. I had, however, imagined the display of goods to be much more varied and magnificent than I found it;

but the reason of this apparent poverty is that the true treasures of art and nature, such as shawls, precious stones, pearls, valuable arms, gold brocades, etc., must not be sought in the bazaars; they are kept securely under lock and key in the dwellings or warehouses of the proprietors, whither the stranger must go if he wishes to see the richest merchandise.

The greatest number of streets occupied by the followers of any one trade are those inhabited by the makers of shoes and slippers. A degree of magnificence is displayed in their shops such as a stranger would scarcely expect to see. There are slippers which are worth 1000 piastres {53} a pair and more. They are embroidered with gold, and ornamented with pearls and precious stones.

The Bazaar is generally so much crowded, that it is a work of no slight difficulty to get through it; yet the space in the middle is very broad, and one has rarely to step aside to allow a carriage or a horseman to pass. But the bazaars and baths are the lounges and gossiping places of the Turkish women. Under the pretence of bathing or of wishing to purchase something, they walk about here for half a day together, amusing themselves with small-talk, love-affairs, and with looking at the wares.

THE MOSQUES.

Without spending a great deal of money, it is very difficult to obtain admittance into the mosques. You are compelled to take out a firmann, which costs from 1000 to 1200 piastres. A guide of an enterprising spirit is frequently sufficiently acute to inquire in the different hotels if there are any guests who wish to visit the mosques. Each person who is desirous of doing so gives four or five colonati {54} to the guide, who thereupon procures the firmann, and frequently clears forty or fifty guilders by the transaction. An opportunity of this description to visit the mosques generally offers itself several times in the course of a month.

I had made up my mind that it would be impossible to quit Constantinople without first seeing the four wonder-mosques, the Aja Sofia, Sultan Achmed, Osmanije, and Soleimanije.

I had the good fortune to obtain admittance on paying a very trifling sum; I think I should regret it to this day if I had paid five colonati for such a purpose.

To an architect these mosques are no doubt highly interesting; to a profane person like myself they offer little attraction. Their principal beauty generally consists in the bold arches of the cupolas. The interior is always empty, with the exception of a few large chandeliers placed at intervals, and furnished with a large number of perfectly plain glass lamps. The marble floors are covered with straw mats. In the Sofia mosque we find a few pillars which have been brought hither from Ephesus and Baalbec, and in a compartment on one side several sarcophagi are deposited.

Before entering the mosque, you must either take off your shoes or put on slippers over them. The outer courts, which are open to all, are very spacious, paved with slabs of marble, and kept scrupulously clean. In the midst stands a fountain, at which the Mussulman washes his hands, his face, and his feet, before entering the mosque. An open colonnade resting on pillars usually runs round the mosques, and splendid plantains and other trees throw a delicious shade around.

The mosque of Sultan Achmed, on the Hippodrome, is surrounded by six minarets. Most of the others have only two, and some few four.

The kitchens for the poor, situated in the immediate neighbourhood of the mosques, are a very praiseworthy institution. Here the poor Mussulman is regaled on simple dishes, such as rice, beans, cucumbers, etc., at the public expense. I marvelled greatly to find no crowding at these places. Another and an equally useful measure is the erection of numerous fountains of clear good water. This is the more welcome when we remember that the Turkish religion forbids the use of all spirituous liquors. At many of these fountains servants are stationed, whose only duty is to keep ten or twelve goblets of shining brass constantly filled with this refreshing nectar, and to offer them to every passer-by, be he Turk or Frank. Beer-houses and wine-shops are not to be found here. Would to Heaven this were every where the case! How many a poor wretch would never have been poor, and how many a madman would never have lost his senses!

Not far from the Osmanije mosque is the

SLAVE-MARKET.

I entered it with a beating heart, and already before I had even seen them, pitied the poor slaves. How glad, therefore, was I when I found them not half so forlorn and neglected as we Europeans are accustomed to imagine! I saw around me friendly smiling faces, from the grimaces and contortions of which I could easily discover that their owners were making quizzical remarks on every passing stranger.

The market is a great yard, surrounded by rooms, in which the slaves live. By day they may walk about in the yard, pay one another visits, and chatter as much as they please.

In a market of this kind we, of course, see every gradation of colour, from light brown to the deepest black. The white slaves, and the most beautiful of the blacks, are not however to be seen by every stranger, but are shut up in the dwellings of the traffickers in human flesh. The dress of these people is simple in the extreme. They either wear only a large linen sheet, which is wrapped round them, or some light garment. Even this they are obliged to take off when a purchaser appears. So long as they are in the hands of the dealers, they are certainly not kept in very good style; so they all look forward with great joy to the prospect of getting a master. When they are once purchased, their fate is generally far from hard. They always adopt the religion of their master, are not overburdened with work, are well clothed

34

and fed, and kindly treated. Europeans also purchase slaves, but may not look upon them and treat them as such; from the moment when a slave is purchased by a Frank he becomes free. Slaves bought in this way, however, generally stay with their masters.

THE OLD SERAIL

is, of course, an object of paramount attraction to us Europeans. I betook myself thither with my expectations at full stretch, and once more found the reality to be far below my anticipations. The effect of the whole is certainly grand; many a little town would not cover so much ground as this place, which consists of a number of houses and buildings, kiosks, and summer-houses, surrounded with plantains and cypress-trees, the latter half hidden amid gardens and arbours. Everywhere there is a total want of symmetry and taste. I saw something of the garden, walked through the first and second courtyard, and even peeped into the third. In the last two yards the buildings are remarkable for the number of cupolas they exhibit. I saw a few rooms and large halls quite full of a number of European things, such as furniture, clocks, vases, etc. My expectations were sadly damped. The place where the heads of pashas who had fallen into disfavour were exhibited is in the third yard. Heaven be praised, no severed heads are now seen stuck on the palings.

I was not fortunate enough to be admitted into the imperial harem; I did not possess sufficient interest to obtain a view of it. At a later period of my journey, however, I succeeded in viewing several harems.

THE HIPPODROME

is the largest and finest open place in Constantinople. After those of Cairo and Padua, it is the most spacious I have seen any where. Two obelisks of red granite, covered with hieroglyphics, are the only ornaments of this place. The houses surrounding it are built, according to the general fashion, of wood, and painted with oil-colours of different tints. I here noticed a great number of pretty children's carriages, drawn by servants. Many parents assembled here to let their children be driven about.

Not far from the Hippodrome are the great cisterns with the thousand and one pillars. Once on a time this gigantic fabric must have presented a magnificent appearance. Now a miserable wooden staircase, lamentably out of repair, leads you down a flight of thirty or forty steps into the depths of one of these cisterns, the roof of which is supported by three hundred pillars. This cistern is no longer filled with water, but serves as a workshop for silk-spinners. The place seems almost as if it had been expressly built for such a purpose, as it receives light from above, and is cool in summer, and warm during the winter. It is now impossible to penetrate into the lower stories, as they are either filled with earth or with water.

The aqueducts of Justinian and Valentinian are stupendous works. They extend from Belgrade to the "Sweet Waters," a distance of about fourteen

miles, and supply the whole of Constantinople with a sufficiency of water.
COFFEE-HOUSES—STORY-TELLERS.

Before I bade farewell to Constantinople for the present and betook me to
Pera, I requested my guide to conduct me to a few coffee-houses, that I
might have a new opportunity of observing the peculiar customs and mode
of life of the Turks. I had already obtained some notion of the appearance
of these places in Giurgewo and Galatz; but in this imperial town I had
fancied I should find them somewhat neater and more ornamental. But
this delusion vanished as soon as I entered the first coffee-house. A
wretchedly dirty room, in which Turks, Greeks, Armenians, and others sat
cross-legged on divans, smoking and drinking coffee, was all I could
discover. In the second house I visited I saw, with great disgust, that the
coffee-room was also used as a barber's shop; on one side they were serving
coffee, and on the other a Turk was having his head shaved. They say that
bleeding is sometimes even carried on in these booths.

In a coffee-house of a rather superior class we found one of the so-called
"story-tellers." The audience sit round in a half-circle, and the narrator
stands in the foreground, and quietly begins a tale from the Thousand and
One Nights; but as he continues he becomes inspired, and at length roars
and gesticulates like the veriest ranter among a company of strolling players.
Sherbet is not drunk in all the coffee-houses; but every where we find stalls
and booths where this cooling and delicious beverage is to be had. It is
made from the juice of fruits, mixed with that of lemons and pomegranates.
In Pera ice is only to be had in the coffee-houses of the Franks, or of
Christian confectioners. All coffee-house keepers are obliged to buy their
coffee ready burnt and ground from the government, the monopoly of this
article being an imperial privilege. A building has been expressly
constructed for its preparation, where the coffee is ground to powder by
machinery. The coffee is made very strong, and poured out without being
strained, a custom which I could not bring myself to like.

It is well worth the traveller's while to make an
EXCURSION TO EJUB,

the greatest suburb of Constantinople, and also the place where the richest
and most noble of the Turks are buried.

Ejub, the standard-bearer of Mahomet, rests here in a magnificent mosque,
built entirely of white marble. None but a Mussulman may tread this
hallowed shrine. A tolerably good view of the interior can, however, be
obtained from without, as the windows are lofty and broad, and reach
nearly to the ground. The sarcophagus stands in a hall; it is covered with a
richly embroidered pall, over which are spread five or six "real" shawls.
The part beneath which the head rests is surmounted by a turban, also of
real shawls. The chief sarcophagus is surrounded by several smaller coffins,
in which repose the wives, children, and nearest relations of Ejub. Hard by

the mosque we find a beautiful fountain of white marble, surrounded by a railing of gilded iron, and furnished with twelve bright drinking-cups of polished brass. A Turk here is appointed expressly to hand these to the passers-by. A little crooked garden occupies the space behind the mosque. The mosques in which the dead sultans are deposited are all built in the same manner as that of Ejub. Instead of the turban, handsome fez-caps, with the heron's feather, lie on the coffins. Among the finest mosques is that in which repose the remains of the late emperor. In Ejub many very costly monuments are to be seen. They are generally surrounded by richly-gilt iron railings, their peaks surmounted by the shining crescent, and forming an arch above a sarcophagus, round which are planted rose-bushes and dwarf cypresses, with ivy and myrtle clinging to their stems. It would, however, be very erroneous to suppose that the rich alone lie buried here. The poor man also finds his nook; and frequently we see close by a splendid monument the modest stone which marks the resting-place of the humble Mussulman.

On my return I met the funeral of a poor Turk. If my attention had not been attracted to the circumstance, I should have passed by without heeding it. The corpse was rolled in a cloth, fastened at the head and at the feet, and laid on a board which a man carried on his shoulder. At the grave the dead man is once more washed, wrapped in clean linen cloths, and thus lowered into the earth. And this is as it should be. Why should the pomp and extravagance of man accompany him to his last resting-place? Were it not well if in this matter we abated something of our conventionality and ostentation? I do not mean to say that interments need be stripped of every thing like ornament; in all things the middle way is the safest. A simple funeral has surely in it more that awakes true religious feeling than the pomp and splendour which are too frequently made the order of the day in these proceedings. In this case are not men sometimes led away to canvass and to criticise the splendour of the show, while they should be deducing a wholesome moral lesson for themselves, or offering up a fervent prayer to the Almighty for the peace of the departed spirit?

HOUSES—THEATRES—CARRIAGES.

The houses in the whole of Constantinople, in which we may include Pera, Topana, etc., are very slightly and carelessly put together. No door, no window, closes and fits well; the floorings frequently exhibit gaps an inch in breadth; and yet rents are very high. The reason of this is to be found in the continual danger of fire to which all towns built of wood are exposed. Every proprietor of a house calculates that he may be burnt out in the course of five or six years, and therefore endeavours to gain back his capital with interest within this period. Thus we do not find the houses so well built or so comfortably furnished as in the generality of European towns. There is a theatre in Pera, which will hold from six to seven hundred spectators. At the time of my sojourn there, a company of Italian singers were giving four representations every week. Operas of the most celebrated masters were here to be heard; but I attended one representation, and had quite enough. The wonder is that such an undertaking answers at all, as the Turks have no taste for music, and the Franks are too fastidious to be easily satisfied.

The carriages—which are, generally speaking, only used by women—are of two kinds. The first is in the shape of a balloon, finely painted and gilt, and furnished with high wheels. On each side is an opening, to enter which the passenger mounts on a wooden stool, placed there by the coachman every time he ascends or descends. The windows or openings can be closed with Venetian blinds. These carriages contain neither seats nor cushion. Every one who drives out takes carpets or bolsters with him, spreads them out inside the coach, and sits down cross-legged. A carriage of this description will hold four persons. The second species of carriage only differs from that already described in having still higher wheels, and consisting of a kind of square box, covered in at the top, but open on all sides. The passengers enter at the back, and there is generally room for eight persons. The former kind of vehicle is drawn by one horse in shafts, and sometimes by two; the latter by one or two oxen, also harnessed in shafts, which are, however, furnished in addition with a wooden arch decorated with flowers, coloured paper, and ribbons. The coachman walks on foot beside his cattle, to guide them with greater security through the uneven ill-paved streets, in which you are continually either ascending or descending a hill.

Wagons there are none; every thing is carried either by men, horses, or asses. This circumstance explains the fact that more porters are found here than in any other city. These men are agile and very strong; a porter often bears a load of from one hundred to a hundred and fifty pounds through the rugged hilly streets. Wood, coals, provisions, and building-materials are carried by horses and asses. This may be one reason why every thing is so dear in Constantinople.

CHAPTER IV.

On Sundays and holydays the "Sweet Waters" of Europe are much frequented. One generally crosses the Golden Horn, into which the sweet water runs, in a kaik. There is, however, another way thither across the mountains.

A large grass-plat, surrounded by trees, is the goal towards which the heaving multitude pours. Here are to be seen people from all quarters of the globe, and of all shades of colour, reclining in perfect harmony on carpets, mats, and pillows, and solacing themselves, pipe in mouth, with coffee and sweetmeats. Many pretty Jewesses, mostly unveiled, are to be seen among the crowd.

On Friday, the holiday of the Turks, the scene in the Asiatic Sweet Waters is just as animated; and here there is much more to interest us Europeans, as the company consists chiefly of Turks, male and female. The latter have, as usual, their faces covered: the most beautiful feature, the flaming eye, is, however, visible.

The trip across the sea to the Asiatic Sweet Waters is incomparably more beautiful and interesting than the journey to the European. We travel up the Bosphorus, in the direction of the Black Sea, past the splendid new palace of the Sultan. Though this palace is chiefly of wood, the pillars, staircases, and the ground-floor, built of marble of dazzling whiteness, are strikingly beautiful. The great gates, of gilded cast-iron, may be called masterpieces; they were purchased in England for the sum of £8000. The roof of the palace is in the form of a terrace, and round this terrace runs a magnificent gallery, built only of wood, but artistically carved. We also pass the two ancient castles which command the approach to Constantinople, and then turn to the right towards the Sweet Waters. The situation of this place is most lovely; it lies in a beautiful valley surrounded by green hills.

Very interesting is also an excursion to Chalcedonia, a peninsula in the Sea of Marmora, on the Asiatic side, adjoining Scutari. We were rowed thither in a two-oared kaik in an hour and a quarter. The finest possible weather favoured our trip. A number of dolphins gambolled around our boat; we saw these tame fishes darting to and fro in all directions, and leaping into the air. It is a peculiar circumstance with regard to these creatures, that they never swim separately, but always either in pairs or larger companies.

The views which we enjoy during these trips are peculiarly lovely. Scutari lies close on our left; the foreground is occupied by mountains of moderate elevation; and above them, in the far distance, gleams the snow-clad summit of Olympus. The uninhabited Prince's Island and the two Dog Islands are not the most picturesque objects to be introduced in such a landscape. To make up for the disadvantage of their presence we have, however, a good view of the Sea of Marmora, and can also distinguish the greater portion of the city of Constantinople.

On Chalcedonia itself there is nothing to be seen but a lighthouse. Beautiful grass-plats, with a few trees and a coffee-house, are the chief points of attraction with the townspeople.

An excursion by sea to Baluklid is also to be recommended. You pass the entire Turkish fleet, which is very considerable, and see the largest ship in the world, the "Mahmud," of 140 guns, built during the reign of the late Sultan Mahmud. Several three-deckers of 120 guns, some of them unrigged, and many men-of-war mounting from forty to sixty cannons, lie in the harbour. For an hour and a half we are riding through the Sea of Marmora, to the left of the great quay which surrounds the walls of

Constantinople. Here, for the first time, we see the giant city in all its magnificent proportions. We also passed the "Seven Towers," of which, however, only five remain standing; the other two, I was told, had fallen in. If these towers really answer no other purpose than that of prisons for the European ambassadors during tumults or in the event of hostilities, I think the sooner the remaining five tumble down the better; for the European powers will certainly not brook such an insult from the Turks, now in the day of their decline.

We disembarked immediately beyond the "Seven Towers," and walked for half an hour through long empty streets, then out at the town-gate, where the cypress-grove for a time conceals from our view a large open space on which is built a pretty Greek church. I was told that during the holidays at Easter such riotous scenes were here enacted that broken heads were far from being phenomena of rare occurrence. In the church there is a cold spring containing little fishes. A legend goes, that on the high days at Easter these poor little creatures swim about half fried and yet alive, because once upon a time, when Constantinople was besieged, a general said that it was no more likely that the city could be taken than that fishes could swim about half fried. Ever since that period the wonderful miracle of the fried fish is said to occur annually at Easter.

On our return to our kaik, we saw near the shore an enormous cuttle-fish, more than fourteen feet in length, which had just been taken and killed. A number of fishermen were trying with ropes and poles to drag the monster ashore.

The walks in the immediate neighbourhood of Pera are the great and little Campo, and somewhat farther distant the great bridge which unites Topana with Constantinople; the latter is a most amusing walk, during which we can view the life and bustle on both shores at the same time. In the little Campo are two Frankish coffee-houses, before which we sit quite in European fashion on handsome chairs and benches, listening to pleasant music, and regaling ourselves with ices.

FEASTS IN CONSTANTINOPLE.

During my residence in Constantinople I had the good fortune to be present at some very entertaining festivities. The most magnificent of these took place on the 23d of April, the anniversary of Mahomet's death.

On the eve of this feast we enjoyed a fairy-like spectacle. The tops of all the minarets were illuminated with hundreds of little lamps; and as there are a great many of these slender spires, it can be readily imagined that this sea of light must have a beautiful effect. The Turkish ships in the harbour presented a similar appearance. At every loop-hole a large lamp occupied the place of the muzzle of the cannon. At nine o'clock in the evening, salvoes were fired from the ships; and at the moment that the cannons were fired, the lamps vanished, flashes of light and gunpowder-smoke filled the air; a few seconds afterwards, as if by magic, the lamps had reappeared. This salute was repeated three times.

The morning of the 23d was ushered in by the booming of the cannon. All the Turkish ships had hoisted their flags, and garlands of coloured paper were twined round the masts to their very tops.

At nine o'clock I proceeded in the company of several friends to Constantinople, to see the grand progress of the Sultan to the mosque. As with us, it is here the custom to post soldiers on either side of the way. The procession was headed by the officers and government officials; but after every couple of officers or statesmen followed their servants, generally to the number of twelve or fifteen persons, in very variegated costumes, partly Turkish, partly European, and withal somewhat military; in fact, a perfect motley. Then came the Emperor's state-horses, splendid creatures, the majority of them of the true Arabian breed, decorated with saddle-cloths richly embroidered with gold, pearls, and precious stones, and proudly moving their plumed heads. Their spirited appearance and beautiful paces excited the admiration of all the learned in such matters. They were followed by a number of pages on foot; these pages are not, however, youths, as in other countries, but men of tried fidelity. In their midst rode the youthful Emperor, wrapped in his cape, and wearing in his fez-cap a fine heron's plume, buckled with the largest diamond in Europe. As the Sultan passed by, he was greeted by the acclamations of the military, but not of the people. The soldiers closed the procession; but their bearing is not nearly so haughty as that of the horses. The reason of this is simple enough—no one dares look upon the Arabians with an evil eye, but the soldiers are entirely subject to the caprice of their officers. I would certainly rather be the Sultan's horse than his soldier.

The uniforms of the officers, in their profusion of gold embroidery, resemble those of our hussars. The privates have very comfortable jackets and trousers of blue cloth with red trimmings; some have jackets entirely of a red colour. The artillerymen wear red facings. Their chaussure is pitiable in the extreme: some have boots, not unfrequently decorated with spurs; others have shoes, trodden down at heel and terribly tattered; and some even appear in slippers. All are without stockings, and thus naked feet peer forth every where. The position of the men with regard to each other is just as irregular; a little dwarf may frequently be seen posted next to a giant, a boy of twelve or fourteen years near a grey-headed veteran, and a negro standing next to a white man.

At this feast a great concourse of people was assembled, and every window was crowded with muffled female heads.

We had been advised not to be present at this ceremony, as it was stated to be of a purely religious nature, and it was feared we should be exposed to annoyance from the fanaticism of the Mussulmen. I am glad to say, however, that the curiosity of my party was stronger than their apprehensions. We pushed through every where, and I had again occasion to feel assured that grievous wrong is frequently done the good Turks. Not only was there no appearance of a disposition to annoy us, but we even obtained very good places without much trouble.

On their Easter days the Greeks have a feast in the great Campo. On all the three holidays, the hamaks (water-carriers and porters), after the service is over, march in large numbers to the Campo with songs and music, with noise and shouting, waving their handkerchiefs in the air. Arrived at their destination, they divide into different groups, and proceed to amuse themselves much after the manner of other nations. A number of tents are erected, where a great deal of cooking and baking is carried on. Large companies are sitting on the ground or on the tombstones, eating and drinking in quiet enjoyment. We see a number of swings laden with men and children; on this side we hear the squeaking of a bagpipe, on that the sound of a pipe and drum, uttering such dismal music that the hearer instinctively puts a finger into each ear. To this music a real bear's dance is going on. Six or eight fellows stand in a half circle round the musician, and two leaders of these light-toed clodhoppers continually wave their handkerchiefs in the air as they stamp slowly and heavily round in a circle. The women are allowed to appear at this feast, but may neither take part in the swinging nor in the dancing. They therefore keep up a brave skirmishing with the sweetmeats, coffee, and delicacies of all kinds. The more wealthy portion of the community employ these days in riding to Baluklid, to gaze and wonder at the miracle of the half-baked and yet living fishes.

As the Greeks are not so good-natured as the Turks, the latter seldom take part in their festivities. Turkish women never appear on these occasions.

On the 8th of May I saw a truly Turkish fête in the neighbourhood of the Achmaidon (place of arrows).

In a plain surrounded on all sides by hills, men of all nations formed a large but closely-packed circle. Kavasses (gens d'arme) were there to keep order among the people, and several officers sat among the circle to keep order among the kavasses. The spectacle began. Two wrestlers or gladiators made their appearance, completely undressed, with the exception of trousers of strong leather. They had rubbed themselves all over with oil, so that their joints might be soft and supple, and also that their adversary should not be able to obtain a firm hold when they grappled together. They made several obeisances to the spectators, began with minor feats of wrestling, and frequently stopped for a few moments in order to husband their strength. Then the battle began afresh, and became hotter and hotter, till at length one of the combatants was hailed as victor by the shouting mob. He is declared the conqueror who succeeds in throwing his opponent in such a manner that he can sit down upon him as on a horse. A combat of this kind usually lasts a quarter of an hour. The victor walks triumphantly round the circle to collect his reward. The unfortunate vanquished conceals himself among the spectators, scarcely daring to lift his eyes. These games last for several hours; as one pair of gladiators retire, they are replaced by another.

Greek, Turkish, and Armenian women may only be spectators of these games from a distance; they therefore occupy the adjoining heights. For the rest, the arrangements are the same as at the Greek Easter feast. People eat, drink, and dance. No signs of beer, wine, or liqueur are to be discovered, and consequently there is no drunkenness.

The Turkish officers were here polite enough to surrender the best places to us strangers. I had many opportunities of noticing the character of the Mussulman, and found, to my great delight, that he is much better and more honest than prejudices generally allow us to believe. Even in matters of commerce and business it is better to have to do with a Turk than with a votary of any other creed, not even excepting my own.

During my stay at Constantinople (from the 5th of April until May 17th) I found the weather just as changeable as in my own country; so much so, in fact, that the temperature frequently varied twelve or fourteen degrees within four-and-twenty hours.

EXCURSION TO BRUSSA.

The two brothers, Baron Charles and Frederick von Buseck, and Herr Sattler, the talented artist, resolved to make an excursion to Brussa; and as I had expressed a similar wish, they were obliging enough to invite me to make a fourth in their party. But when it came to the point, I had almost become irresolute. I was asked by some one if I was a good rider; "for if you are not," said my questioner, "it would be far better for you not to accompany them, as Brussa is four German miles distant from Gemlek, and the road is bad, so that the gentlemen must ride briskly if they wish to reach the town before sundown, starting as they would at half-past two in the afternoon, the general hour of landing at Gemlek. In the event of your being unable to keep up with the rest, you would put them to great inconvenience, or they will be compelled to leave you behind on the road."

I had never mounted a horse, and felt almost inclined to confess the fact; but my curiosity to see Brussa, the beautiful town at the foot of Olympus, gained the day, and I boldly declared that I had no doubt I should be able to keep pace with my companions.

On the 13th of May we left Constantinople at half-past six in the morning, on board a little steamer of forty-horse power. Passing the Prince's and Dog Islands, we swept across the Sea of Marmora towards the snow-crowned Olympus, until, after a voyage of seven hours, we reached Gemlek.

Gemlek, distant thirty sea miles from Constantinople, is a miserable place, but nevertheless does some trade as the harbour of Bithynia. The agent of the Danube Navigation Company was civil enough to procure us good horses, and a genuine, stalwart, and fierce-looking Turkoman for a guide. This man wore in his girdle several pistols and a dagger; a long crooked scimitar hung at his side; and instead of shoes and slippers, large boots decked his feet, bordered at the top by a wide stripe of white cloth, on which were depicted blue flowers and other ornaments. His head was graced by a handsome turban.

At half-past two o'clock the horses arrived. I swung myself boldly upon my Rosinante, called on my good angel to defend me, and away we started, slowly at first, over stock and stone. My joy was boundless when I found that I could sit steadily upon my horse; but shortly afterwards, when we broke into a trot, I began to feel particularly uncomfortable, as I could not get on at all with the stirrup, which was continually slipping to my heel, while sometimes my foot slid out of it altogether, and I ran the risk of losing my balance. Oh, what would I not have given to have asked advice of any one! But unfortunately I could not do so without at once betraying my ignorance of horsemanship. I therefore took care to bring up the rear, under the pretence that my horse was shy, and would not go well unless it saw the others before it. My real reason was that I wished to hide my manœuvres from the gentlemen, for every moment I expected to fall. Frequently I clutched the saddle with both hands, as I swayed from side to side. I looked forward in terror to the gallop, but to my surprise found that I could manage this pace better than the trot. My courage brought its reward, for I reached the goal of our journey thoroughly shaken, but without mishap. During the time that we travelled at a foot-pace, I had found leisure to contemplate the scenery around us. For half the entire distance we ride from one valley into another; as often as a hill is reached, there is a limited prospect before the traveller, who has, however, only to turn his head, and he enjoys a beautiful view over the Sea of Marmora. After a ride of two hours and a half we arrived at a little khan, {71a} where we rested for half an hour. Proceeding thence a short distance, we reached the last hills; and the great valley, at the end of which Brussa is seen leaning against Olympus, lay stretched before our eager eyes, while behind us we could still distinguish, far beyond hill and dale, the distant sea skirting the horizon. Yet, beautiful as this landscape undoubtedly is, I had seen it surpassed in Switzerland. The immense valley which lies spread out before Brussa is uncultivated, deserted, and unwatered; no carpet of luxuriant verdure, no rushing river, no pretty village, gives an air of life to this magnificent and yet monotonous region; and no giant mountains covered with eternal snow look down upon the plain beneath. Pictures like these I had frequently found in Switzerland, in the Tyrol, and also near Salzburg.

Here I saw, indeed, separate beauties, but no harmonious whole. Olympus is a fine majestic mountain, forming an extended barrier; but its height can scarcely exceed 6000 feet; {71b} and during the present month it is totally despoiled of its surface of glittering snow. Brussa, with its innumerable minarets, is the only point of relief to which the eye continually recurs, because there is nothing beyond to attract it. A little brook, crossed by a very high stone bridge, but so shallow already in the middle of May as hardly to cover our horses' hoofs; and towards Brussa, a miserable village, with a few plantations of olives and mulberry-trees,—are the only objects to be discovered throughout the whole wide expanse. Wherever I found the olive-tree—here, near Trieste, and in Sicily,—it was alike ugly. The stem is gnarled, and the leaves are narrow and of a dingy green colour. The mulberry-tree, with its luxuriant bright green foliage, forms an agreeable contrast to the olive. The silk produced in this neighbourhood is peculiarly fine in quality, and the stuffs from Brussa are renowned far and wide.

We reached the town in safety before sunset. It is one of the most disagreeable circumstances that can happen to the traveller to arrive at an Oriental town after evening has closed in. He finds the gates locked, and may clamour for admittance in vain.

In order to gain our inn, we were obliged to ride through the greater part of the town. I had here an opportunity of observing that it is just as unsightly as the interior of Constantinople. The streets are narrow, and the houses built of wood, plaster, and some even of stone; but all wear an aspect of poverty, and at the same time of singularity;—the gables projecting so much that they occupy half the width of the street, and render it completely dark, while they increase its narrowness. The inn, too, at which we put up, looked far from inviting when viewed from the outside, so that we had some dark misgivings respecting the quality of the accommodation that awaited us. But in proportion as the outside had looked unpropitious, were we agreeably surprised on entering. A neat and roomy courtyard, with a basin of pure sparkling water in the midst, surrounded by mulberry-trees, was the first thing we beheld. Round this courtyard were two stories of clean but simply-furnished rooms. The fare was good, and we were even regaled with a bottle of excellent wine from the lower regions of Olympus.

May 14th.

Next morning we visited the town and its environs, under the guidance and protection of a kavasse. The town itself is of great extent, and is reported to contain above 10,000 houses, inhabited exclusively by Turks. The population of the suburbs, which comprise nearly 4000 houses, is a mixed one of Christians, Jews, Greeks, etc. The town numbers three hundred and sixty mosques; but the greater portion of them are so insignificant and in such a dilapidated condition, that we scarcely observed them.

Strangers are here permitted to enter the mosques in company of a kavasse.

We visited some of the principal, among which the Ulla Drchamy may decidedly be reckoned. The cupola of this mosque is considered a masterpiece, and rests upon graceful columns. It is open at the top, thus diffusing a chastened light and a clear atmosphere throughout the building. Immediately beneath this cupola stands a large marble basin, in which small fishes swim merrily about.

The mosque of Sultan Mahomed I. and of Sultan Ildirim Bojasid must also be noticed on account of their splendid architecture; the latter, too, for the fine view which is thence obtained. In the mosque of Murad I. visitors are still shewn weapons and garments which once belonged to that sultan. I saw none of the magnificent regal buildings mentioned by some writers. The imperial kiosk is so simple in its appearance, that if we had not climbed the hill on which it stands for the sake of the view, it would not have been worth the trouble of the walk.

A stone bridge, roofed throughout its entire length, crosses the bed of the river, which has very steep banks, but contains very little water. A double row of small cottages, in which silk-weavers live and ply their trade, lines this bridge, which I was surprised to see here, as its architecture seemed rather to appertain to my own country than to the East. During my whole journey I did not see a second bridge of this kind, either in Syria or Egypt.

The streets are all very dull and deserted, a fact which is rather remarkable in a town of 100,000 inhabitants. In most of the streets more dogs than men are to be seen. Not only in Constantinople, but almost in every Oriental town, vast numbers of these creatures run about in a wild state.

Here, as every where, some degree of bustle is to be found in the bazaars, particularly in those which are covered in. Beautiful and durable silk stuffs, the most valuable of which are kept in warehouses under lock and key, form the chief article of traffic. In the public bazaar we found nothing exposed for sale except provisions. Among these I remarked some small, very unpalatable cherries. Asia Minor is the fatherland of this fruit, but I did not find it in any degree of perfection either here or at Smyrna.

Brussa is peculiarly rich in cold springs, clear as crystal, which burst forth from Mount Olympus. The town is intersected in all directions by subterranean canals; in many streets, the ripple of the waters below can be distinctly heard, and every house is provided with wells and stone basins of the limpid element; in some of the bazaars we find a similar arrangement.

On a nearer approach, the appearance of Mount Olympus is not nearly so grand as when viewed from a distance. The mountain is surrounded by several small hills, which detract from the general effect.

The baths, distant about a mile from the town, are prettily and healthfully situated, and, moreover, abundantly supplied with mineral water. Many strangers resort thither to recruit their weakened frames.

The finest among these baths is called Jeni Caplidche. A lofty circular hall contains a great swimming bath of marble, above which rises a splendid cupola. A number of refracting glasses (six hundred, they told me) diffuse a magic light around.

Our journey back to Constantinople was not accomplished entirely without mishap. One of the gentlemen fell from his horse and broke his watch. The saddles and bridles of hired horses are here generally in such bad condition that there is every moment something to buckle or to cobble up. We were riding at a pretty round pace, when suddenly the girths burst, and the saddle and rider tumbled off together. I arrived without accident at my destination, although I had frequently been in danger of falling from my horse without its being necessary that the girth should break.

The gentlemen were satisfied with my performance, for I had never lagged behind, nor had they once been detained on my account. It was not until we were safely on board the ship that I told them how venturesome I had been, and what terror I had undergone.

CHAPTER V.

The extremely unfavourable reports I heard from Beyrout and Palestine caused me to defer my departure from day to day. When I applied to my consul for a "firmann" (Turkish passport), I was strongly advised not to travel to the Holy Land. The disturbances on Mount Lebanon and the plague were, they assured me, enemies too powerful to be encountered except in cases of the most urgent necessity.

A priest who had arrived from Beyrout about two months previously affirmed positively that, in consequence of the serious disturbances, even he, known though he was far and wide as a physician, had not dared to venture more than a mile from the town without exposing himself to the greatest danger. He advised me to stay in Constantinople until the end of September, and then to travel to Jerusalem with the Greek caravan. This, he said, was the only method to reach that city in safety.

One day I met a pilgrim in a church who came from Palestine. On my asking his advice, he not only confirmed the priest's report, but even added that one of his companions had been murdered whilst journeying homeward, and that he himself had been despoiled of his goods, and had only escaped death through the special interposition of Providence. I did not at all believe the asseverations of this man; he related all his adventures with such a Baron Munchausen air, assumed probably to excite admiration. I continued my investigations on this subject until I was at length fortunate enough to find some one who told an entirely different tale. From this I felt assured at least of the fact, that it would be almost impossible to learn the true state of the case here in Constantinople, and at length made up my mind to avail myself of the earliest opportunity of proceeding as far as

Beyrout, where there was a chance of my getting at the truth.

I was advised to perform this journey in male attire; but I did not think it advisable to do so, as my short, spare figure would have seemed to belong to a youth, and my face to an old man. Moreover, as I had no beard, my disguise would instantly have been seen through, and I should have been exposed to much annoyance. I therefore preferred retaining the simple costume, consisting of a kind of blouse and wide Turkish trousers, which I then wore. The further I travelled, the more I became persuaded how rightly I had acted in not concealing my sex. Every where I was treated with respect, and kindness and consideration were frequently shewn me merely because I was a woman. On

May 17th

I embarked on board a steamboat belonging to the Austrian Lloyd. It was called the Archduke John.

It was with a feeling of painful emotion that I stood on the deck, gazing with an air of abstraction at the preparations for the long voyage which were actively going on around me. Once more I was alone among a crowd of people, with nothing to depend on but my trust in Providence. No friendly sympathetic being accompanied me on board. All was strange. The people, the climate, country, language, the manners and customs—all strange. But a glance upward at the unchanging stars, and the thought came into my soul, "Trust in God, and thou art not alone." And the feeling of despondency passed away, and soon I could once more contemplate with pleasure and interest all that was going on around me.

Near me stood a poor mother who could not bear to part with her son. Time after time she folded him in her arms, and kissed and blessed him. Poor mother! wilt thou see him again, or will the cold ground be a barrier between you till this life is past? Peace be with you both!

A whole tribe of people came noisily towards us;—they were friends of the crew, who bounced about the ship from stem to stern, canvassing its merits in comparison with French and English vessels.

Suddenly there was a great crowding on the swinging ladder, of chests, boxes, and baskets. Men were pushing and crushing backwards and forwards. Turks, Greeks, and others quarrelled and jostled each other for the best places on the upper deck, and in a few moments the whole large expanse wore the appearance of a bivouac. Mats and mattresses were every where spread forth, provisions were piled up in heaps, and culinary utensils placed in order beside them; and before these preparations had been half completed the Turks began washing their faces, hands, and feet, and unfolding their carpets, to perform their devotions. In one corner of the ship I even noticed that a little low tent had been erected; it was so closely locked, that for a long time I could not discern whether human beings or merchandise lay concealed within. No movement of the interior was to be perceived, and it was not until some days afterwards that I was informed by a Turk what the tent really contained. A scheick from the Syrian coast had purchased two girls at Constantinople, and was endeavouring to conceal them from the gaze of the curious. I was for nine days on the same vessel with these poor creatures, and during the whole time had not an opportunity of seeing either of them. At the debarcation, too, they were so closely muffled that it was impossible to discover whether they were white or black.

At six o'clock the bell was rung to warn all strangers to go ashore; and now I could discover who were really to be the companions of my journey. I had flattered myself that I should find several Franks on board, who might be bound to the same destination as myself; but this hope waxed fainter and fainter every moment, as one European after another left the ship, until at length I found myself alone among the strange Oriental nations.

The anchor was now weighed, and we moved slowly out of the harbour. I offered up a short but fervent prayer for protection on my long and dangerous voyage, and with a calmed and strengthened spirit I could once more turn my attention towards my fellow-passengers, who having concluded their devotions were sitting at their frugal meal. During the whole time they remained on the steamer these people subsisted on cold provisions, such as cheese, bread, hard-boiled eggs, anchovies, olives, walnuts, a great number of onions, and dried "mishmish," a kind of small apricot, which instead of being boiled is soaked in water for a few hours. In a sailing vessel it is usual to bring a small stove and some wood, in order to cook pilau, beans, fowls, and to boil coffee, etc. This, of course, is not allowed on board a steamboat.

The beauty of the evening kept me on deck, and I looked with a regretful feeling towards the imperial city, until the increasing distance and the soft veil of evening combined to hide it from my view, though at intervals the graceful minarets were still dimly discernible through the mist. But who shall describe my feelings of joy when I discovered a European among the passengers? Now I was no longer alone; in the first moments we even seemed fellow-countrymen, for the barriers that divide Europeans into different nations fall as they enter a new quarter of the globe. We did not ask each other, Are you from England, France, Italy; we inquired, Whither are you going? and on its appearing that this gentleman intended proceeding, like myself, to Jerusalem, we at once found so much to talk about concerning the journey, that neither of us thought for a moment of inquiring to what country the other belonged. We conversed in the universal French language, and were perfectly satisfied when we found we could understand each other. It was not until the following day that I discovered the gentleman to be an Englishman, and learned that his name was Bartlett. {79}

In Constantinople we had both met with the same fate. He had been, like myself, unable to obtain any certain intelligence, either at his consul's or from the inhabitants, as to the feasibility of a journey to Jerusalem, and so he was going to seek further information at Beyrout. We arranged that we would perform the journey from Beyrout to Jerusalem in company,—if, indeed, we found it possible to penetrate among the savage tribes of Druses and Maronites. So now I no longer stood unprotected in the wide world. I had found a companion as far as Jerusalem, the goal of my journey, which I could now hope to reach.

I was well satisfied with the arrangements on board. I had made up my mind, though not without sundry misgivings, to take a second-class berth; and on entering the steamer of the Austrian Lloyd, I discovered to my surprise how much may be effected by order and good management. Here the men and the women were separately lodged, wash-hand basins were not wanting, we fared well, and could not be cheated when we paid for our board, as the accounts were managed by the first mate: on the remaining steamers belonging to this company I found the arrangements equally good. Crossing the Sea of Marmora, we passed the "Seven Towers," leaving the Prince's Islands behind us on the left.

Early on the following day,

May 18th,

we reached the little town of Galipoli, situate on an eminence near the Hellespont. A few fragments of ruins in the last stage of dilapidation cause us to think of the ages that have fled, as we speed rapidly on. We waited here a quarter of an hour to increase the motley assemblage on deck by some new arrivals.

For the next 20 miles, as far as Sed Bahe, the sea is confined within such narrow bounds, that one could almost fancy it was a channel dug to unite the Sea of Marmora with the Archipelago. It is very appropriately called the STRAIT of the Dardanelles. On the left we have always the mainland of Asia, and on the right a tongue of land belonging to Europe, and terminating at Sed Bahe. The shores on both sides are desert and bare. It is a great contrast to former times, a contrast which every educated traveller must feel as he travels hither from the Bosphorus. What stirring scenes were once enacted here! Of what deeds of daring, chronicled in history, were not these regions the scene! Every moment brought us nearer to the classic ground. Alas, that we were not permitted to land on any of the Greek Islands, past which we flew so closely! I was obliged, perforce, to content myself with thinking of the past, of the history of ancient Greece, without viewing the sites where the great deeds had been done.

The two castles of the Dardanelles, Tschenekalesi and Kilidil Bahar, that on the Asiatic shore looking like a ruin, while its European neighbour wore the appearance of a fortress, let us steam past unchallenged. And how shall I

describe the emotions I felt as we approached the plains of Troy?
I was constantly on deck, lest I should lose any portion of the view, and
scarcely dared to breathe when at length the long-wished-for plain came in
sight.

Here it is, then, that this famous city is supposed to have stood. Yonder
mounds, perchance, cover the resting-places of Achilles, Patroclus, Ajax,
Hector, and many other heroes who may have served their country as
faithfully as these, though their names do not live in the page of history.
How gladly would I have trodden the plain, there to muse on the legends
which in my youth had already awakened in me such deep and awe-struck
interest, and had first aroused the wish to visit these lands—a desire now
partially fulfilled! But we flew by with relentless rapidity. The whole region
is deserted and bare. It seems as if nature and mankind were mourning
together for the days gone by. The inhabitants may indeed weep, for they
will never again be what they once were.

In the course of the day we passed several islands. In the foreground
towered the peak of the Hydræ, shortly afterwards Samothrace rose from
the waves, and we sailed close by the island of Tenedos. At first this island
does not present a striking appearance, but after rounding a small
promontory we obtained a view of the fine fortress skirting the sea; it seems
to have been built for the protection of the town beyond.

After passing Tenedos we lost sight of the Greek islands for a short time
(the mainland of Asia can always be distinguished on our left), but soon
afterwards we reached the most beautiful of them all—Mytelene, which has
justly been sung by many poets as the Island of the Fairies. For seven
hours we glided by its coast. It resembles a garden of olives, orange-trees,
pomegranates, etc. The view is bounded at the back by a double row of
peaked mountains, and the town lies nearly in the midst. It is built in a
circular form, round a hill, strengthened with fortifications. In front the
town is girded by a strong wall, and in the rear extends a deep bay. A few
masts peered forth and shewed us where the bay ended. From this point
we saw numerous villages prettily situated among the luxuriant shade of
large trees. It must be a delightful thing to spend the spring-time on this
island.

I remained on deck till late in the night, so charming, so rich in varied
pictures of verdant isles is this voyage on the Ægæan Sea. Had I been a
magician, I would have fixed the sun in the heavens until we had arrived at
Smyrna. Unfortunately many a beauteous island which we next morning
contemplated ruefully on the map was hidden from us by the shades of
night.

May 19th.

Long before the sun was up, I had resumed my post on deck, to welcome
Smyrna from afar.

A double chain of mountains, rising higher and higher, warned us of our approach to the rich commercial city. At first we can only distinguish the ancient dilapidated castle on a rock, then the city itself, built at the foot of the rock, on the sea-shore; at the back the view is closed by the "Brother Mountains."

The harbour is very spacious, but has rather the appearance of a wharf, with room for whole fleets to anchor. Many ships were lying here, and there was evidently plenty of business going on.

The "Franks' town," which can be distinctly viewed from the steamer, extends along the harbour, and has a decidedly European air.

Herr von Cramer had been previously apprised of my arrival, and was obliging enough to come on board to fetch me. We at once rode to Halizar, the summer residence of many of the citizens, where I was introduced to my host's family.

Halizar is distant about five English miles from Smyrna. The road thither is beautiful beyond description, so that one has no time to think about the distance. Immediately outside the town we pass a large open place near a river, where the camels rest, and where they are loaded and unloaded; I saw a whole herd of these animals. Their Arab or Bedouin drivers were reclining on mats, resting after their labours, while others were still fully employed about their camels. It was a truly Arabian picture, and moreover so new to me, that I involuntarily stopped my long-eared Bucephalus to contemplate it at my leisure.

Not far from this resting-place is the chief place of rendezvous and pastime of the citizens. It consists of a coffee-booth and a few rows of trees, surrounded by numerous gardens, all rich in beautiful fruit-trees. Charming beyond all the rest, the flower of the pomegranate-tree shines with the deepest crimson among the green leaves. Wild oleanders bloomed every where by the roadside. We wandered through beautiful shrubberies of cypress-trees and olives, and never yet had I beheld so rich a luxuriance of vegetation. This valley, with its one side flanked by wild and rugged rocks, in remarkable contrast to the fruitful landscape around, has a peculiar effect when viewed from the hill across which we ride. I was also much amazed by the numerous little troops of from six to ten, or even twenty camels, which sometimes came towards us with their grave majestic pace, and were sometimes overtaken by our fleet donkeys. Surrounded on all sides by objects at once novel and interesting, it will not be wondered at that I found the time passing far too rapidly.

The heat is said not to be more oppressive at Smyrna during the summer than at Constantinople. Spring, however, commences here earlier, and the autumn is longer. This fact, I thought, accounted for the lovely vegetation, which was here so much more forward than at Constantinople.

Herr von Cramer's country-house stands in the midst of a smiling garden; it is spacious and built of stone. The large and lofty apartments are flagged with marble or tiles. In the garden I found the first date-palm, a beautiful tree with a tall slender stem, from the extremity of which depend leaves five or six feet in length, forming a magnificent crown. In these regions and also in Syria, whither my journey afterwards led me, the date-palm does not attain so great a height as in Egypt, nor does it bear any fruit, but only stands as a noble ornament beside the pomegranate and orange trees. My attention was also attracted to numerous kinds of splendid acacias; some of these grew to an immense size, as high as the walnut-trees of my own country.

The villas of the townspeople all strongly resemble each other. The house stands in the midst of the garden, and the whole is surrounded by a wall.

In the evening I visited some of the peasants, in company with Herr von C. This gentleman informed me that these people were very poor, but still I found them decently clad and comfortably lodged in large roomy dwellings built of stone. Altogether, the condition of affairs seems here vastly superior to that in Galicia and in Hungary near the Carpathian mountains.

I reckoned the day I spent with this amiable family among the most pleasant I had yet passed. How gladly would I have accepted their hearty invitation to remain several weeks with them! But I had lost so much time in Constantinople, that on the morning of

May 20th

I was compelled to bid adieu to Frau von C. and her dear children. Herr von C. escorted me back to Smyrna. We took the opportunity of roaming through many streets of the Franks' quarter, which I found, generally speaking, pretty and cheerful enough, and moreover level and well paved. The handsomest street is that in which the consuls reside. The houses are finely built of stone, and the halls are tastefully paved with little coloured pebbles, arranged in the form of wreaths, stars, and squares. The inhabitants generally take up their quarters in these entrance-halls during the day, as it is cooler there than in the rooms. To nearly every house a pretty garden is attached.

The Turkish town is certainly quite different; it is built of wood, and is angular and narrow; dogs lie about in the streets, just as at Brussa and Constantinople. And why should it be otherwise here? Turks live in all this quarter, and they do not feel the necessity of clean and airy dwellings like the fastidious Franks.

The bazaars are not roofed; and here also the costlier portion of the wares is kept under lock and key.

It is well worth the traveller's while to make an excursion to Burnaba, a place lying on the sea-coast not far from the town, and serving, like Halizar, as a retreat for the townspeople during the summer. The views in this direction are various, and the road is good. The whole appearance of the place is that of a very extended village, with all its houses standing in the midst of gardens and surrounded by walls.

From the Acropolis we have a fine view in every direction, and find, in fact, a union of advantages only met with separately elsewhere.

In Smyrna I found the most beautiful women I had yet seen; and even during my further journey I met with few who equalled, and none who surpassed them. These fairy forms are, however, only to be sought among the Greeks. The natural charms of these Graces are heightened by the rich costume they wear. They have a peculiarly tasteful manner of fastening their little round fez-caps, beneath which their rich hair falls in heavy plaits upon their shoulders, or is wound with a richly embroidered handkerchief round the head and brow.

Smyrna is, however, not only celebrated as possessing the loveliest women, but also as the birthplace of one of the greatest men. {85} O Homer, in the Greece of to-day thou wouldst find no materials for thine immortal Iliad!

At five o'clock in the afternoon we quitted the harbour of Smyrna. In this direction the town is seen to much greater advantage after we have advanced a mile than when we approach it from Constantinople; for now the Turks' town lies spread in all its magnitude before us, whereas on the other side it is half hidden by the Franks' quarter.

The sea ran high, and adverse winds checked the speed of our good ship; but I am thankful to say that, except when the gale is very strong, it does not affect my health. I felt perfectly well, and stood enjoying the aspect of the waves as they came dancing towards our vessel. In Smyrna our company had been augmented by the arrival of a few more Franks.

May 21st.

Yesterday evening and all this day we have been sailing among islands. The principal of these were Scio, Samos, and Cos, and even these form a desolate picture of bare, inhospitable mountains and desert regions. On the island of Cos alone we saw a neat town, with strong fortifications.

May 22d.

This morning, shortly after five o'clock, we ran into the superb harbour of Rhodes. Here, for the first time, I obtained a correct notion of a harbour. That of Rhodes is shut in on all sides by walls and masses of rock, leaving only a gap of a hundred and fifty to two hundred paces in width for the ships to enter. Here every vessel can lie in perfect safety, be the sea outside the bar as stormy as it may; the only drawback is, that the entering of this harbour, a task of some difficulty in calm weather, becomes totally impracticable during a storm. A round tower stands as a protection on either side of the entrance to the harbour. The venerable church of St. John and the palace of the Komthur can be distinguished towering high above the houses and fortifications.

Our captain imparted to us the pleasant intelligence that we might spend the hours between this and three o'clock in the afternoon on shore. Our ship had for some time lain surrounded by little boats, and so we lost no time in being conveyed to the land. The first thing we did on reaching it was to ask questions concerning the ancient site of the celebrated Colossus. But we could gain no information, as neither our books nor the people here could point out the place to us with certainty; so we left the coast, to make up for the disappointment by exploring the ancient city.

Rhodes is surrounded with three rows of strong fortifications. We passed over three drawbridges before entering the town. We were quite surprised to see the beautiful streets, the well-kept houses, and the excellent pavement. The principal street, containing the houses of the ancient Knights of St. John, is very broad, with buildings so massively constructed of stone as almost to resemble fortresses. Heraldic bearings, with dates carved in stone, grace many of the Gothic gateways. The French shield, with the three lilies and the date 1402, occurs most frequently. On the highest point in the city are built the church of St. John and the house of the governor.

All the exteriors seem in such good preservation, that one could almost fancy the knights had only departed to plant their victorious banner on the Holy Sepulchre. They have in truth departed—departed to a better home. Centuries have breathed upon their ashes, scattered in all the regions of the earth. But their deeds have been chronicled both in heaven and among men, and the heroes still live in the admiration of posterity.

The churches, the house of the governor, and many other buildings, are not nearly so well preserved inside as a first glance would lead us to imagine. The reason of this is that the upper part of the town is but thinly inhabited. A gloomy air of silence and vacancy reigns around. We could wander about every where without being stared at or annoyed by the vulgar and envious. Mr. Bartlett, the Englishman, made a few sketches in his drawing-book of some of the chief beauties, such as the Gothic gateways, the windows, balconies, etc., and no inhabitant came to disturb him.

The pavement in the city, and even in the streets around the fortifications, consists wholly of handsome slabs of stone, often of different colours, like mosaic, and in such good preservation that we could fancy the work had been but recently concluded. This is certainly partly owing to the fact that no loaded wagon ever crushes over these stones, for the use of vehicles is entirely unknown in these parts; every thing is carried by horses, asses, or camels.

Cannons dating from the time of the Genoese still stand upon the ramparts. The carriages of these guns are very clumsy, the wheels consisting of round discs without spokes.

From our tower of observation we can form a perfect estimate of the extent and strength of the fortifications. The city is completely surrounded by three lofty walls, which seem to have been calculated to last an eternity, for they still stand almost uninjured in all their glory. In some places images of the Virgin, of the size of life, are hewn out of the walls.

The neighbourhood of Rhodes is most charming, and almost resembles a park. Many country houses lie scattered throughout this natural garden. The vegetation is here no less luxuriant than in Smyrna.

The architecture of the houses already begins to assume a new character. Many dwellings have towers attached, and the roofs are flat, forming numerous terraces, which are all built of stone. Some streets in the lower part of the town, inhabited chiefly by Jews, are bordered with cannon-balls, and present a most peculiar appearance.

I was also much struck with the costumes worn by the country-people, who were dressed quite in the Swabian fashion. It was in vain that I inquired the reason of this circumstance. The books we had with us gave no information on the subject, and I could not ask the natives through my ignorance of their language.

By three o'clock in the afternoon we were once more on board, and an hour afterwards we sailed out into the open sea. To-day we saw nothing further, except a high and lengthened mountain-range on the Asiatic mainland. It was a branch of the Taurus. The highest peaks glistened like silver in the evening light, enveloped in a garment of snow.

May 23d.

To-day our organs of vision had a rest, for we were sailing on the high seas. Late in the evening, however, the sailors descried the mountains of Cyprus looming in the far distance like a misty cloud. With my less practised eyes I could see nothing but the sunset at sea—a phenomenon of which I had had a more exalted conception. The rising and setting of the sun at sea is not nearly so striking a spectacle as the same phenomenon in a rocky landscape. At sea the sky is generally cloudless in the evening, and the sun gradually sinks, without refraction of rays or prismatic play of colours, into its ocean-bed, to pursue its unchanging course the next day. How infinitely more grand is this spectacle when seen from the "Rigi Kulm" in Switzerland! There it is really a spectacle, in contemplating which we feel impelled to fall on our knees in speechless adoration, and admire the wisdom of the Almighty in his wondrous works.

May 24th.

On mounting to the deck this morning at five o'clock I could distinguish the island of Cyprus, which looks uglier the nearer we approach. Both the foreground and the mountain-peaks have an uncomfortable barren air. At ten o'clock we entered the harbour of Larnaka. The situation of this town is any thing but fine; the country looks like an Arabian desert, and a few unfruitful date-palms rise beside the roofless stone houses.

I should not have gone on shore at all, if Doctor Faaslanc, whose acquaintance I had made at Constantinople, and who had been appointed quarantine physician here four weeks before my departure, had not come to fetch me. The streets of Larnaka are unpaved, so that we were obliged literally to wade more than ankle-deep in sand and dust. The houses are small, with irregular windows, sometimes high and sometimes low, furnished with wooden grated shutters; and the roofs are in the form of terraces. This style of building I found to be universal throughout Syria.

Of a garden or a green place not a trace was to be seen. The sandy expanse reaches to the foot of the mountains, which viewed from this direction form an equally barren picture. Behind these mountains the appearance of the landscape is said to be very fruitful; but I did not penetrate into the interior, nor did I go to Nikosia, the capital of the island, distant some twelve miles from Larnaka.

Doctor Faaslanc took me to his house, which had an appearance of greater comfort than I had expected to find, for it consisted of two spacious rooms which might almost have been termed halls. An agreeable coolness reigned every where.

Neither stoves nor chimneys were to be seen, as winter is here replaced by a very mild rainy season. The heat in summer is often said to be insupportable, the temperature rising to more than 36° Reaumur. To-day it reached 30° in the sun.

We drank to my safe return to my country, in real old Cyprian wine. Shall I ever see it again? I hope so, if my journey progresses as favourably as it has begun. But Syria is a bad country, and the climate is difficult to bear; yet with courage and perseverance for my companions, I may look forward to the accomplishment of my task. The good doctor seemed much annoyed that he had nothing to offer me but Cyprian wine and a few German biscuits. At this early season fruit is not to be had, and cherries do not flourish here because the climate is too hot for them. In Smyrna I ate the last for this year. When I re-embarked in the afternoon, Mr. Bartlett came with the English consul, who wished, he said, to make the acquaintance of a lady possessing sufficient courage to undertake so long and perilous a journey by herself. His astonishment increased when he was informed that I was an unpretending native of Vienna. The consul was kind enough to offer me the use of his house if I returned by way of Cyprus; he also inquired if he could give me some letters of recommendation to the Syrian consuls. I was touched by this hearty politeness on the part of a perfect stranger—an Englishman moreover, a race on whom we are accustomed to look as cold and exclusive!

CHAPTER VI.

May 25th.

This morning I could discern the Syrian coast, which becomes more glorious the nearer we approach. Beyrout, the goal of our voyage, was jealously hidden from our eyes to the very last moment. We had still to round a promontory, and then this Eden of the earth lay before us in all its glory. How gladly would I have retarded the course of our vessel, as we passed from the last rocky point into the harbour, to have enjoyed this sight a little longer! One pair of eyes does not suffice to take in this view; the objects are too numerous, and the spectator is at a loss whither he should first direct his gaze,—upon the town, with its many ancient towers attached to the houses, giving them the air of knights' castles—upon the numerous country-houses in the shade of luxurious mulberry plantations—upon the beautiful valley between Beyrout and Mount Lebanon—or on the distant mountain-range itself. The towering masses of this magnificent chain, the peculiar colour of its rocks, and its snowclad summits, riveted my attention longer than any thing else.

Scarcely had the anchor descended from the bows, before our ship was besieged by a number of small boats, with more noise and bustle than even at Constantinople. The half-naked and excitable Arabs or Fellahs are so ready with offers of service, that it is difficult to keep them off. It almost becomes necessary to threaten these poor people with a stick, as they obstinately refuse to take a gentler hint. As the water is here very shallow, so that even the little boats cannot come quite close to shore, some others of these brown forms immediately approached, seized us by the arms, took us upon their backs amidst continual shouting and quarrelling, and carried us triumphantly to land.

Before the stranger puts himself into the hands of men of this kind, such as captains of small craft, donkey-drivers, porters, etc., he will find it a very wise precaution to settle the price he is to pay for their services. I generally spoke to the captain, or to some old stager among the passengers, on this subject. Even when I gave these people double their usual price, they were not contented, but demanded an additional backsheesh (gratuity). It is therefore advisable to make the first offer very small, and to retain something for the backsheesh. At length I safely reached the house of Herr Battista (the only inn in the place), and was rejoicing in the prospect of rest and refreshment, when the dismal cry of "no room" was raised. I was thus placed in a deplorable position. There was no second inn, no convent, no place of any kind, where I, poor desolate creature that I was, could find shelter. This circumstance worked so much on the host's feelings, that he introduced me to his wife, and promised to procure me a private lodging.

I had now certainly a roof above my head, but yet I could get no rest, nor even command a corner where I might change my dress. I sat with my hostess from eleven in the morning until five in the afternoon, and a miserably long time it appeared. I could not read, write, or even talk, for neither my hostess nor her children knew any language but Arabic. I had, however, time to notice what was going on around me, and observed that these children were much more lively than those in Constantinople, for here they were continually chattering and running about. According to the custom of the country, the wife does nothing but play with the children or gossip with the neighbours, while her husband attends to kitchen and cellar, makes all the requisite purchases, and besides attending to the guests, even lays the tablecloth for his wife and children. He told me that in a week at furthest, his wife would go with the children to a convent on the Lebanon, to remain there during the hot season of the year. What a difference between an Oriental and a European woman!

I still found the heat at sea far from unendurable; a soft wind continually wafted its cooling influence towards us, and an awning had been spread out to shelter us from the rays of the sun. But what a contrast when we come to land! As I sat in the room here the perspiration dropped continually from my brow, and now I began to understand what is meant by being in the tropics. I could scarcely await the hour when I should be shewn to a room to change my clothes; but to-day I was not to have an opportunity of doing so, for at five o'clock a messenger came from Mr. Bartlett with the welcome intelligence that we could continue our journey, as nothing was to be feared from the Druses and Maronites, and the plague only reigned in isolated places through which it was not necessary that we should pass. He had already engaged a servant who would act as cook and dragoman (interpreter); provisions and cooking utensils had also been bought, and places were engaged on an Arab craft. Nothing, therefore, remained for me to do but to be on the sea-shore by six o'clock, where his servant would be waiting for me. I was much rejoiced on hearing this good news: I forgot that I required rest and a change of clothes, packed up my bundle, and hurried to the beach. Of the town I only saw a few streets, where there was a great bustle. I also noticed many swarthy Arabs and Bedouins, who wore nothing but a shirt. I did not feel particularly anxious to see Beyrout and its vicinity, as I intended to return soon and visit any part I could not examine now.

Before sunset we had already embarked on board the craft that was to carry us to the long-wished-for, the sacred coast of Joppa. Every thing was in readiness, and we lacked only the one thing indispensable—a breeze.

No steamers sail between Joppa and Beyrout; travellers must be content with sailing vessels, deficient alike as regards cleanliness and convenience; they are not provided with a cabin, or even with an awning, so that the passengers remain day and night under the open sky. Our vessel carried a cargo of pottery, besides rice and corn in sacks.

Midnight approached, and still we were in harbour, with not a breath of wind to fill our sails.

Wrapping my cloak tightly round me, I lay down on the sacks, in the absence of a mattress; but I was not yet sufficiently tired out to be able to find rest on such an unusual couch. So I rose again in rather a bad humour, and looked with an evil eye on the Arabs lying on the sacks around me, who were not "slumbering softly," but snoring lustily. By way of forcing myself, if possible, into a poetical train of thought, I endeavoured to concentrate my attention on the contemplation of the beautiful landscape by moonlight; but even this would not keep me from yawning. My companion seemed much in the same mood; for he had also risen from his soft couch, and was staring gloomingly straight before him. At length, towards three o'clock in the morning of

May 26th,

a slight breath of wind arose, we hoisted two or three sails, and glided slowly and noiselessly towards the sea.

Mr. B. had bargained with the captain to keep as close to the shore as possible, in order that we might see the towns as we passed. Excepting in Cæsarea, it was forbidden to cast anchor any where, for the plague was raging at Sur (Tyre) and in several other places.

Bargains of this kind must be taken down in writing at the consulates, and only one-half of the sum agreed should be paid in advance; the other half must be kept in hand, to operate as a check on the crew. After every precaution has been taken, one can seldom escape without some bickering and quarrelling. On these occasions it is always advisable at once to take high ground, and not to give way in the most trifling particular, for this is the only method of gaining peace and quietness.

Towards seven o'clock in the morning we sailed by the town and fortress of Saida. The town looks respectable enough, and contains some spacious houses. The fortress is separated from the town by a small bay, across which a wooden bridge has been built. The fortress seems in a very dilapidated condition; many breaches are still in the same state in which they were left after the taking of the town by the English in 1840, and part of the wall has fallen into the sea. In the background we could descry some ruins on a rock, apparently the remains of an ancient castle.

The next place we saw was Sarepta, where Elijah the prophet was fed by the poor widow during the famine.

The Lebanon range becomes lower and lower, while its namesake, the Anti-Lebanon, begins to rise. It is quite as lofty as the first-named range, which it closely resembles in form. Both are traversed by fields of snow, and between them stands a third colossus, Mount Hermon.

Next came the town of Tyre or Sur, now barren and deserted; for that mighty scourge of humanity, the plague, was raging there to a fearful extent. A few scattered fragments of fortifications and numerous fallen pillars lie strewed on the shore.

And now at length I was about to see places which many have longed to behold, but which few have reached. With a beating heart I gazed unceasingly towards St. Jean d'Acre, which I at length saw rising from the waves, with Mount Carmel in the background. Here, then, was the holy ground on which the Redeemer walked for us fallen creatures! Both St. Jean d'Acre and Mount Carmel can be distinguished a long distance off.

For a second time did a mild and calm night sink gently on the earth without bringing me repose. How unlucky it is that we find it so much harder to miss comforts we have been used to enjoy, than to acquire the habit of using comforts to which we have been unaccustomed! Were this not the case, how much easier would travelling be! As it is, it costs us many an effort ere we can look hardships boldly in the face. "But patience!" thought I to myself; "I shall have more to endure yet; and if I return safely, I shall be as thoroughly case-hardened as any native."

Our meals and our beverage were very simple. In the morning we had pilau, and in the evening we had pilau; our drink was lukewarm water, qualified with a little rum.

From Beyrout to the neighbourhood of St. Jean d'Acre, the coast and a considerable belt of land adjoining it are sandy and barren. Near Acre every thing changed; we once more beheld pretty country-houses surrounded by pomegranate and orange plantations, and a noble aqueduct intersects the plain. Mount Carmel, alone barren and unfruitful, stands in striking contrast to the beauteous landscape around; jutting boldly out towards the sea, it forms the site of a handsome and spacious convent.

The town of St. Jean d'Acre and its fortifications were completely destroyed during the last war (in 1840), and appear to sigh in vain for repairs. The houses and mosques are full of cannon-balls and shot-holes. Every thing stands and lies about as though the enemy had departed but yesterday. Six cannons peer threateningly from the wall. The town and fortifications are both built on a tongue of land washed by the sea.

May 27th.

During the night we reached Cæsarea. With the eloquence of a Demosthenes, our captain endeavoured to dissuade us from our project of landing here; he pointed out to us the dangers to which we were exposing ourselves, and the risks we should run from Bedouins and snakes. The former, he averred, were accustomed to conceal themselves in hordes among the ruins, in order to ease travellers of their effects and money; being well aware that such spots were only visited by curious tourists with well-filled purses, they were continually on the watch, like the robber-knights of the good old German empire. "An enemy no less formidable," said the captain, "was to be encountered in the persons of numerous snakes lurking in the old walls and on the weed-covered ground, which endangered the life of the traveller at every step." We were perfectly well aware of these facts, having gleaned them partly from descriptions of voyages, partly from oral traditions; and so they were not powerful enough to arrest our curiosity. The captain himself was really less actuated by the sense of our danger, in advising us to abandon our undertaking, than by the reflection of the time it lost him; but he exerted himself in vain. He was obliged to cast anchor, and at daybreak to send a boat ashore with us.

Our arms consisted of parasols and sticks (the latter we carried in order to beat the bushes); we were escorted by the captain, his servant, and a couple of sailors.

In the ruins we certainly met with a few suspicious-looking characters in the shape of wandering Bedouins. As it was too late to beat a retreat, we advanced bravely towards them with trusting and friendly looks. The Bedouins did the same, and so there was an end of this dangerous affair. We climbed from one fragment to another, and certainly spent more than two hours among the ruins, without sustaining the slightest injury at the hands of these people. Of the threatened snakes we saw not a single one.

Ruins, indeed, we found every where in plenty. Whole side-walls, which appeared to have belonged to private houses, but not to splendid palaces or temples, stood erect and almost unscathed. Fragments of pillars lay scattered about in great abundance, but without capitals, pedestals, or friezes.

It was with a feeling of awe hitherto unknown to me that I trod the ground where my Redeemer had walked. Every spot, every building became invested with a double interest. "Perchance," I thought, "I may be lingering within the very house where Jesus once sojourned." More than satisfied with my excursion, I returned to our bark.

By three o'clock in the afternoon we were close under the walls of Joppa. To enter this harbour, partially choked up as it is with sand, is described as a difficult feat. We were assured that we should see many wrecks of stranded ships and boats; accordingly I strained my eyes to the utmost, and could discover nothing. We ran safely in; and thus ended a little journey in the course of which I had seen many new and interesting objects, besides gaining some insight into the mode of life among the sailors. Frequently, when it fell calm, our Arabs would recline on the ground in a circle, singing songs of an inconceivably inharmonious and lugubrious character, while they clapped their hands in cadence, and burst at intervals into a barking laugh. I could not find any thing very amusing in this entertainment; on the contrary, it had the effect of making me feel very melancholy, as displaying these good people in a very idiotic and degrading light.

The costume of the sailors was simple in the extreme. A shirt covered them in rather an imperfect manner, and a handkerchief bound round their heads protected them from a coup de soleil. The captain was distinguished from the rest only by his turban, which looked ridiculous enough, surmounting his half-clad form. Their diet consisted of a single warm meal of pilau or beans, eaten in the evening. During the day they stayed their appetites with bread. Their drink was water.

The town of Joppa, extending from the sea-shore to the summit of a rather considerable and completely isolated hill, has a most peculiar appearance. The lower street is surrounded by a wall, and appears sufficiently broad; the remaining streets run up the face of the hills, and seem at a distance to be resting on the houses below. Viewing the town from our boat, I could have sworn that people were walking about on flat house-tops.

As Joppa boasts neither an inn nor a convent which might shelter a traveller, I waited upon the Consul of the Austrian Empire, Herr D---, who received me very kindly and introduced me to his family, which comprised his lady, three sons, and three daughters. They wore the Turkish costume. The daughters, two of whom were exceedingly beautiful, wore wide trousers, a caftan, and a sash round the waist. On their heads they had little fez-caps, and their hair was divided into fifteen or twenty narrow plaits, interwoven with little gold coins, and a larger one at the end of each plait. A necklace of gold coins encircled their necks. The mother was dressed in exactly the same way. When elderly women have little or no hair left, they make up with artificial silk plaits for the deficiencies of nature.

The custom of wearing coins as ornaments is so prevalent throughout Syria, that the very poorest women, girls, and children strive to display as many as possible. Where they cannot sport gold, they content themselves with silver money; and where even this metal is not attainable, with little coins of copper and other baser metals.

The Consul and his son were also clothed in the Turkish garb; but instead of a turban the father wore an old cocked hat, which gave him an indescribably ludicrous appearance. A son and a daughter of this worthy patron of the semi-Turkish, semi-European garb, had but one eye, a defect frequently met with in Syria. It is generally supposed to be caused by the dry heat, the fine particles of sand, and the intense glare of the chalky hills.

As I reached Joppa early in the afternoon, I proceeded in company of the Consul to view the town and its environs. In dirt, bad paving, etc., I found it equal to any of the towns I had yet seen. The lower street, near the sea, alone is broad and bustling, with loaded and unloaded camels passing continually to and fro. The bazaar is composed of some miserable booths containing common provisions and a few cheap wares.

The neighbourhood of Joppa is exceedingly fertile. Numerous large gardens, with trees laden with all kinds of tropical fruits, and guarded by impenetrable hedges of the Indian fig-tree, form a half-circle round the lower portion of the town.

The Indian fig-tree, which I here saw for the first time, has an odd appearance. From its stem, which is very dwarfish, leaves a foot in length, six inches in breadth, and half an inch in thickness, shoot forth. This tree seldom sends forth branches; the leaves grow one out of another, and at the extremity the fruit is formed. Its length is about two or three inches. Ten or twenty such figs are frequently found adhering to a single leaf.

I could not conceive how it happened that in these hot countries, without rain to refresh them, the trees all looked so healthy and beautiful. This fact, I found, was owing to the numerous channels cut through the gardens, which are thus artificially irrigated. The heavy dews and cool nights also tend to restore the drooping vegetation. One great ornament of our gardens was, however, totally wanting—a lawn with wild flowers. Trees and vegetables here grow out of the sandy or stony earth, a circumstance hardly noticed at a distance, but which produces a disagreeable effect on a near view. Flowers I found none.

The whole region round Joppa is so covered with sand, that one sinks ankle-deep at every step.

Consul D--- fulfils the duties of two consulates, the Austrian and the French. From both these offices he derives no benefit but the honour. By some people this honour would be highly valued, but many would rate it at nothing at all. This family, however, seems to have a great idea of honour; for the consul's office is hereditary, and I found the son of the present dignitary already looking forward to filling his place.

In the evening I was present at a real Oriental entertainment in the house of this friendly family.

Mats, carpets, and pillows were spread out on the terrace of the house, and a very low table placed in the centre. Round this the family sat, or rather reclined, cross-legged. I was accommodated with a chair somewhat higher than the table. Beside my plate and that of the Consul were laid a knife and fork, that appeared to have been hunted out from some lumber closet; the rest ate with a species of natural knife and fork, namely—fingers.

The dishes were not at all to my taste. I had still too much of the European about me, and too little appetite, to be able to endure what these good people seemed to consider immense delicacies.

The first dish appeared in the form of a delicate pilau, composed of mutton, cucumbers, and a quantity of spice, which rendered it more unpalatable to me than common pilau. Then followed sliced cucumbers sprinkled with salt; but as the chief ingredients, vinegar and oil, were entirely wanting, I was obliged to force down the cucumber as best I could. Next came rice-milk, so strongly flavoured with attar of roses, that the smell alone was more than enough for me; and now at length the last course was put on the table—stale cheese made of ewe's milk, little unpeeled girkins, which my entertainers coolly discussed rind and all, and burnt hazel-nuts. The bread, which is flat like pancakes, is not baked in ovens, but laid on metal plates or hot stones, and turned when one side is sufficiently done. It tastes better than I should have expected. {101}

Our conversation during dinner was most interesting. Some of the family spoke a little Italian, but this little was pronounced with such a strong Greek accent, that I was obliged to guess at the greater portion of what was said. No doubt they had to do the same with me. The worthy Consul, indeed, affirmed that he knew French very well; but for this evening at least, his memory seemed to have given him the slip. Much was spoken, and little understood. The same thing is said often to be the case in learned societies; so it was not of much consequence.

There are many different kinds of cucumber in Syria, where they are a favourite dish with rich and poor. I found numerous varieties, but none that I found superior to our German one. Another favourite fruit is the water-melon, here called "bastek." These also I found neither larger in size nor better flavoured than the melons I had eaten in southern Hungary.

The Consul's house seems sufficiently large; but the architectural arrangement is so irregular that the extended area contains but few rooms and very little comfort. The apartments are lofty and large, extremely ill-furnished, and not kept in the best possible order.

I slept in the apartment of the married daughter; but had it not been for the beds standing round, I should rather have looked upon it as an old store-closet than a lady's sleeping-room.

May 28th.

At five o'clock in the morning Mr. Bartlett's servant came to fetch me away, as we were at once to continue our journey. I betook myself to the house of the English Consul, where I found neither a horse nor any thing else prepared for our departure. It is necessary to look calmly upon these irregularities here in the East, where it is esteemed a fortunate occurrence if the horses and mukers (as the drivers of horses and donkeys are called) are only a few hours behind their time. Thus our horses made their appearance at half-past five instead of at four, the hour for which they had been ordered. Our baggage was soon securely fixed, for we left the greater portion of our effects at Joppa, and took with us only what was indispensably necessary.

As the clock struck six we rode out of the gate of Joppa, and immediately afterwards reached a large well with a marble basin. Near places of this description a great number of people are always congregated, and more women and girls are seen than appear elsewhere.

The dress of females belonging to the lower orders consists of a long blue garment fastened round the throat, and reaching below the ankle. They completely cover the head and face, frequently without even leaving openings for the eyes. Some females, on the other hand, go abroad with their faces totally uncovered. These are, however, exceptional cases.

The women carry their water-pitchers on their head or shoulder, as their ancestors have done for thousands of years, in the manner we find represented in the oldest pictures. But unfortunately I could discover neither the grace in their gait, the dignity in their movements, nor the physical beauty in their appearance, that I had been led to expect. On the contrary, I found squalor and poverty more prevalent than I had thought possible. We rode on amid the gardens, every moment meeting a little caravan of camels. Immediately beyond the gardens we descry the fruitful valley of Sharon, extending more than eight miles in length, and to a still greater distance in breadth. Here and there we find villages built on hills, and the whole presents the appearance of an extremely fertile and well-populated region. In all directions we saw large herds of sheep and goats; the latter generally of a black or brown colour, with long pendent ears.

The foreground of the picture is formed by the Judæan mountains, a range apparently composed of a number of barren rocks.

A ride of two hours through this plain, which is less sandy than the immediate neighbourhood of Joppa, brought us to a mosque, where we made halt for a quarter of an hour and ate our breakfast, consisting of some hard-boiled eggs, a piece of bread, and a draught of lukewarm water from the cistern. Our poor beasts fared even worse than ourselves—they received nothing but water.

On leaving this place to resume our journey across the plain, we not only suffered dreadfully from the heat, which had reached 30° Reaumur, but were further persecuted by a species of minute gnats, which hovered round us in large swarms, crept into our noses and ears, and annoyed us in such a manner that it required the utmost of our patience and determination to prevent us from turning back at once. Fortunately we only met with these tormentors in those parts where the corn had been cut and was still in the fields. They are not much larger than a pin's head, and look more like flies than gnats. They are always met with in great swarms, and sting so sharply that they frequently raise large boils.

The vegetation was at this season already in so forward a state that we frequently passed stubble-fields, and found that the wheat had in several cases been already garnered up. Throughout the whole of Syria, and in that part of Egypt whither my journey afterwards led me, I never once saw corn or vegetables, wood or stores, carried in wagons; they were invariably borne by horses or asses. In Syria I could understand the reason of this proceeding. With the exception, perhaps, of the eight or ten miles across the valley of Sharon, the road is too stony and uneven to admit the passage of the lightest and smallest carts. In Egypt, however, this is not the case, and yet wagons have not been introduced.

A most comical effect was produced when we met long processions of small donkeys, so completely laden with corn, that neither their heads nor their feet remained visible. The sheaves seemed to be moving spontaneously, or to be propelled by the power of steam. Frequently after a train of this kind has passed, lofty grey heads appear, surrounded by a load piled up to so great a height, that one would suppose large corn-wagons were approaching rather than the "ship of the desert," the camel. The traveller's attention is continually attracted to some novel and curious object totally dissimilar to any thing he has seen at home.

Towards ten o'clock we arrived at Ramla, a place situate on a little hill, and discernible from a great distance. Before reaching the town, we had to pass through an olive-wood. Leaving our horses beneath a shady tree, we entered the coppice on the right: a walk of about a quarter of a mile brought us to the "Tower of the Forty Martyrs," which was converted into a church during the time of the Knights Templars, and now serves as a dwelling for dervishes. It is a complete ruin, and I could scarcely believe that it was still habitable.

We made no stay at Ramda, a place only remarkable for a convent built, it is said, on the site of Joseph of Arimathea's house.

The Syrian convents are built more like fortresses than like peaceful dwellings. They are usually surrounded by strong and lofty walls, furnished with loopholes for cannon. The great gate is kept continually closed, and barred and bolted from within for greater security; a little postern is opened to admit visitors, but even this is only done in time of peace, and when there is no fear of the plague.

At length, towards noon, we approached the mountains of Judæa. Here we must bid farewell to the beautiful fruitful valley and to the charming road, and pursue our journey through a stony region, which we do not pass without difficulty.

At the entrance of the mountain-chain lies a miserable village; near this village is a well, and here we halted to refresh ourselves and water our poor horses. It was not without a great deal of trouble and some expense that we managed to obtain a little water; for all the camels, asses, goats, and sheep from far and wide were collected here, eagerly licking up every drop of the refreshing element they could secure. Little did I think that I should ever be glad to quench my thirst with so disgusting a beverage as the muddy, turbid, and lukewarm water they gave me from this well. We once more filled our leathern bottles, and proceeded with fresh courage up the stony path, which quickly became so narrow, that without great difficulty and danger we could not pass the camels which we frequently met. Fortunately a few camels out of every herd are generally provided with bells, so that their approach is heard at some distance, and one can prepare for them accordingly.

The Bedouins and Arabs generally wear no garment but a shirt barely reaching to the knee. Their head is protected by a linen cloth, to which a thick rope wound twice round the head gives a very good effect. A few have a striped jacket over their shirt, and the rich men or chiefs frequently wear turbans.

Our road now continues to wind upwards, through ravines between rocks and mountains, and over heaps of stones. Here and there single olive-trees are seen sprouting from the rocky clefts. Ugly as this tree is, it still forms a cheerful feature in the desert places where it grows. Now and then we climbed hills whence we had a distant view of the sea. These glimpses increase the awe which inspires the traveller when he considers on what ground he is wandering, and whither he is bending his steps. Every step we now take leads us past places of religious importance; every ruin, every fragment of a fortress or tower, above which the rocky walls rise like terraces, speaks of eventful times long gone by.

An uninterrupted ride of five hours over very bad roads, from the entrance of the mountain-range, added to the extreme heat and total want of proper refreshment, suddenly brought on such a violent giddiness that I could scarcely keep myself from falling off my horse. Although we had been on horseback for eleven hours since leaving Joppa, I was so much afraid that Mr. B. would consider me weak and ailing, and perhaps change his intention of accompanying me from Jerusalem back to Joppa, that I refrained from acquainting him with the condition in which I felt myself. I therefore dismounted (had I not done so, I should soon have fallen down), and walked with tottering steps beside my horse, until I felt so far recovered that I could mount once more. Mr. B. had determined to perform the distance from Joppa to Jerusalem (a sixteen hours' ride) at one stretch. He indeed asked me if I could bear so much fatigue; but I was unwilling to abuse his kindness, and therefore assured him that I could manage to ride on for five or six hours longer. Fortunately for my reputation, my companion was soon afterwards attacked with the same symptoms that troubled me so much; he now began to think that it might, after all, be advisable to rest for a few hours in the next village, especially as we could not hope in any case to reach the gates of Jerusalem before sundown. I felt silently thankful for this opportune occurrence, and left the question of going on or stopping altogether to the decision of my fellow-traveller, particularly as I knew the course he would choose. Thus I accomplished my object without being obliged to confess my weakness. In pursuance of this resolve, we stayed in the neighbouring village of "Kariet el Areb," the ancient Emmaus, where the risen Saviour met the disciples, and where we find a ruin of a Christian church in a tolerable state of preservation. The building is now used as a stable. Some years ago this was the haunt of a famous robber, who was scheikh of the place, and let no Frank pass before he had paid whatever tribute he chose to demand. Since the accession of Mehemet Ali these exactions have ceased both here and in Jerusalem, where money was demanded of the stranger for admission into the Church of the Holy Sepulchre and other sacred places. Even highway robberies, which were once on a time of daily occurrence among these mountains, are now rarely heard of.

We took possession of the entrance-hall of a mosque, near which a delicious spring sparkled forth from a grotto. Seldom has any thing strengthened and refreshed me so much as the water of this spring. I recovered completely from my indisposition, and was able to enjoy the beautiful evening.

As soon as the scheikh of the village heard that a party of Franks had arrived, he despatched four or five dishes of provisions to us. Of all these preparations we could only eat one—the butter-milk. The other dishes, a mixture of honey, cucumbers, hard-boiled eggs, onions, oil, olives, etc., we generously bestowed upon the dragoman and the muker, who caused them quickly to disappear. An hour afterwards the scheikh came in person to pay his respects. We reclined on the steps of the hall; and while the men smoked and drank coffee, a conversation of a very uninteresting kind was kept up, the dragoman acting as interpreter. At length the scheikh seemed seized with the idea that we might possibly be tired with our journey. He took his leave, and offered unasked to send us two men as sentries, which he did. Thus we could go to rest in perfect safety under the open sky in the midst of a Turkish village.

But before we retired to rest, my companion was seized with the rather original idea that we should pursue our journey at midnight. He asked me, indeed, if I was afraid, but at the same time observed, that it would be much safer for us to act upon his suggestion, as no one would suspect our departure by such a dangerous road at midnight. I certainly felt a little afraid, but my pride would not allow me to confess the truth; so our people received the order to be prepared to set out at midnight.

Thus we four persons, alone and totally unarmed, travelled at midnight through the wildest and most dangerous regions. Fortunately the bright moon looked smilingly down upon us, and illuminated our path so brightly, that the horses carried us with firm step over every obstruction. I was, I must confess, grievously frightened by the shadows! I saw living things moving to and fro—forms gigantic and forms dwarfish seemed sometimes approaching us, sometimes hiding behind masses of rock, or sinking back into nothingness. Lights and shadows, fears and anxiety, thus took alternate possession of my imagination.

A couple of miles from our starting-place we came upon a brook crossed by a narrow stone bridge. This brook is remarkable only as having been that from which David collected the five stones wherewith he slew the Philistine giant. At the season of my visit there was no water to be seen; the bed of the stream was completely dry.

About an hour's journey from Jerusalem the valley opens, and little orchards give indication of a more fertile country, as well as of the proximity of the Holy City. Silently and thoughtfully we approached our destination, straining our eyes to the utmost to pierce the jealous twilight that shrouded the distance from our gaze. From the next hill we hoped to behold our sacred goal; but "hope deferred" is often the lot of mortals. We had to ascend another height, and another; at length the Mount of Olives lay spread before us, and lastly JERUSALEM.

## CHAPTER VII.

The red morning dawn had began to tinge the sky as we stood before the walls of Jerusalem, and with it the most beauteous morning of my life dawned upon me! I was so lost in reflection and in thankful emotion, that I saw and heard nothing of what was passing around me. And yet I should find it impossible to describe what I thought, what I felt. My emotion was deep and powerful; my expression of it would be poor and cold.

At half past four o'clock in the morning of the 29th May we arrived at the "Bethlehem Gate." We were obliged to wait half an hour before this gate was opened; then we rode through the still silent and deserted streets of the Nuova Casa (Pilgrim-house), a building devoted by the Franciscan friars to the reception of rich and poor Roman Catholics and Protestants.

I left my baggage in the room allotted to me, and hastened into the church, to lighten the weight on my heart by fervent prayer. The entrance into the church looks like the door of a private house; the building is small, but still sufficiently large for the Roman Catholic congregation. The altar is richly furnished, and the organ is a very bad one. The male and female portions of the congregation are separated from each other, the young as well as the old, and all sit or kneel on the ground. Chairs there are none in this church. The costume of the Christians is precisely the same as that of the Syrians. The women wear boots of yellow morocco, and over these slippers, which they take off on entering the church. In the street their faces are completely, in the church only partially, muffled, and the faces of the girls not at all. Their dress consists of a white linen gown, and a large shawl of the same material, which completely envelops them. They were all cleanly and neatly dressed.

The amount of devotion manifested by these people is very small; the most trifling circumstance suffices to distract their attention. For instance, my appearance seemed to create quite a sensation among them, and they made their remarks upon me to one another so openly both by words and gestures, that I found it quite impossible to give my mind to seriousness and devotion. Some of them pushed purposely against me, and put out their hands to grasp my bonnet, etc. They conversed together a good deal, and prayed very little. The children behaved no better; these little people ate their breakfast while the service was going on, and occasionally jostled each other, probably to keep themselves awake. The good people here must fancy they are doing a meritorious work by passing two or three hours in the church; no one seems to care how this time is spent, or they would assuredly have been taught better.

I had been in the church rather more than an hour when a clergyman stepped up to me and accosted me in my native language. He was a German, and, in fact, an Austrian. He promised to visit me in the course of a few hours. I returned to the Nuova Casa, and now, for the first time, had leisure to examine my apartment. The arrangement was simple in the extreme. An iron bedstead, with a mattress, coverlet, and bolster, a very dingy table, with two chairs, a small bench, and a cupboard, all of deal, composed the whole furniture. These chattels, and also the windows, some panes of which were broken, may once, in very ancient times, have been clean. The walls were of plaster, and the floor was paved with large slabs of stone. Chimneys are no more to be found in this country. I did not see any until my return to Sicily.

I now laid myself down for a couple of hours to get a little rest; for during my journey hither from Constantinople I had scarcely slept at all.

At eleven o'clock the German priest, Father Paul, visited me, in order to explain the domestic arrangements to me. Dinner is eaten at twelve o'clock, and supper at seven. At breakfast we get coffee without sugar or milk; for dinner, mutton-broth, a piece of roast kid, pastry prepared with oil or a dish of cucumbers, and, as a concluding course, roast or spiced mutton. Twice in the week, namely on Fridays and Saturdays, we have fast-day fare; but if the feast of a particular saint falls during the week, a thing that frequently occurs, we hold three fast-days, the one of the saint's day being kept as a time of abstinence. The fare on fast-days consists of a dish of lentils, an omelette, and two dishes of salt fish, one hot and the other cold. Bread and wine, as also these provisions, are doled out in sufficient quantities. But every thing is very indifferently cooked, and it takes a long time for a stranger to accustom himself to the ever-recurring dishes of mutton. In Syria oxen and calves are not killed during the summer season; so that from the 19th of May until my journey to Egypt in the beginning of September, I could get neither beef-soup nor beef.

In this convent no charge is made either for board or lodging, and every visitor may stay there for a whole month. At most it is customary to give a voluntary subscription towards the masses; but no one asks if a traveller has given much, little, or nothing at all, or whether he is a Roman Catholic, a Protestant, or a votary of any other religion. In this respect the Franciscan order is much to be commended. The priests are mostly Spaniards and Italians; very few of them belong to other nations.

Father Paul was kind enough to offer his services as my guide, and to-day I visited several of the holy places in company with him.

We began with the Via Dolorosa, the road which our Lord is said to have trodden when for the last time he wandered as God-man on earth, bowed down by the weight of the cross, on his way to Golgotha. The spots where Christ sank exhausted are marked by fragments of the pillars which St. Helena caused to be attached to the houses on either side of the way. Further on we reach the "Zwerchgasse," the place whither the Virgin Mary is said to have come in haste to see her beloved Son for the last time.

Next we visited Pilate's house, which is partly a ruin, the remaining portion serving as a barrack for Turkish soldiers. I was shewn the spot where the "holy stairs" stood, up which our Lord is said to have walked. On my return, I saw these stairs in the church of S. Giovanni di Laterani. They also pretend to show the place where the Saviour was brought out before the multitude by Pilate. A little distance off, in the midst of a dark vault, they shew the traveller the stone to which Jesus was bound when "they scourged Him."

We ascended the highest terrace of this house, as this spot affords the best view of the magnificent mosque of Omar, standing in a large courtyard. With this exterior view the traveller is fain to be content; for the Turks are here much more fanatical than those in Constantinople and many other towns, so that an attempt to penetrate even into the courtyard would be unsuccessful; the intruder would run the risk of being assailed with a shower of stones. But in proportion as the Turks are strict in the observance of their own ceremonies and customs, so they respect those Christians who are religious and devotional.

Every Christian can go with perfect impunity to pray at all the places which are sacred in his eyes, without fear of being taunted or annoyed by the Turkish passers-by. On the contrary, the Mussulman steps respectfully aside; for even he venerates the Saviour as a great prophet, and the Virgin as his mother.

Not far from Pilate's house stands the building designated as that of Herod; it is, however, a complete ruin. The house of the rich man, at whose gate the beggar Lazarus lay, has shared the same fate; but from the ruins one may conclude how magnificent the building must originally have been.

In the house of Saint Veronica a stone is pointed out on which they shew you a footprint of the Saviour. In another house two footprints of the Virgin Mary are exhibited. Father Paul also drew my attention to the houses which stood on the spot where Mary Magdalene and the other Mary were born. These houses are all inhabited by Turks, but any one may obtain admittance upon payment of a small fee.

The following day I visited the church of the Holy Sepulchre. The way lies through several narrow and dirty streets. In the lanes near the church are booths like those at Maria Zell in Steiermark, and many other places of pilgrimage, where they sell wreaths of roses, shells of mother-of-pearl, crucifixes, etc. The open space before the church is neat enough. Opposite lies the finest house in Jerusalem, its terraces gay with flowers.

Visitors to this church will do wisely to provide themselves with a sufficient number of para, as they may expect to be surrounded by a goodly tribe of beggars. The church is always locked; the key is in the custody of some Turks, who open the sacred edifice when asked to do so. It is customary to give them three or four piastres for their pains, with which sum they are satisfied, and remain at the entrance during the whole time the stranger is in the church, reclining on divans, drinking coffee and smoking tobacco. At the entrance of the church we noticed a long square stone on the ground; this is the "stone of anointing."

In the centre of the nave a little chapel has been built; it is divided into two parts. In the first of these compartments is a stone slab encased in marble. This is vehemently asserted to be the identical stone on which the angel sat when he announced our Lord's resurrection to the women who came to embalm his body. In the second compartment, which is of the same size as the first, stands the sarcophagus or tomb of the Saviour, of white marble. The approach is by such a low door that one has to stoop exceedingly in order to enter. The tomb occupies the whole length of the chapel, and answers the purpose of an altar. We could not look into the sarcophagus. The illumination of this chapel is very grand both by night and day; forty-seven lamps are kept continually burning above the grave. The portion of the chapel containing the tomb is so small, that when the priest reads mass only two or three people have room to stand and listen. The chapel is entirely built of marble, and belongs to the Roman Catholics; but the Greeks have the right of celebrating mass alternately with them.

At the farther end of the chapel the Copts have a little mean-looking altar of wood, surrounded by walls of lath. All round the chapel are niches belonging to the different religious sects.

In this church I was also shewn the subterranean niche in which Jesus is said to have been a prisoner; also the niche where the soldiers cast lots for our Saviour's garments, and the chapel containing the grave of St. Nicodemus. Not far from this chapel is the little Roman Catholic church. A flight of twenty-seven steps leads downwards to the chapel of St. Helena, where the holy woman sat continually and prayed, while she caused search to be made for the true cross. A few steps more lead us down to the spot where the cross was found. A marble slab points out the place.

Mounting the steps once more, we come to the niche containing the pillar to which Jesus was bound when they crowned him with thorns. It is called the pillar of scorn. The pillar at which Jesus was scourged, a piece of which is preserved in Rome, is also shown.

The chapel belonging to the Greeks is very spacious, and may almost be termed a church within a church. It is beautifully decorated.

It is very difficult to find the way in this church, which resembles a labyrinth. Now we are obliged to ascend a flight of stairs, now again to descend. The architect certainly deserves great praise for having managed so cleverly to unite all these holy places under one roof; and St. Helena has performed a most meritorious action in thus rescuing from oblivion the sacred sites in Jerusalem, Bethlehem, and Nazareth.

I was told, that when the Greeks celebrate their Easter here, the ceremonies seldom conclude without much quarrelling and confusion. These irregularities are considerably increased when the Greek Easter happens to fall at the same time as that of the Roman Catholics. On these occasions, there are not only numerous broken heads, but some of the combatants are even frequently carried away dead. The Turks generally find it necessary to interfere, to restore peace and order among the Christians. What opinion can these nations, whom we call Infidels, have of us Christians, when they see with what hatred and virulence each sect of Christians pursues the other? When will this dishonourable bigotry cease?

On the third day after my arrival at Jerusalem, a small caravan of six or seven travellers, two gentlemen namely, and their attendants, applied for admittance at our convent. An arrival of this kind, particularly if the new-comers are Franks, is far too important to admit of our delaying the inquiry from what country the wanderers have arrived. How agreeably was I surprised, when Father Paul came to me with the intelligence that these gentlemen were both Austrian subjects. What a singular coincidence! So far from my native country, I was thus suddenly placed in the midst of my own people. Father Paul was a native of Vienna, and the two counts, Berchtold and Salm Reifferscheit, were Bohemian cavaliers.

As soon as I had completely recovered from the fatigues of my journey, and had collected my thoughts, I passed a whole night in the church of the Holy Sepulchre. I confessed in the afternoon, and afterwards joined the procession, which at four o'clock visits all the places rendered sacred by our Saviour's passion; I carried a wax taper, the remains of which I afterwards took back with me into my native country, as a lasting memorial. This ceremony ended, the priests retired to their cells, and the few people who were present left the church. I alone stayed behind, as I intended to remain there all night. A solemn stillness reigned throughout the church; and now I was enabled to visit, uninterrupted and alone, all the sacred places, and to give myself wholly up to my meditations. Truly these were the most blissful hours of my life; and he who has lived to enjoy such hours has lived long enough.

A place near the organ was pointed out to me where I might enjoy a few hours of repose. An old Spanish woman, who lives like a nun, acts as guide to those who pass a night in the church.

At midnight the different services begin. The Greeks and Armenians beat and hammer upon pendent plates or rods of metal; the Roman Catholics play on the organ, and sing and pray aloud; while the priests of other religions likewise sing and shout. A great and inharmonious din is thus caused. I must confess that this midnight mass did not produce upon me the effect I had anticipated. The constant noise and multifarious ceremonies are calculated rather to disconcert than to inspire the stranger. I much preferred the peace and repose that reigned around, after the service had concluded, to all the pomp and circumstance attending it.

Accompanied by my Spanish guide, I ascended to the Roman Catholics' choir, where prayers were said aloud from midnight until one o'clock. At four o'clock in the morning I heard several masses, and received the Eucharist. At eight o'clock the Turks opened the door at my request, and I went home.

The few Roman Catholic priests who live in the church of the Holy Sepulchre stay there for three months at a time, to perform the services. During this time they are not allowed to quit the church or the convent for a single instant. After the three months have elapsed, they are relieved by other priests.

On the 10th of June I was present at the ceremony of admission into the Order of the Holy Sepulchre. Counts Zichy, Wratislaw, and Salm Reifferscheit were, at their own request, installed as knights of the Sepulchre. The inauguration took place in the chapel.

The chief priest having taken his seat on a chair of state, the candidate for knighthood knelt before him, and took the customary oaths to defend the holy church, to protect widows and orphans, etc. During this time the priests who stood round said prayers. Now one of the spurs of Godfrey de Bouillon was fastened on the heel of the knight; the sword of this hero was put into his hands, the sheath fastened to his side, and a cross with a heavy gold chain, that had also belonged to Godfrey de Bouillon, was put round his neck. Then the kneeling man received the stroke of knighthood on his head and shoulders, the priests embraced the newly-elected knight, and the ceremony was over.

A plentiful feast, given by the new-chosen knights, concluded the solemnity.

Distant somewhat less than a mile from Jerusalem is the Mount of Olives. Emerging from St. Stephen's Gate, we pass the Turkish burial-ground, and reach the spot where St. Stephen was stoned. Not far off we see the bed of the brook Cedron, which is at this season of the year completely dried up. A stone bridge leads across the brook; adjoining it is a stone slab where they shew traces of the footsteps of the Saviour, as He was brought across this bridge from Gethsemane, and stumbled and fell. Crossing this bridge, we arrive at the grotto where Jesus sweat blood. This grotto still retains its original form. A plain wooden altar has been erected there, a few years since, by a Bavarian prince, and the entrance is closed by an iron gate. Not far off is Gethsemane. Eight olive-trees are here to be seen that have attained a great age; nowhere else had I seen these trees with such massive trunks, though I had frequently passed through whole plantations of olives. Those who are learned in natural history assert that the olive-tree cannot live to so great an age as to render it possible that these venerable trunks existed at the time when Jesus passed his last night at Gethsemane in prayer and supplication. As this tree, however, propagates itself, these trees may be sprouts from the ancient stems. The space around the roots has been strengthened with masonry, to afford a support to these patriarchal trunks, and the eight trees are surrounded by a wall three or four feet in height. No layman may enter this spot unaccompanied by a priest, on pain of excommunication; it is also forbidden to pluck a single leaf. The Turks also hold these trees in reverence, and would not injure one of them.

Close by is the spot where the three disciples are said to have slept during the night of their Master's agony. We were shown marks on two rocks, said to have been footsteps of these apostles! The footsteps of the third disciple we could not discover. A little to one side is the place where Judas betrayed his Master.

The little church containing the grave of the Virgin Mary stands near the "Grotto of Anguish." We descend by a broad marble flight of fifty steps to the tomb, which is also used as an altar. About the middle of the staircase are two niches with altars; within these are deposited the bones of the Virgin Mary's parents and of St. Joseph. This chapel belongs to the Greeks. From the foot of the Mount of Olives to its summit is a walk of three quarters of an hour. The whole mountain is desert and sterile; nothing is found growing upon it but olives; and from the summit of this mountain our Saviour ascended into heaven. The spot was once marked by a church, which was afterwards replaced by a mosque: even this building is now in ruins. Only twelve years ago a little chapel, of very humble appearance, was erected here; it now stands in the midst of old walls; but here again a footprint of our Lord is shown and reverenced. On this stone it is asserted that He stood before He was taken up into heaven. Not far off, we are shown the place where the fig-tree grew that Jesus cursed, and the field where Judas hanged himself.

One afternoon I visited many of these sites, in company with Count Berchtold. As we were climbing about the ruins near the mosque, a sturdy goatherd, armed with a formidable bludgeon, came before us, and demanded "backsheesh" (a gift, or an alms) in a very peremptory tone. Neither of us liked to take out our purse, for, fear the insolent beggar should snatch it from our hands; so we gave him nothing. Upon this he seized the Count by the arm, and shouted out something in Arabic which we could not understand, though we could guess pretty accurately what he meant. The Count disengaged his arm, and we proceeded almost to push and wrestle our way into the open field, which was luckily only a few paces off. By good fortune, also, several people appeared near us, upon seeing whom the fellow retired. This incident convinced us of the fact that Franks should not leave the city unattended.

As the Mount of Olives is the highest point in the neighbourhood of Jerusalem, it commands the best view of the town and its environs. The city is large, and lies spread over a considerable area. The number of inhabitants is estimated at 25,000. As in the remaining cities of Syria, the houses here are built of stone, and frequently adorned with round cupolas. Jerusalem is surrounded by a very lofty and well-preserved wall, the lower portion composed of such massive blocks of stone, that one might imagine these huge fragments date from the period of the city's capture by Titus. Of the mosques, that of Omar, with its lead-covered roof, has the best appearance; it lies in an immense courtyard, which is neatly kept. This mosque is said to occupy the site of Solomon's temple.

From the Mount of Olives we can plainly distinguish all the convents, and the different quarters of the Catholics, Armenians, Jews, Greeks, etc. The "Mount of Offence" (so called on account of Solomon's idolatry) rises at the side of the Mount of Olives, and is of no great elevation. Of the temple, and the buildings which Solomon caused to be erected for his wives, but few fragments of walls remain. I had also been told, that the Jordan and the Dead Sea might be seen from this mountain; but I could distinguish neither, probably on account of a mist which obscured the horizon.

At the foot of the Mount of Olives lies the valley of Jehosaphat. The length of this valley does not certainly exceed three miles; neither is it remarkable for its breadth. The brook Cedron intersects this valley; but it only contains water during the rainy season; at other times all trace of it is lost.

The town of Jerusalem is rather bustling, particularly the poor-looking bazaar and the Jews' quarter; the latter portion of the city is very densely populated, and exhales an odour offensive beyond description; and here the plague always seizes its first victims.

The Greek convent is not only very handsome, but of great extent. Hither most of the pilgrims flock, at Easter-time to the number of five or six thousand. Then they are all herded together, and every place is crowded with occupants; even the courtyard and terraces are full. This convent is the richest of all, because every pilgrim received here has to pay an exorbitant price for the very worst accommodation. It is said that the poorest seldom escape for less than four hundred piastres.

Handsomest of all is the Armenian convent; standing in the midst of gardens, it has a most cheerful appearance. It is asserted to be built on the site where St. James was decapitated, an event commemorated by numerous pictures in the church; but most of the pictures, both here and in the remaining churches, are bad beyond conception. Like the Greeks, the Armenian priests enjoy the reputation of thoroughly understanding how to make a harvest out of their visitors, whom they are said generally to send away with empty pockets. As an amends, however, they offer them a great quantity of spiritual food.

In the valley of Jehosaphat we find many tombs of ancient and modern date. The most ancient among these tombs is that of Absolom; a little temple of pieces of rock, but without an entrance. The second is the tomb of Zacharias, also hewn out of the rock, and divided within into two compartments. The third belongs to King Jehosaphat, and is small and unimportant; one might almost call it a mere block of stone. There are many more tombs cut out of the rock. From this place we reach the Jewish burial-ground.

The little village of Sila also lies in this valley. It is so humble, and all its houses (which are constructed of stone) are so small, that wandering continually among tombs, the traveller would rather take them to be ruined resting-places of the dead than habitations of the living.

Opposite this village lies "Mary's Well," so called because the Virgin Mary fetched water here every day. The inhabitants of Siloam follow her example to this day. A little farther on is the pool of Siloam, where our Lord healed the man who was born blind. This pool is said to possess the remarkable property, that the water disappears and returns several times in the course of twenty-four hours.

At the extremity of the valley of Jehosaphat a small hill rises like a keystone; in this hill are several grottoes, formed either by nature or art, which also once served as sepulchres. They are called the "rock-graves." At present the greater portion of them are converted into stables, and are in so filthy a state that it is impossible to enter them. I peeped into one or two, and saw nothing but a cavern divided into two parts. At the summit of these rock-graves lies the "Field of Blood," bought by the priests for the thirty pieces of silver which Judas cast down in the temple.

In the neighbourhood of the Field of Blood rises the hill of Sion. Here, it is said, stood the house of Caiaphas the high-priest, whither our Lord was brought a prisoner. A little Armenian church now occupies the supposed site. The tomb of David, also situated on this hill, has been converted into a mosque, in which we are shewn the place where the Son of Man ate the last Passover with His disciples.

The burial-grounds of the Roman Catholics, Armenians, and Greeks surround this hill.

The "Hill of Bad Counsel," so called because it is said that here the judges determined to crucify Christ, rises in the immediate vicinity of Mount Sion. A few traces of the ruins of Caiaphas' house are yet visible. The "Grotto of Jeremiah" lies beyond the "Gate of Damascus," in front of which we found, near a cistern, an elaborately-sculptured sarcophagus, which is used as a water-trough. This grotto is larger than any I have yet mentioned. At the entrance stands a great stone, called Jeremiah's bed, because the prophet is said generally to have slept upon it. Two miles farther on we come to the graves of the judges and the kings. We descend an open pit, three or four fathoms deep, forming the courtyard. This pit is a square about seventy feet long and as many wide. On one side of this open space we enter a large hall, its broad portal ornamented with beautiful sculpture, in the form of flowers, fruit, and arabesques. This hall leads to the graves, which run round it, and consist of niches hewn in the rock, just sufficiently large to contain a sarcophagus. Most of these niches were choked up with rubbish, but into some we could still see; they were all exactly alike. These long, narrow, rock-hewn graves reminded me exactly of those I had seen in a vault at Gran, in Hungary. I could almost have supposed the architect at Gran had taken the graves of the valley of Jehosaphat for his model.

## CHAPTER VIII.

On the 2d of June I rode, in the company of Counts Berchtold and Salm Reifferscheit and Pater Paul, to Bethlehem. Although, on account of the bad roads, we are obliged to ride nearly the whole distance at a foot-pace, it does not take more than an hour and a half to accomplish the journey. The view we enjoy during this excursion is as grand as it is peculiar. So far as the eye can reach, it rests upon stone; the ground is entirely composed of stones; and yet between the rocky interstices grow fruit-trees of all kinds, and grape-vines trail along, besides fields whose productions force their way upwards from the shingly soil.

I had already wondered when I saw the "Karst," near Trieste, and the desert region of Görz; but these sink into insignificance when compared to the scenery of the Judean mountains.

It is difficult to conceive how these regions can ever have been smiling and fertile. Doubtless they have appeared to better advantage than at the present period, when the poor inhabitants are ground to the bone by their pachas and officers; but I do not think that meadows and woods can ever have existed here to any extent.

On the way we pass a well, surrounded by blocks of stone. At this well the wise men from the East rested, and here the guiding star appeared to them. Midway between Jerusalem and Bethlehem lies the Greek convent dedicated to the prophet Elijah. From hence we can see both towns; on the one hand, the spacious Jerusalem, and on the other, the humble Bethlehem, with some small villages scattered round it. On the right hand we pass "Rachel's grave," a ruined building with a small cupola.

Bethlehem lies on a hill, surrounded by several others; with the exception of the convent, it contains not a single handsome building. The inhabitants, half of whom are Catholics, muster about 2500 strong; many live in grottoes and semi-subterranean domiciles, cutting out garlands and other devices in mother-of-pearl, etc. The number of houses does not exceed a hundred at the most, and the poverty here seems excessive, for nowhere have I been so much pestered with beggar children as in this town. Hardly has the stranger reached the convent-gates before these urchins are seen rapidly approaching from all quarters. One rushes forward to hold the horse, while a second grasps the stirrup; a third and a fourth present their arm to help you to dismount; and in the end the whole swarm unanimously stretch forth their hands for "backsheesh." In cases like these it is quite necessary to come furnished either with a multiplicity of small coins or with a riding-whip, in order to be delivered in one way or another from the horrible importunity of the diminutive mob. It is very fortunate that the horses here are perfectly accustomed to such scenes; were this not the case, they would take fright and gallop headlong away.

The little convent and church are both situated near the town, and are built on the spot where the Saviour was born. The whole is surrounded by a strong fortress-wall, a very low, narrow gate forming the entrance. In front of this fortress extends a handsome well-paved area. So soon as we have passed through the little gate, we find ourselves in the courtyard, or rather in the nave of the church, which is unfortunately more than half destroyed, but must once have been eminent both for its size and beauty. Some traces of mosaic can still be detected on the walls. Two rows of high handsome pillars, forty-eight in number, intersect the interior; and the beam-work, said to be of cedar-wood from Lebanon, looks almost new. Beneath the high altar of this great church is the grotto in which Christ was born. Two staircases lead downwards to it. One of the staircases belongs to the Armenians, the other to the Greeks; the Catholics have none at all. Both the walls and the floor are covered with marble slabs. A marble tablet, with the inscription,

"HIC DE VIRGINE MARIA JESUS CHRISTUS NATUS EST,"

marks the spot whence the true Light shone abroad over the world. A figure of a beaming sun, which receives its light from numerous lamps kept continually burning, is placed in the back-ground of this tablet.

The spot where our Saviour was shewn to the worshipping Magi is but few paces distant. An altar is erected opposite, on the place where the manger stood in which the shepherds found our Lord. The manger itself is deposited in the basilica Santa Maria Maggiore, in Rome. This altar belongs to the Roman Catholics. A little door, quite in the background of the grotto, leads to a subterranean passage communicating with the convent and the Catholic chapel. In this passage another altar has been erected to the memory of the innocents slaughtered and buried here. Proceeding along the passage we come upon the grave of St. Paula and her daughter Eustachia on one side, and that of St. Hieronymus on the other. The body of the latter is, however, deposited at Rome.

Like the church of the Holy Sepulchre at Jerusalem, this great church at Bethlehem belongs at once to the Catholics, the Armenians, and the Greeks. Each of these sects has built for itself a little convent adjoining the church.

After spending at least a couple of hours here, we rode two miles farther, towards Mount Hebron. At the foot of this mountain we turned off to the left towards the three cisterns of Solomon. These reservoirs are very wide and deep, hewn out of the rock, and still partially covered with a kind of cement resembling marble in its consistency and polish. We descended into the third of these cisterns; it was about five hundred paces long, four hundred broad, and a hundred deep.

Not one of these cisterns now contains water; the aqueducts which once communicated with them have entirely vanished. A single rivulet, across which one may easily step, flows beside these giant reservoirs. The region around is barren in the extreme.

On returning to our convent at about two o'clock to partake of our frugal but welcome meal, we were surprised to find that another party of travellers, Franks like ourselves, had arrived. The new-comers proved to be Count Zichy and Count Wratislaw, who had travelled from Vienna to Cairo in company with Counts Berchtold and Salm Reifferscheit. At the last-mentioned place the voyagers parted company, one party proceeding to Jerusalem by way of Alexandria, Damietta, and Joppa, while the other bent their course across the burning sands of Africa towards Mount Sinai, and thence continued their journey to Jerusalem by land. Here at length they had the pleasure of meeting once more. A great and general rejoicing, in which we all joined, was the consequence of this event.

After dinner we once more visited all the holy places in company of the new-comers; we afterwards went to the so-called "Milk Grotto," distant about half a mile from our convent. In this grotto there is nothing to be seen but a simple altar, before which lights are continually burning. It is not locked, and every passer-by is at liberty to enter. This place is held sacred not only by the Christians, but also by the Turks, who bring many a cruise of oil to fill the lamps after they have cleaned them. In this grotto the Holy Family concealed themselves before the flight into Egypt, and the Virgin for a long time nourished the infant Jesus with her milk, from which circumstance the grotto derives its name. The women in the neighbourhood believe that if they feel unwell during the time they are nursing their children, they have merely to scrape some of the sand from the rocks in this grotto, and to take it as a powder, to regain their health.

Half a mile from this grotto we were shown the field in which the angel appeared to announce the birth of the Redeemer to the shepherds. But our newly-arrived friends were not able to visit this spot. They were fain to content themselves with a distant view, as it was high time to think of our return.

ST. JOHN'S.

On the 4th of June I rode out, accompanied by a guide, to the birth-place of St. John the Baptist, distant about four miles from Jerusalem. The way to this convent lies through the Bethlehem Gate, opposite the convent of the "Holy Cross," a building supposed to stand on the site where the wood was felled for our Saviour's cross! Not far off, the place was pointed out to me where a battle was fought between the Israelites and the Philistines, and where David slew Goliath.

Situated in a rocky valley, the convent of St. John is, like all the monasteries in these lands, surrounded by very strong walls. The church of the convent is erected on the spot where the house of Zacharias once stood, and a chapel commemorates the place where St. John first beheld the light. The ascent to this chapel is by a staircase, where a round tablet of stone bears the inscription,

"HIC PRÆCURSOR DOMINI CHRISTI NATUS EST."

Many events of the prophet's life are here portrayed by sculptures in white marble.

About a mile from the convent we find the "Grotto of Visitation," where St. Mary met St. Elizabeth. The remains of the latter are interred here.

On the very first day of my arrival at Jerusalem I had made some observations, during a visit to the church of St. Francis, which gave me any thing but a high opinion of the behaviour of the Catholics here. This unfavourable impression was confirmed by subsequent visits to the church, so that at length I felt obliged to tell Father Paul that I would rather pray at home than among people who seemed to attend to any thing rather than their devotions. My Frankish costume seemed to be such a stumbling-block in the eyes of these people, that at length a priest came to me, and requested that I would make an alteration in my dress, or at any rate exchange my straw hat for a veil, in which I could muffle my head and face. I promised to discard the obnoxious hat and to wear a handkerchief round my head when I attended church, but refused to muffle my face, and begged the reverend gentleman to inform my fellow-worshippers that this was the first time such a thing had been required of a Frankish woman, and that I thought they would be more profitably employed in looking at their prayer-books than at me, for that He whom we go to church to adore is not a respecter of outward things. In spite of this remonstrance, their behaviour remained the same, so that I was compelled almost to discontinue attending public worship.

On great festival-days the high altar of the church of St. Francis is very profusely decorated. It is, in fact, almost overloaded with ornament, and sparkles and glitters with a most dazzling brilliancy. Innumerable candles display the lustre of gold and precious stones. Foremost among the costly ornaments appear a huge gold monstrance presented by the king of Naples, and two splendid candelabra, a gift of the imperial house of Austria.

I happened one day to pass a house, from within which a great screaming was to be heard. On inquiring of my companion what was the matter, I was informed that some person had died in that house the day before, and that the sound I heard was the wail of the "mourning women." I requested admission to the room where the deceased lay. Had it not been for the circumstance that a few pictures of saints and a crucifix decorated the walls, I could never have imagined that the dead man was a Catholic. Several "mourning women" sat near the corpse, uttering every now and then such frantic yells, that the neighbourhood rang with their din. In the intervals between these demonstrations they sat comfortably regaling themselves with coffee; after a little time they would again raise their horrible cry. I had seen enough to feel excessively disgusted, and so went away.

I was also fortunate enough to visit a newly-married pair. The bride was gorgeously dressed in a silk under-garment, wide trousers of peach-blossom satin, and a caftan of the same material; a rich shawl encircled her waist, and on her feet she wore boots of yellow morocco leather; the slippers had been left, according to the Turkish fashion, at the entrance of the chamber. An ornamental head-dress of rich gold brocade and fresh flowers completed the bride's attire; her hair, arranged in a number of thin plaits and decorated with coins, fell down upon her shoulders, and on her neck glittered several rows of ducats and larger gold pieces.

Costumes of this kind are only seen in the family circle, and on the occasion of some great event. Seldom or never are strange men allowed to behold the ladies in their gorgeous apparel; so that it is fruitless to expect to see picturesque female costumes in the public places of the East.

After the marriage ceremony, which is always performed during the forenoon, the young wife is compelled to sit for the remainder of the day in a corner of the room with her face turned towards the wall. She is not allowed to answer any question put by her husband, her parents, or by any one whatever; still less is she permitted to offer a remark herself. This silence is intended to typify the bride's sorrow at changing her condition.

During my visit, the bridegroom sat next to his bride, vainly endeavouring to lure a few words from her. On my rising to depart, the young wife inclined her head towards me, but without raising her eyes from the ground. In Jerusalem, almost all the women and girls wear veils when they go abroad. It was only in church, and in their own houses, that I had an opportunity of fairly seeing these houris. Among the girls I found many an interesting head; but the women who have attained the age of twenty-six or twenty-eight years already look worn and ugly; so that here, as in all tropical countries, we behold a great number of very plain faces, among which handsome ones shine forth at long intervals, like meteors. Thin people are rarely met with in Syria; on the contrary, even the young girls are frequently decidedly stout.

Not far from the bazaar is a great hall, wherein the Turks hold their judicial sittings, decide disputes, and pass sentence on criminals. Some ordinary-looking divans are placed round the interior of this hall, and in one corner a wooden cell, about ten feet long, six wide, and eight feet high, has been erected. This cell, furnished with a little door, and a grated hole by way of window, is intended for the reception of the criminal during his period of punishment.

Throughout the thirteen days I passed at Jerusalem, I did not find the heat excessive. The thermometer generally stood in the shade at from 20° to 22°, and in the sun at 28° (Reaum.), very seldom reaching 30°.

Fruit I saw none, with the exception of the little apricots called mish-mish, which are not larger than a walnut, but nevertheless have a very fine flavour. It is a pity that the inhabitants of these countries contribute absolutely nothing towards the cultivation and improvement of their natural productions; if they would but exert themselves, many a plant would doubtless flourish luxuriantly. But here the people do not even know how to turn those gifts to advantage which nature has bestowed upon them in rich profusion, and of superior quality; for instance, olives. Worse oil can hardly be procured than that which they give you in Syria. The Syrian oil and olives can scarcely be used by Europeans. The oil is of a perfectly green colour, thick, and disgusting alike to the smell and taste; the olives are generally black, a consequence of the negligent manner in which they are prepared. The same remark holds good with regard to the wine, which would be of excellent quality if the people did but understand the proper method of preparing it, and of cultivating the vineyards. At present, however, they adulterate their wine with a kind of herb, which gives it a very sharp and disagreeable taste.

On the whole, the neighbourhood of Jerusalem is very desolate, barren, and sterile. I found the town itself neither more nor less animated than most Syrian cities. I should depart from truth if I were to say, with many travellers, that it appeared as though a peculiar curse rested upon this city. The whole of Judea is a stony country, and this region contains many places with environs as rugged and barren as those of Jerusalem.

Birds and butterflies are rarely seen at the present season of the year, not only in the neighbourhood of Jerusalem, but throughout the whole of Syria. Where, indeed, could a butterfly or a bee find nourishment, while not a flower nor a blade of grass shoots up from the stony earth? And a bird cannot live where there are neither seeds nor insects, but must soar away across the seas to cooler and more fertile climes. Not only here, but throughout the whole of Syria, I missed the delightful minstrels of the air. The sparrow alone can find sustenance every where, for he lives in towns and villages, wherever man is seen. A whole flock of these little twittering birds woke me every morning.

I was as yet much less troubled by insects than I had anticipated. With the exception of the small flies on the plain of Sharon, and of certain little sable jumpers which seem naturalised throughout the whole world, I could not complain of having been annoyed by any creature.

Our common house-flies I saw every where; but they were not more numerous or more troublesome than in Germany.

EXCURSION TO THE RIVER JORDAN AND TO THE DEAD SEA.

To travel with any degree of security in Palestine, Phœnicia, etc., it is necessary to go in large companies, and in some places it even becomes advisable to have an escort. The stranger should further be provided with cooking utensils, provisions, tents, and servants. To provide all these things would have been a hopeless task for me; I had therefore resolved to return from Jerusalem as I had come, namely, via Joppa, and so to proceed to Alexandria or Beyrout, when, luckily for me, the gentlemen whom I have already mentioned arrived at Jerusalem. They intended making several excursions by land, and the first of these was to be a trip to the banks of the Jordan and to the Dead Sea.

I ardently wished to visit these places, and therefore begged the gentlemen, through Father Paul, to permit my accompanying them on their arduous journey. The gentlemen were of opinion that their proposed tour would be too fatiguing for one of my sex, and seemed disinclined to accede to my request. But then Count Wratislaw took my part, and said that he had watched me during our ride from Bethlehem to Jerusalem, and had noticed that I wanted neither courage, skill, nor endurance, so that they might safely take me with them. Father Paul immediately came to me with the joyful intelligence that I was to go, and that I had nothing to do but to provide myself with a horse. He particularly mentioned how kindly Count Wratislaw, to whom I still feel obliged, had interested himself in my behalf. The journey to the Jordan and the Dead Sea should never be undertaken by a small party. The best and safest course is to send for some Arab or Bedouin chiefs, either at Jerusalem or Bethlehem, and to make a contract with them for protection. In consideration of a certain tribute, these chiefs accompany you in person, with some of their tribe, to your place of destination and back again. The Counts paid the two chiefs three hundred piastres, with the travelling expenses for themselves and their twelve men. At three o'clock in the afternoon of the 7th of June our cavalcade started. The caravan consisted of the four counts, Mr. Bartlett, a certain Baron Wrede, two doctors, and myself, besides five or six servants, and the two chiefs with the body-guard of twelve Arabs. All were strongly armed with guns, pistols, swords, and lances, and we really looked as though we sallied forth with the intention of having a sharp skirmish.

Our way lay through the Via Dolorosa, and through St. Stephen's Gate, past the Mount of Olives, over hill and dale. Every where the scene was alike barren. At first we still saw many fruit-trees and olive-trees in bloom, and even vines, but of flowers or grass there was not a trace; the trees, however, stood green and fresh, in spite of the heat of the atmosphere and the total lack of rain. This luxuriance may partly be owing to the coolness and dampness which reigns during the night in tropical countries, quickening and renewing the whole face of nature.

The goal of our journey for to-day lay about eight miles distant from Jerusalem. It was the Greek convent of "St. Saba in the Waste." The appellation already indicates that the region around becomes more and more sterile, until at length not a single tree or shrub can be detected. Throughout the whole expanse not the lowliest human habitation was to be seen. We only passed a horde of Bedouins, who had erected their sooty-black tents in the dry bed of a river. A few goats, horses, and asses climbed about the declivities, laboriously searching for herbs or roots.

About half an hour before we reach the convent we enter upon the wilderness in which our Saviour fasted forty days, and was afterwards "tempted of the devil." Vegetation here entirely ceases; not a shrub nor a root appears; and the bed of the brook Cedron is completely dry. This river only flows during the rainy season, at which period it runs through a deep ravine. Majestic rocky terraces, piled one above the other by nature with such exquisite symmetry that the beholder gazes in silent wonder, overhang both banks of the stream in the form of galleries.

A silence of death brooded over the whole landscape, broken only by the footfalls of our horses echoing sullenly from the rocks, among which the poor animals struggled heavily forward. At intervals some little birds fluttered above our heads, silently and fearfully, as though they had lost their way. At length we turn sharply round an angle of the road,—and what a surprise awaits us! A large handsome building, surrounded by a very strong fortified wall, pierced for cannon in several places, lies spread before us near the bed of the river, and rises in the form of terraces towards the brow of the hill. From the position we occupied, we could see over the whole extent of wall from without and from within. Fortified as it was, it lay open before our gaze. Several buildings, and in front of all a church with a small cupola, told us plainly that St. Saba lay stretched below. On the farther bank, seven or eight hundred paces from the convent, rose a single square tower, apparently of great strength. I little thought that I should soon become much better acquainted with this isolated building. The priests had observed our procession winding down the hill, and at the first knocking the gate was opened. Masters, servants, Arabs, and Bedouins, all passed through; but when my turn came, the cry was, "Shut the gate!" and I was shut out, with the prospect of passing the night in the open air,—a thing which would have been rather disagreeable, considering how unsafe the neighbourhood was. At length, however, a lay brother appeared, and, pointing to the tower, gave me to understand that I should be lodged there. He procured a ladder from the convent, and went with me to the tower, where we mounted by its aid to a little low doorway of iron. My conductor pushed this open, and we crept in. The interior of the tower seemed spacious enough. A wooden staircase led us farther upwards to two tiny rooms, situated about the centre of the tower. One of these apartments, dimly lighted by the rays of a lamp, contained a small altar, and served as a chapel, while the second was used as a sleeping-room for female pilgrims. A wooden divan was the only piece of furniture this room contained. My conductor now took his leave, promising to return in a short time with some provisions, a bolster, and a coverlet for me. So now I was at least sheltered for the night, and guarded like a captive princess by bolt and bar. I could not even have fled had I wished to do so, for my leader had locked the creaking door behind him, and taken away the ladder. After carefully examining the chapel and my neatly-furnished apartment in this dreary prison-house, I mounted the staircase, and gained the summit of the tower. Here I had a splendid view of the country round about, my elevated position enabling me distinctly to trace the greater part of the desert, with its several rows of hills and mountains skirting the horizon. All these hills were alike barren and naked; not a tree nor a shrub, not a human habitation, could I discover. Silence lay heavily on every thing around, and it seemed to me almost as though no earth might here nourish a green tree, but that the place was ordained to remain a desert, as a lasting memorial of our Saviour's fasting. Unheeded by human eye, the sun sank beneath the mountains; I was, perhaps, the only mortal here who was watching its beautiful declining tints. Deeply moved by the scene around me, I fell on my knees, to offer up my prayers and praise to the Almighty, here in the rugged grandeur of the desert.

But I had only to turn away from the death-like silence, and to cast my eye towards the convent as it lay spread out before me, to view once more the bustle and turmoil of life. In the courtyard the Bedouins and Arabs were employed in ministering to the wants of their horses, bringing them water and food; beyond these a group of men was seen spreading mats on the ground, while others, with their faces bowed to the earth, were adoring, with other forms of prayer, the Omnipotent Spirit whose protection I had so lately invoked; others, again, were washing their hands and feet as a preparation for offering up their worship; priests and lay brethren passed hastily across the courtyard, busied in preparations for entertaining and lodging the numerous guests; while some of my fellow-travellers stood apart, in earnest conversation, and Mr. B. and Count Salm Reifferscheit reclined in a quiet spot and made sketches of the convent. Had a painter been standing on my tower, what a picture of the building might he not have drawn as the wild Arab and the thievish Bedouin leant quietly beside the peaceful priest and the curious European! Many a pleasant recollection of this evening have I borne away with me.

I was very unwilling to leave the battlements of the tower; but the increasing darkness at length drove me back into my chamber. Shortly afterwards a priest and a lay brother appeared, and with them Mr. Bartlett. The priest's errand was to bring me my supper and bedding, and my English fellow-traveller had kindly come to inquire if I would have a few servants as a guard, as it must be rather a dreary thing to pass a night quite alone in that solitary tower. I was much flattered by Mr. Bartlett's politeness to a total stranger, but, summoning all my courage, replied that I was not in the least afraid. Thereupon they all took their leave; I heard the door creak, the bolt was drawn, and the ladder removed, and I was left to my meditations for the night.

After a good night's rest, I rose with the sun, and had been waiting some time before my warder appeared with the coffee for my breakfast. He afterwards accompanied me to the convent gate, where my companions greeted me with high praises; some of them even confessed that they would not like to pass a solitary night as I had done.

CHAPTER IX.

June 8th.

At five o'clock in the morning we departed, and bent our course towards the Dead Sea. After a ride of two hours we could see it, apparently at such a short distance, that we thought half an hour at the most would bring us there. But the road wound betwixt the mountains, sometimes ascending, sometimes descending, so that it took us another two hours to reach the shore of the lake. All around us was sand. The rocks seem pulverised; we ride through a labyrinth of monotonous sand-heaps and sand-hills, behind which the robber-tribes of Arabs and Bedouins frequently lurk, making this part of the journey exceedingly unsafe.

Before we reach the shore, we ride across a plain consisting, like the rest, of deep sand, so that the horses sink to the fetlocks at every step. On the whole of our way we had not met with a single human being, with the exception of the horde of Bedouins whom we had found encamped in the river-bed: this was a fortunate circumstance for us, for the people whom the traveller meets during these journeys are generally unable to resist the temptation of seizing upon his goods, so that broken bones are frequently the result of such meetings.

The day was very hot (33° Reaum). We encamped in the hot sand on the shore, under the shelter of our parasols, and made our breakfast of hard-boiled eggs, a piece of bad bread, and some lukewarm water. I tasted the sea-water, and found it much more bitter, salt, and pungent than any I have met with elsewhere. We all dipped our hands into the lake, and afterwards suffered the heat of the air to dry them without having first rinsed them with fresh water; not one of us had to complain that this brought forth an itching or an eruption on our hands, as many travellers have asserted. The temperature of the water was 33° Reaum.; in colour it is a pale green. Near the shore the water is to a certain extent transparent; but as it deepens it seems turbid, and the eye can no longer pierce the surface. We could not even see far across the water, for a light mist seemed to rest upon it, thus preventing us from forming a good estimate of its breadth.

To judge from what we could distinguish, however, the Dead Sea does not appear to be very broad; it may rather be termed an oblong lake, shut in by mountains, than a sea. Not the slightest sign of life can be detected in the water; not a ripple disturbs its sleeping surface. A boat of any kind is of course quite out of the question. Some years since, however, an Englishman made an attempt to navigate this lake; for this purpose he caused a boat to be built, but did not progress far in his undertaking,—a sickness came upon him, he was carried to Jerusalem, and died soon after he had made the experiment. It is rather a remarkable fact that, up to the present moment, no Englishman has been found who was sufficiently weary of his life to imitate his countryman's attempt.

Stunted fragments of drift-wood, most probably driven to shore by tempests, lay scattered every where around. We could, however, discover no fields of salt; neither did we see smoke rising, or find the exhalations from the sea unpleasant. These phenomena are perhaps observed at a different season of the year to that in which I visited the Dead Sea. On the other hand, I saw not only separate birds, but sometimes even flights of twelve or fifteen. Vegetation also existed here to a certain extent. Not far from the shore, I noticed, in a little ravine, a group of eight acicular-leaved trees. On this plain there were also some wild shrubs bearing capers, and a description of tall shrub, not unlike our bramble, bearing a plentiful crop of red berries, very juicy and sweet. We all ate largely of them; and I was the more surprised at finding these plants here, as I had found it uniformly stated that animal and vegetable life was wholly extinct on the shores of the

Dead Sea.

Five cities, of which not a trace now remains, once lay in the plain now filled by this sea—their names were Sodom, Gomorrah, Adama, Zeboin, and Zona. A feeling of painful emotion, mingled with awe, took possession of my soul as I thought of the past, and saw how the works of proud and mighty nations had vanished away, leaving behind them only a name and a memory. It was a relief to me when we prepared, after an hour's rest, to quit this scene of dreary desolation.

For about an hour and a half we rode through an enormous waste covered with trailing weeds, towards the verdant banks of the Jordan, which are known from a distance by the beautiful blooming green of the meadows that surround it. We halted in the so-called "Jordan-vale," where our Saviour was baptised by St. John.

The water of the Jordan is of a dingy clay-colour; its course is very rapid. The breadth of this stream can scarcely exceed twenty-five feet, but its depth is said to be considerable. The moment our Arab companions reached the bank, they flung themselves, heated as they were, into the river. Most of the gentlemen followed their example, but less precipitately. I was fain to be content with washing my face, hands, and feet. We all drank to our hearts' content, for it was long since we had obtained water so cool and fresh. I filled several tin bottles, which I had brought with me for this purpose from Jerusalem, with water from the Jordan, and had them soldered down on my return to the Holy City. This is the only method with which I am acquainted for conveying water to the farthest countries without its turning putrid.

We halted for a few hours beneath the shady trees, and then pursued our journey across the plain. Suddenly a disturbance arose among our Arab protectors; they spoke very anxiously with one another, and continually pointed to some distant object. On inquiring the reason why they were so disturbed, we were told that they saw robbers. We strained our eyes in vain; even with the help of good spy-glasses we could discover nothing, and already began to suspect our escort of having cried "wolf" without reason, or merely to convince us that we had not taken them with us for nothing. But in about a quarter of an hour we could dimly discern figures emerging, one by one, from the far, far distance. Our Bedouins prepared for the combat, and advised us to take the opposite road while they advanced to encounter the enemy. But all the gentlemen wished to take part in the expedition, and joined the Bedouins, lusting for battle. The whole cavalcade rode off at a rapid pace, leaving Count Berchtold and myself behind. But when our steeds saw their companions galloping off in such fiery style, they scorned to remain idly behind, and without consulting our inclinations in the least, they ran of at a pace which fairly took away our breath. The more we attempted to restrain their headlong course, the more rapidly did they pursue their career, so that there appeared every prospect of our becoming the first, instead of the last, among the company. But when the enemy saw such a determined troop advancing to oppose them, they hurried off without awaiting our onset, and left us masters of the field. So we returned in triumph to our old course; when suddenly a wild boar, with its hopeful family, rushed across our path. Away we all went in chase of the poor animals. Count Wratislaw succeeded in cutting down one of the young ones with his sabre, and it was solemnly delivered up to the cook. No further obstacles opposed themselves to our march, and we reached our resting-place for the night without adventure of any kind.

On this occasion I had an opportunity of seeing how the Arabs can manage their horses, and how they can throw their spears and lances in full career, and pick up the lances as they fly by. The horses, too, appear quite different to when they are travelling at their usual sleepy pace. At first sight these horses look any thing but handsome. They are thin, and generally walk at a slow pace, with their heads hanging down. But when skilful riders mount these creatures, they appear as if transformed. Lifting their small graceful heads with the fiery eyes, they throw out their slender feet with matchless swiftness, and bound away over stock and stone with a step so light and yet so secure that accidents very rarely occur. It is quite a treat to see the Arabs exercise. Those who escorted us good-naturedly went through several of their manœuvres for our amusement.

From the valley of the Jordan to the "Sultan's Well," in the vale of Jericho, is a distance of about six miles. The road winds, from the commencement of the valley, through a beautiful natural park of fig-trees and other fruit-trees. Here, too, was the first spot where the eye was gladdened by the sight of a piece of grass, instead of sand and shingle. Such a change is doubly grateful to one who has been travelling so long through the barren, sandy desert.

The village lying beside the Sultan's Well looks most deplorable. The inhabitants seem rather to live under than above the ground. I went into a few of these hollows. I do not know how else to designate these little stoneheap-houses. Many of them are entirely destitute of windows, the light finding its way through the hole left for an entrance. The interiors contained only straw-mats and a few dirty mattresses, not stuffed with feathers, but with leaves of trees. All the domestic utensils are comprised in a few trenchers and water-jugs: the poor people were clothed in rags. In one corner some grain and a number of cucumbers were stored up. A few sheep and goats were roaming about in the open air. A field of cucumbers lies in front of every house. Our Bedouins were in high glee at finding this valuable vegetable in such abundance. We encamped beside the well, under the vault of heaven.

From the appearance of the valley in its present state, it is easy to conclude, in spite of the poverty of the inhabitants and the air of desolation spread over the farther landscape, that it must once have been very blooming and fertile.

On the right, the naked mountains extend in the direction of the Dead Sea; on the left rises the hill on which Moses completed his earthly career, and from which his great spirit fled to a better world. On the face of the mountain three caves are visible, and in the centre one we were told the Saviour had dwelt during his preparation in the wilderness before undertaking his mission of a teacher. High above these caves towers the summit of the rock from which Satan promised to give our Lord the sovereignty of all the earth if He would fall down and worship him.

Baron Wrede, Mr. Bartlett, and myself were desirous of seeing the interior of one of these caves, and started with this intention; but no sooner did one of our Bedouins perceive what we were about, than he came running up in hot haste to assure us that the whole neighbourhood was unsafe. We therefore turned back, the more willingly as the twilight, or rather sunset, was already approaching.

Twilight in these latitudes is of very short duration. At sunrise the shades of night are changed into the blaze of day as suddenly as the daylight vanishes into night.

Our supper consisted of rather a smoky pilau, which we nevertheless relished exceedingly; for people who have eaten nothing throughout the day but a couple of hard-boiled eggs are seldom fastidious about their fare at night. Besides, we had now beautiful fresh water from the spring, and cucumbers in abundance, though without vinegar or oil. But to what purpose would the unnatural mixture have been? Whoever wishes to travel should first strive to disencumber himself of what is artificial, and then he will get on capitally. The ground was our bed, and the dark blue ether, with its myriads of stars, our canopy. On this journey we had not taken a tent with us.

The aspect of the heavens is most beautiful here in Syria. By day the whole firmament is of a clear azure—not a cloud sullies its perfect brightness; and at night it seems spangled with a far greater number of stars than in our northern climes.

Count Zichy ordered the servants to call us betimes in the morning, in order that we might set out before sunrise. For once the servants obeyed; in fact they more than obeyed, for they roused us before midnight, and we began our march. So long as we kept to the plain, all went well; but whenever we were obliged to climb a mountain, one horse after another began to stumble and to stagger, so that we were in continual danger of falling. Under these circumstances it was unanimously resolved that we should halt beneath the next declivity, and there await the coming daylight. June 9th.

At four o'clock the reveille was beaten for the second time. We had now slept for three hours in the immediate neighbourhood of the Dead Sea, a circumstance of which we were not aware until daybreak: not one of our party had noticed any noxious exhalation arising from the water; still less had we been seized with headache or nausea, an effect stated by several travellers to be produced by the smell of the Dead Sea.

Our journey homewards now progressed rapidly, though for three or four hours we were obliged to travel over most formidable mountain-roads and through crooked ravines. In one of the valleys we again came upon a Bedouin's camp. We rode up to the tents and asked for a draught of water, instead of which these people very kindly gave us some dishes of excellent buttermilk. In all my life I never partook of any thing with so keen a relish as that with which I drank this cooling beverage after my fatiguing ride in the burning heat. Count Zichy offered our entertainers some money, but they would not take it. The chief stepped forward and shook several of us by the hand in token of friendship; for from the moment when a stranger has broken bread with Bedouins or Arabs, or has applied to them for protection, he is not only safe among their tribe, but they would defend him with life and limb from the attacks of his enemies. Still it is not advisable to meet them on the open plain; so contradictory are their manners and customs.

We were now advancing with great strides towards a more animated, if not a more picturesque landscape, and frequently met and overtook small caravans. One of these had been attacked the previous evening; the poor Arabs had offered a brave resistance, and had beaten off the foe; but one of them was lying half dead upon his camel, with a ghastly shot-wound in his head.

Nimble long-eared goats were diligently searching among the rocks for their scanty food, and a few grottoes or huts of stone announced to us the proximity of a little town or village. Right thankful were we to emerge safely from these fearful deserts into a less sterile and more populous region.

We passed through Bethany, and I visited the cave in which it is said that Lazarus slumbered before he came forth alive at the voice of the Redeemer. Then we journeyed on to Jerusalem by the same road on which the Saviour travelled when the Jewish people shewed their attachment and respect, for the last time, by strewing olive and palm branches in his way. How soon was this scene of holy rejoicing changed to the ghastly spectacle of the Redeemer's torture and death!

Towards two o'clock in the afternoon we arrived safely at Jerusalem, and were greeted with a hearty welcome by our kind hosts.

A few days after my return from the foregoing excursion, I left Jerusalem for ever. A calm and peaceful feeling of happiness filled my breast; and ever shall I be thankful to the Almighty that He has vouchsafed me to behold these realms. Is this happiness dearly purchased by the dangers, fatigues, and privations attendant upon it? Surely not. And what, indeed, are all the ills that chequer our existence here below to the woes endured by the blessed Founder of our religion! The remembrance of these holy places, and of Him who lived and suffered here, shall surely strengthen and console me wherever I may be and whatever I may be called upon to endure.

## FROM JERUSALEM TO BEYROUT.

My gentleman-protectors wished to journey from Jerusalem to Beyrout by land, and intended taking a circuitous route, by way of Nazareth, Galilee, Canaan, etc., in order to visit as many of these places as possible, which are fraught with such interest to us Christians. They were once more kind enough to admit me into their party, and the 11th of June was fixed for our departure.

June 11th.

Quitting Jerusalem at three o'clock in the afternoon, we emerged from the Damascus Gate, and entered a large elevated plateau. Though this region is essentially a stony one, I saw several stubble-fields, and even a few scanty blades of grass.

The view is very extended; at a distance of four miles the walls of Jerusalem were still in view, till at length the road curved round a hill, and the Holy City was for ever hidden from our sight.

On the left of the road, an old church, said to have been erected in the days of Samuel, stands upon a hill.

At six in the evening we reached the little village of Bir, and fixed our halting-place for the night in a neighbouring stubble-field. During my first journey by land (I mean my ride from Joppa to Jerusalem), I had already had a slight foretaste of what is to be endured by the traveller in these regions. Whoever is not very hardy and courageous, and insensible to hunger, thirst, heat, and cold; whoever cannot sleep on the hard ground, or even on stones, passing the cold nights under the open sky, should not pursue his journey farther than from Joppa to Jerusalem: for, as we proceed, the fatigues become greater and less endurable, and the roads are more formidable to encounter; besides this, the food is so bad that we only eat from fear of starvation; and the only water we can get to drink is lukewarm, and offensive from the leathern jars in which it is kept.

We usually rode for six or seven hours at a time without alighting even for a moment, though the thermometer frequently stood at from 30° to 34° Reaumur. Afterwards we rested for an hour at the most; and this halt was often made in the open plain, where not a tree was in sight. Refreshment was out of the question, either for the riders or the poor beasts, and frequently we had not even water to quench our burning thirst. The horses were compelled to labour unceasingly from sunrise until evening, without even receiving a feed during the day's journey. The Arabian horse is the only one capable of enduring so much hardship. In the evening these poor creatures are relieved of their burdens, but very seldom of the saddle; for the Arabs assert that it is less dangerous for the horse to bear the saddle day and night, than that it should be exposed when heated by the day's toil to the cold night-air. Bridles, saddles, and stirrups were all in such bad condition that we were in continual danger of falling to the ground, saddle and all. In fact, this misfortune happened to many of our party, but luckily it was never attended with serious results.

June 12th.

The night was very chilly; although we slept in a tent, our thick cloaks scarcely sufficed to shield us from the night-air. In the morning the fog was so dense that we could not see thirty paces before us. Towards eight o'clock it rolled away, and a few hours later the heat of the sun began to distress us greatly. It is scarcely possible to guard too carefully against the effects of the heat; the head should in particular be kept always covered, as carelessness in this respect may bring on coup de soleil. I always wore two pocket handkerchiefs round my head, under my straw hat, and continually used a parasol.

From Bir to Jabrud, where we rested for a few hours, we travelled for six hours through a monotonous and sterile country. We had still a good four hours' ride before us to Nablus, our resting-place for the night.

The roads here are bad beyond conception, so that at first the stranger despairs of passing them either on foot or on horseback. Frequently the way leads up hill and down dale, over great masses of rock; and I was truly surprised at the strength and agility of our poor horses, which displayed extraordinary sagacity in picking out the little ledges on which they could place their feet safely in climbing from rock to rock. Sometimes we crossed smooth slabs of stone, where the horses were in imminent danger of slipping; at others, the road led us past frightful chasms, the sight of which was sufficient to make me dizzy. I had read many accounts of these roads, and was prepared to find them bad enough; but my expectations were far surpassed by the reality. All that the traveller can do is to trust in Providence, and abandon himself to fate and to the sagacity of his horse.

An hour and a half before we reached the goal of this day's journey, we passed the grave of the patriarch Jacob. Had our attention not been particularly drawn to this monument, we should have ridden by without noticing it, for a few scattered blocks of stone are all that remain. A little farther on we enter the Samaritan territory, and here is "Jacob's well," where our Saviour held converse with the woman of Samaria. The masonry of the well has altogether vanished, but the spring still gushes forth from a rock.

Nablus, the ancient Sichem, the chief town of Samaria, contains four thousand inhabitants, and is reputed to be one of the most ancient towns in Palestine. It is surrounded by a strong wall, and consists of a long and very dirty street. We rode through the town from one end to the other, and past the poor-looking bazaar, where nothing struck me but the sight of some fresh figs, which were at this early season already exposed for sale. Of course we bought the fruit at once; but it had a very bad flavour.

A number of soldiers are seen in all the towns. They are Arnauts, a wild, savage race of men, who appear to be regarded with more dread by the inhabitants than the wandering tribes whose incursions they are intended to repress.

We pitched our tents on a little hill immediately outside the town. Few things are more disagreeable to the traveller than being compelled to bivouac near a town or village in the East. All the inhabitants, both young and old, flock round in order to examine the European caravan, which is a most unusual sight for them, as closely as possible. They frequently even crowd into the tents, and it becomes necessary to expel the intruders almost by main force. Not only are strangers excessively annoyed at being thus made a gazing-stock, but they also run a risk of being plundered.

Our cook had the good fortune to obtain a kid only three or four days old, which was immediately killed and at once boiled with rice. We made a most sumptuous meal, for it was seldom we could get such good fare.

June 13th.

The morning sun found us already on horseback; we rode through the whole of the beautiful valley at the entrance of which Nablus lies. The situation of this town is very charming. The valley is not broad, and does not exceed a mile and a half in length; it is completely surrounded with low hills. The mountain on the right is called Ebal, and that on the left Grissim. The latter is celebrated as being the meeting-place of the twelve tribes of Israel under Joshua; they there consulted upon the means of conquering the land of Canaan.

The whole valley is sufficiently fertile; even the hills are in some instances covered to their summits with olive, fig, lemon, and orange trees. Some little brooks, clear as crystal, bubble through the beautiful plain. We were frequently compelled to ride through the water; but all the streams are at this season of the year so shallow, that our horses' hoofs were scarcely covered.

After gaining the summit of the neighbouring hill, we turned round with regret to look our last on this valley; seldom has it been my lot to behold a more charming picture of blooming vegetation.

Two hours more brought us to Sebasta, the ancient Samaria, which also lies on a lovely hill, though for beauty of situation it is not to be compared with Nablus. Sebasta is a wretched village. The ruins of the convent built on the place where St. John the Baptist was beheaded were here pointed out to us; but even of the ruins there are few traces left.

Two hours later we reached Djenin, and had now entered the confines of Galilee. Though this province, perhaps, no longer smiles with the rich produce it displayed in the days of old, it still affords a strong contrast to Judæa. Here we again find hedges of the Indian fig-tree, besides palms and large expanses of field; but for flowers and meadows we still search in vain.

The costume of the Samaritan and Galilean women appears as monotonous as it is poor and dirty. They wear only a long dark-blue gown, and the only difference to be observed in their dress is that some muffle their faces and others do not. It would be no loss if all wore veils; for so few pretty women and girls are to be discovered, that they might be searched for, like the honest man of Diogenes, with a lantern. The women have all an ugly brown complexion, their hair is matted, and their busts lack the rounded fullness of the Turkish women. They have a custom of ornamenting both sides of the head, from the crown to the chin, with a row of silver coins; and those women who do not muffle their faces usually wear as head-dress a handkerchief of blue linen.

Djenin is a dirty little town, which we only entered in consequence of having been told that we should behold the place where Queen Jezebel fell from the window and was devoured by dogs. Both window and palace have almost vanished; but dogs, who look even now as though they could relish such royal prey, are seen prowling about the streets. Not only in Constantinople, but in every city of Syria we found these wild dogs; they were, however, nowhere so numerous as in the imperial city.

We halted for an hour or two outside the town, beside a coffee-house, and threw ourselves on the ground beneath the open sky. A kind of hearth made of masonry, on which hot water was continually in readiness, stood close by, and near it some mounds of earth had been thrown up to serve as divans. A ragged boy was busy pounding coffee, while his father, the proprietor of the concern, concocted the cheering beverage, and handed it round to the guests. Straw-mats were spread for our accommodation on the earthen divans, and without being questioned we were immediately served with coffee and argilé. In the background stood a large and lofty stable of brickwork, which might have belonged to a great European inn.

After recruiting ourselves here a little, we once more set forth to finish our day's journey. Immediately after leaving the town, a remarkably fine view opens before us over the great elevated plain Esdralon, to the magnificent range of mountains enclosing this immense plateau. In the far distance they shewed us Mount Carmel, and, somewhat nearer, Mount Tabor. Here, too, the mountains are mostly barren, without, however, being entirely composed of naked masses of rock. Mount Tabor, standing entirely alone and richly clothed with vegetation, has a very fine appearance.

For nearly two hours we rode across the plain of Esdralon, and had thus ample leisure to meditate upon the great events that have occurred here. It is difficult to imagine a grander battlefield, and we can readily believe that in such a plain whole nations may have struggled for victory. From the time of Nabucodonosor to the period of the Crusades, and from the days of the Crusades to those of Napoleon, armies of men from all nations have assembled here to fight for their real or imaginary rights, or for the glory of conquest.

The great and continuous heat had cracked and burst the ground on this plain to such a degree, that we were in continual apprehension lest our horses should catch their feet in one or other of the fissures, and strain or even break them. The soil of the plain seems very good, and is free from stones; it appears, however, generally to lie fallow, being thickly covered with weeds and wild artichokes. The villages are seen in the far distance near the mountains. This plain forms part of Canaan.

We pitched our camp for the night beside a little cistern, near the wretched village of Lagun; and thus slept, for the third night consecutively, on the hard earth.

June 14th.

To-day we rode for an hour across the plain of Esdralon, and once more suffered dreadfully from the stings of the minute gnats which had annoyed us so much on our journey from Joppa to Ramla. These plagues did not leave us until we had partly ascended the mountains skirting the plain, from the summit of which we could see Nazareth, prettily built on a hill at the entrance of a fruitful valley. In the background rises the beautiful Mount Tabor.

From the time we first see Nazareth until we reach the town is a ride of an hour and a half; thus the journey from Lagun to Nazareth occupies four hours and a half, and the entire distance from Jerusalem twenty-six or twenty-seven hours.

CHAPTER X.

It was only nine o'clock when we reached Nazareth, and repaired to the house for strangers in the Franciscan convent, where the priests welcomed us very kindly. As soon as we had made a short survey of our rooms (which resulted in our finding them very like those at Jerusalem, both as regards appearance and arrangement), we set forth once more to visit all the remarkable places, and above all the church which contains the Grotto of Annunciation. This church, to which we were accompanied by a clergyman, was built by St. Helena, and is of no great size. In the background a staircase leads down into the grotto, where it is asserted that the Virgin Mary received the Lord's message from the angel. Three little pillars of granite are still to be seen in this grotto. The lower part of one of these pillars was broken away by the Turks, so that it is only fastened from above. On the strength of this circumstance many have averred that the pillar hangs suspended in air! Had these men but looked beyond their noses, had they only cast their eyes upwards, they could not have had the face to preach a miracle where it is so palpable that none exists. A picture on the wall, not badly executed, represents the Annunciation. The house of the Virgin is not shewn here, because, according to the legend, an angel carried it away to Loretto in Italy. A few steps lead to another grotto, affirmed to be the residence of a neighbour of the Virgin, during whose absence she presided over the house and attended to the duties of the absent Mary.

Another grotto in the town is shewn as "the workshop of Joseph;" it has been left in its primitive state, except that a plain wooden altar has been added. Not far off we find the synagogue where our Lord taught the people, thereby exasperating the Pharisees to such a degree, that they wished to cast Him down from a rock outside the city. In conclusion we were shewn an immense block of stone on which the Saviour is said to have eaten the Passover with His disciples(!).

In the afternoon we went to see "Mary's Well," on the road to Tabarith, at a short distance from Nazareth. This well is fenced round with masonry, and affords pure clear water. Hither, it is said, the Virgin came every day to draw water, and here the women and girls of Nazareth may still be daily seen walking to and fro with pitchers on their shoulders. Those whom we saw were all poorly clad, and looked dirty. Many wore no covering on their head, and, what was far worse, their hair hung down in a most untidy manner. Their bright eyes were the only handsome feature these people possessed. The custom of wearing silver coins round the head also prevailed here.

To-day was a day of misfortunes for me; in the morning, when we departed from Lagun, I had already felt unwell. On the road I was seized with violent headache, nausea, and feverish shiverings, so that I hardly thought I should be able to reach Nazareth. The worst of all this was, that I felt obliged to hide my illness, as I had done on our journey to Jerusalem, for fear I should be left behind. The wish to view all the holy places in Nazareth was also so powerful within me, that I made a great effort, and accompanied the rest of my party for the whole day, though I was obliged every moment to retire into the background that my condition might not be observed. But when we went to table, the smell of the viands produced such an effect upon me, that I hastily held my handkerchief before my face as though my nose were bleeding, and hurried out. Thanks to my sunburnt skin, through which no paleness could penetrate, no one noticed that I was ill. The whole day long I could eat nothing; but towards evening I recovered a little. My appetite now also returned, but unfortunately nothing was to be had but some bad mutton-broth and an omelette made with rancid oil. It is bad enough to be obliged to subsist on such fare when we are in health, but the hardship increases tenfold when we are ill. However, I sent for some bread and wine, and strengthened myself therewith as best I might.

June 15th.

Thanks be to Heaven, I was to-day once more pretty well. In the morning I could already mount my horse and take part in the excursion we desired to make to

TABARITH.

Passing Mary's Well and a mountain crowned by some ruins, the remains of ancient Canaan, we ride for about three miles towards the foot of Mount Tabor, the highest summit of which we do not reach for more than an hour. There were no signs of a beaten road, and we were obliged to ride over all obstacles; a course of proceeding which so tired our horses, that in half an hour's time they were quite knocked up, so that we had to proceed on foot. After much toil and hardship, with a great deal of climbing and much suffering from the heat, we gained the summit, and were repaid for the toil of the ascent, not only by the reflection that we stood on classic ground, but also by the beautiful view which lay spread before our eyes. This prospect is indeed magnificent. We overlook the entire plain of Saphed, as far as the shores of the Galilean Sea. Mount Tabor is also known by the name of the "Mountain of Bliss"—here it was that our Lord preached His exquisite "Sermon on the Mount." Of all the hills I have seen in Syria, Mount Tabor is the only one covered to the summit with oaks and carob-trees. The valleys too are filled with the richest earth, instead of barren sand; but in spite of all this the population is thin, and the few villages are wretched and puny. The poor inhabitants of Syria are woefully ground down; the taxes are too high in proportion to the productions of the soil, so that the peasants cannot possibly grow more produce than they require for their own consumption. Thus, for instance, orchards are not taxed in the aggregate, but according to each separate tree. For every olive-tree the owner must pay a piastre, or a piastre and a half; and the same sum for an orange or lemon tree. And heavily taxed as he is, the poor peasant is never safe in saying, "Such and such a thing belongs to me." The pacha may shift him to another piece of land, or drive him away altogether, if he thinks it advisable to do so; for a pacha's power in his province is as great as that of the Sultan himself in Constantinople.

Porcupines are to be met with on Mount Tabor; we found several of their fine horny quills.

From the farther side of the mountain we descended into the beautiful and spacious valley of Saphed, the scene of the miracle of the loaves and fishes, and rode on for some hours until we reached Tabarith.

A very striking scene opens before the eyes of the traveller on the last mountain before Tabarith. A lovely landscape lies suddenly unrolled before him. The valley sinks deeply down to the Galilean Sea, round the shores of which a glorious chain of mountains rises in varied and picturesque terrace-like forms. More beautiful than all the rest, towers in snowy grandeur the mighty chain of the Anti-Lebanon, its white surface glittering in the rays of the sun, and distinctly mirrored in the clear bosom of the lake. Deep down lies the little town of Tabarith, shadowed by palm-trees, and guarded by a castle raised a little above it. The unexpected beauty of this scene surprised us so much that we alighted from our horses, and passed more than half an hour on the summit of the mountain, to gaze at our leisure upon the wondrous picture. Count S. drew a hurried but very successful sketch of the landscape which we all admired so much, though its mountains were naked and bare. But such is the peculiar character of Eastern scenery; in Europe, meadows, alps, and woods exhibit quite a distinct class of natural beauty. In a mountain region of Europe, a sight like the one we were now admiring would scarcely have charmed us so much. But in these regions, poor alike in inhabitants and in scenery, the traveller is contented with little, and a little thing charms him. For instance, would not a plain piece of beef have been a greater luxury to us on our journey than the most costly delicacies at home? Thus we felt also with regard to scenery.

On entering the town we experienced a feeling of painful emotion. Tabarith lay still half in ruins; for the dreadful earthquake of 1839 had made this place one of the chief victims of its fury. How must the town have looked immediately after the calamity, when even now, in spite of the extensive repairs, it appears almost like a heap of ruins! We saw some houses that had completely fallen in; others were very much damaged, with large cracks in the walls, and shattered terraces and towers: every where, in short, we wandered among ruins. Above 4000 persons, more than half of the entire population, are said to have perished by this earthquake.

We alighted at the house of a Jewish doctor, who entertains strangers, as there is no inn at Tabarith. I was quite surprised to find every thing so clean and neat in this man's house. The little rooms were simply but comfortably furnished, the small courtyard was flagged with large stones, and round the walls of the hall were ranged narrow benches with soft cushions. We were greatly astonished at this appearance of neatness and order; but our wonder rose when we made the discovery that the Jews, who are very numerous at Tabarith, are not clothed in the Turkish or Greek fashion, but quite like their brethren in Poland and Galicia. Most of them also spoke German. I immediately inquired the reason of this peculiarity, and was informed that all the Jewish families resident in this town originally came from Poland or Russia, with the intention of dying in the Promised

Land. As a rule, all Jews seem to cherish a warm desire to pass their last days in the country of their forefathers, and to be buried there.

We requested our young hostess, whose husband was absent, to prepare for us without delay a good quantity of pilau and fowls; adding, that we would in the mean time look at the town and the neighbouring baths at the Sea of Gennesareth, but that we should return in an hour and a half at the most.

We then proceeded to the Sea of Gennesareth, which is a fresh-water lake. We entered a fisherman's boat, in order that we might sail on the waters where our Lord had once bid the winds "be still." We were rowed to the warm springs, which rise near the shore, a few hundred paces from the town. On the lake all was calm; but no sooner had we landed than a storm arose—between the fishermen and ourselves. In this country, if strangers neglect to bargain beforehand for every stage with guides, porters, and people of this description, they are nearly sure of being charged an exorbitant sum in the end. This happened to us on our present little trip, which certainly did not occupy more than half an hour. We took our seats in the boat without arranging for the fares; and on disembarking offered the fishermen a very handsome reward. But these worthies threw down the money, and demanded thirty piastres; whereas, if we had bargained with them at first, they would certainly not have asked ten. We gave them fifteen piastres, to get rid of them; but this did not satisfy their greediness; on the contrary, they yelled and shouted, until the Count's servants threatened to restore peace and quietness with their sticks. At length the fishermen were so far brought to their senses that they walked away, scolding and muttering as they went.

Adjoining the warm springs we found a bathing-house, built in a round form and covered with a cupola. Here we also met a considerable number of pilgrims, mostly Greeks and Armenians from the neighbourhood, who were journeying to Jerusalem. They had encamped beside the bathing-house. Half of these people were in the water, where a most animated conversation was going on. We also wished to enter the building, not for the purpose of bathing, but to view the beauty and arrangements of the interior, which have been the subject of many laudatory descriptions; but at the entrance such a cloud of vapour came rolling towards us that we were unable to penetrate far. I saw enough, however, to feel convinced, that in the description of these baths poetry or exaggeration had led many a pen far beyond the bounds of fact. Neither the exterior of this building, nor the cursory glance I was enabled to throw into the interior, excited either my curiosity or my astonishment. Seen from without, these baths resemble a small-sized house built in a very mediocre style, and with very slender claims to beauty. The interior displayed a large quantity of marble,—for instance, in the floor, the sides of the bath, etc. But marble is not such a rarity in this country that it can raise this bathing-kiosk into a wonder-building, or render it worthy of more than a passing glance. I endeavour to see every thing exactly as it stands before me, and to describe it in my simple diary without addition or ornament.

At eight o'clock in the evening we returned tired and hungry to our comfortable quarters, flattering ourselves that we should find the plain supper we had ordered a few hours before smoking on the covered table, ready for our arrival. But neither in the hall nor in the chamber could we find even a table, much less a covered one. Half dead with exhaustion, we threw ourselves on chairs and benches, looking forward with impatience to the supper and the welcome rest that was to follow it. Messenger after messenger was despatched to the culinary regions, to inquire if the boiled fowls were not yet in an eatable condition. Each time we were promised that supper would be ready "in a quarter of an hour," and each time nothing came of it. At length, at ten o'clock, a table was brought into the room; after some time a single chair, appeared, and then one more; then came another interval of waiting, until at length a clean table-cloth was laid. These arrivals occupied the time until eleven o'clock, when the master of the house, who had been absent on an excursion, made his appearance, and with him came a puny roast fowl. No miracle, alas, took place at our table like that of the plain of Saphed; we were but seven persons, and so the fowl need only have been increased seven times to satisfy us all; but as it was, each person received one rib and no more. Our supper certainly consisted of several courses brought in one after the other. Had we known this, we certainly should soon have arranged the matter, for then each person would have appropriated the whole of a dish to himself. In the space of an hour and a quarter nine or ten little dishes made their appearance; but the portion of food contained in each was so small, that our supper may be said to have consisted of a variety of "tastes." We would greatly have preferred two good-sized dishes to all these kickshaws. The dishes were, a roast, a boiled, and a baked chicken, a little plate of prepared cucumbers, an equally small portion of this vegetable in a raw state, a little pilau, and a few small pieces of mutton.

Our host kindly provided food for the mind during supper by describing to us a series of horrible scenes which had occurred at the time of the earthquake. He, too, had lost his wife and children by this calamity, and only owed his own life to the circumstance that he was absent at a sick-bed when the earthquake took place.

Half an hour after midnight we at length sought our resting-places. The doctor very kindly gave up his three little bedrooms to us, but the heat was so oppressive that we preferred quartering ourselves on the stones in the yard. They made a very hard bed, but we none of us felt symptoms of indigestion after our sumptuous meal.

June 16th.

At five o'clock in the morning we took leave of our host, and returned in six hours to Nazareth by the same road on which we had already travelled. We did not, however, ascend Mount Tabor a second time, but rode along beside its base. To-day I once more visited all the spots I had seen when I was so ill two days before; in this pursuit I passed some very agreeable hours.

June 17th.

In the morning, at half-past four, we once more bade farewell to the worthy priests of Nazareth, and rode without stopping for nine hours and a half, until at two o'clock we reached

MOUNT CARMEL.

It was long since we had travelled on such a good road as that on which we journeyed to-day. Now and then, however, a piece truly Syrian in character had to be encountered, probably lest we should lose the habit of facing hardship and danger. Another comfort was that we were not obliged to-day to endure thirst, as we frequently passed springs of good clear water. At one time our way even led through a small oak-wood, a phenomenon almost unprecedented in Syria. There was certainly not a single tree in all the wood which a painter might have chosen for a study, for they were all small and crippled. Large leafy trees, like those in my own land, are very seldom seen in this country. The carob, which grows here in abundance, is almost the only handsome tree; it has a beautiful leaf, scarcely larger than that of a rose-tree, of an oval form, as thick as the back of a knife, and of a beautiful bright green colour.

Mount Carmel lies on the sea-shore. It is not high, and half an hour suffices the traveller to reach its summit, which is crowned by a spacious and beautiful convent, probably the handsomest in all Palestine, not even excepting the monasteries at Nazareth and Jerusalem. The main front of the building contains a suite of six or seven large rooms, with folding-doors and lofty regular windows. These rooms, together with several in the wings, are devoted to the reception of strangers. They are arranged in European style, with very substantial pieces of furniture, among which neither sofas nor useful chests of drawers are wanting.

About an hour after we arrived our reverend hosts regaled us with a more sumptuous meal than any of which I had partaken since my departure from Constantinople.

In proportion as our fare had been meagre and our accommodation indifferent at Nazareth and Jerusalem, did we find every thing here excellent. In an elegant dining-room stood a large table covered with a fine white cloth, on which cut glass and clean knives, forks, and china plates gleamed invitingly. A servant in European garb placed some capital fast-day fare on the table (it was Friday), and a polite priest kept us company; but not in eating, for he rightly considered that such a hungry company would not require any example to fall to.

During the whole remainder of our journey through Syria this convent occupied a green spot in our memory. How capitally would a few days' rest here have recruited our strength! But the gentlemen had a distant goal before their eyes, and "Forward!" was still the cry.

After dinner we went down to the sea-shore, to visit the large grotto called the "Prophets' school." This grotto has really the appearance of a lofty and spacious hall, where a number of disciples could have sat and listened to the words of the prophet.

The grotto in which Elijah is said to have lived is situated in a church at the top of the mountain. Mount Carmel is quite barren, being only covered here and there with brambles; but the view is magnificent. In the foreground the eye can roam over the boundless expanse of ocean, while at the foot of the mountain it fords a resting-place in the considerable town of Haifa, lying in a fertile plain, which extends to the base of the high mountains, bounded in the distance by the Anti-Libanus, and farther still by the Lebanon itself. Along the line of coast we can distinguish Acre (or Ptolemais), Sur (Tyre), and Soida (Sidon).

June 18th.

This morning we sent our poor over-tired horses on before us to Hese, and walked on foot at midday under a temperature of 33° to Haifas, a distance of more than two miles. Heated and exhausted to the last degree we reached the house of the Consul, who is a Catholic, but seems nevertheless to live quite in Oriental fashion. This gentleman is consul both for France and Austria. Although he was not at home when we arrived, we were immediately shewn into the room of state, where we reclined on soft divans, and were regaled with sherbet of all colours, green, yellow, red, etc., and with coffee flavoured with roses, which we did not like. Hookahs (or tchibuks) were also handed round. At length the Consul's wife appeared, a young and beautiful lady of an imposing figure, dressed in the Oriental garb. She smoked her tchibuk with as much ease as the gentlemen. Luckily a brother of this lady who understood something of Italian was present, and kindly acted as interpreter. I have never found an Oriental woman who knew any language but that of her own country.

After we had rested ourselves, we pursued our journey in a boat to Acre. On my road to Jerusalem I had only seen the outside of this monument of the last war, now I could view its interior; but saw nothing to repay me for my trouble. Considering how ugly the Turkish towns are even when they are in good preservation, it may easily be imagined that the appearance of one of these cities is not improved when it is full of shot-holes, and the streets and interiors of the houses are choked up with rubbish. The entrance to the convent lies through the courtyard of the Turkish barracks, where there seemed to be a great deal of bustle, and where we had an opportunity of noticing how wretchedly clad, and still more miserably shod, the Turkish soldiers are. These blemishes are not so much observed when the men are seen singly at their posts.

The convent here is very small, being in fact only a dwelling-house to which a chapel is attached. Two monks and a lay brother form the whole household.

Scarcely had I established myself in my room, before a very polite lady entered, who introduced herself to me as the wife of a surgeon in the service of the pacha here. She stated that her husband was at present absent at Constantinople, and added that she was in the habit of spending several hours in the convent every evening to do the honours of the house! This assertion struck me as so strange, that I should certainly have remained dumb had not my visitor been a very agreeable, polite French lady. As it was, however, we chatted away the evening pleasantly together, until the supper-bell summoned us to the refectory. All that I saw in this convent was in direct contrast to the arrangement of the comfortable establishment of the Carmelites. The refectory here is astonishingly dirty; the whole furniture consists of two dingy tables and some benches; the table-cloth, plates, etc. wore the prevailing livery; and the fare was quite in keeping with every thing else. We supped at two tables; the gentlemen and the reverend fathers sitting at one, while the French lady and myself occupied the other.

June 19th.

As we were not to travel far to-day, we did not set out until ten o'clock, when we started in company of several Franks who were in the pacha's service. They led us into a park by the roadside belonging to the mother of the Sultan. Here the pacha usually resides during the summer. In half an hour's time we reached this park. The garden is rather handsome, but does not display many plants except lemon, orange, pomegranate, and cypress trees. The display of flowers was not very remarkable; for not only could we discover no rare or foreign plants, but we also missed many flowers which grow plentifully in our gardens at home. A few kiosks are here to be seen, but every thing seemed miserably out of repair.

The residence of the pacha, situated outside the gardens, has a more inviting appearance. We paid our respects to his highness, who received us very graciously, and caused us to be regaled with the usual beverages. No sooner had the high ladies in the harem learnt that a Frankish woman was in their territory, than they sent to invite me to visit them. I gladly accepted this invitation, the more so as it offered an opportunity of gratifying my curiosity. I was conducted to another part of the house, where I stepped into a chamber of middle size, the floor of which was covered with mats and carpets, while on cushions ranged round the walls reclined beauties of various complexions, who seemed to have been collected from every quarter of the globe. One of these women, who was rather elderly, appeared to be the pacha's chief wife, for all the rest pointed to her. The youngest lady seemed about eighteen or nineteen years of age, and was the mother of a child eight months old, with which they were all playing as with a doll; the poor little thing was handed about from hand to hand. These ladies were dressed exactly like the daughters of the consul at Joppa, whose costume I have described. I did not see any signs of particular beauty, unless the stoutness of figure so prevalent here is considered in that light. I saw, however, a woman with one eye, a defect frequently observed in the East. Female slaves were there of all shades of colour. One wore a ring through her nose, and another had tastefully painted her lips blue. Both mistresses and slaves had their eyebrows and eyelashes painted black, and their nails and the palm of the hand stained a light-brown with the juice of the henna.

The Oriental women are ignorant and inquisitive in the highest degree; they can neither read nor write, and the knowledge of a foreign language is quite out of the question. It is very rarely that one of them understands embroidering in gold. Whenever I happened to be writing in my journal, men, women, and children would gather round me, and gaze upon me and my book with many signs and gestures expressive of astonishment.

The ladies of the harem seemed to look with contempt upon employment and work of every kind; for neither here nor elsewhere did I see them do any thing but sit cross-legged on carpets and cushions, drinking coffee, smoking nargilé, and gossiping with one another. They pressed me to sit down on a cushion, and then immediately surrounded me, endeavouring, by signs, to ask many questions. First they took my straw hat and put it upon their heads; then they felt the stuff of my travelling robe; but they seemed most of all astonished at my short hair, {165} the sight of which seemed to impress these poor ignorant women with the idea that nature had denied long hair to the Europeans. They asked me by signs how this came to pass, and every lady came up and felt my hair. They seemed also very much surprised that I was so thin, and offered me their nargilé, besides sherbet and cakes. On the whole, our conversation was not very animated, for we had no dragoman to act as interpreter, so that we were obliged to guess at what was meant, and at length I sat silently among these Orientals, and was heartily glad when, at the expiration of an hour, my friends sent to fetch me away. At a later period of my journey I frequently visited harems, and sometimes considerable ones; but I found them all alike. The only difference lay in the fact that some harems contained more beautiful women and slaves, and that in others the inmates were more richly clad; but every where I found the same idle curiosity, ignorance, and apathy. Perhaps they may be more happy than European women; I should suppose they were, to judge from their comfortable figures and their contented features. Corpulence is said frequently to proceed from a good-natured and quiet disposition; and their features are so entirely without any fixed character and expression, that I do not think these women capable of deep passions or feeling either for good or evil. Exceptions are of course to be found even among the Turkish women; I only report what I observed on the average.

This day we rode altogether for seven hours. We passed a beautiful orange-grove; for the greater part of the way our road led through deep sand, close by the sea-shore; but once we had to pass a dreadfully dangerous place called the "White Mount," one extremity of which rises out of the sea. This once passed, we soon come upon the beautiful far-stretching aqueduct which I noticed on my journey from Joppa to Jerusalem. It traverses a portion of this fruitful plain.

We could not enter the little town of Sur, the goal of this day's journey, as it was closed on account of the plague. We therefore passed by, and pitched our tents beside a village, in the neighbourhood of which large and splendid cisterns of water, hewn in the rock, are to be seen. The superfluous water from these cisterns falls from a height of twenty or thirty feet, and after turning a mill-wheel, flows through the vale in the form of a brook.

## CHAPTER XI.

June 20th.

Shortly after five this morning we were in our saddles, and a few hours afterwards arrived at the beautiful river Mishmir, which is as broad as the Jordan, though it does not contain nearly so much water. Next to the Jordan, however, this river is the largest we find on our journey, besides being a most agreeable object in a region so destitute of streams. Its water is pure as crystal.

In ten hours we reached the town, and at once repaired to the convent, as not one of these cities contains an inn. The little convent, with its tiny church, is situate at the end of a large courtyard, which is so thronged with horses and men, particularly with soldiers, that we had great difficulty in forcing our way through. When we had at length cleared a passage for ourselves to the entrance, we were received with the agreeable intelligence that there was no room for us. What was to be done? We thought ourselves lucky in obtaining a little room where we could pass the night in a house belonging to a Greek family; beds were, however, out of the question; we had to lie on the hard stones. In the courtyard a kind of camp had been pitched, in which twelve state-horses of the Emir {167} of Lebanon (creatures of the true Arab breed) were bivouacking among a quantity of Arnauts.

The Arnaut soldiers are universally feared, but more by friend than foe. They are very turbulent, and behave in an overbearing manner towards the people. The Count, my fellow-traveller, was even insulted in the street, not by a peasant, but by one of these military fellows. These ill-disciplined troops are assembled every where, in order that they may be ready to attack whenever a disturbance occurs between the Druses and Maronites. I consider, however, that the Arnauts are much more to be feared than either the Druses or the Maronites, through whose territories we afterwards journeyed without experiencing, in a single instance, either insult or injury. I hardly think we should have escaped so well had we encountered a troop of these wild horsemen.

Among all the Turkish soldiers the Arnauts are the best dressed; with their short and full white skirts of linen or lawn, and tight trousers of white linen, a scarf round the middle, and a white or a red spencer, they closely resemble the Albanians.

June 21st.

This was a most fatiguing day, although we did not ride for more than ten hours; but this ten hours' journey was performed without even a quarter of an hour's rest, though the thermometer stood at 33° Reaumur. Our path lay through a sandy desert, about two miles in breadth, running parallel with the mountain-range from Saida to Beyrout. The monotony of the steppe is only broken at intervals by heaps of sand. The surface of the sand presents the appearance of a series of waves; the particles of which it is composed are very minute, and of a fine yellowish-brown colour. A beautiful fertile valley adjoins this desert, and stretches towards Mount Lebanon, on whose brown rocky surface several villages can be descried.

This mountain-range has a most imposing appearance. White rocks and strata of white sand shine forth from its broad and generally barren expanse like fields of snow.

The residence of the late Lady Hester Stanhope can be seen in the distance on the declivity of the mountain.

During our long ride of ten hours we did not pass a single tank, spring, or even pool, and all the river-beds on our way were completely dried up by the heat. Not a tree could we see that could shelter us for a moment from the glaring heat of the sun. It was a day of torment for us and for our poor beasts. Two of our brave horses sank from exhaustion, and could go no farther, though relieved of their burdens; we were obliged to leave the poor creatures to perish by the wayside.

At three in the afternoon we at length arrived at Beyrout, after having bravely encountered, during ten consecutive days, the toil and hardship inseparable from a journey through Syria.

The distance from Jerusalem to Beyrout is about 200 miles, allowing for the circuitous route by way of Tabarith, which travellers are not, however, compelled to take. From Jerusalem to Nazareth is 54 miles; from Nazareth across Mount Tabor to Tabarith and back again 31 miles; from Nazareth to

Mount Carmel, Haifas, and Acre, 46 miles; and from Acre to Beyrout 69 miles; making the total 200 miles.

Our poor horses suffered dreadfully during this journey; for they were continually obliged either to climb over rocks, stones, and mountains, or to wade through hot sand, in which they sank above the fetlocks at every step. It would have been a better plan had we only engaged our horses from Jerusalem to Nazareth, where we could have procured fresh ones to carry us on to Beyrout. We had been told at Jerusalem that it was sometimes impossible to obtain horses at Nazareth, and so preferred engaging our beasts at once for the whole journey. On arriving at Nazareth we certainly discovered that we had been deceived, for horses are always to be had there in plenty; but as the contract was once made, we were obliged to abide by it. During the ten days of our journey the temperature varied exceedingly. By day the heat fluctuated between 18° and 39° Reaumur; the nights too were very changeable, being sometimes sultry, and sometimes bitterly cold.

BEYROUT

lies in a sandy plain; but the mulberry-trees by which it is surrounded impart to this city an air of picturesque beauty. Still we wade every where, in the streets, gardens, and alleys, through deep sand. Viewed from a distance, Beyrout has a striking effect, a circumstance I had remarked on my first arrival there from Constantinople; but it loses considerably on a nearer approach. I did not enjoy walking through the town and its environs; but it was a great pleasure to me to sit on a high terrace in the evening, and look down upon the landscape. The dark-blue sky rose above the distant mountains, the fruitful valley, and the glittering expanse of ocean. The golden sun was still illumining the peaks of the mountains with its farewell rays, until at length it sunk from view, shrouding every thing in a soft twilight. Then I saw the innumerable stars shine forth, and the moon shed its magic light over the nocturnal landscape; and that mind can scarcely be called human which does not feel the stirring of better feelings within it at such a spectacle. Truly the temple of the Lord is every where; and throughout all nature there is a mysterious something that tells even the infidel of the omnipresence of the Great Spirit. How many beautiful evenings did I not enjoy at Beyrout! they were, in fact, the only compensation for the grievous hardships I was obliged to endure during my stay in this town.

In the inn I could again not find a single room, and was this time much more at a loss to find a place of shelter than I had been before; for our host's wife had gone out of town with her children, and had let her private house; so I sat, in the fullest sense of the word, "in the street." A clergyman, whose acquaintance I had made in Constantinople, and who happened just then to be at Beyrout, took compassion upon me, and procured me a lodging in the house of a worthy Arab family just outside the town. Now I certainly had a roof above my head, but I could not make myself understood; for not a soul spoke Italian, and my whole knowledge of Arabic was comprised in the four words: taib, moi, sut, mafish— beautiful, water, milk, and nothing.

With so limited a stock of expressions at my command, I naturally could not make much way, and the next day I was placed in a very disagreeable dilemma. I had hired a boy to show me the way to a church, and explained to him by signs that he was to wait to conduct me home again. On emerging from the church I could see nothing of my guide. After waiting for some time in vain, I was at length compelled to try and find my way alone.

The house in which I lived stood in a garden of mulberry-trees, but all the houses in the neighbourhood were built in the same style, each having a tower attached, in which there is a habitable room; all these dwellings stand in gardens planted with mulberry-trees, some of them not separated from each other at all, and the rest merely by little sand-hills. Flowers and vegetables are nowhere to be seen, nor is the suburb divided into regular streets; so that I wandered in an endless labyrinth of trees and houses. I met none but Arabs, whose language I did not understand, and who could, therefore, give me no information. So I rushed to and fro, until at length, after a long and fatiguing pilgrimage, I was lucky enough to stumble on the house I wanted. Unwilling to expose myself to such a disagreeable adventure a second time, I thought it would be preferable to dwell within the town; and therefore hired the young guide before mentioned to conduct me to the house of the Austrian Consul-General Herr von A. Unfortunately this gentleman was not visible to such an insignificant personage as myself, and sent me word that I might come again in a few hours. This was a true "Job's message" for me, as far as consolation went. The heat was most oppressive; I had now entered the town for the second time, to be sent once more back to the glowing sands, with permission to "come again in a few hours." Had I not been uncommonly hardy, I should have succumbed. But luckily I knew a method to help myself. I ordered my little guide to lead me to the house in which the wife of Battista the innkeeper had lived.

During my previous residence at Beyrout I had accidentally heard that a French lady lodged in the same house, and occupied herself with the education of the children. I went to call on this French lady, and was lucky enough to find her; so I had, at any rate, so far succeeded that I had found a being with whom I could converse, and of whom I might request advice and assistance. My new acquaintance was an extremely cordial maiden lady about forty years of age. Her name was Pauline Kandis. My unfortunate position awakened her compassion so much, that she placed her own room at my disposal for the time being. I certainly saw that my present quarters left much to be desired, for my kind entertainer's lodging consisted of a single room, divided into two parts by several tall chests; the foremost division contained a large table, at which four girls sat and stood at their lessons. The second division formed a kind of lumber-room, redolent of boxes, baskets, and pots, and furnished with a board, laid on an old tub, to answer the purposes of a table. My condition was, however, so forlorn, that I took joyful possession of the lumber-room assigned to me. I immediately departed with my boy-guide, and by noon I was already installed, with bag and baggage, in the dwelling of my kind hostess. But there was no more walking for me that day. What with the journey and my morning's peregrinations I was so exhausted that I requested nothing but a resting-place, which I found among the old chests and baskets on the floor. I was right glad to lie down, and court the rest that I needed so much.

At seven o'clock in the evening the school closed. Miss K. then took her leave, and I remained sole occupant of her two rooms, which she only uses as school-rooms, for she sleeps at her brother's house.

My lodging at Miss K.'s was, however, the most uncomfortable of any I had yet occupied during my entire journey.

From eight o'clock in the morning until seven at night four or five girls, who did any thing rather than study, were continually in the room. The whole day long there was such a noise of shouting, screaming, and jumping about, that I could not hear the sound of my own voice. Moreover, the higher regions of this hall of audience contained eight pigeons' nests; and the old birds, which were so tame that they not only took the food from our plates, but stole it out of our very mouths, fluttered continually about the room, so that we were obliged to look very attentively at every chair on which we intended to sit down. On the floor a cock was continually fighting with his three wives; and a motherly hen, with a brood of eleven hopeful ducks, cackled merrily between. I wonder that I did not contract a squint, for I was obliged continually to look upwards and downwards lest I should cause mischief, and lest mischief should befall me. During the night the heat and the stench were almost insupportable; and immediately after midnight the cock always began to crow, as if he earned his living by the noise he made. I used to open the window every night to make a passage of escape for the heat and the foul air, while I lay down before the door, like Napoleon's Mameluke, to guard the treasures entrusted to my care. But on the second night two wandering cats had already discovered my whereabouts—without the least compunction they stepped quietly over me into the chamber, and began to raise a murderous chase. I instantly jumped up and drove away the robbers; and from that time forward I was obliged to remain in the interior of my fortress, carefully to barricade all the windows, and bear my torments with what fortitude I might.

Our diet was also of a very light description. A sister-in-law of the good

Pauline was accustomed to send in our dinner, which consisted one day of a thimbleful of saffron-coloured pilau, while the next would perhaps bring half the shoulder of a small fish. Had I boarded with my hostess, I should have kept fast-day five days in the week, and have had nothing to eat on the remaining two. I therefore at once left off dining with them, and used to cook a good German dish for myself every day. In the morning I asked for some milk, in order to make my coffee after the German fashion. Yet I think that some of our adulterators of milk must have penetrated even to Syria, for I found it as difficult to obtain pure goats' milk here as to get good milk from the cow in my own country.

My bedstead was formed out of an old chest, and my sole employment and amusement was idling. I had not a book to read, no table to write on; and if I once really succeeded in getting something to read or made an attempt at writing, the whole tribe of youngsters would come clustering round, staring at my book or at my paper. It would certainly have been useless to complain, but yet I could not always entirely conceal the annoyance I felt.

My friends must pardon me for describing my cares so minutely, but I only do so to warn all those who would wish to undertake a journey like mine, without being either very rich, very high-born, or very hardy, that they had much better remain at home.

As I happened to be neither rich nor high-born, the Consul would not receive me at all the first time I called upon him, although the captain of a steamer had been admitted to an audience just before I applied. A few days afterwards I once more waited upon the Consul, told him of my troubles, and stated plainly how thankful I should feel if any one would assist me so far as to procure me a respectable lodging, for which I would gladly pay, and where I could remain until an opportunity offered to go to Alexandria; the worthy Consul was kind enough to reply to my request with a shake of the head, and with the comforting admission that "he was very sorry for me—it was really extremely unfortunate." I think the good gentleman must have left all his feeling at home before settling in Syria, otherwise he would never have dismissed me with a few frivolous speeches, particularly as I assured him that I was perfectly well provided with money, and would bear any expense, but added that it was possible to be placed in positions where want of advice was more keenly felt than want of means. During the whole of my residence at Beyrout, my countryman never troubled himself any more about me.

During my stay here I made an excursion to the grotto, said to be the scene of St. George's combat with the dragon; this grotto is situate to the right of the road, near the quarantine-house. The ride thither offers many fine views, but the grotto itself is not worth seeing.

Frequently in the evening I went to visit an Arab family, when I would sit upon the top of the tower and enjoy the sight of the beautiful sunset.

A very strong military force was posted at Beyrout, consisting entirely of Arnauts. They had pitched their tents outside the town, which thus wore the appearance of a camp. Many of these towns do not contain barracks; and as the soldiers are not here quartered in private houses, they are compelled to bivouack in the open field.

The bazaar is very large and straggling. On one occasion I had the misfortune to lose myself among its numerous lanes, from which it took me some time to extricate myself; I had an opportunity of seeing many of the articles of merchandise, and an immense number of shops, but none which contained any thing very remarkable. Once more I found how prone people are to exaggerate. I had been warned to abstain from walking in the streets, and, above all, to avoid venturing into the bazaar. I neglected both pieces of advice, and walked out once or twice every day during my stay, without once meeting with an adventure of any kind.

I had already been at Beyrout ten long, long days, and still no opportunity offered of getting to Alexandria. But at the end of June the worthy artist Sattler, whose acquaintance I had made at Constantinople, arrived here. He found me out, and proposed that I should travel to Damascus with Count Berchtold, a French gentleman of the name of De Rousseau, and himself, instead of wasting my time here. This proposition was a welcome one to me, for I ardently desired to be released from my fowls' nest. My arrangements were soon completed, for I took nothing with me except some linen and a mattress, which were packed on my horse's back.

JOURNEY FROM BEYROUT TO DAMASCUS, BALBECK, AND MOUNT LEBANON. July 1st.

At one o'clock in the afternoon we were all assembled before the door of M. Battista's inn, and an hour later we were in our saddles hastening towards the town-gate. At first we rode through a deep sea of sand surrounding the town; but soon we reached the beautiful valley which lies stretched at the foot of the Anti-Libanus, and afterwards proceeded towards the range by pleasant paths, shaded by pine-woods and mulberry-plantations.

But now the ascent of the magnificent Anti-Libanus became steeper and more dangerous, as we advanced on rocky paths, often scarcely a foot in breadth, and frequently crossed by fissures and brooklets. Some time elapsed before I could quite subdue my fear, and could deliver myself wholly up to the delight of contemplating these grand scenes, so completely new to us Europeans, leaving my horse, which planted its feet firmly and without once stumbling among the blocks of stone lying loosely on each other, to carry me as its instinct directed; for these horses are exceedingly careful, being well used to these dangerous roads. We could not help laughing heartily at our French companion, who could not screw up his courage sufficiently to remain on his horse at the very dangerous points. At first he always dismounted when we came to such a spot; but at length he grew weary of eternally mounting and dismounting, and conquered his fear, particularly when he observed that we depended so entirely on the sagacity of our steeds, and gave ourselves completely up to the contemplation of the mountains around us. It is impossible adequately to describe the incomparable forms of this mountain-range. The giant rocks, piled one above the other, glow with the richest colours; lovely green valleys lie scattered between; while numerous villages are seen, sometimes standing isolated on the rocks, and at others peering forth from among the deep shade of the olive and mulberry trees.

The sun sinking into the sea shot its last rays through the clear pure air towards the highest peaks of the mighty rocks. Every thing united to form a picture which when once seen can never be forgotten.

The tints of the rocky masses are peculiarly remarkable; exhibiting not only the primary colours, but many gradations, such as bluish-green, violet, etc. Many rocks were covered with a red coating resembling cinnabar, in several places we found small veins of pure sulphur, and each moment something new and wonderful met our gaze. The five hours which we occupied in riding from Beyrout to the village of Elhemsin passed like five minutes. The khan of Elhemsin was already occupied by a caravan bringing wares and fruit from Damascus, so that we had nothing for it but to raise our tent and encamp beneath it.

July 2d.

The rising sun found us prepared for departure, and soon we had reached an acclivity from whence we enjoyed a magnificent view. Before us rose the lofty peaks of Lebanon and Anti-Libanus, partly covered with snow; while behind us the mountains, rich in vineyards, olive-plantations, and pine-woods, stretched downward to the sea-shore. We had mounted to such a height, that the clouds soaring above the sea and the town of Beyrout lay far beneath us, shrouding the city from our gaze.

Vineyards are very common on these mountains. The vines do not, however, cling round trees for support, nor are they trained up poles as in Austria; they grow almost wild, the stem shooting upwards to a short distance from the ground, towards which the vine then bends. The wine made on these mountains is of excellent quality, rather sweet in flavour, of a golden-yellow colour, and exceedingly fiery.

We still continued to climb, without experiencing much inconvenience from the heat, up a fearful dizzy path, over rocks and stones, and past frightful chasms. Our leathern bottles were here useless to us, for we had no lack of water; from every crevice in the rocks a clear crystal flood gushed forth, in which the gorgeously-coloured masses of stone were beautifully mirrored.

After a very fatiguing ride of five hours we at length reached the ridge of the Anti-Libanus, where we found a khan, and allowed ourselves an hour's rest. The view from this point is very splendid. The two loftiest mountain-ridges of Lebanon and Anti-Libanus enclose between them a valley which may be about six miles long, and ten or twelve broad. Our way led across the mountain's brow and down into this picturesque valley, through which we journeyed for some miles to the village of Maschdalanscher, in the neighbourhood of which place we pitched our tents.

It is, of course, seldom that a European woman is seen in these regions, and thus I seemed to be quite a spectacle to the inhabitants; at every place where we halted many women and children would gather round me, busily feeling my dress, putting on my straw hat, and looking at me from all sides, while they endeavoured to converse with me by signs. If they happened to have any thing eatable at hand, such as cucumbers, fruits, or articles of that description, they never failed to offer them with the greatest good-nature, and seemed highly rejoiced when I accepted some. On the present evening several of these people were assembled round me, and I had an opportunity of noticing the costume of this mountain tribe. Excepting the head-dress, it is the same as that worn throughout all Palestine, and indeed in the whole of Syria; the women have blue gowns, and the men, white blouses, wide trousers, and a sash: sometimes the women wear spencers, and the more wealthy among them even display caftans and turbans. The head-dress of the women is very original, but does not look remarkably becoming. They wear on their foreheads a tin horn more than a foot in length, and over this a white handkerchief, fastened at the back and hanging down in folds. This rule, however, only applies to the wealthier portion of the community, which is here limited enough. The poorer women wear a much smaller horn, over which they display an exceedingly dingy handkerchief. During working hours they ordinarily divest themselves of these ornaments, as they would render it impossible to carry loads on the head. The rich inhabitants of the mountains, both male and female, dress in the Oriental fashion; but the women still retain the horn, which is then made of silver.

The village of Maschdalanscher is built of clay huts thatched with straw. I saw many goats and horned cattle, and a good store of corn lay piled up before the doors.

We were assured that the roads through the mountains inhabited by the Druses and Maronites were very unsafe, and we were strongly urged to take an escort with us; but as we met caravans almost every hour, we considered this an unnecessary precaution, and arrived safely without adventure of any kind at Damascus.

July 3d.

This morning we rode at first over a very good road, till at length we came upon a ravine, which seemed hardly to afford us room to pass. Closer and more closely yet did the rocky masses approach each other, as we passed amongst the loose shingle over the dry bed of a river. Frequently the space hardly admitted of our stepping aside to allow the caravans we met to pass us. Sometimes we thought, after having painfully laboured through a ravine of this kind, that we should emerge into the open field; but each time it was only to enter a wilder and more desert pass. So we proceeded for some hours, till the rocky masses changed to heaps of sand, and every trace of vegetation disappeared. At length we had climbed the last hill, and Damascus, "the vaunted city of the East," lay before us.

It is certainly a striking sight when, escaping from the inhospitable domains of the mountain and the sandhill, we see stretched at our feet a great and luxuriant valley, forming in the freshness of its vegetation a singular contrast to the desert region around. In this valley, amid gardens and trees innumerable, extends the town, with its pretty mosques and slender lofty minarets; but I was far from finding the scene so charming that I could have exclaimed with other travellers, "This is the most beauteous spot on earth!"

The plain in which Damascus lies runs on at the foot of the Anti-Libanus as far as the mountain of Scheik, and is shut in on three sides by sandhills of an incomparably dreary appearance. On the fourth side the plain loses itself in the sandy desert. This valley is exceedingly well watered by springs descending from all the mountains, which we could not, however, see on our approach; but no river exists here. The water rushes forth but to disappear beneath the sand, and displays its richness only in the town and its immediate neighbourhood.

From the hill whence we had obtained the first view of Damascus, we have still a good two miles to ride before we reach the plantations. These are large gardens of mish-mish, walnut, pomegranate, orange, and lemon trees, fenced in with clay walls, traversed by long broad streets, and watered by bubbling brooks. For a long time we journeyed on in the shade of these fruitful woods, till at length we entered the town through a large gate. Our enthusiastic conceptions of this renowned city were more and more toned down as we continued to advance.

The houses in Damascus are almost all built of clay and earth, and many ugly wooden gables and heavy window-frames give a disagreeable ponderous air to the whole. Damascus is divided into several parts by gates, which are closed soon after sunset. We passed through a number of these gates, and also through the greater portion of the bazaar, on our road to the Franciscan convent.

We had this day accomplished a journey of more than twenty-four miles, in a temperature of 35° to 36° Reaum., and had suffered much from the scorching wind, which came laden with particles of dust. Our faces were so browned, that we might easily have been taken for descendants of the Bedouins. This was the only day that I felt my eyes affected by the glare.

Although we were much fatigued on arriving at the convent, the first thing we did, after cleansing ourselves from dust and washing our burning eyes, was to hasten to the French and English consuls, so eager were we to see the interior of some of these clay huts.

A low door brought us into a passage leading to a large yard. We could have fancied ourselves transported by magic to the scene of one of the fantastic "Arabian Nights," for all the glory of the East seemed spread before our delighted gaze. In the midst of the courtyard, which was paved with large stones, a large reservoir, with a sparkling fountain, spread a delightful coolness around. Orange and lemon trees dipped their golden fruit into the crystal flood; while at the sides flower-beds, filled with fragrant roses, balsams, oleanders, etc., extended to the stairs leading to the reception-room. Every thing seemed to have been done that could contribute to ornament this large and lofty apartment, which opened into the courtyard. Swelling divans, covered with the richest stuffs, lined the walls, which, tastefully ornamented with mirrors and painted and sculptured arabesques, and further decked with mosaic and gilding, displayed a magnificence of which I could not have formed a conception. In the foreground of this fairy apartment a jet of water shot upwards from a marble basin. The floor was also of marble, forming beautiful pictures in the most varied colours; and over the whole scene was spread that charm so peculiar to the Orientals, a charm combining the tasteful with the rich and gorgeous. The apartment in which the women dwell, and where they receive their more confidential visitors, are similar to the one I have just described, except that they are smaller, less richly furnished, and completely open in front. The remaining apartments also look into the courtyard; they are simply, but comfortably and prettily arranged.

All the houses of the Orientals are similar to this one, except that the apartments of the women open into another courtyard than those of the men.

After examining and admiring every thing to our heart's content, we returned to our hospitable convent. This evening the clerical gentlemen entertained us. A tolerably nice meal, with wine and good bread, restored our exhausted energies to a certain extent.

At Beyrout we were quite alarmed at the warnings we received concerning the numbers of certain creeping things we should find here in the bedsteads. I therefore betook myself to bed with many qualms and misgivings; but I slept undisturbed, both on this night and on the following one.

CHAPTER XII.

July 4th.

Damascus is one of the most ancient cities of the East, but yet we see no ruins; a proof that no grand buildings ever existed here, and that therefore the houses, as they became old and useless, were replaced by new ones.

To-day we visited the seat of all the riches—the great bazaar. It is mostly covered in, but only with beams and straw mats. On both sides are rows of wooden booths, containing all kinds of articles, but a great preponderance of eatables, which are sold at an extraordinarily cheap rate. We found the "mish-mish" particularly good.

As in Constantinople, the rarest and most costly of the wares are not exposed for sale, but must be sought for in closed store-houses. The booths look like inferior hucksters' shops, and each merchant is seen sitting in the midst of his goods. We passed hastily through the bazaar, in order soon to reach the great mosque, situate in the midst of it. As we were forbidden, however, not only to enter the mosque, but even the courtyard, we were obliged to content ourselves with wondering at the immense portals, and stealing furtive glances at the interior of the open space beyond. This mosque was originally a Christian church; and a legend tells that St. George was decapitated here.

The khan, also situate in the midst of the bazaar, is peculiarly fine, and is said to be the best in all the East. The high and boldly-arched portal is covered with marble, and enriched with beautiful sculptures. The interior forms a vast rotunda, surrounded by galleries, divided from each other, and furnished with writing-tables for the use of the merchants. Below in the hall the bales and chests are piled up, and at the side are apartments for travelling dealers. The greater portion of the floor and the walls is covered with marble.

Altogether, marble seems to be much sought after at Damascus. Every thing that passes for beautiful or valuable is either entirely composed of this stone, or at least is inlaid with it. Thus a pretty fountain in a little square near the bazaar is of marble; and a coffee-house opposite the fountain, the largest and most frequented of any in Damascus, is ornamented with a few small marble pillars. But all these buildings, not even excepting the great bathing-house, would be far less praised and looked at if they stood in a better neighbourhood. As the case is, however, they shine forth nobly from among the clay houses of Damascus.

In the afternoon we visited the Grotto of St. Paul, lying immediately outside the town. On the ramparts we were shewn the place where the apostle is said to have leaped from the wall on horseback, reaching the ground in safety, and taking refuge from his enemies in the neighbouring grotto, which is said to have closed behind him by miracle, and not to have opened again until his persecutors had ceased their pursuit. At present, nothing is to be seen of this grotto excepting a small stone archway, like that of a bridge. Tombs of modern date, consisting of vaults covered with large blocks of stone, are very numerous near this grotto.

We paid several more visits, and every where found great pomp of inner arrangement and decoration, varying of course in different houses. We were always served with coffee, sherbet, and argilé; and in the houses of the Turks a dreary conversation was carried on through the medium of an interpreter.

Walks and places of amusement there are none. The number of Franks resident here is too small to call for a place of general recreation, and the Turk never feels a want of this kind. The most he does is to saunter slowly from the bath to the coffee-house, and there to kill his time with the help of a pipe and a cup of coffee, staring vacantly on the ground before him. Although the coffee-houses are more frequented than any other buildings in the East, they are often miserable sheds, being all small, and generally built only of wood.

The inhabitants of Damascus wear the usual Oriental garb, but as a rule I thought them better dressed than in any Eastern town. Some of the women are veiled, but others go abroad with their faces uncovered. I saw here some very attractive countenances; and an unusual number of lovely children's heads looked at me from all sides with an inquisitive smile.

In reference to religious matters, these people seem very fanatical; they particularly dislike strangers. For instance, the painter S. wished to make sketches of the khan, the fountain, and a few other interesting objects or views. For this purpose he sat down before the great coffee-house to begin with the fountain; but scarcely had he opened his portfolio before a crowd of curious idlers had gathered around him, who, as soon as they saw his intention, began to annoy him in every possible way. They pushed the children who stood near against him, so that he received a shock every moment, and was hindered in his drawing. As he continued to work in spite of their rudeness, several Turks came and stood directly before the painter, to prevent him from seeing the fountain. On his still continuing to persevere, they began to spit upon him. It was now high time to be gone, and so Mr. S. hastily gathered his materials together and turned to depart. Then the rage of the rabble broke noisily forth. They followed the artist yelling and screaming, and a few even threw stones at him. Luckily he succeeded in reaching our convent unharmed.

Mr. S. had been allowed to draw without opposition at Constantinople, Brussa, Ephesus, and several other cities of the East, but here he was obliged to flee. Such is the disposition of these people, whom many describe as being so friendly.

The following morning at sunrise Mr. S. betook himself to the terrace of the convent, to make a sketch of the town. Here too he was discovered, but luckily not until he had been at work some hours, and had almost completed his task; so that as soon as the first stone came flying towards him, he was able quietly to evacuate the field.

July 5th.

In Damascus we met Count Zichy, who had arrived there with his servants a few days before ourselves, and intended continuing his journey to Balbeck to-day.

Count Zichy's original intention had been to make an excursion from this place to the celebrated town of Palmyra, an undertaking which would have occupied ten days. He therefore applied to the pacha for a sufficient escort for his excursion. This request was, however, refused; the pacha observing, that he had ceased for some time to allow travellers to undertake this dangerous journey, as until now all strangers had been plundered by the wandering Arabs, and in some instances men had even been murdered. The pacha added, that it was not in his power to furnish so large an escort as would be required to render this journey safe, by enabling the travellers to resist all aggressions. After receiving this answer, Count Zichy communicated with some Bedouin chiefs, who could not guarantee a safe journey, but nevertheless required 6000 piastres for accompanying him. Thus it became necessary to give up the idea altogether, and to proceed instead to Balbeck and to the heights of Lebanon.

At the hour of noon we rode out of the gate of Damascus in company with Count Zichy. The thermometer stood at 40° Reaumur. Our procession presented quite a splendid appearance; for the pacha had sent a guard of honour to escort the Count to Balbeck, to testify his respect for a relation of Prince M---.

At first our way led through a portion of the bazaar; afterwards we reached a large and splendid street which traverses the entire city, and is said to be more than four miles in length. It is so broad, that three carriages can pass each other with ease, without annoyance to the pedestrians. It is a pity that this street, which is probably the finest in the whole kingdom, should be so little used, for carriages are not seen here any more than in the remaining portion of Syria.

Scarcely have we quitted this road, before we are riding through gardens and meadows, among which the country-houses of the citizens lie scattered here and there. On this side of the city springs also gush forth and water the fresh groves and the grassy sward. A stone bridge, of very simple construction, led us across the largest stream in the neighbourhood, the Barada, which is, however, neither so broad nor so full of water as the Jordan.

But soon we had left these smiling scenes behind us, and were wending our way towards the lonely desert. We passed several sepulchres, a number of which lie scattered over the sandy hills and plains round us. On the summit of one of these hills a little monument was pointed out to us, with the assertion that it was the grave of Abraham. We now rode for hours over flats, hills, and ridges of sand and loose stones; and this day's journey was as fatiguing as that of our arrival at Damascus. From twelve o'clock at noon until about five in the evening we continued our journey through this wilderness, suffering lamentably from the heat. But now the wilderness was passed; and suddenly a picture so lovely and grand unfolded itself before our gaze, that we could have fancied ourselves transported to the romantic vales of Switzerland. A valley enriched with every charm of nature, and shut in by gigantic rocks of marvellous and fantastic forms, opened at our feet. A mountain torrent gushed from rock to rock, foaming and chafing among mighty blocks of stone, which, hurled from above, had here found their resting-place. A natural rocky bridge led across the roaring flood. Many a friendly hut, the inhabitants of which looked forth with stealthy curiosity upon the strange visitors, lay half hidden between the lofty walls. And so our way continued; valley lay bordered on valley, and the little river which ran bubbling by the roadside led us past gardens and villages, through a region of surpassing loveliness, to the great village of Zabdeni, where we at length halted, after an uninterrupted ride of ten hours and a half.

The escort which accompanied us consisted of twelve men, with a superior and a petty officer. These troopers looked very picturesque when, as we travelled along the level road, they went through some small manœuvres for our amusement, rushing along on their swift steeds and attacking each other, one party flying across the plain, and the other pursuing them as victors.

The character of these children of nature is, on the whole, a very amiable one. They behaved towards us in an exceedingly friendly and courteous manner, bringing us fruit and water whenever they could procure them, leading us carefully by the safest roads, and shewing us as much attention as any European could have done. But their idea of mine and thine does not always appear to be very clearly defined. Once, for instance, we passed through fields in which grew a plant resembling our pea, on a reduced scale. Each plant contained several pods, and each pod two peas. Our escort picked a large quantity, ate the fruit with an appearance of great relish, and very politely gave us a share of their prize. I found these peas less tender and eatable than those of my own country, and returned them to the soldier who had offered them to me, observing at the same time that I would rather have had mish-mish. On hearing this he immediately galloped off, and shortly afterwards returned with a whole cargo of mish-mish and little apples, which had probably been borrowed for an indefinite period from one of the neighbouring gardens. I mention these little circumstances, as they appeared to me to be characteristic. On the one hand, Mr. S. had been threatened with the fate of St. Stephen for wishing to make a few sketches; and yet, on the other, these people were so kind and so ready to oblige.

This region produces abundance of fruit, and is particularly rich in mish-mish, or apricots. The finest of these are dried; while those which are over-ripe, or half decayed, are boiled to a pulp in large pots, and afterwards spread to dry on long smooth boards, in the form of cakes, about half an inch in thickness. These cakes, which look like coarse brown leather, are afterwards folded up, and form, together with the dried mish-mish, a staple article of commerce, which is exported far and wide. In Constantinople, and even in Servia, I saw cakes of this description which came from these parts.

The Turks are particularly fond of taking this dried pulp with them on their journeys. They cut it into little pieces, which they afterwards leave for several hours in a cup of water to dissolve; it then forms a really aromatic and refreshing drink, which they partake of with bread.

From Damascus to Balbeck is a ride of eighteen hours. Count Zichy wished to be in Balbeck by the next day at noon; we therefore had but a short night's rest.

The night was so mild and beautiful, that we did not want the tents at all, but lay down on the bank of a streamlet, beneath the shade of a large tree. For a long time sleep refused to visit us, for our encampment was opposite to a coffee-house, where a great hubbub was kept up until a very late hour. Small caravans were continually arriving or departing, and so there was no chance of rest. At length we dropped quietly asleep from very weariness, to be awakened a few hours afterwards to start once more on our arduous journey.

July 6th.

We rode without halting for eight hours, sometimes through pleasant valleys, at others over barren unvarying regions, upon and between the heights of the Anti-Libanus. At the hour of noon we reached the last hill, and

HELIOPOLIS OR BALBECK,

the "city of the sun," lay stretched before us.

We entered a valley shut in by the highest snow-covered peaks of Lebanon and Anti-Libanus, more than six miles in breadth and fourteen or sixteen miles long, belonging to Cælosyria. Many travellers praise this vale as one of the most beautiful in all Syria.

It certainly deserves the title of the 'most remarkable' valley, for excepting at Thebes and Palmyra we may search in vain for the grand antique ruins which are here met with; the title of the 'most beautiful' does not, according to my idea, appertain to it. The mountains around are desert and bare. The immeasurable plain is sparingly cultivated, and still more thinly peopled. With the exception of the town of Balbeck, which has arisen from the ruins of the ancient city, not a village nor a hut is to be seen. The corn, which still partly covered the fields, looked stunted and poor; the beds of the streams were dry, and the grass was burnt up. The majestic ruins, which become visible directly the brow of the last hill is gained, atone in a measure for these drawbacks; but we were not satisfied, for we had expected to see much more than met our gaze.

We wended our way along stony paths, past several quarries, towards the ruins. On reaching these quarries we dismounted, to obtain a closer view of them. In the right hand one lies a colossal block of stone, cut and shaped on all sides; it is sixty feet in length, eighteen in breadth, and thirteen in diameter. This giant block was probably intended to form part of the Cyclops wall surrounding the Temple of the Sun, for we afterwards noticed several stones of equal length and breadth among the ruins. Another to the left side of the road was remarkable for several grottoes and fragments of rock picturesquely grouped.

We had sent our horses on to the convent, and now hastened towards the ruined temples. At the foot of a little acclivity a wall rose lofty and majestic; it was constructed of colossal blocks of rock, which seemed to rest firmly upon each other by their own weight, without requiring the aid of mortar. Three of these stones were exactly the size of one we had seen in the quarry. Many appeared to be sixty feet in length, and broad and thick in proportion. This is the Cyclops wall surrounding the hill on which the temples stand. A difficult path, over piled-up fragments of marble and pieces of rock and rubbish, serves as a natural rampart against the intrusion of camels and horses; and this circumstance alone has prevented these sanctuaries of the heathen deities from being converted into dirty stables.

When we had once passed this obstruction, delight and wonder arrested our footsteps. For some moments our glances wandered irresolutely from point to point; we could fix our attention on nothing, so great was the number of beauties surrounding us: splendid architecture—arches rising boldly into the air, supported on lofty pillars—every thing wore an air so severely classic, and yet all was gorgeously elegant, and at the same time perfectly tasteful.

At first we reviewed every thing in a very hasty manner, for our impulse hurried us along, and we wished to take in every thing at one glance. Afterwards we began a new and a more deliberate survey.

As we enter a large open courtyard, our eye is caught by numerous pieces of marble and fragments of columns, some of the latter resting on tastefully sculptured plinths. Almost every thing here is prostrate, covered with rubbish and broken fragments, but yet all looks grand and majestic in its ruin. We next enter a second and a larger courtyard, above two hundred paces in length and about a hundred in breadth. Round the walls are niches cut in marble, and ornamented with the prettiest arabesques. These niches were probably occupied in former times by statues of the numerous heathen gods. Behind these are little cells, the dwellings of the priests; and in the foreground rise six Corinthian pillars, the only trace left of the great Temple of the Sun. These six pillars, which have hitherto bid defiance to time, devastation, and earthquakes, are supposed to be the loftiest and most magnificent in the world. Nearly seventy feet in height, each pillar a rocky colossus, resting on a basement twenty-seven feet high, covered with excellent workmanship, a masterpiece of ancient architecture, they tower above the Cyclops wall, and look far away into the distance—giant monuments of the hoary past.

How vast thus temple must originally have been is shewn by the remaining pedestals, from which the pillars have fallen, and lay strewed around in weather-stained fragments. I counted twenty such pedestals along the length of the temple, and ten across its breadth.

The lesser temple, separated from the greater merely by a wall, lies deeper and more sheltered from the wind and weather; consequently it is in better preservation. A covered hall, resting on pillars fifty feet in height, leads round this temple. Statues of gods and heroes, beautifully sculptured in marble, and surrounded by arabesques, deck the lofty arches of this corridor. The pillars consist of three pieces fastened together with such amazing strength, that when the last earthquake threw down a column it did not break, but fell with its top buried in the earth, where it is seen leaning its majestic height against a hill.

From this hall we pass through a splendid portal into the interior of the little sanctuary. An eagle with outspread wings overshadows the upper part of the gate, which is thirty feet in height by twenty in breadth. The two sides are enriched with small figures prettily executed, in a tastefully-carved border of flowers, fruit, ears of corn, and arabesques. This portal is in very good preservation, excepting that the keystone has slipped from its place, and hangs threateningly over the entrance, to the terror of all who pass beneath. But we entered and afterwards returned unhurt, and many will yet pass unharmed like ourselves beneath the loose stone. We shall have returned to dust, while the pendent mass will still see generation after generation roll on.

This lesser temple would not look small by any means, were it not for its colossal neighbour. On one side nine, and on the other six pillars are still erect, besides several pedestals from which the pillars have fallen. Walls, niches, every thing around us, in fact, is of marble, enriched with sculptured work of every kind. The sanctuary of the Sun is separated from the nave of the temple by a row of pillars, most of them prostrate.

To judge from what remains of both these temples, they must originally have been decorated with profuse splendour. The costliest statues and bas-reliefs, sculptured in a stone resembling marble, once filled the niches and halls, and the remains of tasteful ornaments and arabesques bear witness to the luxury which once existed here. The only fault seems to have been a redundancy of decoration.

A subterranean vaulted passage, two hundred and fifty paces in length and thirty in breadth, traverses this temple. In the midst of this walk a colossal head is hewn out of the rocky ceiling representing probably some hero of antiquity. This place is now converted into a stable for horses and camels! The little brook Litany winds round the foot of the hill on which these ruins stand.

We had been cautioned at Damascus to abstain from wandering alone among these temples; but our interest in all we saw was so great that we forgot the warning and our fears, and hastened to and fro without the least protection. We spent several hours here, exploring every corner, and meeting no one but a few curious inhabitants, who wished to see the newly-arrived Franks. Herr S. even wandered through the ruins at night quite alone, without meeting with an adventure of any kind.

I am almost inclined to think that travellers sometimes detail attacks by robbers, and dangers which they have not experienced, in order to render their narrative more interesting. My journey was a very long one through very dangerous regions; on some occasions I travelled alone with only one Arab servant, and yet nothing serious ever happened to me.

Heliopolis is in such a ruined state, that no estimate can be formed of the pristine size and splendour of this celebrated town. Excepting the two temples of the Sun, and a very small building in their vicinity, built in a circular form and richly covered with sculpture and arabesques, and a few broken pillars, not a trace of the ancient city remains.

The present town of Balbeck is partly built on the site occupied by its predecessor; it lies to the right of the temples, and consists of a heap of small wretched-looking houses and huts. The largest buildings in the place are the convent and the barracks; the latter of these presents an exceedingly ridiculous appearance; fragments of ancient pillars, statues, friezes, etc. having been collected from all sides, and put together to form a modern building according to Turkish notions of taste.

We were received into the convent, but could command no further accommodation than an empty room and a few straw mats. Our attendant brought us pilau, the every-day dish of the East; but to-day he surprised us with a boiled fowl, buried beneath a heap of the Turkish fare. Count Zichy added a few bottles of excellent wine from Lebanon to the feast; and so we sat down to dinner without tables or chairs, as merry as mortals need desire to be.

Here, as in most other Eastern towns, I had only to step out on the terrace-roof of the house to cause a crowd of old and young to collect, eager to see a Frankish woman in the costume of her country. Whoever wishes to create a sensation, without possessing either genius or talent, has only to betake himself, without loss of time, to the East, and he will have his ambition gratified to the fullest extent. But whoever has as great an objection to being stared at as I have, will easily understand that I reckoned this among the greatest inconveniences of my journey.

July 7th.

At five o'clock in the morning we again mounted our horses, and rode for three hours through an immense plain, where nothing was to be seen but scattered columns, towards the foremost promontories of the Lebanon range. The road towards the heights was sufficiently good and easy; we were little disturbed by the heat, and brooks caused by the thawing of snow-fields afforded us most grateful refreshment. In the middle of the day we took an hour's nap under the shady trees beside a gushing stream; then we proceeded to climb the heights. As we journeyed onwards the trees became fewer and farther between, until at length no soil was left in which they could grow.

The way was so confined by chasms and abysses on the one side, and walls of rock on the other, that there was scarcely room for a horse to pass. Suddenly a loud voice before us cried, "Halt!" Startled by the sound, we looked up to find that the call came from a soldier, who was escorting a woman afflicted with the plague from a village where she had been the first victim of the terrible disease to another where it was raging fearfully. It was impossible to turn aside; so the soldier had no resource but to drag the sick person some paces up the steep rocky wall, and then we had to pass close by her. The soldier called out to us to cover our mouths and noses. He himself had anointed the lower part of his face with tar, as a preventive against contagion.

This was the first plague-stricken person I had seen; and as we were compelled to pass close by her, I had an opportunity of observing the unfortunate creature closely. She was bound on an ass, appeared resigned to her fate, and turned her sunken eyes upon us with an aspect of indifference. I could see no trace of the terrible disease, except a yellow appearance of the face. The soldier who accompanied her seemed as cool and indifferent as though he were walking beside a person in perfect health.

As the plague prevailed to a considerable extent throughout the valleys of the Lebanon, we were frequently obliged to go some distance out of our way to avoid the villages afflicted with the scourge; we usually encamped for the night in the open fields, far from any habitation.

On the whole long distance from Balbeck to the cedars of Lebanon we found not a human habitation, excepting a little shepherd's hut near the mountains. Not more than a mile and a half from the heights we came upon small fields of snow. Several of our attendants dismounted and began a snow-balling match,—a wintry scene which reminded me of my fatherland. Although we were travelling on snow, the temperature was so mild that not one of our party put on a cloak. We could not imagine how it was possible for snow to exist in such a high temperature. The thermometer stood at 9° Reaumur.

A fatiguing and dangerous ride of five hours at length brought us from the foot to the highest point of Mount Lebanon. Here, for the first time, we can see the magnitude and the peculiar construction of the range.

Steep walls of rock, with isolated villages scattered here and there like beehives, and built on natural rocky terraces, rise on all sides; deep valleys lie between, contrasting beautifully in their verdant freshness with the bare rocky barriers. Farther on lie stretched elevated plateaux, with cows and goats feeding at intervals; and in the remote distance glitters a mighty stripe of bluish-green, encircling the landscape like a broad girdle—this is the Mediterranean. On the flat extended coast several places can be distinguished, among which the most remarkable is Tripoli. On the right the "Grove of Cedars" lay at our feet.

For a long time we stood on this spot, and turned and turned again, for fear of losing any part of this gigantic panorama. On one side the mountain-range, with its valleys, rocks, and gorges; on the other the immense plain of Cælosyria, on the verge of which the ruins of the Sun-temple were visible, glittering in the noontide rays. Then we climbed downwards and upwards, then downwards once more, through ravines and over rocks, along a frightful path, to a little grove of the far-famed cedars of Lebanon. In this direction the peculiar pointed formation which constitutes the principal charm of these mountains once more predominates.

The celebrated Grove of Cedars is distant about two miles and a half from the summit of Lebanon; it consists of between five and six hundred trees: about twenty of these are very aged, and five peculiarly large and fine specimens are said to have existed in the days of Solomon. One tree is more than twenty-five feet in circumference; at about five feet from the ground it divides into four portions, and forms as many good-sized trunks.

For more than an hour we rested beneath these ancient monuments of the vegetable world. The setting sun warned us to depart speedily; for our destination for the night was above three miles away, and it was not prudent to travel on these fearful paths in the darkness.

Our party here separated. Count Zichy proceeded with his attendants to Huma, while the rest of us bent our course towards Tripoli. After a hearty leave-taking, one company turned to the right and the other to the left.

We had hardly held on our way for half an hour, before one of the loveliest valleys I have ever beheld opened at our feet; immense and lofty walls of rock, of the most varied and fantastic shapes, surrounded this fairy vale on all sides: in the foreground rose a gigantic table-rock, on which was built a beautiful village, with a church smiling in the midst. Suddenly the sound of chimes was borne upwards towards us on the still clear air; they were the first I had heard in Syria. I cannot describe the feeling of delicious emotion this familiar sound caused in me. The Turkish government every where prohibits the ringing of bells; but here on the mountains, among the free Maronites, every thing is free. The sound of church-bells is a simple earnest music for Christian ears, too intimately associated with the usages of our religion to be heard with indifference. Here, so far from my native country, they appeared like links in the mysterious chain which binds the Christians of all countries in one unity. I felt, as it were, nearer to my hearth and to my dear ones, who were, perhaps, at the same moment listening to similar sounds, and thinking of the distant wanderer.

The road leading into this valley was fearfully steep. We were obliged to make a considerable détour round the lovely village of Bscharai; for the plague was raging there, which made it forbidden ground for us. Some distance beyond the village we pitched our camp beside a small stream. This night we suffered much from cold and damp.

The inhabitants of Bscharai paid us a visit for the purpose of demanding backsheesh. We had considerable difficulty in getting rid of them, and were obliged almost to beat them off with sticks to escape from their contagious touch.

The practice of begging is universal in the East. So soon as an inhabitant comes in sight, he is sure to be holding out his hand. In those parts where poverty is every where apparent, we cannot wonder at this importunity; but we are justly surprised when we find it in these fruitful valleys, which offer every thing that man can require; where the inhabitants are well clothed, and where their stone dwellings look cheerful and commodious; where corn, the grape-vine, the fig and mulberry tree, and even the valuable potato-plant, which cannot flourish throughout the greater part of Syria on account of the heat and the stony soil, are found in abundance. Every spot of earth is carefully cultivated and turned to the best account, so that I could have fancied myself among the industrious German peasantry; and yet these free people beg and steal quite as much as the Bedouins and Arabs. We were obliged to keep a sharp watch on every thing. My riding-whip was stolen almost before my very eyes, and one of the gentlemen had his pocket picked of his handkerchief.

Our march to-day had been very fatiguing; we had ridden for eleven hours, and the greater part of the road had been very bad. The night brought us but little relaxation, for our cloaks did not sufficiently protect us from the cold.

CHAPTER XIII.

July 8th.

To-day we quitted our cold hard couch at six o'clock in the morning, and travelled agreeably for two hours through this romantic valley, which appeared almost at every step in a new aspect of increased beauty. Above the village a foaming stream bursts from the mighty rocks in a beautiful waterfall, irrigates the valley, and then vanishes imperceptibly among the windings of the ravine. Brooks similar to this one, but smaller, leapt from the mountains round about. On the rocky peaks we seem to behold ruined castles and towers, but discover with astonishment, as we approach nearer, that what we supposed to be ruins are delusive pictures, formed by the wonderful masses of rock, grouped one above the other in the most fantastic forms. In the depths on the one side, grottoes upon grottoes are seen, some with their entrances half concealed, others with gigantic portals, above which the wild rocks tower high; on the other a rich soil is spread in the form of terraces on the rocky cliffs, forming a lovely picture of refreshing vegetation. Had I been a painter, it would have been difficult to tear me away from the contemplation of these regions.

Below the greater waterfall a narrow stone bridge, without balustrades or railing, leads across a deep ravine, through which the stream rushes foaming, to the opposite shore. After having once crossed, we enter upon a more inhabited tract of country, and travel on between rows of houses and gardens. But many of the houses stood empty, the inhabitants having fled into the fields, and there erected huts of branches of trees, to escape the plague. The Maronites, the real inhabitants of these mountains, are strong people, gifted with a determined will; they cannot be easily brought under a foreign yoke, but are ready to defend their liberty to the death among the natural strongholds of their rocky passes. Their religion resembles that of the Christians, and their priests are permitted to marry. The women do not wear veils, but I saw few such handsome countenances among them as I have frequently observed in the Tyrol.

On the first mountain-range of Lebanon, in the direction of Cælosyria, many Druses are found, besides a few tribes of "Mutualis." The former incline to the Christian faith, while the latter are generally termed "calf-worshippers." They practise their religion so secretly, that nothing certain is known concerning it; the general supposition is, however, that they worship their deity under the form of a calf.

Our way led onwards, for about six miles from Bscharai, through the beautiful valleys of the Lebanon. Then the smiling nature changed, and we were again wandering through sterile regions. The heat, too, became very oppressive; but every thing would have been borne cheerfully had there not been an invalid among us.

Herr Sattler had felt rather unwell on the previous day; to-day he grew so much worse that he could not keep his seat in his saddle, and fell to the ground half insensible. Luckily we found a cistern not far off, and near it some trees, beneath which we made a bed of cloaks for our sick friend. A little water mixed with a few drops of strong vinegar restored him to consciousness. After the lapse of an hour, the patient was indeed able to resume his journey; but lassitude, headache, and feverish shiverings still remained, and we had a ride of many hours before us ere we could reach our resting-place for the night. From every hill we climbed the ocean could be seen at so short a distance that we thought an hour's journeying must bring us there. But each time another mountain thrust itself between, which it was necessary to climb. So it went on for many hours, till at length we reached a small valley with a lofty isolated mass of rock in the midst, crowned by a ruined castle. The approach to this stronghold was by a flight of stairs cut in the rock. From this point our journey lay at least over a better road, between meadows and fruit-trees, to the little town which we reached at night-fall. We had a long and weary search before we could obtain for our sick comrade even a room, destitute of every appearance of comfort. Poor Herr Sattler, more dead than alive, was compelled, after a ride of thirteen hours, to take up his lodging on the hard ground. The room was perfectly bare, the windows were broken, and the door would not lock. We were fain to search for a few boards, with which we closed up the windows, that the sick man might at least be sheltered from the current of air.

I then prepared him a dish of rice with vinegar; this was the only refreshment we were able to procure.

The rest of us lay down in the yard; but the anxiety we felt concerning our sick friend prevented us from sleeping much. He exhibited every symptom of the plague; in this short time his countenance was quite changed; violent headache and exhaustion prevented him from moving, and the burning heat added the pangs of thirst to his other ills. As we had been travelling for the last day and a half through regions where the pestilence prevailed, it appeared but too probable that Herr Sattler had been attacked by it. Luckily the patient himself had not any idea of the kind, and we took especial care that he should not read our anxiety in our countenances.

July 9th.

Heaven be praised, Herr Sattler was better to-day, though too weak to continue his journey. As we had thus some time on our hands, the French gentleman and I resolved to embark in a boat to witness the operation of fishing for sponges, by which a number of the poorer inhabitants of the Syrian coast gain their livelihood.

A fisherman rowed us about half a mile out to sea, till he came to a place where he hoped to find something. Here he immersed a plummet in the sea to sound its depth, and on finding that some thing was to be gained here, he dived downwards armed with a knife to cut the sponge he expected to find from the rocks; and after remaining below the surface for two or three minutes, reappeared with his booty, When first loosened from the rocks, these sponges are usually full of shells and small stones, which give them a very strong and disagreeable smell. They require to be thoroughly cleansed from dirt and well washed with sea-water before being put into fresh.

After our little water-party, we sallied forth to see the town, which is very prettily situated among plantations of mulberry-trees in the vicinity of the sea-coast. The women here are not only unveiled, but frequently wear their necks bare; we saw some of them working in their gardens and washing linen; they were half undressed. We visited the bazaar, intending to purchase a few eggs and cucumbers for our dinner, and some oranges for our convalescent friend. But we could not obtain any; and moderate as our wishes were, it was out of our power to gratify them.

By the afternoon Herr Sattler had so far regained his strength, that he could venture to undertake a short journey of ten miles to the little town of Djäebbehl. This stage was the less difficult for our worthy invalid from the fact that the road lay pleasantly across a fruitful plain skirting the sea, while a cool sea-breeze took away the oppressiveness of the heat. The majestic Lebanon bounded the distant view on the left, and several convents on the foremost chain of mountains looked down upon the broad vale.

We seemed to have but just mounted our horses when we already descried the castle of the town to which we were bound rising above its walls, and soon after halted at a large khan in its immediate neighbourhood. There were large rooms here in plenty, but all were empty, and the unglazed windows could not even be closed by shutters.

Houses of entertainment of this description barely shield the traveller from the weather. We took possession of a large entrance-hall for our night's quarters, and made ourselves as comfortable as we could.

Count Berchtold and I walked into the town of Djäebbehl (Byblus). This place is, as I have already mentioned, surrounded by a wall; it contains also a small bazaar, where we did not find much to buy. The majority of dwellings are built in gardens of mulberry-trees. The castle lies rather high, and is still in the condition to which it was reduced after the siege by the English in 1840; the side fronting the ocean has sustained most damage. This castle is now uninhabited, but some of the lower rooms are converted into stables. Not far off we found some fragments of ancient pillars; an amphitheatre is said to have once stood here.

July 10th.

To-day Herr Sattler had quite recovered his health, so that we could again commence our journey, according to custom, early in the morning. Our road lay continually by the sea-shore. The views were always picturesque and beautiful, as on the way from Batrun to Djäebbehl; but to-day we had the additional luxury of frequently coming upon brooks which flowed from the neighbouring Lebanon, and of passing springs bursting forth near the seashore; one indeed so close to the sea, that the waves continually dashed over it.

After riding forward for four hours, we reached the so-called "Dog's-river," the greatest and deepest on the whole journey. This stream also has its origin in the heights of the Lebanon, and after a short course falls into the neighbouring sea.

At the entrance of the valley where the Dog's-river flowed lay a simple khan. Here we made halt to rest for an hour.

Generally we got nothing to eat during the day, as we seldom or never passed a village; even when we came upon a house, there was rarely any thing to be had but coffee: we were therefore the more astonished to find here fresh figs, cucumbers, butter-milk, and wine,—things which in Syria make a feast for the gods. We revelled in this unwonted profusion, and afterwards rode into the valley, which smiled upon us in verdant luxuriance. This vale cannot be more than five or six hundred feet in breadth. On either side high walls rise towering up; and on the left we see the ruins of an aqueduct quite overgrown with ivy. This aqueduct is seven or eight hundred paces in length, and extends as far as the spot where the Dog's-river rushes over rocks and stones, forming not a lofty, but yet a fine waterfall. Just below this fall a bridge of Roman architecture, supported boldly on rocky buttresses, unites the two shores. The road to this bridge is by a broad flight of stone stairs, upon which our good Syrian horses carried us in perfect safety both upwards and downwards; it was a fearful, dizzy road. The river derives its name from a stone lying near it, which is said to resemble a dog in form. Stones and pieces of rock, against which the stream rushed foaming, we saw in plenty, but none in which we could discover any resemblance to a dog. Perhaps the contour has been destroyed by the action of wind and weather.

Scarcely had we crossed this dangerous bridge when the road wound sharply round a rock in the small but blooming valley, and we journeyed towards the heights up almost perpendicular rocks, and past abysses that overhung the sea.

The rocky mountain we were now climbing juts far out into the sea, and forms a pass towards the territory of Beyrout which a handful of men might easily hold against an army. Such a pass may that of Thermopylæ have been; and had these mountaineers but a Leonidas, they would certainly not be far behind the ancient Spartans.

A Latin inscription on a massive stone slab, and higher up four niches, two of which contain statues, while the others display similar inscriptions, seemed to indicate that the Romans had already known and appreciated the importance of this pass. Unfortunately both statues and writing were so much injured by the all-destroying hand of time, that only a man learned in these matters could have deciphered their meaning. In our party there was no one equal to such a task.

We rode on for another half-hour, after which the path led downwards into the territory of Beyrout; and we rode quietly and comfortably by the seaside towards this city. Mulberry trees and vineyards bloomed around us, country-houses and villages lay half hidden between, and convents crowned the lower peaks of the Lebanon, which on this side displays only naked rocks, the majority of a bluish-grey colour.

At a little distance from Beyrout we came upon a second giant bridge, similar to that over the Dog's-river. Broad staircases, on which four or five horsemen could conveniently ride abreast, led upwards and downwards. The steps are so steep, and lie so far apart, that it seems almost incredible that the poor horses should be able to ascend and descend upon them. We looked down from a dizzy height, not upon a river, but upon a dry river-bed.

At five o'clock in the evening we arrived safely at Beyrout; and thus ended our excursion to the "lovely and incomparable city of the East," to the world-renowned ruin, and to the venerable Grove of Cedars. Our tour had occupied ten days; the distance was about 180 miles; namely, from Beyrout to Damascus about 60, from Damascus to Balbeck 40, and from Balbeck across the Lebanon to Beyrout about 80 miles.

Of four-footed beasts, amphibious creatures, birds, or insects, we had seen nothing. Count Berchtold caught a chameleon, which unfortunately effected its escape from its prison a few days afterwards. At night we frequently heard the howling of jackals, but never experienced any annoyance from them. We had not to complain of the attacks of insects; but suffered much from the dreadful heat, besides being frequently obliged to endure hunger and thirst: the thermometer one day rose to 40°.

In Beyrout I once more put up at the house of the kind French lady. The first piece of news I heard was that I had arrived twenty-four hours too late, and had thus missed the English packet-boat; this was a most annoying circumstance, for the boat in question only starts for Alexandria once a month (on the 8th or 9th), and at other times it is a great chance if an opportunity of journeying thither can be found. On the very next day I hastened to the Austrian consulate, and begged the Vice-consul, Herr C., to let me know when a ship was about to start for Egypt, and also to engage a place for me. I was told that a Greek vessel would start for that country in two or three days; but these two or three days grew into nineteen.

Never shall I forget what I had to endure in Beyrout. When I could no longer bear the state of things at night in the Noah's ark of my good Pauline, I used to creep through the window on to a terrace, and sleep there; but was obliged each time to retire to my room before daybreak lest I should be discovered. It is said that misfortunes seldom happen singly, and my case was not an exception to the rule. One night I must have caught cold; for in the morning when I hastened back to my prison, and lay down on the bed to recover from the effects of my stone couch, I experienced such an acute pain in my back and hips that I was unable to rise. It happened to be a Sunday morning, a day on which my kind Pauline did not come to the house, as there was no school to keep; and so I lay for twenty-four hours in the greatest pain, without help, unable even to obtain a drop of water. I was totally unable to drag myself to the door, or to the place where the water-jug stood. The next day, I am thankful to say, I felt somewhat better; my Pauline also came, and prepared me some mutton-broth. By the fourth day I was once more up, and had almost recovered from the attack.

JOURNEY FROM BEYROUT TO CAIRO AND ALEXANDRIA.

It was not until the 28th of July that a Greek brig set sail for Alexandria. At ten o'clock in the evening I betook myself on board, and the next morning at two we weighed anchor. Never have I bid adieu to any place with so much joy as I felt on leaving the town of Beyrout; my only regret was the parting from my kind Pauline. I had met many good people during my journey, but she was certainly one of the best.

Unhappily, my cruel fate was not yet weary of pursuing me; and in my experience I fully realised the old proverb of, "out of the frying-pan into the fire." On this vessel, and during the time we had to keep quarantine in Alexandria, I was almost worse off than during my stay in Beyrout. It is necessary, in dealing with the captain of a vessel of this description, to have a written contract for every thing—stating, for instance, where he is to land, how long he may stay at each place, etc. I mentioned this fact at the consulate, and begged the gentlemen to do what was necessary; but they assured me the captain was known to be a man of honour, and that the precaution I wished to take would be quite superfluous. Upon this assumption, I placed myself fearlessly in the hands of the man; but scarcely had we lost sight of land, when he frankly declared that there were not sufficient provisions and water on board to allow of our proceeding to Alexandria, but that he must make for the harbour of Limasol in Cyprus. I was exceedingly angry at this barefaced fraud, and at the loss of time it would occasion me, and offered all the opposition I could. But nothing would avail me; I had no written contract, and the rest of the company offered no active resistance—so to Cyprus we went.

A voyage in an ordinary sailing-vessel, which is not a packet-boat, is as wearisome a thing as can be well conceived. The lower portion of the ship is generally so crammed with merchandise, that the deck alone remains for the passengers. This was the case on the present occasion. I was obliged to remain continually on deck: during the daytime, when I had only my umbrella to shield me from the piercing rays of the sun; at night, when the dews fell so heavily, that after an hour my cloak would be quite wet through, in cold and in stormy weather. They did not even spread a piece of sailcloth by way of awning. This state of things continued for ten days and eleven nights, during which time I had not even an opportunity to change my clothes. This was a double hardship; for if there is a place above all others where cleanliness becomes imperative to comfort, it is certainly on board a Greek ship, the generality of which are exceedingly dirty and disgusting. The company I found did not make amends for the accommodation. The only Europeans on board were two young men, who had received some unimportant situation in a quarantine office from the Turkish government. The behaviour of both was conceited, stupid, and withal terribly vulgar. Then there were four students from Alexandria, who boarded at Beyrout, and were going home to spend the vacation—good-natured but much-neglected lads of fourteen or fifteen years, who seemed particularly partial to the society of the sailors, and were always talking, playing, or quarrelling with them. The remainder of the company consisted of a rich Arab family, with several male and female negro slaves, and a few very poor people. And in such society I was to pass a weary time. Many will say that this was a good opportunity for obtaining an insight into the customs and behaviour of these people; but I would gladly have declined the opportunity, for it requires an almost angelic patience to bear such a complication of evils with equanimity. Among the Arabs and the lower class of Greeks, moreover, every thing possessed by one member of the community is looked upon as public property. A knife, a pair of scissors, a drinking-glass, or any other small article, is taken from its owner without permission, and is given back after use without being cleaned. On the mat, the carpet, or the mattress, which you have brought on board as bedding, a negro and his master will lie down; and wherever a vacant space is left, some one is sure to stand or lie down. Take what precautions you may, it is impossible to avoid having your person and garments infested by certain very disgusting parasitical creatures. One day I cleaned my teeth with a toothbrush; one of the Greek sailors, noticing what I was about, came towards me, and when I laid the brush down for an instant, took it up. I thought he only wished to examine it; but no, he did exactly as I had done, and after cleaning his teeth returned me my brush, expressing himself entirely satisfied with it.

The diet on board a vessel of this kind is also exceedingly bad. For dinner we have pilau, stale cheese, and onions; in the evening, we get anchovies, olives, stale cheese again, and ship-biscuit instead of bread. These appetising dishes are placed in a tray on the ground, round which the captains (of whom there are frequently two or three), the mate, and those passengers who have not come furnished with provisions of their own, take their places. I did not take part in these entertainments; for I had brought a few live fowls, besides some rice, butter, dried bread, and coffee, and prepared my own meals. The voyage in one of these agreeable ships is certainly not very dear, if we do not take the discomforts and privations into account; but these I can really not estimate at too high a price. For the voyage to Alexandria (a distance of 2000 sea-miles) I paid sixty piastres; the provisions I took with me cost thirty more; and thus the entire journey came only to ninety piastres.

In general the wind was very unfavourable, so that we frequently cruised about for whole nights, and awoke in the morning to find ourselves in almost the same position we had occupied the previous evening.

This is one of the most disagreeable impressions, and one which can scarcely be described, to be continually driving and driving without approaching the conclusion of your journey. To my shame I must confess that I sometimes shed tears of regret and annoyance. My fellow-passengers could not at all understand why I was so impatient; for, with their constitutional indolence, they were quite indifferent as to whether they spent their time for a week or a fortnight longer in smoking, sleeping, and idling on board or on shore—whether they were carried to Cyprus or Alexandria. It was not until the fourth day that we landed at

LIMASOL.

This place contains pretty houses, some of which are even provided with slated roofs, and resemble European habitations. Here, for the first time since my departure from Constantinople, I saw a vehicle; it was not, however, a coach, but simply a wooden two-wheeled cart, and is used to transport stones, earth, and merchandise. The region around Limasol is barren in the extreme, almost like that of Larnaca, except that the mountains are here much nearer.

We stayed in this port the whole of the day; and now I learnt for the first time that the captain had not put in here so much on account of scarcity of provisions, as because he wanted to take in wine and endeavour to take in passengers. Of the latter, however, none presented themselves. The wine is very cheap; I bought a bottle containing about three pints for a piastre. As soon as we were again at sea, our worthy captain gave out that he wished to call at Damietta. My patience was at length exhausted. I called him a cheat, and insisted that he should bend his course to no other port than to Alexandria, otherwise I should have him brought before a judge if it cost me a hundred piastres. This remonstrance produced so much effect upon the captain, that he promised me not to cast anchor any where else; and, marvellous to relate, he kept his word.

One other circumstance occurred during this journey which is interesting as furnishing a sample of the heroism of the modern Greeks.

On the 5th of August, about noon, our sailors discovered a two-masted ship in the distance, which altered her course immediately on perceiving our vessel, and came sailing towards us. It was at once concluded by all that this ship must be a pirate, else why did she alter her course and give chase to us? The circumstance was indeed singular; yet these maritime heroes ought to have been used to all kinds of adventures, and not at once to have feared the worst, particularly as, so far as I am aware, the pirate's trade is very nearly broken up, and attempts of this kind are unprecedented—at least in these regions.

A painter like Hogarth should have been on board our ship, to mark the expression of fear and cowardice depicted on the several countenances. It was wonderful to behold how the poor captains ran from one end of the ship to the other, and huddled us travellers together into a heap, recommending us to sit still and keep silence; how they then hurried away and ran to and fro, making signs and gestures, while the pale sailors tumbled after them with scared faces, wringing their hands. Any one who had not witnessed the scene would think this description exaggerated. What would the Grecian heroes of antiquity say if they could throw a glance upon their gallant descendants! Instead of arming themselves and making preparations, the men ran about in the greatest confusion. We were in this enviable state when the dreaded pirate came within gunshot; and the reason of her approach turned out to be that her compass was broken. The whole scene at once changed, as though a beneficent fairy had waved her wand. The captains instantly recovered their dignity, the sailors embraced and jumped about like children, and we poor travellers were released from durance and permitted to take part in the friendly interview between the two heroic crews.

The captain who had spoken us asked our gallant leader in what latitude we were, and hearing that we were sailing to Alexandria, requested that a lantern should be hung at the mainmast-head, at which he might look as at a guiding-star.

With the exception of Cyprus, we had seen no land during all our weary journey. We could only judge when we arrived in the neighbourhood of Damietta by the altered colour of the sea; as far as the eye could reach, the beautiful dark-blue wave had turned to the colour of the yellow Nile. From these tokens I could judge of the magnitude and volume of that river, which at this season of the year increases greatly, and had already been rising for two months.

August 7th.

At eight o'clock in the morning we safely reached the quay of Alexandria.

CHAPTER XIV.

At first we could only perceive the tops of masts, behind which low objects seemed to be hiding as they rose from the sea. In a little time a whole forest of masts appeared, while the objects before mentioned took the shape of houses peering forth amongst them. At length the land itself could be distinguished from the surrounding ocean, and we discerned hills, shrubberies, and gardens in the vicinity of the town, the appearance of which is not calculated to delight the traveller, for a large desert region of sand girdles both city and gardens, giving an air of dreariness to the whole scene.

We cast anchor between the lighthouse and the new hospital. No friendly boat was permitted to approach and carry us to the wished-for shore; we came from the land of the plague to enter another region afflicted with the same scourge, and yet we were compelled to keep quarantine, for the Egyptians asserted that the Syrian plague was more malignant than the variety of the disease raging among them. Thus a compulsory quarantine is always enforced in these regions, a circumstance alike prejudicial to visitors, commerce, and shipping.

We waited with fear and trembling to hear how long a period of banishment in the hospital should be awarded us. At length came a little skiff, bringing two guardians (servants of the hospital), and with them the news that we must remain in the hospital ten days from the period of our entrance, but that we could not disembark to-day, as it was Sunday. Excepting at the arrival of the English packet-boats, the officials have no time to examine vessels on Sundays or holidays,—a truly Egyptian arrangement. Why could not an officer be appointed for these days to take care of the poor travellers? Why should fifty persons suffer for the convenience of one, and be deprived of their liberty for an extra day? We came from Beyrout furnished with a Teshkeret (certificate of health) by the government, besides the voucher of our personal appearance, and yet we were condemned to a lengthened imprisonment. But Mehemet Ali is far more mighty and despotic in Egypt than the Sultan in Constantinople; he commands, and what can we do but obey, and submit to his superior power?

From the deck of our ship I obtained a view of the city and the desert region around. The town seems tolerably spacious, and is built quite in European style.

Of the Turkish town, which lies in the background, we can distinguish nothing; the proper harbour, situate at the opposite side of the city, is also invisible, and its situation can only be discerned from the forest of masts that towers upwards. The eye is principally caught by two high sand-hills, on one of which stands Fort Napoleon, while the other is only surmounted by several cannon; the foreground is occupied by rocky ridges of moderate elevation, flanked on one side by the lighthouse, and on the other by the new quarantine buildings. The old quarantine-house lies opposite to the new one. In several places we notice little plantations of date-palms, which make a very agreeable impression on the European, as their appearance is quite new to him.

August 8th.

At seven o'clock this morning we disembarked, and were delivered with bag and baggage at the quarantine-house. I now trod a new quarter of the globe, Africa. When I sit calmly down to think of the past, I frequently wonder how it was that my courage and perseverance never once left me while I followed out my project step by step. This only serves to convince me that, if the resolution be firm, things can be achieved which would appear almost impossible.

I had expected to find neither comfort nor pleasure in the quarantine-house, and unfortunately I had judged but too well. The courtyard into which we were shewn was closely locked, and furnished on all sides with wooden bars; the rooms displayed only four bare walls, with windows guarded in the same manner. It is customary to quarter several persons in the same room, and then each pays a share of the expense. I requested a separate apartment, which one can also have, but of course at a higher charge. Such a thing as a chair, a table, or a piece of furniture, was quite out of the question; whoever wishes to enjoy such a luxury must apply by letter to an innkeeper of the town, who lends any thing of the kind, but at an enormously high rate. Diet must be obtained in the same way. In the quarantine establishment there is no host, every thing must be procured from without. An innkeeper generally demands between thirty and forty piastres per diem for dinner and supper. This I considered a little too exorbitant, and therefore ordered a few articles of food through one of the keepers. He promised to provide every thing punctually; but I fear he cannot have understood me, for I waited in vain, and during the whole of the first day had nothing to eat. On the second day my appetite was quite ravenous, and I did not know what to do. I betook myself to the room of the Arab family who had come in the same ship with me, and were therefore also in quarantine; I asked for a piece of bread, for which I offered to pay but the kind woman not only gave me bread, but pressed upon me a share of all the provisions she was preparing for her family, and would not be prevailed upon to accept any remuneration; on the contrary, she explained to me by signs that I was to come to her whenever I wanted any thing.

It was not until the evening of the second day that, perceiving it was hopeless to expect any thing from my stupid messenger, I applied to the chief superintendent of the hospital, who came every evening at sunset to examine us and to lock us in our rooms. I ordered my provisions of him, and from this time forward always received them in proper time.

The keepers were all Arabs, and not one of them could understand or speak any language but their own; this is also a truly Egyptian arrangement. I think that in an establishment of this kind, where travellers from all parts of the world are assembled, it would at least be advisable to have a person who understands Italian, even if he cannot speak it. An individual of this kind could easily be obtained; for Italian, as I afterwards found, is such a well-known language throughout the East, but particularly at Alexandria and Cairo, that many people are to be met with, even among the lowest classes, who understand and can speak it.

The supply of water is also very badly managed. Every morning, immediately after sunrise, a few skins of water are brought for the purpose of cleaning the cooking utensils; at nine o'clock in the morning and five in the afternoon a few camels come laden with skins of fresh water, which are emptied into two stone tanks in the courtyard. Then all fill their cooking and drinking vessels, but in such an untidy way that I felt not the slightest inclination to drink. One man was ladling out the water with a dirty pot, while another dabbled in the tank with his filthy hands; and some even put their dirty feet on the run and washed them, so that some of the water ran back into the tank. This receptacle is moreover never cleaned, so that dirt accumulates upon dirt, and the only way to obtain clear water is by filtering it.

On the second day of my residence here I was exceedingly surprised to observe that the courtyard, the staircases, the rooms, etc. were being cleaned and swept with particular care. The mystery was soon solved; the commissioner appeared with a great stick, and paused at the threshold of the door to see that the linen, clothes, etc. were hung up to air, the books opened, and the letters or papers suspended by strings. No idea can be formed of the stupid nervous fear of this commissioner. For instance, on passing through the first room on his way to my apartment, he saw the stalk of a bunch of grapes lying on the ground. With fearful haste he thrust this trifling object aside with his stick, for fear his foot should strike against it in passing; and as he went he continually held his stick in rest, to keep us plague-struck people at a respectful distance.

On the seventh day of our incarceration we were all sent to our rooms at nine o'clock in the morning. Doors and windows were then locked, and great chafing-dishes were brought, and a dreadful odour of brimstone, herbs, burnt feathers, and other ingredients filled the air. After we had been compelled to endure this stifling atmosphere for four or five minutes, the windows and doors were once more opened. A person of a consumptive habit could scarcely have survived this inhuman ordeal.

On the ninth day the men were drawn up in a row, to undergo an examination by the doctor. The old gentleman entered the room, with a spy-glass in one hand and a stick in the other, to review the troop. Every man had to strike himself a blow on the chest and another in the side; if he could do this without feeling pain, it was considered a sign of health, because the plague-spots appear first on these parts of the body. On the same day, the women were led into a large room, where a great female dragoon was waiting for us to put us through a similar ceremony. Neither men nor women are, however, required to undress.

A few hours later we were summoned to the iron grating which separated us from the disinfected people. On the farther side were seated several officers, to whom we paid the fee for our rooms and the keepers—the charge was very trifling. My room, with attendance, only cost me three piastres per diem. But how gladly would every traveller pay a higher price if he could only have a table and a few chairs in his apartment, and an attendant who understood what was said to him!

So far as cleanliness is concerned, there is nothing to complain of; the rooms, the staircases and the courtyard were kept very neatly, and the latter was even profusely watered twice a day. We were not at all annoyed by insects, and we were but little incommoded by the heat. In the sun the temperature never exceeded 33°; and in the shade the greatest heat was 22° Reaumur.

August 17th.

At seven o'clock this morning our cage was at length opened. Now all the world rushed in; friends and relations of the voyagers, ambassadors from innkeepers, porters, and donkey-drivers, all were merry and joyous, for every one found a friend or an acquaintance, and I only stood friendless and alone, for nobody hastened towards me or took an interest in me; but the envoys of the innkeepers, the porters, and donkey-drivers, cruel generation that they were, quarrelled and hustled each other for the possession of the solitary one.

I collected my baggage, mounted a donkey, and rode to "Colombier," one of the best inns in Alexandria. Swerving a little from the direct road, I passed "Cleopatra's Needles," two obelisks of granite, one of which is still erect, while the other lies prostrate in the sand at a short distance. We rode through a miserable poverty-stricken village; the huts were built of stones, but were so small and low that we can hardly understand how a man can stand upright in them. The doors were so low that we had to stoop considerably in entering. I could not discover any signs of windows. And this wretched village lay within the bounds of the city, and even within the walls, which inclose such an immense space, that they not only comprise Alexandria itself, but several small villages, besides numerous country-houses and a few shrubberies and cemeteries.

In this village I saw many women with yellowish-brown countenances. They looked wretched and dirty, and were all clothed in long blue garments, sitting before their doors at work, or nursing children. These women were employed in basket-making and in picking corn. I did not notice any men; they were probably employed in the fields.

I now rode forward across the sandy plain on which the whole of Alexandria is built, and suddenly, without having passed through any street, found myself in the great square.

I can scarcely describe the astonishment I felt at the scene before me. Every where I saw large beautiful houses, with lofty gates, regular windows, and balconies, like European dwellings; equipages, as graceful and beautiful as any that can be found in the great cities of Europe, rolled to and fro amid a busy crowd of men of various nations. Franks, in the costume of their country, were distinguished among the turbans and fez-caps of the Orientals; and tall women, in their blue gowns, wandered amidst the half-naked forms of the Arabs and Bedouins. Here a negro was running with argilé behind his master, who trotted along on his noble horse; there Frankish or Egyptian ladies were to be seen mounted on asses. Coming from the dreary monotony of the quarantine-house, this sight made a peculiar impression upon me.

Scarcely had I arrived at the hotel before I hastened to the Austrian consulate, where Herr von L., the government councillor, received me very kindly. I begged this gentleman to let me know what would be the first opportunity for me to continue my journey to Cairo; I did not wish to take passage on board an English steamboat, as the charge on this vessel for the short distance of about 400 sea miles is five pounds. The councillor was polite enough to procure me a berth on board an Arabian barque, which was to start from Atfé the same evening.

I also learnt at the consulate, that Herr Sattler, the painter, had arrived by the packet-boat a few days previously, and was now at the old quarantine-house. I rode out in company with a gentleman to visit him, and was glad to find him looking very well. He was just returning from his journey to Palestine.

I found the arrangements in the old quarantine-building rather more comfortable than those in the new; the establishment is moreover nearer the town, so that it is easier to obtain the necessaries of life. On my return, my companion was so kind as to conduct me through the greater portion of the Turkish town, which appeared to be better built and more neatly kept than any city of the Turks I had yet seen. The bazaar is not handsome; it consists of wooden booths, displaying only the most ordinary articles of merchandise.

On the same day that I quitted the quarantine-house, I rode in the evening to the Nile Canal, which is twenty-four feet broad and about twenty-six miles long. A number of vessels lay there, on one of which a place had been taken for me (the smaller division of the cabin) as far as Atfé, for the sum of fifteen piastres. I at once took possession of my berth, made my arrangements for the night and for the following day, and waited hour after hour till we should depart. Late in the night I was at length told that we could not set out to-night at all. To pack up my things again, and to set off to walk to the inn, a distance of two miles, and to return next morning, would have been a rather laborious proceeding; I therefore resolved to remain on board, and sat down among the Arabs and Bedouins to eat my frugal supper, which consisted of cold provisions.

Next day I was told every half-hour that we should depart immediately, and each time I was again disappointed.

Herr von L. had wished to supply me with wine and provisions for the passage; but as I had calculated upon being in Atfé to-day at noon, I had declined his offer with many thanks. But now I had no provisions; I could not venture into the town on account of the distance, and found it quite impossible to make the sailors understand that they were to bring me some bread and baked fish from the neighbouring bazaar. At length hunger compelled me to venture out alone: I pushed through the crowd, who looked at me curiously, but suffered me to pass unmolested, and bought some provisions.

In Alexandria I procured beef and beef-soup, for the first time since my departure from Smyrna. In Alexandria and throughout the whole of Egypt the white bread is very delicious.

At four in the afternoon we at length set sail. The time had passed rapidly enough with me, for there was a great deal of bustle around this canal. Barques came and departed, took in or discharged cargo; long processions of camels moved to and fro with their drivers to fetch and carry goods; the soldiers passed by, to the sound of military music, to exercise in the neighbouring square; there was continually something new to see, so that when four o'clock arrived, I could not imagine what had become of the time.

With the exception of the crew, I was the only person on board. These vessels are long and narrow, and are fitted up with a cabin and an awning. The cabin is divided into two little rooms; the first and larger of these contains two little windows on each side. The second and smaller one is often only six feet long by five broad. The space under the awning is appropriated to the poorer class of passengers and to the servants. It is necessary to take on board, besides provisions, a little stove, wood for fuel, kitchen-utensils and articles of this kind, a supply of water. The water of the Nile is, indeed, very good and thoroughly tasteless, so that it is universally drunk in Alexandria, Cairo, and elsewhere; but it is very turbid and of a yellowish colour, so that it must be filtered to render it clear and pure. Thus it happens that even on the river we are obliged to take water with us.

Handsome country-houses with gardens skirt the sides of the canal; the finest of these belongs to a pacha, the son-in-law of Mehemet Ali. As we passed this palace I saw the Egyptian Napoleon for the first time; he is a very little old man, with a long snow-white beard; his eyes and his gestures are very animated. Several Europeans stood around him, and a number of servants, some of them clothed in Greek, others in Turkish costume. In the avenue his carriage was waiting, a splendid double-seated vehicle, with four beautiful horses, harnessed in the English style. The Franks are favourably disposed towards this despot, whose subjects cherish a very opposite feeling. His government is very lenient to Christians, while the Mussulmen are obliged to bend their necks beneath a yoke of iron slavery.

This view of villas and gardens only lasts for two hours at the most. Afterwards we continue our journey to Atfé through a very uniform and unsatisfactory region of sandy hills and plains. On the right we pass the Mariotic Sea; and on both sides lie villages of a very wretched appearance.

August 19th.

At eleven in the forenoon we reached Atfé, and had therefore travelled about 180 sea-miles in sixteen hours. Atfé is a very small town, or rather a mere heap of stones.

The landing-places were always the scenes of my chief troubles. It was seldom that I could find a Frank, and was generally obliged to address several of the bystanders before I succeeded in finding one who could speak Italian and give me the information I required. I requested to be taken at once to the Austrian consulate, where this difficulty was usually removed. This was also the case here. The consul immediately sent to inquire how I could best get to Cairo, and offered me a room in his house in the mean time. A ship was soon found, for Atfé is a harbour of some importance. The canal joins the Nile at this place; and as larger vessels are used on the stream itself, all goods are transhipped here, so that barques are continually starting for Alexandria and Cairo. In a few hours I was obliged to re-embark, and had only time to provide myself with provisions and a supply of water, and to partake of a sumptuous dinner at the consul's, whose hospitality was doubly grateful to me as I had fasted the previous day. The chief compartment of the cabin had been engaged for me, at an expense of 100 piastres. On embarking, however, I found that this place had been so filled with goods, that hardly a vacant space remained for the poor occupant. I at once hastened back to the consulate and complained of the captain, whereupon the consul sent for that worthy and desired him to clear my cabin, and to refrain from annoying me during the voyage, if he wished to be paid on our arrival at Cairo. This command was strictly obeyed, and until we reached our destination I was left in undisturbed possession of my berth. At two in the afternoon I once more set sail alone in the company of Arabs and Bedouins.

I would counsel any one who can only make this journey to Cairo once in his lifetime to do it at the end of August or the beginning of September. A more lovely picture, and one more peculiar in its character, can scarcely be imagined. In many places the plain is covered as far as the eye can trace by the Nile-sea (it can scarcely be called river in its immense expanse), and every where little islands are seen rising from the waters, covered with villages surrounded by date-palms, and other trees, while in the background the high-masted boats, with their pyramidal sails, are gliding to and fro. Numbers of sheep, goats, and poultry cover the hills, and near the shore the heads of the dark-grey buffaloes, which are here found in large herds, peer forth from the water. These creatures are fond of immersing their bodies in the cool flood, where they stand gazing at the passing ships. Here and there little plantations of twenty to thirty trees are seen, which appear, as the ground is completely overflowed, to be growing out of the Nile. The water here is much more muddy and of a darker colour than in the canal between Atfé and Alexandria. The sailors pour this water into great iron vessels, and leave it to settle and become clearer; this is, however, of little use, for it remains almost as muddy as the river. Notwithstanding this circumstance, however, this Nile-water is not at all prejudicial to health; on the contrary, the inhabitants of the valley assert that they possess the best and wholesomest water in the world. The Franks are accustomed, as I have already stated, to take filtered water with them. When the supply becomes exhausted, they have only to put a few kernels of apricots or almonds chopped small into a vessel of Nile-water to render it tolerably clear within the space of five or six hours. I learnt this art from an Arab woman during my voyage on the Nile.

The population of the region around the Nile must be very considerable, for the villages almost adjoin each other. The ground consists every where of sand, and only becomes fruitful through the mud which the Nile leaves behind after its inundation. Thus the luxuriant vegetation here only commences after the waters of the Nile have retired.

The villages cannot be called handsome, as the houses are mostly built of earth and clay, or of bricks made of the Nile mud. Man, the "crown of creation," does not appear to advantage here; the poverty, the want of cleanliness, and rude savage state of the people, cannot be witnessed without a feeling of painful emotion.

The dress of the women consists of the usual long blue garment, and the men wear nothing but a shirt reaching to the knee. Some of the women veil their faces, but others do not.

I was astonished at the difference between the fine strongly-built men and the ugly disgusting women and neglected children. In general the latter present a most lamentable appearance, with faces covered with scabs and sores, on which a quantity of flies are continually settling. Frequently also they have inflamed eyes. In spite of the oppressive heat, I remained nearly the whole day seated on the roof of my cabin, enjoying the landscape, and gazing at the moving panorama to my heart's content.

The company on board could be called good or bad; bad, because there was not a soul present to whom I could impart my feelings and sentiments on the marvels of nature around me; good, because all, but particularly the Arab women who occupied the little cabin in the forepart of the vessel, were very good-natured and attentive to me.

They wished me to accept a share of every thing they possessed, and gave me a portion of each of their dishes, which generally consisted either of pilau, beans, or cucumbers, and which I did not find palatable; when they drank coffee in the morning, the first cup was always handed to me. In return I gave them some of my provisions, all of which they liked, excepting the coffee, which had milk in it. When we landed at a village, the inhabitants would inquire by signs if I wished for any thing. I wanted some milk, eggs, and bread, but did not know how to ask for them in Arabic. I therefore had recourse to drawing; for instance, I made a portrait of a cow, gave an Arab woman a bottle and some money, and made signs to her to milk her cow and to fill my bottle. In the same way I drew a hen, and some eggs beside her; pointed to the hen with a shake of my head, and then to the eggs with a nod, counting on the woman's fingers how many she was to bring me. In this way I could always manage to get on, by limiting my wants to such objects as I could represent by drawings.

When they brought me the milk, and I explained to the Arab woman by signs that, after she had finished cooking, I wished to have the use of the fire to prepare my milk and eggs, she immediately took off her pot from the fire and compelled me, in spite of all remonstrances, to cook my dinner first. If I walked forward towards the prow to obtain a better view of the landscape, the best place was immediately vacated on my behalf; and, in short, they all behaved in such a courteous and obliging way, that these uncultivated people might have put to shame many a civilised European. They certainly, however, requested a few favours of me, which, I am ashamed to say, it cost me a great effort to grant. For instance, the oldest among them begged permission to sleep in my apartment, as they only possessed a small cabin, while I had the larger one all to myself. Then they performed their devotions, even to the preliminary washing of face and feet, in my cabin: this I permitted, as I was more on deck than below. At first these women called me Mary, imagining, probably, that every Christian lady must bear the name of the Virgin. I told them my baptismal name, which they accurately remembered; they told me theirs in return, which I very soon forgot. I mention this trifling circumstance, because I afterwards was frequently surprised at the retentive memory of these people during my journey through the desert towards the Red Sea.

August 21st.

Although I felt solitary among all the voyagers on the barque, these two days passed swiftly and agreeably away. The flatter the land grew, the broader did the lordly river become. The villages increased in size; and the huts, mostly resembling a sugar-loaf, with a number of doves roosting on its apex, wore an appearance of greater comfort. Mosques and large country-houses presently appeared; and, in short, the nearer we approached towards Cairo, the more distinct became these indications of affluence. The sand-hills appeared less frequently, though on the route between Atfé and Cairo I still saw five or six large barren places which had quite the look of deserts. Once the wind blew directly towards us from one of these burning wastes with such an oppressive influence, that I could easily imagine how dreadful the hot winds (chamsir) must be, and I no longer wondered at the continual instances of blindness among the poor inhabitants of these regions. The heat is unendurable, and the fine dust and heated particles of sand which are carried into the air by these winds cannot fail to cause inflammation of the eyes.

Little towers of masonry, on the tops of which telegraphs have been fixed, are seen at intervals along the road between Alexandria and Cairo.

Our vessel was unfortunate enough to strike several times on sand-banks, besides getting entangled among the shallows—a circumstance of frequent occurrence during the time that the Nile is rising. On these occasions I could not sufficiently admire the strength, agility, and hard-working perseverance of our sailors, who were obliged to jump overboard and push off the ship with poles, and afterwards were repeatedly compelled to drag it for half an hour together through shallow places. These people are also very expert at climbing. They could ascend without ratlines to the very tops of the slanting masts, and take in or unloose the sails. I could not repress a shudder on seeing these poor creatures hanging betwixt earth and heaven, so far above me that they appeared like dwarfs. They work with one hand, while they cling to the mast with the other. I do not think that a better, or a more active, agile, and temperate race of sailors exists than these. Their fare consists of bread or ship-biscuit in the morning, with sometimes a raw cucumber, a piece of cheese, or a handful of dates in addition. For dinner they have the same diet, and for supper they have a dish of warm beans, or a kind of broth or pilau. Roast mutton is a rare delicacy with them, and their drink is nothing but the Nile water.

During the period of the inundation, the river is twice as full of vessels as at other times. When the river is swollen, the only method of communication is by boats.

On the last day of this expedition a most beauteous spectacle awaited me— the Delta! Here the mighty Nile, which irrigates the whole country with the hundreds of canals cut from its banks through every region, divides itself into two principal branches, one of which falls into the sea at Rosetta, and the other at Damietta. If the separate aims of the river could be compared to seas, how much more does its united vastness merit the appellation!

When I was thus carried away by the beauty and grandeur of nature, when I thus saw myself placed in the midst of new and interesting scenes, it would appear to me incredible how people can exist, possessing in abundance the gifts of riches, health, and leisure time, and yet without a taste for travelling. The petty comforts of life and enjoyments of luxury are indeed worth more in the eyes of some than the opportunity of contemplating the exalted beauties of nature or the monuments of history, and of gaining information concerning the manners and customs of foreign nations. Although I was at times very badly situated, and had to encounter more hardships and disagreeables than fall to the lot of many a man, I would be thankful that I had had resolution given me to continue my wanderings whenever one of these grand spectacles opened itself before me. What, indeed, are the entertainments of a large town compared to the Delta of the Nile, and many similar scenes? The pure and perfect enjoyment afforded by the contemplation of the beauty of nature is not for a moment to be found in the ball-room or the theatre; and all the ease and luxury in the world should not buy from me my recollections of this journey.

Not far from the Delta we can behold the Libyan Desert, of which we afterwards never entirely lose sight, though we sometimes approach and sometimes recede from it. I became conscious of certain dark objects in the far distance; they developed themselves more and more, and at length I recognised in them the wonder-buildings of ancient times, the Pyramids; far behind them rises the chain of mountains, or rather hills, of Mokattam.

Evening was closing in when we at length arrived at Bulak, the harbour of Cairo. If we could have landed at once, I might, perhaps, have reached the town itself this evening; as the harbour is, however, always over-crowded with vessels, the captain is often compelled to wait for an hour before he can find a place to moor his craft. By the time I could disembark it had already grown quite dark, and the town-gates were shut. I was thus obliged to pass the night on board.

The journey from Atfé to Cairo had occupied two days and a half. This passage had been one of the most interesting, although the heat became more and more oppressive, and the burning winds of the desert were sometimes wafted over to us. The highest temperature at midday was 36°, and in the shade from 24° to 25° Reaumur. The sky was far less beautiful and clear than in Syria; it was here frequently overcast with white clouds.

CHAPTER XV.

August 22d.

The aspect of this great Egyptian metropolis is not nearly so imposing as I had fancied it to be; its situation is too flat, and from on board we can only discern scattered portions of its extended area. The gardens skirting the shore are luxuriant and lovely.

At my debarcation, and on the road to the consulate, I met with several adventures, which I relate circumstantially, trifling as they may appear, in order to give a hint as to the best method of dealing with the people here. At the very commencement I became involved in a dispute with the captain of the vessel. I had still to pay him three dollars and a half, and gave him four dollars, in the expectation that he would return me my change. This, however, he refused to do, and persisted in keeping the half-dollar. He said it should be divided as backsheesh among the crew; but I am sure they would have seen nothing of it. Luckily, however, he was stupid enough not to put the money in his pocket, but kept it open in his hand. I quickly snatched a coin from him, and put it into my pocket, explaining to him at the same time that he should not have it back until he had given me my change, adding that I would give the men a gratuity myself. He shouted and stormed, and kept on asking for the money. I took no heed of him, but continued quietly packing up my things. Seeing, at length, that nothing was to be done with me, he gave me back my half-dollar; whereupon we parted good friends. This affair concluded, I had to look about for a couple of asses; one for myself, and another for my luggage. If I had stepped ashore I should have been almost torn in pieces by contending donkey-drivers, each of whom would have lugged me in a different direction. I therefore remained quietly for a time in my cabin, until the drivers ceased to suspect that any one was there. In the meantime I had been looking upon the shore from the cabin-window, and speculating upon which animal I should take; then I quickly rushed out, and before the proprietors of the long-eared steeds were aware of my intention, I had seized one by the bridle and pointed to another. This concluded the matter at once; for the proprietors of the chosen animals defended me from the rest, and returned with me to the boat to carry my baggage.

A fellow came up and arranged my little trunk on the back of the ass. For this trifling service I gave him a piastre; but observing that I was alone, he probably thought he could soon intimidate me into giving whatever he demanded. So he returned me my piastre, and demanded four. I took the money, and told him (for fortunately he understood a little Italian) that if he felt dissatisfied with this reward he might accompany me to the consulate, where his four piastres would be paid so soon as it appeared that he had earned them. He shouted and blustered, just as the captain had done; but I remained deaf, and rode forward towards the custom-house. Then he came down to three piastres, then to two, and finally said he would be content with one, which I threw to him. When I reached the custom-house, hands were stretched out towards me from all sides; I gave something to the chief person, and let the remaining ones clamour on. When, after experiencing these various annoyances, I rode on towards the town, a new obstacle arose. My Arab guide inquired whither he should conduct me. I endeavoured in vain to explain to him where I wanted to go; he could not be made to understand me. Nothing now remained for me but to accost every well-dressed Oriental whom I met, until I should find one who could understand either French or Italian. The third person I addressed fortunately knew something of the latter language, and I begged him to tell my guide to take me to the Austrian consulate. This was done, and my troubles concluded.

A ride of three quarters of an hour in a very broad handsome street, planted with a double row of a kind of acacia altogether strange to me, among a crowd of men, camels, asses, etc., brought me to the town, the streets of which are in general narrow. There is so much noise and crowding every where, that one would suppose a tumult had broken out. But as I approached, the immense mass always opened as if by magic, and I pursued my way without hindrance to the consulate, which lies hidden in a little narrow blind alley.

I went immediately to the office, and presented myself to the consul, with the request that he would recommend me a respectable inn of the second class. Herr Chamgion, the consul, interested himself for me with heartfelt kindness; he immediately despatched a kavasse to an innkeeper whom he knew, paid my guide, and recommended the host strongly to take good care of me; in short, he behaved towards me with true Christian kindliness. His house was ever open to me, and I could go to him with any petition I wished to make. It is a real pleasure to me to be able publicly once more to thank this worthy man.

I had been furnished with a letter of recommendation to a certain Herr Palm. The consul kindly sent at once for this gentleman, who soon appeared, and accompanied me to the inn.

I requested Herr P. to recommend me a servant who could either speak Italian or French, and afterwards to tell me the best method to set about seeing the lions of the town. Herr P. very willingly undertook to do so; and after the lapse of an hour, the dragoman had already been found, and two asses stood before the door to carry me and my servant through the whole town.

The animated bustle and hum of business in the streets of Cairo is very great. I can even say that in the most populous cities of Italy I never saw any thing I could compare to it; and certainly this is a bold assertion.

Many of the streets are so narrow, that when loaded camels meet, one party must always be led into a by-street until the other has passed. In these narrow lanes I continually encountered crowds of passengers, so that I really felt quite anxious, and wondered how I should find my way through. People mounted on horses and donkeys tower above the moving mass; but the asses themselves appear like pigmies beside the high, lofty-looking camels, which do not lose their proud demeanour even under their heavy burdens. Men often slip by under the heads of the camels. The riders keep as close as possible to the houses, and the mass of pedestrians winds dexterously between. There are water-carriers, vendors of goods, numerous blind men groping their way with sticks, and bearing baskets with fruit, bread, and other provisions for sale; numerous children, some of them running about the streets, and others playing before the house-doors; and lastly, the Egyptian ladies, who ride on asses to pay their visits, and come in long processions with their children and negro servants. Let the reader further imagine the cries of the vendors, the shouting of the drivers and passengers, the terrified screams of flying women and children, the quarrels which frequently arise, and the peculiar noisiness and talkativeness of these people, and he can fancy what an effect this must have on the nerves of a stranger. I was in mortal fear at every step, and on reaching home in the evening felt quite unwell; but as I never once saw an accident occur, I at length accustomed myself to the hubbub, and could follow my guide where the crowd was thickest without feeling uneasy.

The streets, or, as they may be more properly called, the lanes of Cairo, are sprinkled with water several times in the day; fountains and large vessels of water are also placed every where for the convenience of the passers-by. In the broad streets straw-mats are hung up to keep off the sun's rays.

The richer class of people wear the Oriental garb, with the exception that the women merely have their heads and faces wrapped in a light muslin veil; they wear also a kind of mantilla of black silk, which gives them a peculiar appearance. When they came riding along, and the wind caught this garment and spread it out, they looked exactly like bats with outstretched wings.

Many of the Franks also dress in the Oriental style; the Fellahs go almost naked, and their women only wear a single blue garment.

Here, as throughout all the East, the rich people are always seen on horseback. I was not so much pleased with the Egyptian as with the Syrian horses, for the former appeared to me less slim and gracefully built.

The population of Cairo is estimated at 200,000, and is a mixed one, consisting of Arabs, Mamelukes, Turks, Berbers, Negroes, Bedouins, Christians, Greeks, Jews, etc. Thanks to the powerful arm of Mehemet Ali, they all live peacefully together.

Cairo contains 25,000 houses, which are as unsightly and irregular as the streets. They are built of clay, unburnt bricks, and stones, and have little narrow entrances; the unsymmetrical windows are furnished with wooden shutters impenetrable to the eye. The interiors are decorated like the houses in Damascus, but in a less costly style; neither is there such an abundance of fresh water at Cairo.

The Jews' quarter is the most hideous of all; the houses are dirty, and the streets so narrow that two persons can only just push by each other. The entire town is surrounded by walls and towers, guarded by a castle, and divided into several quarters, separated from each other by gates, which are closed after sunset. On the heights around Cairo are to be seen some castles from the time of the Saracens.

As I rode to and fro in the town, my guide suddenly stopped, bought a quantity of bread, and motioned me to follow him. I thought he was going to take me to a menagerie, and that this bread was intended for the wild animals. We entered a courtyard with windows all round reaching to the ground, and strengthened with iron bars. Stopping before the first window, my servant threw in a piece of bread; what was my horror when I saw, instead of a lion or tiger, a naked emaciated old man rush forth, seize the bread, and devour it ravenously. I was in the mad-house. In the midst of each dark and filthy dungeon is fixed a stone, with two iron chains, to which one or two of these wretched creatures are attached by an iron ring fastened round the neck. There they sit staring with fearfully distorted faces, their hair and beard unkempt, their bodies emaciated, and the marrow of life drying up within them. In these foul and loathsome dens they must pine until the Almighty in his mercy loosens the chains which bind them to their miserable existence by a welcome death. There is not one instance of a cure, and truly the treatment to which they are subjected is calculated to drive a half-witted person quite mad. And yet the Europeans can praise Mehemet Ali! Ye wretched madmen, ye poor fellahs, are ye too ready to join in this praise?

Quitting this abode of misery, my dragoman led me to "Joseph's well," which is deeply hewn out of the rock. I descended more than two hundred and seventy steps, and had got half-way to the bottom of the gigantic structure. On looking downward into its depths a feeling of giddiness came over me.

The new palace of Mehemet Ali is rather a handsome building, arranged chiefly in the European style. The rooms, or rather the halls, are very lofty, and are either tastefully painted or hung with silk, tapestry, etc. Large pier-glasses multiply the objects around, rich divans are attached to the walls, and costly tables, some of marble, others of inlaid work, enriched with beautiful paintings, stand in the rooms, in one of which I even noticed a billiard-table. The dining-hall is quite European in its character. In the centre stands a large table; two sideboards are placed against one side of the wall, and handsome chairs stand opposite. In one of the rooms hangs an oil-painting representing Ibrahim Pasha, {236} Mehemet Ali's son.

This palace stands in the midst of a little garden, neither remarkable for the rarity of the plants it contains, nor for the beauty of their arrangement. The views from some of the apartments, as well as that from the garden, are very lovely.

Opposite the palace a great mosque is being built as a mausoleum for Mehemet Ali. The despot probably reckons on having some years yet to live, for much remains to be done before the beautiful structure is completed. The pillars and the walls of the mosque are covered with the most splendid marble, of a yellowish-white colour.

The before-mentioned buildings, namely, Joseph's well, the palace and gardens, and the mosque, are all situate on a high rock, to which a single broad road leads from Cairo. Here we behold a threefold sea, namely, of houses, of the Nile, and a sea of sand, on which the lofty Pyramids rise in the distance like isolated rocks. The mountains of Mokattam close the background, and a number of lovely gardens and plantations of date-palms surround the town. With one glance we can behold the most striking contrasts. A wreath of the most luxurious vegetation runs round the town, and beyond lies the dreary monotony of the desert. The colour of the Nile is so exactly similar to that of the sand forming its shores, that at a distance the line of demarcation cannot be traced.

On my way homewards I met several fellahs carrying large baskets full of dates, and stopped one of them, in order to purchase some of this celebrated fruit. Unfortunately for me, the dates were still unripe, hard, of a brick-red colour, and so unpalatable that I could not eat one of them. A week or ten days afterwards I was able to procure some ripe ones; they were of a brown colour like the dried fruit, the tender skin could easily be peeled off, and I liked them better than dried dates, because they were more pulpy and not so sweet. A much more precious fruit, the finest production of Egypt and Syria, almost superior to the pine-apple in taste, is the banana, which is so delicate that it almost melts in the mouth. This fruit cannot be dried, and is therefore never exported. Sugar melons and peaches are to be had in abundance, but their flavour is not very good. I also preferred the Alexandrian grape to that of Cairo.

The bazaars, through which we rode in all directions, displayed nothing very remarkable in manufactures or in productions of nature and art.

From first to last I spent a week at Cairo, and occupied the whole of my time from morning till night in viewing the curiosities of the town.

I only saw two mosques, that of Sultan Hassan and of Sultan Amru. Before I was permitted to enter the first of these edifices, they compelled me to take off my shoes, and walk in my stockings over a courtyard paved with great stones. The stones had become so heated by the solar rays, that I was obliged to run fast, to avoid scorching the soles of my feet. I cannot give an opinion touching the architectural beauty of this building, which is built in such a simple style that none but a connoisseur would discover its merits. I was better pleased with the mosque of Sultan Amru, which contains several halls, and is supported on numerous columns. The mosques in Cairo struck me as having a more ancient and venerable appearance than those of Constantinople, while the latter, on the other hand, were larger and more elegant.

I also visited the island of Rodda, which is worthy the name of a beautiful garden. It lies opposite to old Cairo, on the Nile, and is said to be a favourite walk of the townspeople, though I was there twice without meeting any one. The garden is spacious, and contains all kinds of tropical productions: here I saw the sugar-cane, which greatly resembles the stem of the Indian maize; the cotton-tree, growing to a height of five or six feet; the banana-tree, the short-stemmed date-palm, the coffee-tree, and many others. Flowers were also there in quantities which must be cultivated with great care in the hot-houses of my native country. The whole of this collection of plants is very tastefully arranged, and shines forth in the height of luxuriant beauty. It is customary to lay the entire island under water every evening by means of artificial canals. This system is universally carried out throughout the Egyptian plantations, and is, in fact, the only method by which vegetation can be preserved in its freshest green in spite of the burning heat. The care of this fairy grove is entrusted to a German ornamental gardener; unfortunately I was informed of this fact too late, otherwise I should have visited my countryman and requested an explanation of many things which appeared strange to me.

In the midst of the garden is a beautiful grotto, ornamented within and without by a great variety of shells from the Red Sea, which give it a most striking appearance. At this spot, towards which many paths lead, all strewed with minute shells instead of gravel, Moses is said to have been found in his cradle of bulrushes(?). Immediately adjoining the garden we find a summer residence belonging to Mehemet Ali.

The well shewn as that into which Joseph was thrust by his brethren lies about two miles distant from the town, in a village on the road to Suez. Half a mile off a very large and venerable sycamore-tree was pointed out to me as the one in the shade of which the holy family rested on their way to Egypt; and a walk of another quarter of a mile brings us to the garden of Boghos Bey, in the midst of which stands one of the finest and largest obelisks of Upper Egypt: it is still in good condition, and completely covered with hieroglyphics. The garden, however, offers nothing remarkable. The ancient city of Heliopolis is said to have been built not far off; but at the present day not a vestige of it remains.

The road to this garden already lies partly in the desert. At first the way winds through avenues of trees and past gardens; but soon the vast desert extends to the right, while beautiful orange and citron groves still skirt the left side of the path. Here we continually meet herds of camels, but a dromedary is a rare sight.

EXCURSION TO THE PYRAMIDS OF GIZEH.August 25th, 1842.

At four in the afternoon I quitted Cairo, crossed two arms of the Nile, and a couple of hours afterwards arrived safely at Gizeh. As the Nile had overflowed several parts of the country, we were compelled frequently to turn out of our way, and sometimes to cross canals and ride through water; now and then, where it was too deep for our asses, we were obliged to be carried across. As there is no inn at Gizeh I betook myself to Herr Klinger, to whom I brought a letter of recommendation from Cairo. Herr K. is a Bohemian by birth, and stands in the service of the viceroy of Egypt, as musical instructor to the young military band. I was made very welcome here, and Herr Klinger seemed quite rejoiced at seeing a visitor with whom he could talk in German. Our conversation was of Beethoven and Mozart, of Strauss and Lanne. The fame of the bravura composers of the present day, Liszt and Thalberg, had not yet penetrated to these regions. I requested my kind host to shew me the establishment for hatching eggs that exists at Gizeh. He immediately sent for the superintendent, who happened however to be absent, and to have locked up the keys. In this place about 8000 eggs are hatched by artificial warmth during the months of March and April. The eggs are laid on large flat plates, which are continually kept at an equal temperature by heat applied below the surface: they are turned several times during the day. As the thousands of little chickens burst their shells, they are sold, not by number or weight, but by the measure. This egg-hatching house has the effect of rendering poultry plentiful and cheap.

After chatting away the evening very pleasantly I sought my couch, tired with my ride and with the heat, and rejoicing at the sight of the soft divan, which seemed to smile upon me, and promise rest and strength for the following day. But as I was about to take possession of my couch, I noticed on the wall a great number of black spots. I took the candle to examine what it could be, and nearly dropped the light with horror on discovering that the wall was covered with bugs. I had never seen such a disgusting sight. All hopes of rest on the divan were now effectually put to flight. I sat down on a chair, and waited until every thing was perfectly still; then I slipped into the entrance-hall, and lay down on the stones, wrapped in my cloak.

Though I had escaped from one description of vermin, I became a prey to innumerable gnats. I had passed many uncomfortable nights during my journey, but this was worse than any thing I had yet endured.

However, this was only an additional inducement for rising early, and long before sunrise I was ready to continue my journey. Before daybreak I took leave of my kind host, and rode with my servant towards the gigantic structures. To-day we were again obliged frequently to go out of our route on account of the rising of the Nile; owing to this delay, two hours elapsed before we reached the broad arm of the Nile, dividing us from the Libyan desert, on which the Pyramids stand, and over which two Arabs carried me. This was one of the most disagreeable things that can be imagined. Two large powerful men stood side by side; I mounted on their shoulders, and held fast by their heads, while they supported my feet in a horizontal position above the waters, which at some places reached almost to their armpits, so that I feared every moment that I should sit in the water. Besides this, my supporters continually swayed to and fro, because they could only withstand the force of the current by a great exertion of strength, and I was apprehensive of falling off. This disagreeable passage lasted above a quarter of an hour. After wading for another fifteen minutes through deep sand, we arrived at the goal of our little journey.

The two colossal pyramids are of course visible directly we quit the town, and we keep them almost continually in sight. But here the expectations I had cherished were again disappointed, for the aspect of these giant structures did not astonish me greatly. Their height appears less remarkable than it otherwise would, from the circumstance that their base is buried in sand, and thus hidden from view. There is also neither a tree nor a hut, nor any other object which could serve to display their huge proportions by the force of contrast.

As it was still early in the day and not very hot, I preferred ascending the pyramid before venturing into its interior. My servant took off my rings and concealed them carefully, telling me that this was a very necessary precaution, as the fellows who take the travellers by the hands to assist them in mounting the pyramids have such a dexterous knack of drawing the rings from their fingers, that they seldom perceive their loss until too late.

I took two Arabs with me, who gave me their hands, and pulled me up the very large stones. Any one who is at all subject to dizziness would do very wrong in attempting this feat, for he might be lost without remedy. Let the reader picture to himself a height of 500 feet, without a railing or a regular staircase by which to make the ascent. At one angle only the immense blocks of stone have been hewn in such a manner that they form a flight of steps, but a very inconvenient one, as many of these stone blocks are above four feet in height, and offer no projection on which you can place your foot in mounting. The two Arabs ascended first, and then stretched out their hands to pull me from one block to another. I preferred climbing over the smaller blocks without assistance. In three quarters of an hour's time I had gained the summit of the pyramid.

For a long time I stood lost in thought, and could hardly realise the fact that I was really one of the favoured few who are happy enough to be able to contemplate the most stupendous and imperishable monument ever erected by human hands. At the first moment I was scarcely able to gaze down from the dizzy height into the deep distance; I could only examine the pyramid itself, and seek to familiarise myself with the idea that I was not dreaming. Gradually, however, I came to myself, and contemplated the landscape which lay extended beneath me. From my elevated position I could form a better estimate of the gigantic structure, for here the fact that the base was buried in sand did not prejudice the general effect. I saw the

Nile flowing far beneath me, and a few Bedouins, whom curiosity had attracted to the spot, looked like very pigmies. In ascending I had seen the immense blocks of stone singly, and ceased to marvel that these monuments are reckoned among the seven wonders of the world.

On the castle the view had been fine, but here, where the prospect was bounded only by the horizon and by the Mokattam mountains, it is grander by far. I could follow the windings of the river, with its innumerable arms and canals, until it melted into the far horizon, which closed the picture on this side. Many blooming gardens, and the large extensive town with its environs; the immense desert, with its plains and hills of sand, and the lengthened mountain-range of Mokattam,—all lay spread before me; and for a long time I sat gazing around me, and wishing that the dear ones at home had been with me, to share in my wonder and delight.

But now the time came not only to look down, but to descend. Most people find this even more difficult than the ascent; but with me the contrary was the case. I never grow giddy, and so I advanced in the following manner, without the aid of the Arabs. On the smaller blocks I sprang from one to the other; when a stone of three or four feet in height was to be encountered, I let myself glide gently down; and I accomplished my descent with so much grace and agility, that I reached the base of the pyramid long before my servant. Even the Arabs expressed their pleasure at my fearlessness on this dangerous passage.

After eating my breakfast and resting for a short time, I proceeded to explore the interior. At first I was obliged to cross a heap of sand and rubbish; for we have to go downwards towards the entrance, which is so low and narrow that we cannot always stand upright. I could not have passed along the passage leading into the interior if the Arabs had not helped me, for it is so steep and so smoothly paved that, in spite of my conductor's assistance, I slid rather than walked. The apartment of the king is more spacious, and resembles a small hall. On one side stands a little empty sarcophagus without a lid. The walls of the chambers and of the passages are covered with large and beautifully polished slabs of granite and marble. The remaining passages, or rather dens, which are shown here, I did not see. It may be very interesting for learned men and antiquarians thus to search every corner; but for a woman like myself, brought hither only by an insatiable desire to travel, and capable of judging of the beauties of nature and art only by her own simple feelings, it was enough to have ascended the pyramid of Cheops, and to have seen something of its interior. This pyramid is said to be the loftiest of all. It stands on a rock 150 feet in height, which is invisible, being altogether buried in sand. The height of the vast structure is above 500 feet. It was erected by Cheops more than 3000 years ago, and 100,000 men are said to have been employed in its construction for twenty-six years. It is a most interesting structure, built of immense masses of rock, fixed together with a great deal of art, and seemingly calculated to last an eternity. They look so strong and so well preserved, that many travellers will no doubt repair hither in coming generations, and continue the researches commenced long ago.

The Sphynx, a statue of most colossal dimensions, situate at no great distance from the great pyramid, is so covered with sand that only the head and a small portion of the bust remain visible. The head alone is twenty-two feet in height.

After walking about and inspecting every thing, I commenced my journey back. On the way I once more visited Herr Klinger, strengthened myself with a hearty meal, and arrived safely at Cairo late in the evening. Here I wished to take my little purse out of my pocket, and found that it was gone. Luckily I had only taken one collonato (Spanish dollar) with me. No one can imagine what dexterity the Bedouins and Arabs possess in the art of stealing. I always kept a sharp eye upon my effects, and notwithstanding my vigilance several articles were pilfered from me, and my purse must also have been stolen during this excursion. The loss was very disagreeable to me because it involved that of my box-key. I was, however, fortunate in finding an expert Arabian locksmith, who opened my chest and made me a new key, on which occasion I had another opportunity of seeing how careful it is necessary to be in all our dealings with these people to avoid being cheated. The key locked and unlocked my box well, and I paid for it; but immediately afterwards observed that it was very slightly joined in the middle, and would presently break. The Arab's tools still lay on the ground; I immediately seized one of them, and told the man I would not give it up until he had made me a new key. It was in vain that he assured me he could not work without his tools; he would not give my money back, and I kept the implement: by this means I obtained from him a new and a good key.

## CHAPTER XVI.

I visited many Christian churches, the finest among which was the Greek one. On my way thither I saw many streets where there can hardly have been room for a horseman to pass. The road to the Armenian church leads through such narrow lanes and gates, that we were compelled to leave our asses behind; there was hardly room for two people to pass each other.

On the other hand, I had nowhere seen a more spacious square than the Esbekie-place in Cairo. The square in Padua is perhaps the only one that can compare with it in point of size; but this place looks like a complete chaos. Miserable houses and ruined huts surround it; and here and there we sometimes come upon a part of an alley or an unfinished canal. The centre is very uneven, and is filled with building materials, such as stones, wood, bricks, and beams. The largest and handsomest house in this square is remarkable as having been inhabited by Napoleon during his residence at Cairo: it is now converted into a splendid hotel.

Herr Chamgion, the consul, was kind enough to send me a card of invitation for the theatre. The building looks like a private house, and contains a gallery capable of accommodating three or four hundred people; this gallery is devoted to the use of the ladies. The performers were all amateurs; they acted an Italian comedy in a very creditable manner. The orchestra comprised only four musicians. At the conclusion of the second act the consul's son, a boy of twelve years, played some variations on the violin very prettily.

The women, all natives of the Levant, were very elegantly dressed; they wore the European garb, white muslin dresses with their hair beautifully braided and ornamented with flowers. Nearly all the women and girls were handsome, with complexions of a dazzling whiteness, which we rarely see equalled in Europe. The reason of this is, perhaps, that they always stay in their houses, and avoid exposing themselves to the sun and wind.

The following day I visited the abode of the howling dervishes, in whom I took a lively interest since I had seen their brethren at Constantinople. The hall, or rather the mosque, in which they perform their devotions is very splendid. I was not allowed here to stand among the men as I had done at Constantinople, but was conducted to a raised gallery, from which I could look down through a grated window.

The style of devotion and excitement of these dervishes is like that I had witnessed at Constantinople, without being quite so wild in its character. Not one of them sank exhausted, and the screeching and howling were not so loud. Towards the end of their performance many of the dervishes seized a small tambourine, on which they beat and produced a most diabolical music.

In the slave-market there was but a meagre selection; all the wares had been bought, and a new cargo of these unfortunates was daily expected. I pretended that I wished to purchase a boy and a girl, in order to gain admittance into the private department. Here I saw a couple of negro girls of most uncommon beauty. I had not deemed it possible to find any thing so perfect. Their skin was of a velvety black, and shone with a peculiar lustre. Their teeth were beautifully formed and of dazzling whiteness, their eyes large and lustrous, and their lips thinner than we usually find them among these people. They wore their hair neatly parted, and arranged in pretty curls round the head. Poor creatures, who knows into what hands they might fall! They bowed their heads in anguish, without uttering a syllable. The sight of the slave-market here inspired me with a feeling of deep melancholy. The poor creatures did not seem so careless and merry as those whom I had seen on the market-place at Constantinople. In Cairo the slaves seemed badly kept; they lay in little tents, and were driven out, when a purchaser appeared, very much in the manner of cattle. They were only partially clothed in some old rags, and looked exhausted and unhappy. During my short stay at Cairo one of the chief feasts of the Mahommedans—namely, the Mashdalansher, or birthday of the Prophet—occurred. This feast is celebrated on a great open space outside the town. A number of large tents are erected; they are open in front, and beneath their shelter all kinds of things are carried on. In one tent, Mahommedans are praying; in another, a party of dervishes throw themselves with their faces to the ground and call upon Allah; while in a third, a juggler or storyteller may be driving his trade. In the midst of all stood a large tent, the entrance to which was concealed by curtains. Here the "bayaderes" were dancing; any one can obtain admission by paying a trifling sum. Of course I went in to see these celebrated dancers. There were, however, only two pairs; two boys were elegantly clothed in a female garb, richly decorated with gold coins. They looked very pretty and delicate, so that I really thought they were girls. The dance itself is very monotonous, slow, and wearisome; it consists only of some steps to and fro, accompanied by some rather indecorous movements of the upper part of the body. These gestures are said to be very difficult, as the dancer must stand perfectly still, and only move the upper part of his person. The music consisted of a tambourine, a flageolet, and a bagpipe. Much has been written concerning the indecency of these dances; but I am of opinion that many of our ballets afford much greater cause of complaint. It may, however, be that other dances are performed of which the general public are not allowed to be spectators; but I only speak of what is done openly. I would also by far prefer a popular festival in the East to a fair in our highly-civilised states. The Oriental feasts were to me a source of much enjoyment, for the people always behaved most decorously. They certainly shouted, and pushed, and elbowed each other like an European mob; but no drunken men were to be seen, and it was very seldom that a serious quarrel occurred. The commonest man, too, would never think of offering an insult to one of the opposite sex. I should feel no compunction in sending a young girl to this festival, though I should never think of letting her go to the fair held at Vienna on St. Bridget's day.

The people were assembled in vast numbers, and the crowd was very great, yet we could pass every where on our donkeys.

At about three o'clock my servant sought out an elevated place for me, for the great spectacle was soon to come, and the crushing and bustle had already reached their highest pitch. At length a portly priest could be descried riding along on a splendid horse; before him marched eight or ten dervishes with flags flying, and behind him a number of men, among whom were also many dervishes. In the midst of the square the procession halted; a few soldiers pushed their way among the people, whom they forced to stand back and leave a road. Whenever the spectators did not obey quickly, a stick was brought into action, which soon established order in a most satisfactory manner.

The procession now moved on once more, the standard-bearers and dervishes making all kinds of frantic gestures, as though they had just escaped from a madhouse. On reaching the place where the spectators formed a lane, the dervishes and several other men threw themselves down with their faces to the ground in a long row, with their heads side by side. And then—oh horror!—the priest rode over the backs of these miserable men as upon a bridge. Then they all sprang up again as though nothing had happened, and rejoined the advancing train with their former antics and grimaces. One man stayed behind, writhing to and fro as if his back had been broken, but in a few moments' time he went away as unconcernedly as his comrades. Each of the actors in this scene considers himself extremely fortunate in having attained to such a distinction, and this feeling even extends to his relations and friends.

SHUBRA.

One afternoon I paid a visit to the beautiful garden and country-house of the Viceroy of Egypt. A broad handsome street leads between alleys of sycamores, and the journey occupies about an hour and a half. Immediately upon my arrival I was conducted to an out-building, in the yard belonging to which a fine large elephant was to be shewn. I had already seen several of these creatures, but never such a fine specimen as this. Its bulk was truly marvellous; its body clean and smooth, and of a dark-brown colour.

The park is most lovely; and the rarest plants are here seen flourishing in the open air, in the fulness of bloom and beauty, beside those we are accustomed to see every day. On the whole, however, I was better pleased with the garden at Rodda. The palace, too, is very fine. The ceilings of the rooms are lofty, and richly ornamented with gilding, paintings, and marble. The rooms appropriated to the viceroy's consort are no less magnificent; the ascent to them is by a broad staircase on each side. On the ground-floor is situate the favourite apartment of the autocrat of Cairo, furnished in the style of the reception-halls at Damascus. A fountain of excellent water diffuses a delicious coolness around. In the palace itself we find several large cages for parrots and other beautiful birds. What pleased me most of all was, however, the incomparable kiosk, lying in the garden at some distance from the palace. It is 130 paces long and 100 broad, surrounded by arcades of glorious pillars. This kiosk contains in its interior a large and beautiful fountain; and at the four corners of the building are terraces, from which the water falls in the form of little cataracts, afterwards uniting with the fountain, and shooting upwards in the shape of a mighty pillar. All things around us, the pavilion and the pillars, the walls and the fountain, are alike covered with beautiful marble of a white or light-brown colour; the pavilion is even arranged so that it can be lighted with gas.

From this paradise of the living I rode to the abode of the dead, the celebrated "world of graves," which is to be seen in the desert. Here are to be found a number of ancient sepulchres, but most of them resemble ruins, and to find out their boasted beauty is a thing left to the imagination of every traveller. I only admired the sepulchre of Mehemet Ali's two sons, in which the bones of his wife also rest: this is a beautiful building of stone; five cupolas rise above the magnificent chambers where the sarcophagi are deposited.

The petrified date-wood lies about eight miles distant from Cairo; I rode out there, but did not find much to see, excepting here and there some fragments of stems and a few petrifactions lying about. It is said that the finest part of this "petrified wood" begins some miles away; but I did not penetrate so far.

During my residence in Cairo the heat once reached 36° Reaumur, and yet I found it much more endurable than I had expected. I was not annoyed at all by insects or vermin; but I was obliged to be careful not to leave any provisions in my room throughout the night. An immense swarm of minute ants would seize upon every kind of eatable, particularly bread. One evening I left a roll upon the table, and the next morning found it half eaten away, and covered with ants within and without. It is here an universal custom to place the feet of the tables in little dishes filled with water, to keep off these insects.

EXCURSION TO SUEZ.

It had originally been my intention to stay at Cairo a week at the furthest, and afterwards to return to Alexandria. But the more I saw, the more my curiosity became excited, and I felt irresistibly impelled to proceed. I had now travelled in almost every way, but I had not yet tried an excursion on a camel. I therefore made inquiry as to the distance, danger, and expense of a journey to Suez on the Red Sea. The distance was a thirty-six hours' journey, the danger was said to be nil, and the expense they estimated at about 250 piastres.

I therefore hired two strong camels, one for me, the other for my servant and the camel-driver, and took nothing with me in the way of provisions but bread, dates, a piece of roast meat, and hardboiled eggs. Skins of water were hung at each side of the camels, for we had to take a supply which would last us the journey and during our return.

If we ride every day for twelve hours, this journey occupies six days, there and back. But as I was unable to depart until the afternoon of the 26th, and was obliged to be in Alexandria at latest by the 30th, in order not to miss the steamer, I had only four days and a half to accomplish it in. Thus this excursion was the most fatiguing I had ever undertaken.

At four in the afternoon I rode through the town-gate, where the camels were waiting for us; we mounted them and commenced our journey. The desert begins at the town-gates, but for the first few miles we have a sight of some very fruitful country on the left, until at length we leave town and trees behind us, and with them all the verdure, and find ourselves surrounded on all sides by a sea of sand.

For the first four or five hours I was not ill-pleased with this mode of travelling. I had plenty of room on my camel, and could sit farther back or forward as I chose, and had provisions and a bottle of water at my side. Besides this, the heat was not oppressive; I felt very comfortable, and could look down from my high throne almost with a feeling of pride upon the passing caravans. Even the swaying motion of the camel, which causes in some travellers a feeling of sickness and nausea like that produced by a sea-voyage, did not affect me. But after a few hours I began to feel the fatigues and discomforts of a journey of this kind. The swinging motion pained and fatigued me, as I had no support against which I could lean. The desire to sleep also arose within me, and it can be imagined how uncomfortable I felt. But I was resolved to go to Suez; and if all my hardships had been far worse, I would not have turned back. I summoned all my fortitude, and rode without halting for fifteen hours, from four in the afternoon until seven the next morning.

During the night we passed several trains of camels, some in motion, some at rest, often consisting of more than a hundred. We were not exposed to the least annoyance, although we had attached ourselves to no caravan, but were pursuing our way alone.

From Cairo to Suez posts are established at every five or six hours' journey, and at each of these posts there stands a little house of two rooms for the convenience of travellers. These huts were built by an English innkeeper established at Cairo; but they can only be used by very rich people, as the prices charged are most exorbitant. Thus, for instance, a bed for one night costs a hundred piastres, a little chicken twenty, and a bottle of water two piastres. The generality of travellers encamp before the house, and I followed the same plan, lying down for an hour in the sand while the camels ate their scanty meal. My health and bodily strength are, I am happy to say, so excellent, that I am ready after a very short rest to encounter new fatigues. After this hour of repose I once more mounted my camel to continue my journey.

August 27th.

It may easily be imagined that the whole scene by which we are here surrounded has over it an air of profound and deathlike stillness. The sea, where we behold nothing but water around us, presents more of life to divert the mind. The very rushing and splash of the wheels, the bounding waves, the bustle of bending or reefing sails, and the crowding of people on the steamer, brings varied pictures to temper the monotony around. Even the ride through the stony deserts which I had traversed in Syria has not so much sameness, for there we at least hear the tramp of the horse and the sound of many a rolling stone; the traveller's attention is, besides, kept continually on the stretch in guiding each step that his horse takes, to avoid the risk of a fall. But all this is wanting in a journey through a sandy desert. No bird hovers in the air, not a butterfly is here to gladden the eye, not even an insect or a worm crawls on the ground; not a living creature is, in fact, to be seen, but the little vultures preying on the carcasses of fallen camels. Even the tread of the heavy-footed camel is muffled by the deep sand, and nothing is ever heard but the moaning of these poor animals when their driver forces them to lie down to take off their burden; most probably the exertion of stooping hurts them. The driver beats the camel on the knee with a stick, and pulls its head towards him by a rope fastened to it like a halter. During this operation the rider must hold very fast in order not to fall off, for suddenly the creature drops on its fore-knees, then on its hind legs, and at length sits completely down on the ground. When you mount the animal again, it becomes necessary to keep a vigilant eye upon him, for as soon as he feels your foot on his neck he wishes to rise.

As I have already said, we see nothing on this journey but many and large companies of camels, which march one behind the other, while their drivers shorten the way with dreary inharmonious songs. Half-devoured carcasses of these "ships of the desert" lie every where, with jackals and vultures gnawing at them. Even living camels are sometimes seen staggering about, which have been left to starve by their masters as unfit for further service. I shall never forget the piteous look of one of these poor creatures which I saw dragging itself to and fro in the desert, anxiously seeking for food and drink. What a cruel being is man! Why could he not put an end to the poor camel's pain by a blow with a knife? One would imagine that the air in the vicinity of these fallen animals was poisoned; but here this is less the case than it would be in more temperate regions, for the pure air and the great heat of the desert rather dry up than decompose corpses.

From the same cause our piece of roast beef was still good on the fifth day. The hard-boiled eggs, which my servant packed so clumsily that they got smashed in the very first hour, did not become foul. Both meat and eggs were shrunk and dried up. On the third day the white bread had become as hard as ship-biscuit, so that we had to break it up and soak it in water. Our drinking water became worse day by day, and smelt abominably of the leathern receptacles in which we were compelled to keep it. Until we reached Suez our poor camels got not a drop to drink, and their food consisted of a scanty meal of bad provender once a day.

At eight in the morning we set off once more, and rode until about five in the afternoon. At about four I suddenly descried the Red Sea and its shores. This circumstance delighted me, for I felt assured that we should reach the coast in the course of another hour, and then our laborious journey to Suez would be accomplished. I called to my servant, pointed out the sea to him, and expressed my surprise that we had sighted it so soon. He maintained, however, that what I beheld was not the sea, but a fata morgana. At first I refused to believe him, because the thing seemed so real. But after an hour had elapsed we were as far from the sea as ever, and at length the mirage vanished; and I did not behold the real sea until six o'clock on the following morning, when it appeared in exactly the same way as the phantom of the previous evening.

At five in the afternoon we at length halted. I lay down on the earth completely exhausted, and enjoyed a refreshing sleep for more than three hours, when I was awakened by my servant, who informed me that a caravan was just before us, which we should do well to join, as the remainder of our road was far less safe than the portion we had already traversed. I was at once ready to mount my camel, and at eight o'clock we were again in motion.

In a short time we had overtaken the caravan, and our camels were placed in the procession, each beast being tethered to the preceding one by a rope. It was already quite dark, and I could barely distinguish that the people sitting on the camels before me were an Arab family. They travelled in boxes resembling hen-coops, about a foot and a half in height, four feet in length, and as many broad. In a box of this kind two or three men sat cross-legged; many had even spread a light tent over their heads. Suddenly I heard my name called by a female voice. I started, and thought I must be mistaken, for whom in the world could I meet here who knew my Christian name? But once more a voice cried very distinctly, "Ida! Ida!" and a servant came up, and told me that some Arab women, who had made the voyage from Atfé to Cairo in company with me, were seated on the first camel. They sent to tell me that they were on their way to Mecca, and rejoiced to meet me once more. I was indeed surprised that I should have made such an impression on these good people that they had not forgotten my name.

To-night I saw a glorious natural phenomenon, which so surprised me that I could not refrain from uttering a slight scream. It may have been about eleven o'clock, when suddenly the sky on my left was lighted up, as though every thing were in flames; a great fiery ball shot through the air with lightning speed, and disappeared on the horizon, while at the same moment the gleam in the atmosphere vanished, and darkness descended once more on all around. We travelled on throughout the whole of this night.

August 28th.

At six o'clock this morning we came in sight of the Red Sea. The mountain-chain of Mokattam can be discerned some time previously. Some way from Suez we came upon a well of bad, brackish water. Notwithstanding all drawbacks, the supply was eagerly hailed. Our people shouted, scolded, and pushed each other to get the best places; camels, horses, asses, and men rushed pell-mell towards the well, and happy was he who could seize upon a little water. There are barracks near this well, and soldiers are posted here to promote peace—by means of the stick.

The little town of Suez lies spread out on the sea-shore, and can be very distinctly seen from here. The unhappy inhabitants are compelled to draw their supplies either from this well, or from one on the sea-coast four miles below Suez. In the first case the water is brought on camels, horses, or asses; in the second it is transported by sea in boats or small ships.

The Red Sea is here rather narrow, and surrounded by sand of a yellowish-brown hue; immediately beyond the isthmus is the continuation of the great Libyan Desert. The mountain-range of Mokattam skirts the plain on the right, from Cairo to the Red Sea. We quite lose sight of this range until within the last ten or twelve hours before reaching Suez. The mountains are of moderate elevation and perfectly bare; but still the eye rests with pleasure on the varied forms of the rocks.

After an hour's rest beside the well, we were still unable to procure water for our poor beasts, and hastened, therefore, to reach the town. At nine in the morning we were already within its walls. Of the town and its environs I can say nothing, excepting that they both present a very melancholy appearance, as there is nowhere a garden or a cluster of trees to be seen.

I paid my respects to the consul, and introduced myself to him as an Austrian subject. He was kind enough to assign me a room in his own house, and would on no account permit me to take up my quarters in an inn. It was a pity that I could only converse with this gentleman by means of a dragoman; he was a Greek by birth, and only knew the Arabic language and his own. He is the richest merchant in Suez (his wealth is estimated at 150,000 collonati), and only discharges the functions of French and Austrian consul as an honorary duty.

In the little town itself there is nothing remarkable to be seen. On the sea-coast they shewed me the place where Moses led the children of Israel through the Red Sea. The sinking of the tide at its ebb is here so remarkable that whole islands are left bare, and large caravans are able to march through the sea, as the water only reaches to the girths of the camels, and the Arabs and Bedouins even walk through. As it happened to be ebb-tide when I arrived, I rode through also, for the glory of the thing. On these shores I found several pretty shells; but the real treasures of this kind are fished out of the deep at Ton, a few days' journey higher up. I saw whole cargoes of mother-of-pearl shells carried away.

I remained at Suez until four in the afternoon, and recruited my energies perfectly with an excellent dinner, at which tolerably good water was not wanting. The consul kindly gave me a bottle, as provision for my journey. He has it fetched from a distance of twelve miles, as all the water that can be procured in the neighbourhood tastes brackish and salt. In the inn a bottle of water costs two piastres.

The first night of my homeward journey was passed partly in a Bedouin encampment and partly on the road, in the company of different caravans. I found the Bedouins to be very good, obliging people, among whom I might wander as I pleased, without being exposed to injury. On the contrary, while I was in their encampment they brought me a straw-mat and a chest, in order that I might have a comfortable seat.

The homeward journey was just as monotonous and wearisome as that to Suez, with the additional fact that I had a quarrel with my people the day before its termination. Feeling exceedingly fatigued by a lengthened ride, I ordered my servant to stop the camels, as I wished to sleep for a few hours. The rascals refused to obey, alleging that the road was not safe, and that we should endeavour to overtake a caravan. This was, however, nothing but an excuse to get home as quickly as possible. But I was not to be frightened, and insisted that my desire should be complied with, telling them moreover that I had inquired of the consul at Suez concerning the safety of the roads, and had once more heard that there was nothing to fear. Notwithstanding all this they would not obey, but continued to advance. I now became angry, and desired the servant once more to stop my camel, as I was fully determined not to proceed another step.

I told him I had hired both camels and men, and had therefore a right to be mistress; if he did not choose to obey me, he might go his way with the camel-driver, and I would join the first caravan I met, and bring him to justice, let it cost me what it would. The fellow now stopped my camel, and went away with the other and the camel-driver. He probably expected to frighten me by this demonstration, and to compel me to follow; but he was vastly mistaken. I remained standing where I was, and as often as he turned to look at me, made signs that he might go his way, but that I should stay. When he saw how fearless and determined I was, he turned back, came to me, made my camel kneel down, and after helping me to alight, prepared me a resting-place on a heap of sand, where I slept delightfully for five hours; then I ordered my things to be packed up, mounted my camel, and continued my journey.

My conduct astonished my followers to such a degree, that they afterwards asked me every few hours if I wished to rest. On our arrival at Cairo the camel-driver had not even the heart to make the customary demand for backsheesh, and my servant begged pardon for his conduct, and hoped that I would not mention the difference we had had to the consul.

The maximum temperature during this journey was 43° Reaumur, and when it was perfectly calm I really felt as if I should be stifled.

This journey from Cairo to Suez can, however, be accomplished in a carriage in the space of twenty hours. The English innkeeper established at

Cairo has had a very light carriage, with seats for four, built expressly for this purpose; but a place in this vehicle costs five pounds for the journey there, and the same sum for the return.

On the following day I once more embarked on board an Arabian vessel for Alexandria. Before my departure I had a terrible quarrel with the donkey-driver whom I usually employed. These men, as in fact all fellahs, are accustomed to cheat strangers in every possible way, but particularly with coins. They usually carry bad money about with them, which they can substitute for the good at the moment when they are paid, with the dexterity of jugglers. My donkey-driver endeavoured to play me this trick when I rode to the ship; he saw that I should not require his services any more, and therefore wished to cheat me as a parting mark of attention. This attempt disgusted me so much that I could not refrain from brandishing my whip at him in a very threatening manner, although I was alone among a number of his class. My gesture had the desired effect; the driver instantly retreated, and I remained victor.

My reader would do me a great wrong by the supposition that I mention these circumstances to make a vaunt of my courage; I am sure that the fact of my having undertaken this journey alone will be sufficient to clear me from the imputation of cowardice. I wish merely to give future travellers a hint as to the best method of dealing with these people. Their respect can only be secured by the display of a firm will; and I am sure that in my case they were the more intimidated as they had never expected to find so much determination in a woman.

## CHAPTER XVII.

September 5th.

At five o'clock in the evening of the 2d of September I commenced my journey back to Alexandria. During the fortnight I remained at Cairo the Nile had continued to rise considerably, and the interest of the region had increased in proportion. In three days' time I arrived safely at Alexandria, and again put up at Colombier's. Two days had still to elapse before the departure of the French steam-vessel, and I made use of this time to take a closer survey of the town and its environs.

On my arrival at Alexandria I met two Egyptian funerals. The first was that of a poor man, and not a soul followed the coffin. The corpse lay in a wooden box without a lid, a coarse blanket had been spread over it, and four men carried the coffin. The second funeral had a more respectable air. The coffin, indeed, was not less rude, but the dead man was covered with a handsome shawl, and four "mourning women" followed the body, raising a most dolorous howl from time to time. A motley crowd of people closed the procession. The corpse was laid in the grave without the coffin.

The catacombs of Alexandria are very extensive, and well worth a visit. A couple of miles from them we see the celebrated plain on which the army of Julius Cæsar was once posted. The cistern and bath of Cleopatra were both under water. I could, therefore, only see the place where they stood.

The viceroy's palace, a spacious building inclining to the European style, has a pleasing effect. Its interior arrangement is also almost wholly European.

The bazaar contains nothing worthy of remark. The arsenal looks very magnificent when viewed from without. It is difficult to obtain admission into this building, and you run the risk of being insulted by the workmen. The hospital has the appearance of a private house.

I was astonished at the high commission which is here demanded on changing small sums of money. In changing a collonato, a coin very much used in this country, and worth about two guilders, the applicant must lose from half a piastre to two piastres, according to the description of coin he requires. If beshliks {261} are taken, the commission charged is half a piastre; but if piastres are wanted, two must be paid. The government value of a collonato is twenty piastres; in general exchange it is reckoned at twenty-two, and at the consulate's at twenty-one piastres.

DEPARTURE FROM ALEXANDRIA.

September 7th.

At eight o'clock in the morning I betook myself on board the French steam-packet Eurotas, a beautiful large vessel of 160-horse power. At nine o'clock we weighed anchor.

The weather was very unfavourable. Though it did not rain, we continually had contrary winds, and the sea generally ran high. In consequence we did not sight the island of Candia until the evening of the third day, four-and-twenty hours later than we should have done under ordinary circumstances.

Two women, who came on board as passengers to Syra, were so violently attacked by sea-sickness, that they left the deck a few hours after we got under way, and did not reappear until they landed at Syra. A very useful arrangement on board the French vessel is the engagement of a female attendant, whose assistance sometimes becomes very necessary. Heaven be praised, I had not much to fear from the attacks of sea-sickness. The weather must be very bad—as, for instance, during our passage through the Black Sea—before my health is affected, and even then I recover rapidly. During our whole voyage, even when the weather was wretched, I remained continually on deck, so that during the day-time I could not miss seeing even the smallest islet. On

September 10th,

late in the evening, we discovered the island of Candia or Crete, and the next morning we were pretty close to it. We could, however, distinguish nothing but bare unfruitful mountains, the tallest among which, my namesake Mount Ida, does not look more fertile than the rest. On the right loomed the island of Scarpanto. We soon left it in our wake, and also passed the Brothers' Islands, and many others, some of them small and uninhabited, besides separate colossal rocks, towering majestically into the sea. Soon afterwards we passed the islands Santorin and Anaph.

The latter of these islands is peculiarly beautiful. In the foreground a village lies at the foot of a high mountain, with its peak surmounted by a little church. On the side towards the sea this rock shoots downwards so perpendicularly, that we might fancy it had been cut off with a saw.

Since we had come in sight of Candia, we had not been sailing on the high seas. Scarcely did one island vanish from our view, before it was replaced by another. On

September 11th,

between three and four in the morning, we reached Syra. The terrible contrary winds with which we had been obliged to contend during almost the whole of our passage had caused us to arrive a day behind our time, to make up for which delay we only stayed half a day here, instead of a day and a half. This was a matter of indifference to those of us who were travelling further, for as we came from Egypt, we should not have been allowed in any case to disembark. Those who landed here proceeded at once to the quarantine-house.

Syra possesses a fine harbour. From our vessel we had a view over the whole town and its environs. An isolated mountain, crowned by a convent and church, the seat of the bishop, rises boldly from the very verge of the shore. The town winds round this mountain in the form of several wreaths, until it almost reaches the episcopal buildings. The background closes with the melancholy picture of a barren mountain-chain. A lighthouse stands on a little neighbouring island. The quarantine establishment looks cheerful enough, and is situate at a little distance from the town on the sea-shore.

It was Sunday when we arrived here; and as Syra belongs to Greece, I here heard the sound of bells like those of Mount Lebanon, and once more their strain filled me with deep and indescribable emotion. Never do we think so warmly of our home as when we are solitary and alone among strange people in a far-distant land!

I would gladly have turned aside from my route to visit Athens, which I might have reached in a few hours; but then I should once more have been compelled to keep quarantine, and perhaps on leaving Greece the infliction would have to be borne a third time, a risk which I did not wish to run. I therefore preferred keeping quarantine at Malta, and having done with it at once.

On the same day at two o'clock we once more set sail. This day and the following I remained on deck as much as possible, bidding defiance to wind and rain, and gazing at the islands as we glided past one after another. As one island disappeared, another rose in its place. Groups of isolated rocks also rose at intervals, like giants from the main, to form a feature in the changing panorama.

On the right, in the far distance, we could distinguish Paros and Antiparos, on the left the larger Chermian Isles; and at length we passed close to Cervo (Stag's Island), which is particularly distinguished by the beauty of its mountain-range. Here, as at Syra, we find an isolated mountain, round which a town winds almost to its summit.

September 12th.

As I came on deck to-day with the sun, the mainland of the Morea was in sight on our right,—a great plain, with many villages scattered over its surface, and a background of bare hills. After losing sight of the Morea we sailed once more on the high seas.

This day might have had a tragical termination for us. I was sitting as usual on deck, when I noticed an unusual stir among the sailors and officers, and even the commander ran hastily towards me. Nevertheless I did not dare to ask what had happened; for in proportion as the French are generally polite, they are proud and overbearing on board their steamers. I therefore remained quietly seated, and contented myself with watching every movement of the officers and men. Several descended to the coal-magazine, returning heated, blackened by the coals, and dripping with water. At length a cabin-boy came hurrying by me; and upon my asking him what was the matter, he replied in a whisper, that fire had broken out in the coal-room. Now I knew the whole extent of our danger, and yet could do nothing but keep my seat, and await whatever fate should bring us. It was most fortunate for us that the fire occurred during the daytime, and had been immediately discovered by the engine-man. Double chain-pumps were rigged, and the whole magazine was laid under water,—a proceeding which had the effect of extinguishing the flames. The other passengers knew nothing of our danger; they were all asleep or sitting quietly in the cabins; the sailors were forbidden to tell them what had happened, and even my informant the cabin-boy begged me not to betray him. We had three hundredweight of gunpowder on board.

September 14th.

We did not come in sight of land until this evening, when the goal of our journey appeared.

MALTA.

We cast anchor in the harbour of Lavalette at seven o'clock.

During the whole of our journey from Alexandria the wind had been very unfavourable; the sea was frequently so agitated, that we could not walk across the deck without the assistance of a sailor.

The distance from Alexandria via Syra to Malta is 950 sea-miles. We took eight days to accomplish this distance, landing only at Syra. The heat was moderate enough, seldom reaching 28° or 29° Reaumur.

The appearance of Malta is picturesque; it contains no mountains, and consists entirely of hills and rocks.

The town of Lavalette is surrounded by three lines of fortifications, winding like steps up the hill on which the town lies; the latter contains large fine houses, all built of stone.

September 15th.

This morning at eight o'clock we disembarked, and were marched off to keep quarantine in the magnificent castle of the Knights of St. John.

This building stands on a hill, affording a view over the whole island in the direction of Civita Vecchia. We found here a number of clean rooms, and were immediately supplied with furniture, bedding, etc. by the establishment at a very reasonable charge. Our host at once despatched to every guest a bill of fare for breakfast and dinner, so that each one can choose what he wishes, without being cheated as to the prices. The keepers here are very obliging and attentive; they almost all know something of Italian, and execute any commission with which they are entrusted punctually and well. The building for the incarcerated ones is situate on an elevated plateau. It has two large wings, one on each side, one story high, containing apartments each with a separate entrance. Adjoining the courtyard is the inn, and not far from it the church; neither, however, may be visited by the new-comers. The requisite provisions are procured for them by a keeper, who takes them to the purchasers. The church is always kept locked. A broad handsome terrace, with a prospect over the sea, the town of Lavalette, and the whole island, forms the foreground of the picture. This terrace and the ramparts behind the houses form very agreeable walks. The courtyard of our prison is very spacious, and we are allowed to walk about in it as far as a statue which stands in the middle. Until ten o'clock at night we enjoy our liberty; but when this hour arrives, we are sent to our respective rooms and locked up. The apartments of the keepers are quite separate from ours.

The arrangements of the whole establishment are so good and comfortable, that we almost forget that we are prisoners. What a contrast to the quarantine-house at Alexandria!

If a traveller receives a visitor, he is not separated from his guest by ditches and bars, but stands only two steps from him in the courtyard. The windows here are not grated; and though our clothes were hung on horses to air, neither we nor our effects were smoked out. If it had not been for the delay it caused, I should really have spent the eighteen days of my detention here very pleasantly. But I wished to ascend Mount Etna, and was a fixture here until the 2d of October.

October 1st.

The quarantine doctor examined us in a very superficial manner, and

pronounced that we should be free to-morrow. Upon this a boisterous hilarity prevailed. The prisoners rejoiced at the prospect of speedy release, and shouted, sang, and danced in the courtyard. The keepers caught the infection, and all was mirth and good-humour until late in the night.
October 2d.
At seven o'clock this morning we were released from thraldom. A scene similar to that at Alexandria then took place; every one rushed to seize upon the strangers. It is here necessary that the traveller should be as much upon his guard as in Egypt among the Arabs, in the matters of boat-fares, porterage, etc. If a bargain is not struck beforehand, the people are most exorbitant in their demands.
A few days before our release, I had made an arrangement with an innkeeper for board, lodging, and transport. Today he came to fetch me and my luggage, and we crossed the arm of the sea which divides Fort Manuel from the town of Lavalette.
A flight of steps leads from the shore into the town, past the three rows of fortifications rising in tiers above each other. In each of these divisions we find streets and houses. The town, properly speaking, lies quite at the top; it is therefore necessary to mount and descend frequently, though not nearly so often as at Constantinople. The streets are broad and well paved, the houses spacious and finely built; the place of roofs is supplied by terraces, frequently parcelled out into little flower-beds, which present a very agreeable appearance.
My host gave me a tiny room, and meals on the same principle—coffee with milk morning and evening, and three dishes at dinner-time; but for all this I did not pay more than forty-five kreutzers, or about one shilling and sixpence.
The first thing I did after taking up my quarters here was to hasten to a church to return thanks to the Almighty for the protection He had so manifestly extended to me upon my long and dangerous journey. The first church which I entered at Lavalette was dedicated to St. Augustine. I was particularly pleased with it, for since my departure from Vienna I had not seen one so neatly or so well built. Afterwards I visited the church of St. John, and was much struck with its splendour. This building is very spacious, and the floor is completely covered with monumental slabs of marble, covering the graves of the knights. The ceiling is ornamented with beautiful frescoes, and the walls are sculptured from ceiling to floor with arabesques, leaves, and flowers, in sandstone.
All these ornaments are richly gilt, and present a peculiarly imposing appearance. The side-chapels contain numerous monuments, mostly of white marble, and one single one of black, in memory of celebrated Maltese knights. At the right-hand corner of the church is the so-called "rose-coloured" chapel. It is hung round with a heavy silk stuff of a red colour,

which diffuses a roseate halo over all the objects around. The altar is surrounded by a high massive railing. Two only of the paintings are well executed—namely, that over the high altar, and a piece representing Christ on the cross. The pillars round the altar are of marble; and at each side of the grand altar rise lofty canopies of red velvet fringed with gold, reaching almost to the vaulted cupola.

The uncomfortable custom of carrying chairs to and fro during church-time, which is so universal throughout Italy, begins already at Malta.

The predilection for the clerical profession seems to prevail here, as it does throughout Italy; I could almost say that every fifteenth person we meet either is a clergyman or intends to become one. Children of ten or twelve years already run about in the black gown and three-cornered hat.

The streets are handsome and cleanly kept, particularly the one which intersects the town; some of them are even watered. The counters of the dealers' shops contain the most exquisite wares; in fact, every where we find indications that we are once more on European ground.

When we see the Fachini here, with their dark worked caps or round straw hats, their short jackets and comfortable trousers, with jaunty red sashes round their waists, and their bold free glance,—when we contrast them with the wretched fellahs of Egypt, and consider that these men both belong to the same class in society, and that the fellahs even inhabit the more fruitful country, we begin to have our doubts of Mehemet Ali's benignant rule.

The governor's palace, a great square building, stands on a magnificent open space; next to it is the library; and opposite, the chief guard-house rears its splendid front, graced with pillars. The coffee-houses here are very large; they are kept comfortably and clean, particularly that on the great square, which is brilliantly illuminated every evening.

Women and girls appear dressed in black; they are usually accustomed to throw a wide cloak over their other garments, and wear a mantilla which conceals arms, chest, and head. The face is left uncovered, and I saw some very lovely ones smiling forth from the black drapery. Rich people wear these upper garments of silk; the cloaks of the poorer classes are made of merino or cheap woollen stuffs.

It was Sunday when I entered Lavalette for the first time. Every street and church was thronged with people, all of whom were neatly and decently dressed. I saw but few beggars, and those whom I met were less ragged than the generality of their class.

The military, the finest I had ever seen, consisted entirely of tall handsome men, mostly Scotchmen. Their uniforms were very tasteful. One regiment wore scarlet jackets and white linen trousers; another, black jackets and shoulder-knots,—in fact, the whole uniform is black, with the exception of the trousers, which are of white linen.

175

It seemed much more the fashion to drive than to ride here. The coaches are of a very peculiar kind, which I hardly think can be found elsewhere. They consist of a venerable old rattling double-seated box, swinging upon two immense wheels, and drawn by a single horse in shafts. The coachman generally runs beside his vehicle.

October 3d.

To-day I drove in a carriage (for the first time since my departure from Vienna, a period of six months and a half) to Civita Vecchia, to view this ancient town of Malta, and particularly the celebrated church of St. Peter and St. Paul. On this occasion I traversed the whole length of the island, and had an opportunity of viewing the interior.

Malta consists of a number of little elevations, and is intersected in all directions by excellent roads. I also continually passed handsome villages, some of them so large that they looked like thriving little towns. The heights are frequently crowned by churches of considerable extent and beauty; although the whole island consists of rock and sandstone, vegetation is sufficiently luxurious. Fig, lemon, and orange trees grow every where, and plantations of the cotton-shrub are as common as potato-fields in my own country. The stems of these shrubs are not higher than potato-plants, and are here cultivated exactly in the same way. I was told that they had been stunted this year by the excessive drought, but that in general they grew a foot higher.

The peasants were every where neatly dressed, and live in commodious well-built houses, universally constructed of stone, and furnished with terraces in lieu of roofs.

CIVITA VECCHIA

is a town of splendid houses and very elegant country-seats. Many inhabitants of Lavalette spend the summer here, in the highest portion of the island.

The church of St. Peter and St. Paul is a spacious building, with a simple interior. The floor is covered merely with stone slabs; the walls are white-washed to the ceiling, but the upper portion is richly ornamented with arabesques. A beautiful picture hanging behind the high altar represents a storm at sea. The view from the hall of the convent is magnificent; we can overlook almost the entire island, and beyond our gaze loses itself in the boundless expanse of ocean.

Near the church stands a chapel, beneath which is St. Paul's grotto, divided into two parts: in the first of these divisions we find a splendid statue of St. Paul in white marble; the second was the dungeon of the apostle.

Not far from this chapel, at the extremity of the town, are the catacombs, which resemble those at Rome, Naples, and other towns.

During our drive back we made a little detour to see the gorgeous summer-palace and garden of the governor.

The whole excursion occupied about seven hours. During my residence in Malta the heat varied from 20° to 25° Reaumur in the sun.

## CHAPTER XVIII.

October 4th.
At eight o'clock in the evening I embarked on board the Sicilian steamer Hercules, of 260-horse power, the largest and finest vessel I had yet seen. The officers here were not nearly so haughty and disobliging as those on board the Eurotas. Even now I cannot think without a smile of the airs the captain of the latter vessel gave himself. He appeared to consider that he had as good a right to be an admiral as Bruys.
At ten o'clock we steamed out of the harbour of Lavalette. As it was already dark night, I went below and retired to rest.
October 5th.
When I hurried on deck this morning I found we were already in sight of the Sicilian coast, and—oh happiness!—I could distinguish green hills, wooded mountains, glorious dells, and smiling meadows,—a spectacle I had enjoyed neither in Syria, in Egypt, nor even at Malta. Now I thought at length to behold Europe, for Malta resembles the Syrian regions too closely to favour the idea that we are really in Europe. Towards eleven o'clock we reached
SYRACUSE.
Unfortunately we could only get four hours' leave of absence. As several gentlemen among the passengers wished to devote these few hours to seeing all the lions of this once rich and famous town, I joined their party and went ashore with them. Scarcely had we landed before we were surrounded by a number of servants and a mob of curious people, so that we were almost obliged to make our way forcibly through the crowd. The gentlemen hired a guide, and desired to be at once conducted to a restaurateur, who promised to prepare them a modest luncheon within half an hour. The prospect of a good meal seemed of more importance in the eyes of my fellow-passengers than any thing else. They resolved to have luncheon first, and afterwards to take a little walk through the city.
On hearing this I immediately made a bargain with a cicerone to shew me what he could in four hours, and went with him, leaving the company seated at table. Though I got nothing to eat to-day but a piece of bread and a few figs, which I despatched on the road, I saw some sights which I would not have missed for the most sumptuous entertainment.
Of the once spacious town nothing remains but a very small portion, inhabited by 10,000 persons at most. The dirty streets were every where crowded with people, as though they dwelt out of doors, while the houses stood empty.

Accompanied by my guide, I passed hastily through the new town, and over three or four wooden bridges to Neapolis, the part of ancient Syracuse in which monuments of the past are seen in the best state of preservation. First we came to the theatre. This building is tolerably well preserved, and several of the stone seats are still seen rising in terrace form one above the other. From this place we betook ourselves into the amphitheatre, which is finer by far, and where we find passages leading to the wild beasts' dens, and above them rows of seats for spectators; all is in such good condition that it might, at a trifling expense, be so far repaired as to be made again available for its original purpose. Now we proceeded to the "Ear of Dionysius," with which I was particularly struck. It consists of a number of chambers, partly hewn out of the rock by art, partly formed by nature, and all opening into an immensely lofty hall, which becomes narrower and narrower towards the top, until it at length terminates in an aperture so minute as to be invisible from below. To this aperture Dionysius is said to have applied his ear, in order to overhear what the captives spoke. (This place is stated to have been used as a prison for slaves and malefactors.) It is usual to fire a pistol here, that the stranger may hear the reverberating echoes. A lofty opening, resembling a great gate, forms the entrance to these rocky passages. Overgrown with ivy, it has rather the appearance of a bower than of a place of terror and anguish. Several of these side halls are now used as workshops by rope-makers, while in others the manufacture of saltpetre is carried on. The region around is rocky, but without displaying any high mountains. I saw numerous grottoes, some of them with magnificent entrances, which looked as though they had been cut in the rocks by art. In one of these grottoes water fell from above, forming a very pretty cataract.

During this excursion the time had passed so rapidly that I was soon compelled to think, not of a visit to the catacombs, but of my return on board.

I proceeded to the sea-shore, where the Syracusans have built a very pretty promenade, and was rowed back to the steamer.

Of all the passengers I was the only one who had seen any thing of Syracuse; all the rest had spent the greater part of the time allowed them in the inn, and at most had been for a short walk in the town. But they had obtained an exceedingly good dinner; and thus we had each enjoyed ourselves in our own way.

At three o'clock we quitted the beautiful harbour of Syracuse, and three hours brought us to

CATANEA.

This voyage was one of the most beautiful and interesting that can be imagined. The traveller continually sees the most charming landscapes of blooming Sicily; and at Syracuse we can already descry on a clear day the giant Etna rearing its head 10,000 feet above the level of the sea. At six in the evening we disembarked; but those going farther had to be on board again by midnight. I had intended to remain at Catanea and ascend Mount Etna; but on making inquiries I was assured that the season was too far advanced for such an undertaking, and therefore resolved to set sail again at midnight. I went on shore in company with a Neapolitan and his wife, for the purpose of visiting some of the churches, a few public buildings, and the town itself. The buildings, however, were already closed, though the exteriors promised much. We could only deplore that we had arrived an hour too late, and take a walk round the town. I could scarcely wonder enough at the bustle in the crowded squares and chief streets, and at the shouting and screaming of the people. The number of inhabitants is about 50,000. The two chief streets, leading in different directions from the great square, are long, broad, and particularly well paved with large stone slabs: they contain many magnificent houses. The only circumstance which displeased me was, that every where, even in the chief streets, the people dry clothes on large poles at balconies and windows. This makes the town look as though it were inhabited by a race of washerwomen. I should not even mind so much if they were clean clothes; but I frequently saw the most disgusting rags fluttering in front of splendid houses. Unfortunately this barbarous custom prevails throughout the whole of Sicily; and even in Naples the hanging out of clothes is only forbidden in the principal street, the Toledo: all the other streets are full of linen.

Among the equipages, which were rolling to and fro in great numbers, I noticed some very handsome ones. Some were standing still in the great square, while their occupants amused themselves by looking at the bustle around them, and chatted with friends and acquaintances who crowded round the carriages. I found a greater appearance of life here than either at Naples or Palermo.

The convent of St. Nicholas was unfortunately closed, so that we could only view its exterior. It is a spacious magnificent building, the largest, in fact, in the whole town. We also looked at the walks on the sea-shore, which at our first arrival we had traversed in haste in order to reach the town quickly. Beautiful avenues extend along each side of the harbour; they are, however, less frequented than the streets and squares. We had a beautiful moonlight night; the promontory of Etna, with its luxurious vegetation, as well as the giant mountain itself, were distinctly visible in all their glory. The summit rose cloudless and free; no smoke came from the crater, nor could we discover a trace of snow as we returned to our ship. We noticed several heaps of lava piled upon the sea-shore, of a perfectly black colour.

Late in the evening we adjourned to an inn to refresh ourselves with some good dishes, and afterwards returned to the steamer, which weighed anchor at midnight.

October 6th.

We awoke in the harbour of Messina. The situation of this town is lovely beyond description. I was so charmed with it that I stood for a long time on deck without thinking of landing.

A chain of beautiful hills and huge masses of rock in the background surround the harbour and town. Every where the greatest fertility reigns, and all things are in the most thriving and flourishing condition. In the direction of Palermo the boundless ocean is visible.

I now bade farewell to the splendid steamer Hercules, because I did not intend to proceed direct to Naples, but to make a detour by way of Palermo.

As soon as I had landed, I proceeded to the office of the merchant M., to whom I had a letter of recommendation. I requested Herr M. to procure me a cicerone as soon as possible, as I wished to see the sights of Messina, and afterwards to continue my journey to Palermo. Herr M. was kind enough to send one of his clerks with me. I rested for half an hour, and then commenced my peregrination.

From the steamer Messina had appeared to me a very narrow place, but on entering the town I found that I had made quite a false estimate of its dimensions. Messina is certainly built in a very straggling oblong form, but still its breadth is not inconsiderable.

I saw many very beautiful squares; for instance, the chief square, with its splendid fountain ornamented with figures, and a bas-relief of carved work in bronze. Every square contains a fountain, but we seldom find any thing particularly tasteful. The churches are not remarkable for the beauty of their façades, nor do they present any thing in the way of marble statues or finely executed pictures.

The houses are generally well built, with flat roofs; the streets, with few exceptions, are narrow, small, and very dirty. An uncommonly broad street runs parallel with the harbour, and contains, on one side at least, some very handsome houses. This is a favourite place for a walk, for we can here see all the bustle and activity of the port. Several of the palaces also are pretty; that appropriated to the senate is the only one which can be called fine, the staircase being constructed entirely of white marble, in a splendid style of architecture: the halls and apartments are lofty, and generally arched. The regal palace is also a handsome pile.

In the midst of the town I found an agreeable public garden. The Italians appear, however, to choose the streets as places of rendezvous, in preference to enclosures of this kind; for every where I noticed that the garden-walks were empty, and the streets full. But on the whole there is not nearly so much life here as at Catanea. In order to obtain a view of the whole of Messina and its environs I ascended a hill near the town, surmounted by a Capuchin convent; here I enjoyed a prospect which I have seldom seen equalled. As I gazed upon it I could easily imagine that an inhabitant of Messina can find no place in the world so beautiful as his native town.

The promontory against which the town leans is clothed with a carpet of the brightest green, planted with fruit-trees of all kinds, and enlivened with scattered towns, villages, and country seats. Beautiful roads, appearing like white bands, intersect the mountains on every side in the direction of the town. The background is closed by high mountains, sometimes wooded, sometimes bare, now rising in the form of alps, now in the shape of rocky masses. At the foot of the hills we see the long-drawn town, the harbour with its numerous ships, and beyond it groups of alps and rocks. The boundless sea flows on the spectator's right and left towards Palermo and Naples, while in the direction of Catanea the eye is caught by mountains, with Etna towering among them.

The same evening I embarked on board the Duke of Calabria, for the short trip of twelve or fourteen hours to Palermo. This steamer has only engines of 80 horse-power, and every thing connected with it is small and confined. The first-class accommodation is indeed pretty good, but the second-class places are only calculated to contain very few passengers. Though completely exhausted by my long and fatiguing walk through Messina, I remained on deck, for I could not be happy without seeing Stromboli. Unfortunately I could distinguish very little of it. We had started from Messina at about six o'clock in the evening, and did not come in sight of the mountain until two hours later, when the shades of night were already descending; we were, besides, at such a distance from it that I could descry nothing but a colossal mass rising from the sea and towering towards heaven. I stayed on deck until past ten o'clock in the hope of obtaining a nearer view of Stromboli; but we had soon left it behind us in the far distance, with other islands which lay on the surface like misty clouds.

October 7th.

To-day I hastened on deck before sunrise, to see as much as possible of the Sicilian coast, and to obtain an early view of Palermo. At ten o'clock we ran into the harbour of this town.

I had been so charmed with the situation of Messina that I did not expect ever to behold any thing more lovely; and yet the remembrance of this town faded from my mind when

PALERMO

rose before me, surrounded by magnificent mountains, among which the colossal rock of St. Rosalia, a huge slab of porphyry and granite, towered high in the blue air. The combination of various colours unites with its immense height and its peculiar construction to render this mountain one of the most remarkable in existence. Its summit is crowned by a temple;

and a good road, partly cut out of the rock, partly supported on lofty pillars of masonry, which we can see from on board our vessel, leads to the convent of St. Rosalia, and to a chapel hidden among the hills and dedicated to the same saint.

At the foot of this mountain lies a gorgeous castle, inhabited, as my captain told me, by an English family, who pay a yearly rent of 30,000 florins for the use of it. To the left of Palermo the mountains open and shew the entrance into a broad and transcendently beautiful valley, in which the town of Monreal lies with magical effect. Several of these gaps occur along the coast, affording glimpses of the most lovely vales, with scattered villages and pretty country-seats.

The harbour of Palermo is picturesque and eminently safe. The town numbers about 130,000 inhabitants. Here, too, our deck was crowded with Fachini, innkeepers, and guides, before the anchor was fairly lowered. I inquired of the captain respecting the price of board and lodging, and afterwards made a bargain with a host before leaving the ship. By following this plan I generally escaped overcharge and inconvenience.

Arrived at the inn, I sent to Herr Schmidt, to whom I had been recommended, with the request that he would despatch a trustworthy cicerone to me, and make me a kind of daily scheme of what I was to see. This was soon done, and after hurrying over my dinner I commenced my wanderings.

I entered almost every church I passed on my way, and found them all neat and pretty. Every where I came upon picturesque villas and handsome houses, with glass doors instead of windows, their lower portion guarded by iron railings and forming little balconies. Here the women and girls sit of an evening working and talking to their heart's content.

The streets of Palermo are far handsomer and cleaner than those of Messina. The principal among them, Toledo and Casaro, divide the town into four parts, and join in the chief square. The streets, as we pass from one into another, present a peculiar appearance, filled with bustling crowds of people moving noisily to and fro. In the Toledo Street all the tailors seem congregated together, for the shops on each side of the way are uniformly occupied by the votaries of this trade, who sit at work half in their houses and half in the street. The coffee-houses and shops are all open, so that the passers-by can obtain a full view of the wares and of the buyers and sellers.

The regal palace is the handsomest in the town. It contains a gothic chapel, richly decorated; the walls are entirely covered with paintings in mosaic, of which the drawings do not display remarkable taste, and the ceiling is over-crowded with decorations and arabesques. An ancient chandelier, in the form of a pillar, made of beautiful marble and also covered with arabesques, stands beside the pulpit. On holydays an immense candle is put in this candlestick and lighted.

I wished to enter this chapel, but was refused admittance until I had taken off my hat, like the men, and carried it in my hand. This custom prevails in several churches of Palermo. The space in front of the palace resembles a garden, from the number of avenues and beds of flowers with which it is ornamented. Second in beauty is the palace of the senate, but it cannot be compared with that at Messina.

The town contains several very handsome squares, in all of which we find several statues and fountains.

Foremost among the churches the Cathedral must be mentioned; its gothic façade occupies one entire side of a square. A spacious entrance-hall, with two monuments, not executed in a very fine style of art, leads into the interior of the church, which is of considerable extent, but built in a very simple style. The pillars, two of which always stand together, and the four royal monuments at the entrance, are all of Egyptian granite. The finest part of the church is the chapel of St. Rosalia on the right, not far from the high altar; both its walls are decorated with large bas-reliefs in marble, beautifully executed: one of these represents the banishment of the plague, and the finding of St. Rosalia's bones. A splendid pillar of lapis-lazuli, said to be the largest and finest specimen of this stone in existence, stands beside the high altar. The two basins with raised figures at the entrance of the church also deserve notice. The left side of the square is occupied by the episcopal palace, a building of no pretensions.

Santa Theresia is a small church, containing nothing remarkable except a splendid bas-relief in marble, representing the Holy Family, which an Englishman once offered to purchase for an immense sum. The neighbouring church of St. Pieta, on the contrary, can be called large and grand. The façades are ornamented with pillars of marble, the altar is richly gilt, and handsome frescoes deck the ceiling. St. Domenigo, another fine church, possesses, my cicerone assured me, the largest organ in the world. If he had said the greatest he had seen, I could readily have believed him.

In St. Ignazio, or Olivazo, near a minor altar at one side, we find a painting representing the Virgin and the infant Jesus. The sacristan persisted that this was a work of Raphael's. The colouring appeared to me not quite to resemble that of the great master, but I understand too little of these things to be able to judge on such a subject. At any rate it is a fine piece. A few steps below the church lies the oratory, which nearly equals it in size, and also contains a handsome painting over the altar. "St. Augustine" also repays the trouble of a visit; it displays great wealth in marble, sculptures, frescoes, and arabesques. "St. Joseph" is also rich in various kinds of marble. Several of its large columns have been made from a single block. A clear cold stream issues from this church.

I have still to notice the lovely public gardens, which I visited after dining with the consul-general, Herr Wallenburg. I cannot omit this opportunity of gratefully mentioning the friendly sympathy and kindness I experienced on the part of this gentleman and his lady. To return to the gardens,—the most interesting to me was the botanical, where a number of rare trees and plants flourish famously in the open air.

The catacombs of the Augustine convent are most peculiar; they are situate immediately outside the town. From the church, which offers nothing of remarkable interest, a broad flight of stairs leads downwards into long and lofty passages cut in the rock, and receiving light from above. The skeletons of the dead line the walls, in little niches close beside each other; they are clothed in a kind of monkish robe, and each man's hands are crossed on his chest, with a ticket bearing his name, age, and the date of his death depending therefrom. A more horrible sight can scarcely be imagined than these dressed-up skeletons and death's-heads. Many have still hair on the scalp, and some even beard. The niches in which they stand are surmounted by planks displaying skulls and bones, and the corridors are crowded with whole rows of coffins, their inmates waiting for a vacant place. If the relations of one of the favoured skeletons neglect to supply a certain number of wax-tapers on All-Saints' day, the poor man is banished from his position, and one of the candidates steps in and occupies his niche.

The corpses of women and girls are deposited in another compartment, and look as though they were lying in state in their glass coffins, dressed in handsome silks, with ornamental coifs on their heads, ruffs and lace collars round their necks, and silk shoes and stockings, which however soon burst, on their feet. A wreath of flowers decks the brow of each girl, and beneath all this ornament the skull appears with its hollow eyes—a parody upon life and death.

Whenever any one wishes to be immortalised in this way, his friends and relations must pay a certain sum for a place on the day of his burial, and afterwards bring wax-tapers every year. The body is then laid in a chamber of lime, which remains for eight months hermetically closed, until the flesh has been entirely eaten away; then the bones are fastened together, dressed, and placed in a niche.

On All-Saints' day these corridors of death are crowded with gazers; friends and relations of the deceased resort thither to light candles and perform their devotions. I was glad to have had an opportunity of seeing these audience-halls of the dead, but still I rejoiced when I hastened upwards to sojourn once more among the living.

From here I drove to Olivuzza, to view the Moorish castle of Ziza, celebrated for the beauty of its situation and of the region around. Not far from the old castle stands a new one, with a garden of much beauty, containing also a number of fantastic toys, such as little grottoes and huts, hollow trees in which secret doors fly suddenly open, disclosing to view a nun, a monk, or some figure of the kind, etc. Here I still found a species of date-tree growing in the open air; but the fruit it bears is very small, and never becomes completely ripe: this was the last date-tree I saw.

The royal villa "Favourite," about a mile from the town, is situated in a lovely spot. It is built in the Chinese style, with a quantity of points, gables, and little bells; its interior is, however, arranged according to European design, in a rich, tasteful, and artistic manner. We linger with pleasure in the rooms, each of which offers some attractive feature. Thus, for instance, one apartment contains beautiful fresco paintings; another, life-size portraits of the royal family in Chinese costume; in a third, the effects of damp on walls and ceiling are so accurately portrayed that at first I was deceived by the resemblance, and regretted to find a room in such a condition among all the pomp and splendour around. One small cabinet is entirely inlaid with little pieces of all the various kinds of marble that are to be found in Sicily. The large tables are made of petrified and polished woods, etc. Besides these minor attractions, a much greater one exists in the splendid view which we obtain from the terraces and from the summit of the Chinese tower. I found it difficult to tear myself from contemplating this charming prospect; a painter would become embarrassed by the very richness of the materials around him. Every thing I had seen from on board here appeared before my eyes with increased loveliness, because I here saw it from a higher position, and obtained a more extended view.

An ornamental garden lies close to the palace. It is flagged with large blocks of stone, between which spaces are left for earth. These beds are parcelled out according to plans, bordered with box a foot in height, and arranged so as to form immense leaves, flowers, and arabesques; while in the midst stand vases of natural flowers. The park fills up the background; it consists merely of a few avenues and meadows, extending to the foot of Mount Rosalia.

This mountain I also ascended. The finest paved street, which is sufficiently broad for three carriages to pass each other, winds in a serpentine manner round the rocky heights, so that we can mount upwards without the slightest difficulty.

The convent is small and very simply constructed; the courtyard behind it, on the contrary, is exceedingly imposing. It is shut in on all sides by steep walls of rock, covered with clinging ivy in a most picturesque manner. On the left we find a little grotto containing an altar. In the foreground, on the right, a lofty gate, formed by nature and beautified by art, leads into a chapel wonderfully formed of pieces of rock and stalactites. A feeling of astonishment and admiration almost amounting to awe came upon me as I entered. The walls near the chief altar are overgrown with a kind of delicate moss of an emerald-green colour, with the white rock shining through here and there; and in the midst rises a natural cupola, terminating in a point. The extreme summit of this dome cannot be distinguished; it is lost in obscurity. Here and there natural niches occur, in which statues of saints have been placed. To the left of the high altar I saw the monument of St. Rosalia, beautifully executed in white marble. She is represented in a recumbent posture, the size of life; the statue rests on a pedestal two feet in height. In the most highly-decorated or the most gorgeous church I could not have felt myself more irresistibly impelled to devotion than in this grand temple of nature.

From the 15th to the 18th of July in every year a great feast is held in honour of St. Rosalia, the patron saint of the city, in the town and on the mountain. On these days a number of people make a pilgrimage to the grotto above described, where the bones of the saint were found at a time when the plague was raging at Palermo. They were carried with great pomp into the town, and from that moment the plague ceased.

The road from the convent to the temple, built on the summit of a rock, and visible to the sailors from a great distance, leads us for about half a mile over loose stones. Its construction is extremely simple, and not remarkable in any way. In former times its summit was decked by a colossal statue of the saint. This fell down, and the head alone remained unmutilated. Like the statue, the fane is now in ruins, and its site is only visited for the sake of the beautiful view.

On our way back to the convent, my guide drew my attention to a spot where a large tree had stood. Some years before, a family was sitting quietly beneath its shade, partaking of a frugal meal, when the tree suddenly came crashing down, and caused the death of four persons.

The excursion to St. Rosalia's Hill can easily be made in four or five hours. It is usual to ride up the mountain on donkeys; these animals are, however, so sluggish, compared with those of Egypt, that I often preferred dismounting and proceeding on foot. The Neapolitan donkeys are just as lazy.

I wished still to visit Bagaria, the summer residence of many of the townspeople. One morning I drove to this lovely spot in the company of an amiable Swiss family. The distance from Palermo is about two miles and a half, and the road frequently winding close to the sea, presents a rich variety of beautiful pictures.

We went to view the palace of Prince Fascello: the proprietor appears, however, seldom to reside here, for every thing wears an air of neglect. Two halls in this building are worthy of notice; the walls of the smaller one are covered with figures and ornaments, beautifully carved in wood, with pieces of mirror glass placed between them. The vaulted ceiling is also decorated with mirrors, some of which are unfortunately already broken. The walls of the larger hall are completely lined with the finest Sicilian marble. Above the cornices the marble has been covered with thin glass, which gives it a peculiar appearance of polish. The immense ceiling of the great hall is vaulted like that of the smaller one, and completely covered with mirrors, all of them in good preservation. Both apartments, but particularly the large one, are said to have a magical effect when lighted up with tapers.

I spent a Sunday in Palermo, and was much pleased at seeing the peasants in their festive garb, in which, however, I could discover nothing handsome; nor, indeed, any thing peculiar, save the long pendent nightcaps. The men wear jackets and breeches, and have the before-mentioned caps on their heads; the dress of the women is a spencer, a petticoat, and a kerchief of white or coloured linen round the head and neck.

The common people appeared to be neither cleanly nor wealthy. The rich are dressed according to the fashions of London, Paris, and Vienna.

In all the Sicilian towns I found the mob more boisterous and impudent than in the East, and frequently it was my lot to witness most diabolical quarrels and fights. It is necessary to be much more on one's guard against theft and roguery among these people than among the Arabs and Bedouins. Now I acknowledge how falsely I had judged the poor denizens of the East when I took them for the most thievish of tribes. The people here and at Naples were far worse than they. I was doubly pained on making this discovery, from the fact that I saw more fasting and praying, and more clergymen in these countries than any where else. To judge from appearances, I should have taken the Sicilians and Neapolitans for the most pious people in the world. But their behaviour towards strangers is rude in the extreme. Never had I been so impudently stared out of countenance as in these Sicilian towns: fingers were pointed at me amidst roars of laughter; the boys even ran after me and jeered at me—and all because I wore a round straw hat. In Messina I threw this article away, and dressed according to the fashion which prevails here and in my own country; but still the gaping did not cease. In Palermo it was not only the street boys who stood still to gaze at me, the grandees also did me the same honour, whether I drove or walked. I once asked a lady the reason of this, and requested to know if my appearance was calculated either to give offence or to excite ridicule; she replied that neither was the case, but that the only thing the citizens remarked in me was that I went about alone with a servant. In Sicily this was quite an uncommon circumstance, for there I always saw two ladies walking together, or a lady and gentleman. Now the grand mystery was solved; but notwithstanding this, I did not alter my mode of action, but continued to walk quietly about the town with my servant, for I preferred being laughed at a little to giving any one the trouble of accompanying me about every where. At first this staring made me very uncomfortable; but man can adapt himself to every thing, and I am no exception to the rule.

The vegetation in Sicily is eminent for its luxuriant loveliness. Flowers, plants, and shrubs attain a greater height and magnitude than we find elsewhere. I saw here numerous species of aloes, which we cultivate laboriously in hot-houses, growing wild, or planted as hedges around gardens. The stems, from which blossoms burst forth, often attain a height of from twenty to thirty feet. Their flowering season was already past. October 10th.

After a sojourn of five days I bade farewell to Palermo, and took my departure in wet weather. This was the first rain I had seen fall since the 20th of April. The temperature remained very warm; on fine days the thermometer still stood at 20° or 22° Reaumur in the sun at noon.

The vessel on which I now embarked was a royal mail-steamer. We left Palermo at noon; towards evening the sea became rather rough, so that the spray dashed over me once or twice, although I continually kept near the steersman.

At the commencement of our journey nothing was to be seen but sky and water. But the next day, as we approached the Neapolitan coast, island after island rose from the sea, and at length the mainland itself could be discerned. Capri was the first island we approached closely. Soon afterwards my attention was drawn to a great cloud rising towards the sky; it was a smoky column from the glowing hearth of Vesuvius. At length a white line glittered on the verge of the horizon, like a band through the clear air. There was a joyful cry of "Napoli! Napoli!" and Naples lay spread before me.

## CHAPTER XIX.

My imagination was so powerfully excited, I may say over-excited, by the accounts I had heard and read concerning this fairy city, that here once more my expectations were far from being realised. This was, perhaps, partly owing to the circumstance that I had already seen Constantinople and had just quitted Palermo, the situation of which latter town had so enchanted me that my enthusiasm was here confined within very narrow bounds, and I felt inclined to prefer Palermo to Naples.

At two o'clock in the afternoon I landed, and the kind assistance of Herr Brettschneider at once procured me an excellent room in Santa Lucia, with a prospect of the harbour and the bay, besides a view of Vesuvius and the region surrounding it. As usual, I wished to commence my researches at once; but already in Palermo I had felt an unceasing pain in my side, so that my last walks there had been attended with considerable difficulty.

Here I became really ill, and was unable to quit my room. I had a boil on my back, which required the care of the surgeon, and kept me in my room for a fortnight, until the fever had abated.

If this misfortune had happened to me in the East, or even while I was in quarantine at Malta, who knows whether I should not have been looked upon as having a "plague-boil," and shut up for forty days?

During my imprisonment here, my only relaxation during the hours when I was free from fever and it did not rain, was to sit on the balcony, contemplating the beautiful prospect, and looking on the bustling, lively populace. The Neapolitans appeared to me very ill-behaved, boisterous, and quarrelsome, and seemed to entertain a great horror of work. The latter circumstance seems natural enough, for they require little for their daily support, and we hardly find that the common people any where work more than is necessary to shield them from immediate want; this is particularly the case in Italy, where the heat is oppressive during the day, and the temperature of the evening so agreeable, every one wishes to enjoy himself rather than to work.

I sometimes saw men employ themselves for half a day together in pushing bullets with a little stick through a ring fastened to the ground: this is one of the most popular games. The women are always sitting or standing in front of the houses, chattering or quarrelling; and the children lie about in the streets all day long. The veriest trifle suffices to breed a quarrel among old or young, and then they kick one another with their feet—a very graceful practice for women or girls! Even with their knives they are ready on all occasions.

For making observations on the Neapolitans no better post can be chosen than a lodging in the quarter St. Lucia. The fishermen, lazzaroni, and sailors live in the little side lanes, and spend the greater part of the day in the large street of St. Lucia, the chief resort both for pedestrians and people on horse-back and in carriages. In and about the harbour we find numerous vendors of oysters and crabs, which they bring fresh from the sea. The lazzaroni no longer go about half naked, and the common people are dressed in a decent though not in a picturesque manner.

Here a number of handsome equipages rolled by; their lady occupants were very fashionably attired.

Even among the better classes it is usual for the men to purchase all the household necessaries, such as fish, bread, poultry, etc. Poultry is very much eaten in Italy, particularly turkeys, which are sometimes sold ready cut up, according to weight. On Sundays and holydays the shops containing wares and provisions, and the meat and poultry stalls, are opened in the same way as on a week-day. Throughout all Italy we do not see them closed for the observance of a Sunday or holyday.

On the fifteenth day I had so far recovered that I could begin my tour of observation, using, however, certain precautions.

At first I confined my researches to churches, palaces, and the museum,

189

particularly as the weather was unprecedentedly bad. It rained, or rather poured, almost every day, and in these cases the water rushes in streams out of the by-lanes towards the sea. The greater part of Naples is built on an acclivity, and there are no gutters, so that the water must force its way along the streets: this has its peculiar advantages; for the side-lanes, which are filthy beyond description, thus get a partial cleansing by the stream.

As I am not a connoisseur, it would be foolish in me to attempt a criticism upon the splendid productions of art which I beheld here, in Rome, and at Florence and other places. I can only recount what I saw.

During my excursions I generally regulated my movements according to the divisions and instructions contained in August Lewald's hand-book, a work which every traveller will find very serviceable and correct.

I began with the royal palace, which was situate near my lodging at St. Lucia, with one front facing the sea, and the other turned towards the fine large square. This building contains forty-two windows in a row. I could see nothing of its interior excepting the richly decorated chapel, as the royal family resided there during the whole time of my stay, and thus the apartments were not accessible to strangers.

Opposite the castle stands the magnificent Rotunda, called also the church of San Francesco de Paula. Adjoining this church on either side were arcades in the form of a half circle, supported by handsome pillars, beneath which several shops are established. The roof of the Rotunda is formed by a splendid cupola resting on thirty-four marble pillars. The altars, with the niches between, occupied by colossal statues, are ranged round the walls, and in some instances decorated by splendid modern paintings. A great quantity of lapis lazuli has been used in the construction of the grand altar. In the higher regions of the cupola two galleries, with tasteful iron railings, are to be seen. The entire church, and even the confessionals, are covered with a species of grey marble. The peculiar appearance of this place of worship is exceedingly calculated to excite the visitor's wonder, for to judge from its exterior he would scarcely take the splendid building before him for a church. It was built on the model of the famous rotunda at Rome; but the idea of the porticoes is taken from St. Peter's.

Two large equestrian statues of bronze form the ornaments of the square before this church. Quitting this square, we emerge into the two finest and most frequented streets in the town, namely, the Chiaga and Toledo. Not far off is the imposing theatre of St. Carlo, said to be not only the largest in Italy, but in all Europe. Its exterior aspect is very splendid. A large and broad entrance extends in front, with pillars, beneath the shelter of which the carriages drive up, so that the spectators can arrive and depart without the chance of getting wet. This evening there was to be a "particularly grand performance." I entered the theatre, and was much struck with its appearance. It contains six tiers, all parcelled off into boxes, of which I counted four-and-twenty on the grand circle. Each box is almost the size of a small room, and can easily accommodate from twelve to fifteen people. A fairy-like spectacle is said to be produced when, on occasions of peculiar festivity, the whole exterior is lighted up. Here, as in nearly all the Italian theatres, a clock, shewing not only the hours but the minutes, is fixed over the front of the stage. A "particular performance" commences at six o'clock, and usually terminates an hour or two before midnight. This evening I saw a little ballet, then two acts of an opera, and afterwards a comedy, the whole concluding with a grand ballet. It is usual on benefit-nights to give a great variety of entertainments in order to attract the public; on these occasions the prices are also reduced one-fifth.

The greatest square, Largo del Castello, almost adjoins the theatre; it is of an oblong form, and contains many palace-like buildings, including the finance and police offices. A pretty spring, the water of which falls down some rocks and forms a cascade, is also worthy of mention.

A little to the left we come upon the Medina-square, boasting the finest fountain in Naples. Between these two squares, beside the sea-shore, lies Castel Nuovo, said to be built quite in the form of the Bastille. It is strongly fortified, and serves as a defence for the harbour. This is a very lively neighbourhood. Many an hour's amusement have I had, watching the motley crowd, particularly on Sundays and holydays, when it is frequented by improvisators, singers, musicians, and mountebanks of every description. Not far from the harbour is a long street in which numerous kitchens and many provision-stalls are established. Here I walked in the evenings to see the people assembled round the macaroni-pots: it is advisable, however, to leave watch and purse at home, and even one's pocket-handkerchief is not safe.

Of the shouting and crowding here no conception can be formed. Large kettles are placed in front of the shops, and the proprietors sit beside them, plunging a great wooden fork and spoon into the cauldron to fill the plates of expectant customers. Some eat their favourite dish with fat and cheese, others without, according to the state of their exchequer for the time being; but one and all eat with their fingers. The army of hungry mortals seems innumerable; and during feeding-time the stranger finds no little difficulty in forcing a passage, notwithstanding the breadth of the street. Not far from this thoroughfare of the people two "Punchinellos" are erected. In one of these the Marionettes are a foot and a half, and in the other no less than three feet high.

There is, besides, a theatre for the people, where pieces of tragic and comic character are performed, in all of which the clown plays a prominent part. The remaining theatres, the Nuovo, the Carlini, and others, are about the size of those in the Leopold- and Josephstadt at Vienna, and can accommodate about 800 spectators. Their exteriors and interiors are alike undistinguished; but in some of them the singing and playing are very creditable. In one of these theatres we are obliged to descend instead of to ascend to reach the pit and the first tier of boxes.

Naples contains more than three hundred churches and chapels. I visited a number of them, for I entered every church that came in my way. St. Fernando, a church of no great size, but of very pleasing appearance, struck me particularly. The ceiling of this edifice is covered with frescoes, and the walls enriched with marble. At the two side altars we find a pair of very fine half-length pictures of saints.

St. Jesu Nuovo, another exceedingly handsome church, stands on the borders of the Lago Maggiore, and is full of magnificent frescoes, surrounded by arabesque borders. The latter appear as though they were gilded, and the effect thus produced is remarkably fine. This spacious building contains a number of small chapels, partitioned off by massive gratings. The great cupola is exceedingly handsome, and every chapel boasts a separate one.

St. Jesu Maggiore does not carry out its appellation, for it is a small unpretending church, though some splendid gothic ornaments beautify the exterior.

St. Maria di Piedigrotta, another little church, is much frequented, from the fact that the common people place great confidence in the picture of the Virgin there displayed. The church contains nothing worthy of notice.

The grotto of Pausilipp, a cavern of immense length, now called Puzzoli, is not far distant. This grotto, hewn out of a rock, is about 1200 paces long, between 50 and 60 feet in height, and of such breadth that two carriages can easily pass each other. A little chapel cut out of the rock occupies the middle of the cavern, and both grotto and chapel are illuminated night and day. As in the whole of Naples, the pavement here is formed of lava from Mount Vesuvius.

Immediately above the grotto, in the direction of the town, we come upon a simple gravestone of white marble—the monument of the poet Virgil. A long flight of steps leads to the garden containing this monument: the poet's ashes do not, however, rest here; the spot where he sleeps cannot be accurately determined, and this monument is only raised to his memory. The prospect from these heights as well repays a visit as the grotto of Pausilipp, where we wander for a long time in deep darkness, until we suddenly emerge into the broad light of day, to find ourselves surrounded by a most lovely landscape.

The public garden of Naples is also situate in this quarter of the town. It extends to the lower portion of the Strada Chiaga, is of great length without being broad, and displays a vast number of beautiful statues, prospects, and rare plants; a large and handsome street, containing many fine houses, adjoins it on one side. I also rode to the Vomero, on which are erected the king's pleasure-palace and a small convent. A glorious prospect here unfolds itself: Naples with its bay, Puzzoli, and a number of beautiful islands, the lake Agnaro, the extinct craters of Solfatara, Baiæ, Vesuvius with its chain of mountains, and the stupendous ocean, lie grouped, in varied forms and gorgeously blending colours, before the gaze of the astonished spectator. This is the place of which the Neapolitans say, with some justice, "Hither should men come, and gaze, and die!"

Still the prospects from St. Rosalia's Mount, and from the royal palace Favorita at Palermo, had pleased me better; for there the beauties of nature are more crowded together, are nearer to the spectator: he can obtain a more complete view of them, while in varied gorgeousness they do not yield the palm even to the fairy pictures of Naples.

I more than once spent half a day in the Academy "degli Studii," for in this place much was to be seen. The entrance to the building is indescribably beautiful; both the portico and the handsome staircases are ornamented with statues and busts executed in most artistic style. A door on the right leads us to a hall in which the paintings from Pompeii and Herculaneum are displayed; several of these relics have no small pretensions to beauty, and the colours of almost all are still wonderfully bright and fresh. In the great hall at the end of the courtyard we find on one side the Farnese Hercules, and on the other the Bull, both works of the Athenian Glycon. These two antiques, particularly the latter, have been in a great measure restored.

The gallery of great bronzes is considered the first in the world, for here we find united the finest works of ancient times. So many beautiful creations of art were here brought together, that if I attempted a description of them I should not know where to begin.

Opposite the gallery of bronzes is that allotted to the marbles, among which a beautiful Venus stands prominently forth.

In the gallery of Flora, a statue of the same goddess, called the Farnese, is also the principal attraction.

A statue of Apollo playing on the lyre, of porphyry, is the greatest masterpiece in the hall of coloured marbles; while in the gallery of the Muses a basin of Athenian porphyry occupies the first place.

In the Adonis room the beautiful Venus Anadyomene engrossed my chief attention; and in the cabinet of Venus the Venus Callipygos forms an exquisite sidepiece to the Venus de Medicis.

The upper regions of this splendid building contain an extensive library and a picture-gallery.

I also paid a visit to the catacombs of St. Januarius, which extend three stories high on a mountain, and are full of little niches, five or six of which are often found one above the other.

In the chapel Santa Maria della Pieta, in the palace St. Severino, I admired three of the finest and most valuable marble statues that can be found any where; I mean, "Veiled Innocence," "Malice in a Net," and a veiled recumbent figure of Christ. All three are by the sculptor Bernini.

The largest church in the town is the cathedral dedicated to St. Januarius. This structure rests on a hundred and ten columns of Egyptian and African granite, standing three by three, embedded in the walls. The church has not a very imposing appearance. The chief altar, beneath which the body of St. Januarius is deposited, is ornamented with many kinds of valuable marble. Here I saw a great number of pictures, most of them of considerable merit. The chapel of St. Januarius, also called the "chapel of the treasure," is one of the most gorgeous shrines that can be conceived. The Neapolitans built it as a thank-offering at the cessation of a plague. The cost was above a million of ducats, and the wealth of this chapel is greater than that of any church in Christendom. It is built in a circular form, and all the resources of art have been lavished on the decoration of the chief altar. Every spot is covered with treasures and works of art, and the roof is supported by forty-two Corinthian pillars of dark-red stone. All the decorations of the high altar, the immense candelabra and massive flower-vases, are of silver. At a grand festival, when every thing is richly illuminated, the appearance of this chapel must be gorgeous in the extreme. The head and two bottles of the blood of St. Januarius are preserved here; the people assert that this blood liquefies every year. The frescoes on the ceiling are splendidly painted; and on the square before the church is to be seen an obelisk surmounted by a statue of St. Januarius.

St. Jeronimo has an imposing appearance when one first enters. The whole roof of this church as far downwards as the pillars is covered with beautiful arabesques and figures. It also contains some fine paintings, and is, besides, renowned for its architecture.

St. Paula Maggiore, another spacious church, is well worth seeing on account of its magnificent arabesques and fresco-paintings; besides these it also contains some handsome monuments and statues of marble. Two very ancient pillars stand in front of this church.

St. Chiara, a fine large church, offers some fine monuments and oil-paintings.

Among the excursions in the neighbourhood of Naples, that to Puzzoli is certainly the most interesting. After passing through the great grotto, we reach the ancient and rather important town of Puzzoli, with 8000 inhabitants. Cicero called this place a little Rome. In the centre of the town stands the church of St. Proculus, which was converted from a heathen into a Christian temple, and is surrounded by fine-looking Corinthian pillars.

Remarkable beyond all else is the ruined temple of Seropis. Almost the entire magnitude and arrangement of this magnificent building can yet be discerned. A few of the pillars that once supported the cupola are still erect, and several of the cells, which surrounded the temple and were once used as baths, can still be seen. Every thing here is of fine white marble. The greater portion of the ruin was dismantled, to be used in the construction of the royal villa of Caserta.

The harbour of Puzzoli is related to have been the finest in Italy. From this place Caligula had a bridge erected to Baiæ, about 4000 paces in length. He undertook this gigantic work in consequence of a prophecy that was made to him, that he would no more become emperor than he could ride to Baiæ on horseback. This prophecy he confuted, and became emperor. Of the amphitheatre and the colosseum not a trace remains. A little chapel now occupies the site on which they stood; tradition asserts that it is built on the very spot where St. Januarius was thrown to the bears.

Not far from this chapel we are shewn the labyrinth of Dædalus; several of its winding walks still exist, through which it would be difficult to find the way without a cicerone.

We ascended the hill immediately beyond the city, on which some remains of Cicero's villa are yet to be seen: here we enjoyed a splendid prospect.

In this region we continually wander among ruins, and see every where around us the relics of the past. Thus a short walk brought us from Cicero's villa to the ruins of three temples—those of Diana, Venus, and Mercury. Of the first, one side and a few little cells, called the "baths of Venus," alone remain. Part of Venus's temple stands in the rotunda. It was built on acoustic principles, so that any one who puts his ear to a certain part of the wall can hear what is whispered at the opposite extremity. A few fragments of the rotunda were the only trace left of the temple of Diana.

The vapour baths of Nero, hewn out of the rock, consist of several passages, into which it is impossible to penetrate far on account of the heat. A boy ran to the spring and brought us some boiling water; he returned from his expedition fiery red in the face, and covered with perspiration. These poor lads are accustomed to remain at the spring until they have succeeded in boiling some eggs; but I would not allow any such cruelty, and did not even wish them to fetch me the water, but Herr Brettschneider would have it so in spite of me.

From this place we crossed by sea to Baiæ, where at one time many of the rich people had their villas. Their proceedings here are said, however, to have been of so immoral a character, that at length it was considered wrong to have resided here any time. Every visitor must be enchanted with the fertility of this region, and with its lovely aspect. A castle, now used as a barrack for veterans, crowns the summit of a rock which stands prominently forth. A few unimportant traces can still be here discovered of an ancient temple of Hercules. Some masonry, in the form of a monument, marks the alleged spot where Agrippina was murdered and buried by order of her son.

The immense reservoir built by order of the emperor Augustus for the purpose of supplying the fleet with fresh water, is situate in the neighbourhood of Baiæ; it is called Piscina. This giant structure contains several large chambers, their roofs supported by numerous columns. To view this reservoir we are compelled to descend a flight of steps.

Not far from the before-mentioned building we come upon the "Cento Camarelle," a prison consisting of a multitude of small cells.

On our way back we visited Solfatara, the celebrated crater plain, about 1000 feet in length by 800 in breadth, skirted by hills. Its volcanic power is not yet wholly extinct; in several places brimstone-fumes (whence the plain derives its name,) are still seen rising into the air, which they impregnate with a most noxious odour. On striking the ground with a stick a sound is produced, from which we can judge that the whole space beneath us is hollow. This excursion is a very disagreeable one; we are continually marching across a mere crust of earth, which may give way any moment. I found here a manufactory of brimstone and alum. A little church belonging to the Capuchins, where we are shewn a stone on which St. Januarius was decapitated after the bears had refused to tear him to pieces, stands on a hill near the Solfatara.

Towards evening we reached the "Dog's Grotto." A huntsman from the royal preserve Astroni accompanied us, and fetched the man who keeps the keys of the grotto. This functionary soon appeared with a couple of dogs, to furnish us with a practical illustration of the convulsions caused by the foul air of the cavern. But I declined the experiment, and contented myself with viewing the grotto. It is of small extent, about eight or ten feet long, not more than five in breadth, and six or eight high. I entered the cave, and so long as I remained erect felt no inconvenience. So soon as I bent towards the ground, however, and the lower stratum of air blew upon my face, I experienced a most horrible choking sensation.

After we had satisfied our curiosity the huntsman led us to the neighbouring hunting-lodge, and to a little lake where a number of ducks are fattened. This man spoke of another and a much more remarkable grotto, of which he possessed the keys, and which he should have great pleasure in shewing us. Though twilight was rapidly approaching we determined to go, as the place was not far off. The man opened the door, and invited us to enter the cavern, advising us at the same time to bend down open-mouthed, as we had done in the Dog's Grotto, and at the same time to fan the air upwards with our hands, that we might the better inhale it,—a proceeding which he asserted to be peculiarly good for the digestive organs. His eloquence was so powerful, that we could not help suspecting the man; and it struck us as very strange that he was so particularly anxious we should enter the cavern together. This, therefore, we refused to do; and

Herr Brettschneider remained outside with our guide, while I entered alone and did as he had directed. Though the lower stratum of air in the Dog's Grotto had been highly mephitic, the atmosphere here was more stifling still. I rushed forth with the speed of lightning; and now we clearly saw through the fellow's intention. If Herr Brettschneider and myself had entered together, he would undoubtedly have shut the door, and we should have been stifled in a few moments. We did not allow him to notice our suspicions, but merely said that we could not spend any more time here to-day on account of the lateness of the hour. Our worthy friend accompanied us through a wild and gloomy region, with his gun on his shoulder; and I was not a little afraid of him, for he kept talking about his honesty and the good intentions he had towards us. We kept, however, close beside him, and watched him narrowly, without betraying any symptom of apprehension; and at length, to our great relief, we gained the open road.

The royal villa of Portici lies about four "miglia" from Naples, and we made an excursion thither by railway. Both the palace and the gardens are handsome, and of considerable size. Thence we proceeded to Resina. Portici and Resina are so closely connected together by villas and houses, that a stranger would take them for one place. Beneath Resina lies Herculaneum, a city destroyed seventy-nine years after the birth of our Saviour. In the year 1689 a marquis caused a well to be dug in his garden, when, at a depth of sixty-five feet, the labourers came upon fragments of marble with divers inscriptions. It was not until 1720 that systematic excavations were made. Even then great caution was necessary, as Resina is unfortunately built upon Herculaneum, and the safety of the houses became endangered.

At Resina we procured torches and a guide, and descended to view the subterranean city. We saw the theatre, a number of houses, several temples, and the forum. Some fine frescoes are still to be distinguished on the walls of the apartments. The floors are covered with mosaic; but still this place does not offer nearly so many objects of interest as another which was overwhelmed at the same time—Pompeii.

Pompeii is without doubt the most remarkable city of its kind that exists. A great portion of the town is surrounded by walls, and entire rows of houses, several temples, the theatre, the forum, in short a vast number of buildings, streets, and squares lay open before us. The more I wandered through the streets and open places, the more I involuntarily wondered not to find the inhabitants and labourers employed in repairing the houses; I could hardly realise the idea that so many beautiful houses and well preserved apartments should be untenanted. The deserted aspect of this town had a very melancholy effect in my eyes.

Though a great portion of the town has already been dug out, only three hundred skeletons have been found,—a proof that the greater portion of the inhabitants effected their escape.

In many houses I found splendid tesselated pavements, representing flowers, wreaths, animals, and arabesques; even the halls and courtyards were decorated with a larger kind of mosaic work. The walls of the rooms are plastered over with a description of firm polished enamel, frequently looking like marble, and covered with beautiful frescoes. In Sallust's house a whole row of wine jugs still stands in the cellar. In the houses the division of the rooms, and the purposes to which the different apartments were devoted, can still be distinctly traced. In general they are very small, and the windows seldom look out upon the street. Deep ruts of carriages can be seen in the streets. All the treasures of art which could be removed, such as statues, pictures, etc., were carried off to Naples, and placed in the museum there.

VESUVIUS.

In the agreeable society of Herr M. and Madame Brettschneider, I rode away from Resina at eleven in the forenoon. A pleasant road, winding among vineyards, brought us in an hour's time to the neighbourhood of the great lava-field, Torre del Greco. It is a fearful sight to behold these grand mounds of lava towering in the most various forms around us. All traces of vegetation have vanished; far and wide we can descry nothing but hardened masses, which once rushed in molten streams down the mountain. A capitally-constructed road leads us, without the slightest fatigue, through the midst of this scene of devastation to the usual resting-place of travellers, the "Hermitage."

At this dwelling we made halt, ascended to the upper story, and called for a bottle of Lacrimæ Christi. The view here, and at several other points of our ascent, is most charming.

The hermit seems, however, to lead any thing but a solitary life, for a day seldom passes on which strangers do not call in to claim his attention in proportion as they run up a score. The clerical gentleman is, in fact, no more and no less than a very common innkeeper, and partakes of the goodly obesity frequently noticed among persons of his class. We stayed three quarters of an hour in the domicile of this hermit-host, and afterwards rode on towards the heights, along a beautiful road among fields of lava. In half an hour's time, however, we were completely shut in by lava-fields, and here the beaten track ended. We now dismounted, and continued our ascent on foot. It is difficult for one who has not seen it to picture to himself the scene that lay around us. Devastation every where; lava covering the whole region in heaps upon heaps, fantastically piled one on the other. Here a huge isolated mound rises, seemingly cut off on all sides from the lava around; there we see how a mighty stream once rushed down the mountain-side, and cooled gradually into stone. Immense chasms are filled with lava masses, which have lain here for many years cold and motionless, and will probably remain for as many more, for their fury has spent itself.

The lava is of different colours, according as it has been exposed to the atmosphere for a longer or a shorter period. The oldest lava has the hue of granite, and almost its hardness, for which reasons it is largely used for building houses and paving streets.

From the place where we left our donkeys we had to climb upwards for nearly an hour over the lava before reaching the crater. The ascent is somewhat fatiguing, as we are obliged to be very careful at every step to avoid entangling our feet among the blocks of lava; still the difficulty is not nearly so great as people make out. It is merely necessary to wear good thick boots, and then all goes extremely well. The higher we mount, the more numerous do the fissures become from which smoke bursts forth. In one of these clefts we placed some eggs, which were completely boiled in four minutes' time. Near these places the ground is so hot that we could not have stood still for many minutes; still we did not get burnt feet or any thing of the kind.

On reaching the crater we found ourselves enveloped in so thick a fog that we could not see ten paces in advance. There was nothing for it but to sit down and wait patiently until the sun could penetrate the mist and spread light and cheerfulness among us. Then we descended into the crater, and approached as closely as possible to the place from which the smoky column whirls into the air. The road was a gloomy one, for we were shut in as in a bowl, and could discern around us nothing but mountains of lava, while before us rose the huge smoky column, threatening each moment to shroud us in darkness as the wind blew it in clouds in our direction. When the ground was struck with a stick, it gave forth a hollow rumbling sound like at Solfatara. In the neighbourhood of the column of smoke we could see nothing more than at the edge from which we had climbed downwards—a peculiar picture of unparalleled devastation. The circumference of the crater seems not to have changed since the visit of Herr Lewald, who a few years ago estimated its dimensions at 5000 feet. After once more mounting to the brim, we walked round a great part of the edge of the basin.

At the particular desire of Herr M., who was well acquainted with all the remarkable points about the volcano, our guide now led the way to the so-called "hell," a little crater which formed itself it in the year 1834. To reach it we had to climb about over fields of lava for half an hour. The aspect of this hell did not strike me as particularly grand. An uneven wall of lava suddenly rose fifteen paces in advance of us, with whole strata of pure sulphur and other beautifully-coloured substances depending from its projecting angles. One of these substances was of a snowy-white colour, light, and very porous. I took a piece with me, but the next day on proceeding to pack it carefully, I found that above half had melted and become quite soft and damp, so that I was compelled to throw the whole away. The same thing happened to a mass of a red colour that I had brought away with me, and which had a beautiful effect, like glowing lava, clinging to the fissures and sides of the rocks. We held pieces of paper to the fissures in this wall, and they immediately became ignited. Herr M. then threw in a cigar, which also burst into a flame. The heat proceeding from these clefts was so great, that we could not bear to hold our hands there for an instant. At one place, near a fissure, we laid our ears to the ground, and could hear a rushing bubbling sound as though water was boiling beneath us. There was really much to see in this hell, without the discomfort of being enveloped in the offensive sulphurous smoke of the chief crater.

After staying for several hours in and about the crater we left it, and returned by the steep way over the cone of cinders. The descent here is almost perpendicular, and we could hardly escape with whole skins if it were not for the fact that we sink ankle-deep into sand and cinders at every step.

To avoid falling, it is requisite to bend the body backwards and step upon the heel. By observing this precaution, the worst that can happen to one is to sit down involuntarily once or twice, without danger to life or limb. In twelve minutes we had reached the spot where our donkeys stood. We reached Resina during the darkness of night, having spent eight hours in our excursion.

My last trip was to the Castle of Caserta, distant sixteen miglia from Naples, in the direction of Capua. It is considered one of the finest pleasure-palaces in Europe, and I was exceedingly pleased with its appearance. The building is of a square form, with a portico 507 feet long, supported by ninety-eight columns of the finest marble. The staircase and halls in the upper story alone must have cost enormous sums, as well as the chapel on the first floor, which is very rich and gorgeous. The saloons and apartments are decorated in a peculiarly splendid manner with a multiplicity of frescoes, oil-paintings, sculptures, gildings, costly silk-hangings, marbles, etc. A pretty little theatre, with well-painted scenery, is to be found in the palace. The garden is extensive, particularly as regards length. A hill, from which a considerable stream rushes foaming over artificial rockwork into the deeper recesses of the garden, rises at its extremity. Scarcely has this river sunk to rest, flowing slowly and majestically through a bed formed of large square stones, before it is compelled to form another cascade, and another, and one more, until it almost reaches the castle, near which a large basin has been constructed, from whence the water is led into the town. Seen from the portico, these waterfalls have a lovely appearance. From Caserta we drove ten miles farther on to the celebrated aqueduct which supplies the whole of Naples with water. It is truly a marvellous work. Over three stupendous arched ways, one above the other, the necessary quantity of water flows into the city.

This was my last excursion; on the following day, the 7th of November, at three in the morning, I left Naples. Apart from the delightful reminiscences of lovely natural scenes, I shall always think with pleasure on my sojourn in Naples in connexion with Herr Brettschneider and his lady. I was a complete stranger to them when I delivered my note of introduction, and yet they at once welcomed me as kindly and heartily as though I had belonged to their family. How many hours, and even days, did they not devote to me, to accompany me sometimes to one place, sometimes to another; how eagerly did they seek to shew me all the riches of nature and art displayed in this favoured city! I was truly proud and delighted at having found such friends; and once more do I offer them my sincere thanks.

## CHAPTER XX.

November 7th.

I travelled by the mail-carriage. By seven in the morning we were at Caserta, and an hour later at Capua, a pretty bustling town on the banks of a river. Our road was most picturesque; we drove among vineyards and gardens through the midst of a lovely plain. On the right were mountains, increasing in number as we proceeded, and imparting a rich variety to the landscape. At noon we halted before a lovely inn. From this point the country increases in beauty at every step. The heights are strikingly fertile, and in the valley an excellent road winds amid pleasant gardens. The mountains frequently seem to approach as though about to form an impenetrable pass; while ruins crown the summits of the rocks, and give a romantic appearance to the whole. At about three o'clock we reached the little town of Jeromania, lying in the midst of vegetable-gardens. Above this town the handsome convent of Monte Cassino stands on a rock, and in its neighbourhood we notice the ruins of an amphitheatre.

To-day the weather was not in the least Italian, being, on the contrary, gloomy and rough, as we generally find it in Austria at the same season of the year. Yesterday it was so cold at Naples that Mount Vesuvius was covered with snow during several hours.

The dress of the peasants in these regions is of a more national character than I had yet found it. The women wear short and scanty petticoats of blue or red cloth, tight-fitting bodices, and gaily-striped aprons. Their head-dress consists of a white handkerchief, with a second above it folded in a square form. The men look like robbers; with their long dark-blue or brown cloaks, in which they wrap themselves so closely that it is difficult to get a glimpse of their faces, and their steeple-crowned black hats, they quite resemble the pictures of the bandits in the Abruzzi. They glide about in so spectral a manner, and eye travellers with such a sinister look, that I almost became uncomfortable.

From Jeromania we had still a few miles to travel until we entered the Roman territory near Ceprano.

In Naples, and in fact throughout the whole of Italy, the passports are continually called for,—a great annoyance to the traveller. In the course of to-day my passport was "visé" five times, making once in every little town through which we had passed.

It was our fortune at Ceprano to lodge with a very cheating host. In the evening, when I inquired the price of a bedroom and breakfast, they told me a bed would cost two pauls, and breakfast half a paul; but when I came to pay, the host asked three pauls for my bed-room, and another for a cup of the worst coffee I have ever drunk; and the whole company was subjected to the same extortion. We expostulated and complained, but were at length compelled to comply with the demand.

November 8th.

The landscape remains the same, but the appearance of the towns and villages is not nearly so neat and pretty as in the Neapolitan domain. The costume of the peasants is like that worn by the people whom we met yesterday, excepting that the women have a stiff stomacher, fastened with a red lace, instead of the spencer. The dress of the men consists of short knee-breeches, brown stockings, heavy shoes, and a jacket of some dark colour. Some wear, in addition to this, a red waistcoat, and a green sash round the waist. All wear the conical hat. In cold weather the dark bandit's cloak is also seen.

ROME.

As we approach Rome the country becomes more and more barren; the mountains recede, and the extended plains have a desert, uncultivated look. Towns and villages become so thinly scattered, that it seems as though the whole region were depopulated. The road is rather narrow, and as the country is in many places exceedingly marshy, a great portion of it has been paved. For many miles before we enter Rome we do not pass a single town or village. At length, some three hours before we reach the city, the dome of St. Peter's is seen looming in the distance; one church after another appears, and at length the whole city lies spread before us.

Many ruins of aqueducts and buildings of every kind shewed at every step what treasures of the past here awaited us. I was particularly pleased with the old town-gate Lateran, by which we entered.

It was already quite dark when we reached the Dogana. I at once betook myself to my room and retired to rest.

I remained a fortnight at Rome, and walked about the streets from morning till night. I visited St. Peter's almost every day, and went to the Vatican several times.

All the squares in Rome (and there are a great many) are decorated with fountains, and still more frequently with obelisks. The finest is the Piazza del Popolo. To the right rises the terrace-hill Picino, rich in pillars, statues, fountains, and other ornaments,—a favourite walk of the citizens. On this hill, which is arranged after the manner of a beautiful garden, we have a splendid view. The city of Rome here appears to much greater advantage than when we approach it from the direction of Naples. We can see the whole town at one glance, with the yellow Tiber flowing through the midst, and a vast plain all around. The background is closed by beautiful mountain-ranges, with villas, little towns, and cottages on the declivities. But I missed one feature, to which I had become so accustomed that the most beautiful view appeared incomplete without it—the sea. To make up for this drawback, we here encounter wherever we walk such a number of ruins, that we soon become forgetful of all around us, and live only in the past.

The Piazza del Popolo forms the termination of the three principal streets in Rome; on the largest and finest of these, the Corso, many palaces are to be seen.

The splendid post-office, of white marble, rises on the Colonna square. Two clocks are erected on this building; one with our dial, one with the Italian. At night both are illuminated,—a very useful as well as an ornamental arrangement. The ancient column of Antoninus also stands in this square.

The façade of the Dogana boasts some pillars from the temple of Antonius Pius.

The objects I have just enumerated struck me particularly as I wended my way to St. Peter's. I cannot describe how deeply I was impressed by the sight of this colossal structure. I need only state the fact, that on the first day I entered the cathedral at nine in the morning, and did not emerge from its gates until three in the afternoon.

I sat down before the pictures in mosaic, underneath the huge dome and the canopy; then I stood before the statues and monuments, and could only gaze in wonder at every thing.

The expense of building and decorating this church is said to have amounted to 45,852,000 dollars. It occupies the site of Nero's circus. Two arcades, with four rows of pillars and ninety-six statues, surround the square leading to the church.

The façade of St. Peter's is decorated with Corinthian pillars, and on its parapet stand statues fifty-two feet in height.

The entrance is so crowded with statues, carved work, and gilding, that several hours may be spent in examining its wonders. The traveller's attention is particularly attracted by the gigantic gates of bronze.

I cannot adequately describe the splendour of the interior, nor have I seen any thing with which I could compare it.

The most beautiful mosaics, monuments, statues, carvings in bronze, gilded ornaments, in short every thing that art can produce, are here to be found in the highest perfection. Oil-paintings alone are excluded. Every thing here is in mosaic; even the cupola displays mosaic work instead of the usual fresco-paintings. Immense statues of white marble occupy the niches.

Beneath the cupola, the finest portion of the building, stands the great altar, at which none but the Pope may read mass. Over this altar extends a giant canopy of bronze, with spiral pillars richly decorated with arabesques. The weight of metal used in its construction was 186,392 pounds, and the cost of the gold for gilding was 40,000 dollars; the entire canopy is worth above 150,000 dollars. The cupola was executed by Michael Angelo; it rests on four massive pillars, each of them furnished with a balcony. In the interior of these pillars chapels are constructed, where the chief relics are kept, and only displayed to the people from the balcony at particular times. I was in the church at the time when the handkerchief which wiped the drops of agony from our Lord's brow, and a piece of the true cross, were shewn.

The pulpit stands in a very elevated position, and was executed in bronze by Bernini; 219,161 pounds of metal, and 172,000 dollars, were spent upon its construction. In the interior is concealed the wooden pulpit from which St. Peter preached; and immediately beside this we find a pillar of white marble, said to have belonged to Solomon's temple at Jerusalem.

The lions on the monument of Clement XIII., by Canova, are considered the finest that were ever sculptured.

I was fortunate enough to penetrate into the catacombs of St. Peter's, a favour which women rarely obtain, and which I only owed to my having been a pilgrimage to Jerusalem. These catacombs consist of handsome passages and pillars of masonry, which do not, however, exceed eight or nine feet in height. A number of sarcophagi, containing the remains of emperors and popes, are here deposited.

The roof of St. Peter's covers an immense area, and is divided into a number of cupolas, chambers, and buildings. A fountain of running water is even found here. From this roof we have a splendid view as far as the sea and the Apennines; we can descry the entire Vatican, which adjoins the church, as well as the Pope's gardens.

I ascended to the ball in the great cupola, where there is nothing to be seen, as there is not the slightest opening, much less a window, left in it. Nothing is to be gained by mounting into this dark narrow receptacle but the glory of being able to say, "I have been there!" It is far more interesting to look down from the windows and galleries of the great cupola into the body of the church itself; for then we can estimate the grandeur of the colossal building, and the people who walk about beneath appear like dwarfs.

Two noble fountains deck the square in front of St. Peter's, and in the midst towers a magnificent obelisk from Heliopolis, said to weigh 992,789 pounds. Near this obelisk are two slabs, by standing on either of which we can see all the rows of columns melted as it were into one.

My journey to Jerusalem also obtained for me an audience of the Pope. His Holiness received me in a great hall adjoining the Sixtine Chapel. Considering his great age of seventy-eight years, the Pope has still a noble presence and most amiable manners. He asked me some questions, gave me his blessing, and permitted me at parting to kiss the embroidered slipper.

My second walk was to the Vatican. Here I saw the immense halls of Raphael, the staircases of Bramante and Bernini, and the Sixtine Chapel, containing Michael Angelo's masterpieces, the world-renowned frescoes. The immense wall behind the high altar represents the last judgment, while the ceilings are covered with prophets and sybils.

The picture-gallery contains many works of the great masters, as does also the gallery of vases and candelabra.

The Biga chamber. The biga is an antique carriage of white marble, drawn by two horses.

In the gallery of statues the figure representing Nero as Apollo playing on the lyre is the finest.

In the gallery of busts those of Menelaus and Jupiter pre-eminently attract attention.

The name of the Laocoon cabinet indicates the masterpiece it contains, as also the cabinet of the Apollo Belvidere. The latter statue was found in Nero's baths at Porto d'Anzio.

The celebrated torso of the Belvidere, a fragment of Greek art, which Michael partly used as his model, is placed in the square vestibule. Never was flesh so pliably counterfeited in stone as in this masterpiece.

A long gallery contains a series of tapestries, the designs for which were drawn by Raphael.

The Vatican contains ten thousand rooms, twenty large halls, eight large and about two hundred small staircases.

The Quirinal palace, the summer residence of the Pope, lies on the hill of the same name (Monte Cavallo), which is quite covered with villas and beautiful houses, on account of the salubrity of the air.

I visited most of the private palaces and picture-galleries. The principal are, the Colonna palace, on the Quirinal hill; and the Barberini palace, where we find a portrait of Raphael's mistress, Fornarina, painted by himself, and an original picture of Beatrice Cenci by Guidosteri.

The finest of all the Roman palaces is that of Borghese; from its form, which resembles a piano, this building has obtained the name of "il Cembalo di Borghese." The gallery contains sixteen hundred paintings, most of them masterpieces by celebrated artists.

The Farnese palace is remarkable for its architecture, and the Stoppani for its architect, Raphael. Besides these there are many other palaces. I saw but few villas, for the weather was generally bad, and it rained almost every day.

I visited the Villa Borghese on a Sunday, when there is a great bustle here; for a stream of people on foot, on horseback, and in carriages, sets in towards its beautiful park, situate just beyond the Piazza del Popolo, in the same way that the crowds flock to our beloved "Prater" on a fine day in spring. I also saw the Villa Medicis and the Villa Pamfili. The latter boasts a very extensive park.

I took care to visit most of the churches. My plan was to go out early in the morning, and to inspect several churches until about eleven o'clock, when it was time to repair to the galleries. When I went to the principal churches,—for instance, those of St. John of Lateran, St. Paul, St. Maria Maggiore, St. Lawrence, and St. Sebastian,—I was always accompanied by a guide specially appointed to conduct strangers to the churches. I could fill volumes with the description of the riches and magnificence they display.

The church of St. John of Lateran possesses the wooden altar at which St. Peter is said to have read mass, the wooden table at which Jesus sat to eat the last supper, and the heads of the disciples Peter and Paul. Near this church, in a building specially constructed for it, is the Scala Santa (holy staircase), which was brought from Jerusalem and deposited here. This is a flight of twenty-eight steps of white marble, covered with boards, which no one is allowed to ascend or descend in the regular way, every man being required to shuffle up and down on his knees. Near this holy stair a common one is built, which it is lawful to ascend in the regular way.

The basilica of St. Paul lies beyond the gate of the same name, in a very insalubrious neighbourhood. It is only just rebuilt, after having been destroyed by fire.

The basilica Maria Maggiore, in which is deposited the "holy gate," has the highest belfry in Rome, and above its portico we see a beautiful chamber where the new Pope stands to dispense the first blessing among the people. In the chapel of the Crucifix five pieces of the wood of the Saviour's manger are preserved in a silver urn.

St. Lorenzo, a mile from the town, is a very plain-looking edifice. Here we find the Campo Santo, or cemetery. The graves are covered with large blocks of stone.

St. Bessoriana is also called the church of the Holy Cross of Jerusalem, from the fact that a piece of the cross is preserved here, besides the letters I.N.R.I., some thorns, and a nail.

St. Sebastian in the suburbs, one of the most ancient Roman churches, is built over the great catacombs, in which 174,000 Christians were buried.

The catacombs are some stories deep, and extend over a large area.
All the above-named basilicas are so empty, and stand on such lonely spots, that I was almost afraid to visit them alone.
The handsome church of Sta. Maria in Trastavare contrasts strangely with the quarter of the town in which it lies. This part of Rome is inhabited by people calling themselves descendants of the ancient Trojans.
Sta. Maria ad Martyres, or the Rotunda, once the Pantheon of Agrippa, is in better preservation than any other monument of ancient Rome. The interior is almost in its pristine condition; it contains no less than fifteen altars. In this church Raphael is buried. The Rotunda has no windows, but receives air and light through a circular opening in the cupola.
The best view of ancient Rome is to be obtained from the tower of the Senate-house. From this place we see stretched out beneath us, Mount Palatine, the site of ancient Rome; the Capitol, in the midst of the city; the Quirinal hill (Monte Cavallo), with the summer residence of the Pope; the Esquiline mount, the loftiest of the hills; Mount Aventine; the Vatican; and lastly, Monte Testaccio, consisting entirely of broken pottery which the Romans throw down here.
I also paid a visit to the Ponte Publicius, the most ancient bridge in Rome, in the neighbourhood of which Horatius Cocles achieved his heroic action; and the Tullian prison, beneath the church of St. Joseph of Falignani, where Jugurtha was starved to death. The staircase leading up to the building is called "the steps of sighs." The Capitol has unfortunately fallen into decay; we can barely distinguish a few remains of temples and other buildings.
Of the graves of the Scipios I could also discover little more than the site; the subterranean passages are nearly all destroyed.
The Marsfield is partly covered with buildings, and partly used as a promenade.
Cestius' grave is uncommonly well preserved, and a pyramid of large square stones surrounds the sarcophagus. The aqueducts are built of large blocks of stone fastened together without mortar. They are now no longer used, as they have partly fallen into decay, and some of the springs have dried up.
The hot baths of Titus are well worthy a visit, though in a ruined condition. Here the celebrated Laocoon group was found. Near these baths is the great reservoir called the "Seven Halls of Titus."
One of the greatest and best-preserved buildings of ancient Rome is the amphitheatre of Flavius, or the Colliseum, once the scene of the combats with wild beasts. It was capable of holding 87,000 spectators. Four stories yet remain. This building is seen to the greatest advantage by torchlight. I was fortunate enough to find an opportunity of joining a large party, and we were thus enabled to divide the expense. The triumphal arch of Titus, of white marble, covered with glorious sculptures; the arches of Septimus Severus, that of Janus, and several other antique monuments, are to be seen

near the Colliseum.

The beautiful bridge of St. Angelo, constructed entirely of square blocks of stone, leads across the Tiber to the castle of the same name, the tomb of Hadrian. The emperor caused this large round building to be erected for his future mausoleum. It is built of immense stone blocks, and now serves as a fortress and state-prison.

The temple of Marcus Aurelius is converted into the Dogana. That of Minerva Medica lies in the midst of a vineyard, and is built in the form of a rotunda. The upper part has sunk in.

There are twelve obelisks in the different public squares of Rome, all brought from Egypt.

I have still to mention the 108 fountains, from which fresh water continually spouts into the air. Foremost among them in size and beauty is the Fontana Trevi.

I was prevented by the bad weather from making trips to any distance, but one afternoon I drove to Tivoli. The road leading thither is called the Tiburtinian. After travelling for about six miles we become conscious of a dreadfully offensive sulphurous smell, and soon find that it proceeds from a little river running through the Solfatara. A ride of eighteen Italian miles brought us to the town of Tivoli, lying amidst olive-woods on the declivity of the Apennines, and numbering about 7000 inhabitants. Towards evening I took a short walk in the town, beneath the protection of an umbrella, and was not much pleased. Next morning I left the house early, and proceeded first to the temple of Sybilla, built on a rock opposite to the waterfall. Afterwards I went to view the grotto of Neptune, and that through which the Arno flows, rushing out of the cavern to fall headlong over a ledge of lofty rocks, and form the cascade of Tivoli. The best view of this fall is obtained from the bridge. Besides many pretty minor cascades, I saw a number of ruins; the most remarkable among these was the villa of Mecænas.

November 23d.

At six o'clock this morning I commenced my journey to Florence with a Veturino. Almost the whole distance the weather was in the highest degree unfavourable—it was foggy, rainy, and very cold. A journey through Italy during autumn or winter is far from agreeable; for there are generally cold and rain to be encountered, and no warm rooms to be found in the inns, where fires are never kindled until after the guests have arrived. And the fires they light in the grates are, after all, quite inadequate to warm the damp, unaired rooms, and the traveller feels scorched and cold almost at the same moment. The floors are all of stone, but a few straw-mats are sometimes spread beneath the dining-tables.

The landscape through which we travelled to-day did not possess many attractions. For about forty miles, as far as Ronciglione, we saw neither town nor village. The aspect of Ronciglione is rather melancholy, though it boasts a broad street and many houses of two stories. But the latter all have a gloomy look, and the town itself appears to be thinly populated. We passed the night here.

According to Italian custom, I had made a bargain with the proprietor of our vehicle for the journey, including lodging and board. I was well satisfied, for he strictly kept his contract. But whoever expects more than one meal a day under an arrangement of this sort will find himself grievously mistaken; the traveller who wishes to take any thing in the morning or in the middle of the day must pay out of his own pocket. I found every thing here exceedingly expensive and very bad.

November 24th.

To-day we passed through some very pretty, though not populous districts. In the afternoon we at length reached two towns,—namely, Viterbo, with 13,000 inhabitants, lying in a fruitful plain; and Montefiascone, built on a high hill, and backed by lofty mountains, on which a celebrated vine is cultivated. At the foot of the hill, near Montefiascone, lies a small lake, and farther on one of considerable size, the Lago de Balsana, with a little town of the same name, once the capital of the Volsci. An ancient fortress rises in the midst of this town, surrounded by tall and venerable houses as with a wreath.

We had now to cross a considerable mountain, an undertaking of some difficulty when we consider how heavily the rain had fallen. By the aid of an extra pair of horses we passed safely over the miserable roads, and took up our quarters for the night in the little village of Lorenzo. We had already reached the domain of the Apennines.

November 25th.

We had now only a few more hours to travel through the papal dominions. The river Centino forms the boundary between the States of the Church and Tuscany. The greater portion of the region around us gave tokens of its volcanic origin. We saw several grottoes and caverns of broken stone resembling lava, basaltic columns, etc.

The Dogana of Tuscany, a handsome building, stands in the neighbourhood of Ponte Centino. The country here wears a wild aspect; as far as the eye can stretch, it rests upon mountains of different elevations. The little town of Radicofani lies on the plateau of a considerable hill, surrounded by rocks and huge blocks of stone. A citadel or ancient fortress towers romantically above the little town, and old towers look down from the summit of many a hill and cliff. The character of the lower mountain-range is exceedingly peculiar; it is split into gaps and fissures in all directions, as though it had but recently emerged from the main.

For many hours we almost rode through a flood. The water streamed down the streets, and the wind howled round our carriage with such violence that we seriously anticipated being blown over. Luckily the streets in the Tuscan are better than those in the Roman territory, and the rivers are crossed by firm stone bridges.

November 26th.

To-day our poor horses had a hard time of it. Up hill and down hill, and past yawning chasms, our way lay for a long time through a desert and barren district, until, at a little distance from the village of Buonconvento, the scene suddenly changed, and a widely-extended, hilly country, with beautiful plains, the lovely town of Siena, numerous villages great and small, with homesteads and handsome farms, and solitary churches built on hills, lay spread before us. Every thing shewed traces of cultivation and opulence.

Most of the women and girls we met were employed in plaiting straw. Here all wear straw hats—men, women, and children. At five in the evening we at length reached

SIENA.

Our poor horses were so exhausted by the bad roads of the Apennines, that the driver requested leave to make a day's halt here. This interruption to our journey was far from being unwelcome to me, for Siena is well worthy to be explored.

November 27th.

The town numbers 16,000 inhabitants, and is divided almost into two halves by a long handsome street. The remaining streets are small, irregular, and dirty. The Piazza del Campo is very large, and derives a certain splendour of appearance from some palaces built in the gothic style. In the midst stands a granite pillar, bearing a representation in bronze of Romulus and Remus suckled by the she-wolf. I saw several other pillars of equal beauty in different parts of the town, while in Rome, where they would certainly have been more appropriate, I did not find a single one. All the houses in the streets of Siena have a gloomy appearance; many of them are built like castles, of great square blocks of stone, and furnished with loopholes.

The finest building is undoubtedly the cathedral. Though I came from the "city of churches," the beauty of this edifice struck me so forcibly, that for a long time I stood silently regarding it. It is, in truth, considered one of the handsomest churches in Italy. It stands on a little elevation in the midst of a large square, and is covered outside and inside with white marble. The lofty arches of the windows, supported by columns, have a peculiarly fine effect; and the frescoes in the sacristy are remarkable alike for the correctness of outline and brilliancy of colour.

The drawings are said to be by Raphael; and the freshness of colour observed in these frescoes is ascribed to the good qualities of the Siena earth. The mass-books preserved in the sacristy contain some very delicate miniatures on parchment.

Some of the wards in the neighbouring hospital are also decorated with beautiful frescoes, which appear to date from the time of Raphael.

The grace and beauty of the women of Siena have been extolled by many writers. As to-day was Sunday, I attended high mass for the purpose of meeting some of these graceful beauties. I found that they were present in the usual average, and no more; beauty and grace are no common gifts.

In the afternoon I visited the promenade, the Prato di Lizza, where I found but little company. A fine prospect is obtained from the walls of the town.

November 28th.

The country now becomes very beautiful. The mountains are less high, the valleys widen, and at length hills only appear at intervals, clothed with trees, meadows, and fields. In the Tuscan dominions I noticed many cypresses, a tree I had not seen since my departure from Constantinople and Smyrna. The country seems well populated, and villages frequently appear.

At five in the evening we reached

FLORENCE,

but I did not arrive at Madame Mocalli's hotel until an hour and a half later; for the examination of luggage and passes, and other business of this kind, always occupies a long time.

The country round Florence is exceedingly lovely, without being grand. The charming Arno flows through the town: it is crossed by four stone bridges, one of them roofed and lined with booths on either side. Florence contains 8000 houses and 90,000 inhabitants. The exterior of the palaces here is very peculiar. Constructed chiefly of huge blocks of stone, they almost resemble fortresses, and look massive and venerable.

The cathedral is said to be the finest church in Christendom; I thought it too simple, particularly the interior. The walls are only whitewashed, and the painted windows render the church extremely dark. I was best pleased with the doors of the sacristy, with the celebrated works of Luca del Robbin, and the richly decorated high altar.

The Battisterio, once a temple of Mars, with eight very fine doors of bronze, which Michael Angelo pronounced worthy to be the gates of Paradise, stands beside the cathedral.

The other principal churches are:—St. Lorenzo, also with a white interior and grey pillars, containing some fine oil paintings, and the chapel of the Medici, a splendid structure, decorated with costly stones, and monuments of several members of the royal family.

St. Croce, a handsome church, full of monuments of eminent men, is also called the Italian Pantheon; the sculptures are beautiful, and the paintings good. The remains of Michael Angelo rest here, and the Buonaparte family possess a vault beneath a side chapel. Another chapel of considerable size contains some exquisite statues of white marble.

St. Annunciate is rich in splendid frescoes; those placed round the walls in the courtyard of the church, and surrounded by a glass gallery, are particularly handsome. On the left as we enter we find the costly chapel of our Lady "dell' Annunciata," in which the altar, the immense candelabra, the angels and draperies, in short every thing is of silver. This wealthy church contains in addition some good pictures and a quantity of marble.

St. Michele is outwardly beautified by some excellent statues. The interior displays several valuable paintings and an altar of great beauty, beneath a white marble canopy in the Gothic style.

St. Spirito contains many sculptures, among which a statue of the Saviour in white marble claims particular attention.

All these churches are rather dark from having stained windows.

Foremost among the palaces we may reckon the Palais Pitti, built on a little hill. This structure has a noble appearance; constructed entirely of pieces of granite, it seems calculated to last an eternity. Of all the palaces I had seen, this one pleased me most; it would be difficult to find a building in the same style which should surpass it. As a rule, indeed, I particularly admired the Florentine buildings, which seemed to me to possess a much more decided national appearance than the palaces of modern Rome.

The picture-gallery of this palace numbers five hundred paintings, most of them masterpieces, among which we find Raphael's Madonna della Sedia. Besides the pictures, each apartment contains gorgeous tables of valuable stone.

Behind the palace the Boboli garden rises, somewhat in the form of a terrace. Here I found numerous statues distributed with much taste throughout charming alleys, groves, and open places. From the higher points a splendid view is obtained.

The palace degli Ufizzi, on the Arno, has an imposing effect, from its magnificent proportions and peculiar style of architecture. Some of the greatest artistic treasures of the world are united in the twenty halls and cabinets and three immense galleries of this building.

The Tribuna contains the Venus de Medicis, found at Tivoli, and executed by Cleomenes, a son of Apollodorus of Athens. Opposite to it stands a statue of Apollino.

In the centre of the hall of the artists' portrait-gallery we find the celebrated Medician vase.

The cabinet of jewels boasts the largest and finest onyx in existence.

The Palazzo Vecchio resembles a fortified castle. The large courtyard, surrounded by lofty arcades, is crowded with paintings and sculptures. A beautiful fountain stands in the midst; and two splendid statues, one representing Hercules and the other David, adorn the entrance. The glorious fountain of Ammanato, drawn by sea-horses and surrounded by Tritons, is not far off.

In the Gherardeska palace we find a fresco representing the horrible story of Ugolino.

The Palazzo Strozzi should not be left out of the catalogue; it has already stood for 360 years, and looks as though it had been completed but yesterday.

In the Speccola we are shewn the human body and its diseases, modelled in wax by the same artist who established a similar cabinet at Vienna (in the Josephinum). In the museum of natural history stuffed animals and their skeletons are preserved.

The traveller should not depart without visiting the "workshops for hard stones," where beautiful pictures, table-slabs, etc. are put together of Florentine marble. Splendid works are produced here; I saw flowers and fruits constructed of stone which would not have dishonoured the finest pencil. The enormous table in the palace degli Ufizzi is said to have cost 40,000 ducats. Twenty-five men were employed for twenty years in its construction; it is composed of Florentine mosaic. This table did not strike me particularly; it appeared overloaded with ornament.

Of the environs of Florence I only saw the Grand Duke's milk-farm, a pleasant place near the Arno, amid beautiful avenues and meadows.

DEPARTURE FROM FLORENCE.December 3d.

At seven in the evening I quitted Florence, and proceeded in the mail-carriage to Bologna, distant about eighty miles. When the day broke, we found ourselves on an acclivity commanding a really splendid view. Numerous valleys, extending between low hills, opened before our eyes, the snow-clad Apennines formed the background, and in the far distance shone a gleaming stripe—the Adriatic sea. At five in the evening of

December 4th

we reached Bologna.

This town is of considerable extent, numbers 50,000 inhabitants, and has many fine houses and streets; all of these, however, are dull, with the exception of a few principal streets. Beggars swarm at every corner—an unmistakable token that we are once more in the States of the Church.

December 5th.

This was a day of rest. I proceeded at once to visit the cathedral, which is rich in frescoes, gilding, and arabesques. A few oil-paintings are also not to be overlooked.

In the church of St. Dominic I viewed with most interest the monument of King Enzio.

The picture-gallery contains a St. Cecilia, one of the earlier productions of Raphael.

A fine fountain, with a figure of Neptune, graces the principal square. In the Palazzo Publico I saw a staircase up which it is possible to ride.

The most remarkable edifices at Bologna are the two square leaning towers at the Porta Romagna. One of these towers is five, and the other seven feet out of the perpendicular. Their aspect inspired me with a kind of nervous dread; on standing close to the wall to look up at them it really appeared as though they were toppling down. In themselves these towers are not interesting, being simply constructed of masonry, and not very lofty.

The finest spot in Bologna is the Campo Santo, the immense cemetery, with its long covered ways and neat chapels, displaying a number of costly monuments, the works of the first modern sculptors. Three large and pleasant spots near these buildings serve as burial-places for the poorer classes. In one the men are interred, in the second the women, and in the third the children.

A hall three miglia in length, resting on 640 columns, leads from this cemetery to a little hill, surmounted by the church of the Madonna di St. Luca, and from thence almost back into the town. The church just mentioned contains a miraculous picture, namely, a true likeness of the Virgin, painted by St. Luke after a vision. The complexion of this picture is much darker than that of the commonest women I have seen in Syria. But faith is every thing, and so I will not doubt the authenticity of the picture. The prospect from the mountains is exceedingly fine.

I returned in the evening completely exhausted, and half an hour afterwards was already seated in the post-carriage to pursue my journey to Ferrara.

On the whole the weather was unfavourable; it rained frequently, and the roads were mostly very bad, particularly in the domains of the Pope, where we stuck fast four or five times during the night. On one occasion of this kind we were detained more than an hour, until horses and oxen could be collected to drag us onwards. We were twelve hours getting over these fifty-four miles, from six in the evening till the same hour in the morning. December 6th.

This morning I awoke at Ferrara, where the carriage was to be changed once more. I availed myself of a few spare hours to view the town, which, on the whole, rather resembles a German than an Italian place. It has fine broad streets, nice houses, and few arched ways in front of them. In the centre of the town stands a strong castle, surrounded by fortifications; this was once the residence of the bishop.

At nine o'clock we quitted this pretty town, and reached the Po an hour afterwards. We were ferried across the stream; and now, after a long absence, I once more stood on Austrian ground. We continued our journey through a lovely plain to Rovigo, a place possessing no object of interest. Here we stayed to dine, and afterwards passed the Adige, a stream considerably smaller than the Po. The country between Rovigo and Padua was hidden from us by an impenetrable fog, which prevented our seeing fifty paces in advance. At six o'clock in the evening we reached Padua, our resting-place for the night.

Early next morning I hastened onwards, for I had already seen Padua, Venice, Trieste, etc. in the year 1840.

I reached my native town safely and in perfect health, and had the happiness of finding that my beloved ones were all well and cheerful.

During my journey I had seen much and endured many hardships; I had found very few things as I had imagined them to be.

Friends and relations have expressed a wish to read a description of my lonely wanderings. I could not send my diary to each one; so I have dared, upon the representations of my friends, and at the particular request of the publisher of this book, to tell my adventures in a plain unvarnished way.

I am no authoress; I have never written anything but letters; and my diary must not, therefore, be judged as a literary production. It is a simple narration, in which I have described every circumstance as it occurred; a collection of notes which I wrote down for private reference, without dreaming that they would ever find their way into the great world. Therefore I would entreat the indulgence of my kind readers; for—I repeat it—nothing can be farther from my thoughts than any idea of thrusting myself forward into the ranks of those gifted women who have received in their cradle the Muses' initiatory kiss.